Edgar Allan Poe and the Dupin Mysteries

Edgar Allan Poe and the Dupin Mysteries

Richard Kopley

First published in hardcover in 2008 by
PALGRAVE MACMILLAN®
in the United States—a division of St. Martin's Press LLC,
175 Fifth Avenue, New York, NY 10010.

Where this book is distributed in the UK, Europe and the rest of the world,
this is by Palgrave Macmillan, a division of Macmillan Publishers Limited,
registered in England, company number 785998, of Houndmills,
Basingstoke, Hampshire RG21 6XS.

Palgrave Macmillan is the global academic imprint of the above companies
and has companies and representatives throughout the world.

Palgrave® and Macmillan® are registered trademarks in the United States,
the United Kingdom, Europe and other countries.

ISBN: 978–0–230–12038–9

Library of Congress Cataloging-in-Publication Data is available from the
Library of Congress.

A catalogue record for this book is available from the British Library.

Design by Newgen Imaging Systems (P) Ltd., Chennai, India.

First PALGRAVE MACMILLAN paperback edition: August 2011

10 9 8 7 6 5 4 3 2 1

Printed in the United States of America.

Transferred to Digital Printing in 2011

For Richard Wilbur

CONTENTS

ACKNOWLEDGMENTS

I am happy to thank the Penn State administrators who have directly and indirectly supported this project: John J. Romano, Vice President of Penn State Commonwealth Campuses; Sandra E. Gleason, Associate Dean for Faculty and Research, Penn State University College; Raymond E. Lombra, Associate Dean for Administration and Research, College of the Liberal Arts, Penn State; Robin Schulze, Head, Department of English, Penn State; Robert L. Caserio Jr., former Head, Department of English, Penn State; Anita D. McDonald, Chancellor, Penn State DuBois; Mary-Beth Krogh-Jespersen, Chancellor, Penn State Worthington Scranton; Maureen Horan and Mary Mino, Co-Interim Directors of Academic Affairs, Penn State DuBois; and Robert E. Loeb, former Director of Academic Affairs, Penn State DuBois. Important support was provided also by James L. West III, Director of Penn State's Center for the History of the Book, and Hester Blum, Director of Penn State's Center for American Literary Studies.

I am pleased to express my appreciation, as well, to the libraries where I conducted research for this book, including the New York Public Library (and its Rare Books Division and its Science, Industry, and Business Library); the New-York Historical Society library; the New York Society Library; the Library of Congress; the American Antiquarian Society library; Butler Library of Columbia University; the library of the Historical Society of Moorestown (NJ); the library of Christ Church, Riverton (NJ); the Pattee/Paterno Library of Penn State; the Holland/New Library of Washington State University; and the Colindale Branch of the British Public Library. I am also grateful to Whitlock Farm Booksellers, where I found *Death-Bed Confessions*.

For permission to publish "Edgar Allan Poe and *The Philadelphia Saturday News*" (1991), now lightly revised, as chapter II of this book, I am pleased to thank Jeffrey A. Savoye, Secretary/Treasurer of the

Edgar Allan Poe Society of Baltimore. For permission to reprint the three Dupin tales from the Mabbott edition, *The Collected Works of Edgar Allan Poe*, I am glad to express my appreciation to Scarlett Huffman of the Permissions Department of Harvard University Press.

For conversations related to this project, I acknowledge, with thanks, Kent P. Ljungquist (Worcester Polytechnic Institute) and Theodore Price (Montclair State University).

And I am indebted to Grace Farrell, the perceptive reader for Palgrave Macmillan and to the editorial staff, Farideh Koohi-Kamali, Julia Cohen, Brigitte Shull, and Joanna Robert.

It has been a pleasure to share this work with my family—my wife Amy Golahny, our daughter Emily, our son Gabe, and my mother Irene Kopley. And I thank my father-in-law Yuda Golahny for his support.

INTRODUCTION

Jorge Luis Borges wrote in his 1973 *An Introduction to American Literature* that Poe's tales "of intellect" "inaugurate a new genre, the detective story, which has conquered the entire world. . . ." Of these tales, Poe's Dupin tales are especially honored; indeed, Arthur Conan Doyle referred in 1908 to "those admirable stories of Monsieur Dupin, so wonderful in their masterful force, their reticence, their quick dramatic point," and T. S. Eliot stated in 1927, "In real keenness of wit and the way in which this keenness is exhibited no one has ever surpassed Poe's Monsieur Dupin."[1]

Each of the three tales has had its advocates. Mark Twain wrote in 1896, "What a curious thing a 'detective' story is. And was there ever one that the author needn't be ashamed of, except 'The Murders in the Rue Morgue'?" G. K. Chesterton asserted in 1939, ". . . I do not think that the standard set by a certain Mr. Edgar A. Poe in a story called *The Murders of the Rue Morgue*, has ever been definitely and indisputably surpassed." And Philip Van Doren Stern agreed, stating in 1941, "Like printing, the detective story has been improved upon only in a mechanical way since it was first invented; as artistic products, Gutenberg's Bible and Poe's 'The Murders in the Rue Morgue' have never been surpassed." Yet Dorothy Sayers considered "The Mystery of Marie Rogêt" in 1929 "the most interesting of all [of the Dupin stories] to the connoisseur," and Richard P. Benton supported this judgment in 1969: "One would have to agree with Dorothy Sayers that 'The Mystery of Marie Rogêt' is caviar for the gourmet. . . ."; it is "a masterpiece of detective fiction. . . ." However, Poe described "The Purloined Letter" in 1844 as "perhaps, the best of my tales of ratiocination" (*Letters* 1:450). Ellery Queen concurred, terming this tale in 1968 "artistically Poe's finest achievement in the genre he himself invented," and T. O. Mabbott characterized it in 1951 as "surely unsurpassed in detective fiction and perhaps unequaled."[2]

No matter which assessment we share, we recognize that with these three tales Poe invented conventions that have lasted 170 years, shaping diverse subgenres of detective fiction, from the hard-boiled to the metaphysical.[3] Meriting particular attention is Dupin's ratiocinative process. In each tale, the detective brilliantly works to solve the mystery of the crime that has been committed.[4] Yet also in each tale, another mystery remains—that of the literary work itself. For this mystery, we may learn from Dupin to become our own Dupin. His detection may be taken as an allegory of our own potential reading. Poe's sleuth may help us to sleuth Poe.

Monsieur Dupin employs a methodology involving close attention to relevant evidence ("a minuteness of attention" [*Collected Works* 2:546; see also 3:753]), including evidence seemingly outside the case ("things external to the game" [2:530; see also 3:752]), with particular concern for the unusual ("deviations from the plane of the ordinary" [2:548; see also 2:549n, 3:736–37]) and the too-evident (the "excessively obvious" [3:989–90]), and a willingness to identify with another's point of view ("...the analyst throws himself into the spirit of his opponent..." [2:529; see also 3:984–85]). With varying elements of this blended approach, Dupin is able to infer what must have happened, identify the culprit (in "Rue Morgue" and "Marie Rogêt"), and find the letter (in "The Purloined Letter"). Using a similar blended approach, but attending to literary creation rather than crime, we may understand anew the origins of a genre. The principle of identification invites our application of the methods of Poe's detective to solve the mysteries of Poe's detective fiction—to detect what has hitherto gone undetected.

The "minuteness of attention," with concern for the unusual and the too-evident, may be seen as corresponding to a close reading of the text, a formal analysis. This approach enjoyed its heyday in the 1940s and 1950s as the New Criticism, and, despite the ascendancy of other approaches since then, close reading has remained a powerful method of investigating a literary work. And we now see discussion of a "new formalism," an effort "to reinstate close reading."[5] Close reading is especially rewarding in the case of a writer of such consummate artistry—and hermetic inclination—as Poe. Richard Wilbur has said, "I think that if he's read word by word, he turns out, at his best, to be a very rich and intentional writer."[6] And Poe intimated the need for close reading himself in January 1842: "The analysis of a book is a matter of time and of mental exertion. For many classes of composition there is required a deliberate perusal, with notes, and subsequent generalization" (*Collected Works* 2:3).

Chapter I, "Formal Considerations of the Dupin Tales," offers a "deliberate perusal" of "The Murders in the Rue Morgue," "The Mystery of Marie Rogêt," and "The Purloined Letter." We find that like the "words" that "stretch, in large characters, from one end of the chart to the other"—words that are so "excessively obvious" that they are missed (*Collected Works* 3:989–90)—the pattern of language established over the entirety of a Dupin tale is similarly missed. We should read each Dupin tale closely with a sense of the whole in mind, much as we might read a sonnet. (Notably, Wilbur also said, "We must give Poe the trustful attention that we're used to giving John Donne...")[7] Reading a part in terms of the whole and the whole in terms of its parts—the "hermeneutic circle"—may be highly rewarding. Close attention to Poe's pattern of language reveals that each Dupin tale has a clear symmetrical structure framing a significant midpoint. These tales constitute "*une espéce de trilogie*" (a phrase that John H. Ingram quotes from Charles Baudelaire)[8]—a sort of trilogy, each element of which is aesthetically complete. Here, a "minuteness of attention" illuminates the design of the work; formalism reveals form.

Furthermore, identification with Poe leads to an interest in "things external to the game"—that is, to works outside the text—his reading. We thus become involved with genetic criticism, an analysis of a text through study of the author's reading and transformation of that reading. John Livingston Lowes's study of Samuel Taylor Coleridge's "The Rime of the Ancient Mariner" and "Kubla Khan," *The Road to Xanadu*, is the classic early example of genetic criticism, and the approach continues to thrive across a range of authors.[9] "Intertextuality" is a useful term, but so, too, is an earlier one, "source study," since it retains a sense of chronology (implying not a cause, but an artistic opportunity taken). A concern with sources is often prompted by what has been aptly termed "a curiosity, and sometimes an awe, about how such and such a work came to exist."[10] Chapters II, III, and IV examine Poe's reading and his adaptation of it for each of the Dupin tales.

Chapter II, "'The Murders in the Rue Morgue' and *The Philadelphia Saturday News*," offers an examination of a neglected but vital contemporary newspaper. This study reveals not only that *The Philadelphia Saturday News* offers sources for the orangutan, the L'Espanayes, the French sailor, and the murder itself, among much else, but also that Poe's transformation of his sources sheds light on his artistry. Consideration of what Poe deleted or altered, in particular, enhances our understanding of what he wrote. Reading the popular press, Poe transformed the unconventional even as he created literary convention. Our close attention to *The Philadelphia Saturday News* yields important interpretive consequences concerning race and, eventually, gender.

Chapter III, "'The Mystery of Marie Rogêt' and 'Various Newspaper Files,'" explores a number of contemporary newspapers, including those that Poe named in his notes to his second Dupin tale, as it appeared in the 1845 volume *Tales*. Many of Poe's newspaper sources for "Marie Rogêt" have long been known, but continued identification with Poe as a reader reveals that an extract that he included in the work—one considered by scholars to have been fabricated by Poe—was based on fact. Furthermore, the newspaper context for Poe's tale leads to an understanding that the 1799 murder of Gulielma Sands in New York City informed his imagining that Marie Rogêt's murderer had blamed someone else. And it leads, as well, to a recognition that Poe's antagonism toward a contemporary newspaper editor informed his negative treatment of the *Brother Jonathan* ("L'Etoile"). This recognition calls to mind the first line of "The Cask of Amontillado" (1846): "The thousand injuries of Fortunato I had borne as I best could; but when he ventured upon insult, I vowed revenge" (*Collected Works* 3:1256).

Chapter IV, "'The Purloined Letter' and *Death-Bed Confessions*," continues with an identification with Poe as a reader. Having left England in June 1820 just as Queen Caroline was returning to face charges of adultery and, she hoped, to be crowned, young Poe would have known—unusually well for an American boy—about the unhappy monarch and the people's support for her. A volume that exonerated both Caroline and her husband George IV, *Death-Bed Confessions* was a popular item in London in 1822, a year after the Queen had died, and it was reprinted in the United States. For his third and final Dupin tale, Poe returned to the long-remembered Caroline and transformed elements of *Death-Bed Confessions* with regard to the theft from Princess Caroline in 1813 of what is termed in that work "the purloined letter." Poe's transformation of an incident from this neglected volume sheds light on both his tale and his compositional practice. Furthermore, the study of *Death-Bed Confessions* contributes to the growing field of book history. And chapters II, III, and IV instance not only genetic criticism, but cultural studies, as well.

Finally, in chapter V, "Autobiographical Considerations of the Dupin Tales," the technique of identification leads inevitably to our considering anew the life of Poe. Here, genetic criticism supports biographical criticism. That is, one of the "deviations from the plane of the ordinary" regarding the Dupin tales is the presence in a major source for each of them of a woman of uncertain reputation.

Especially helpful in this connection is a confiding remark that Poe made to his friend Marie Louise Shew Houghton concerning his feelings about his mother. Upon consideration of this evidence, we may fairly infer that Poe wrote the Dupin tales, in part, to try to come to terms with his abiding sense of guilt.

Throughout this study, Dupin's blended critical approach helps us to understand the Dupin tales. And the combination of close reading, genetic criticism, and biographical criticism may certainly be applicable to other literary works, as well. Dupin's method of detection is a kind of practical criticism, one with an affinity to the synthesis that David S. Reynolds once termed "reconstructive criticism."[11] It is true, as Borges has noted, that Poe invented a genre that "conquered the...world"; we should add that through this genre—especially the Dupin tales—Poe also taught the world.

CHAPTER I

FORMAL CONSIDERATIONS OF THE DUPIN TALES

Our close reading of the Dupin tales may be guided by a review that Poe wrote for the April 1841 issue of *Graham's Magazine*, where he first published "The Murders in the Rue Morgue." He asserted, with regard to Edward Bulwer's novel *Night and Morning*, that "[t]he interest of plot" appeals to "considerations analogous with those which are the essence of sculptural taste" (*Complete Works* 10:120).[1] Relevant to the implied matter of form is the narrator's stating in "Rue Morgue" that with regard to "the processes of invention or creation" and "the processes of resolution," "the former" is "nearly, if not absolutely, the latter conversed" (*Collected Works* 2:527n). This point is reinforced when the narrator imagines "a double Dupin—the creative and the resolvent" (2:533). Through his narrator, Poe thus conveys a sense of mirroring halves—a sense that proves relevant to the structure of "Rue Morgue" itself—and indeed, of "The Mystery of Marie Rogêt" and "The Purloined Letter," as well.

This should not be surprising, for in Poe's 1838 novel *The Narrative of Arthur Gordon Pym* a pattern of phrases is "conversed," and the reflecting patterns frame a significant midpoint —the infinitely reflected image of Pym's friend Augustus dying on 1 August (*Collected Writings* 1:142). That image suggests Poe's infinite memory of his brother Henry dying on 1 August 1831. And Poe's 1843 short work "The Tell-Tale Heart" offers a framed central chiasmus (the pattern ABBA)—the phrase describing the old man's "Evil Eye," "the damned spot": "open—wide, wide open" (*Collected Works* 3:795). Thus, X marks "the spot."[2]

Pertinently, at the front of the house of Madame L'Espanaye and her daughter Camille on Rue Morgue is "'a double or folding gate'" (*Collected Works* 2:540). Thus may be suggested the reflecting halves of "The Murders in the Rue Morgue." And what may be further revealed is the significant midpoint between them.

The symmetry of Poe's first detective tale has been discussed by Richard Wilbur, who notes that the setting of the murder of the L'Espanayes is the fourth floor of a building even as the setting of the sailor's confirmation of Dupin's theory regarding the murderer is *"au troisième"*—again, the fourth floor of a building.[3] The symmetry of the story is developed further with a pattern of repeated language. Even as "a minuteness of attention" (*Collected Works* 2:546) helped Dupin to solve the mystery of Rue Morgue, so too will it help us to recognize the structure of "Rue Morgue." And even as he engaged in this "minuteness of attention" while he walked with his companion to "the rear of the building," after which they "[r]etrac[ed]" their "steps" "to the front" (2:546; see also 535), so may we, with "a minuteness of attention," follow Poe's path from the beginning to the end of his pattern of language, and then, after the story's center, retrace his steps from the end of this pattern to its beginning. (Emphasis in the following parallels is my own, except where otherwise indicated.)

The symmetrical phrasing in "Rue Morgue" involves four pairs of corresponding language clusters framing the center. The first half of the outermost pair of clusters, drawn from the imaginary article "Extraordinary Murders" in "Gazette des Tribunaux," includes early mention of *"furniture broken and thrown about,"* "A small *iron safe*" "under *the bed* [Poe's emphasis] (not under *the bedstead*)" with "a few old letters, and other *papers* of little consequence," *"the corpse of the daughter*...dragged"* down after having been *"thrust up"* the chimney after "the deceased had been *throttled to death*," *"the corpse of the old lady*, with her *throat so entirely cut that*, upon an attempt to raise her, *the head fell off*," and "[t]he body" and "the head" "fearfully *mutilated*" (*Collected Works* 2:537–38). The second half of the outermost pair, drawn from the narrator's account of the sailor's story, involves mention of the L'Espanayes's "arranging some *papers* in the *iron chest*," the orangutan's having *"nearly severed her* [Madame L'Espanaye's] *head from her body"* and *"retain[ed] its grasp until she* [Mademoiselle L'Espanaye] *expired*," its *"throwing down and breaking the furniture"* and "dragging *the bed* from *the bedstead*," and its having "seized first *the corpse of the daughter*, and *thrust* it *up* the chimney...then that *of the old lady*," and having approached the window with "its *mutilated* burden" (2:566–67). The correspondences of elements of the outer pair of clusters may be seen to continue as we turn to the next pair of clusters.

In the first half of the next pair, according to Dupin, physician Paul Dumas suggests that a *"A heavy club of wood"* may have been the murder weapon; then Alexandre Etienne states that *"The police are entirely at fault.*... There is *not*, however, *the shadow of a clew* apparent," and the narrator adds, "I saw no means by which *it would be possible* to *trace the murderer" (Collected Works* 2:544). Similarly, later, in the second half of the second pair of clusters, Dupin imagines the thinking of the sailor, *"'The police are at fault*—they have *failed to produce the slightest clew*. Should they even *trace* the animal, *it* would *be impossible* to prove me cognizant of *the murder...*'"; then the narrator describes the sailor as holding *"a huge oaken cudgel"* (2:561–62).

As we approach the center, we encounter the third pair of corresponding clusters. Both of these involve Dupin's recounting the evidence. In the first cluster of the pair, the detective notes "the *outré* [Poe's emphasis] character of its [the mystery's] features," *"the seeming absence of motive," "the atrocity of the murder," "the assassinated* Mademoiselle L'Espanaye," and *"the corpse thrust, with the head downward, up the chimney" (Collected Works* 2:547). In the second cluster of the pair, Dupin mentions *"that startling absence of motive* in *a murder* so singularly *atrocious," "a* woman strangled to death ... and *thrust up a chimney, head downward," "assassins,"* again *"thrusting the corpse up the chimney,"* and "something *excessively outré* [Poe's emphasis]" about the treatment of the daughter's corpse (2:556–57).

And nearly at the center, we reach the fourth pair of corresponding clusters. In the first cluster of this pair, Dupin states, *"I merely wish you to bear in mind that,* with myself, it [the suspicion] was sufficiently forcible to give a definite form—a certain tendency—to my inquiries in the chamber.... It is not too much to say that neither of us believe in *præternatural* events.... *The impossibility of egress* [is] ... thus absolute..." *(Collected Works* 2:550–51). In the second cluster of the pair, Dupin asserts that "...*no egress* could have been made...." "*I wish you to bear* especially *in mind that* I have spoken of a *very* [Poe's emphasis] unusual degree of activity...." "... I wish to impress upon your understanding the *very extraordinary* [Poe's emphasis]—the almost *præternatural* character of that agility..." (2:554–55). With these four corresponding clusters of language, Poe frames the center of his tale.

And so we approach that center. Determining that the murderer must have escaped through one of the two windows of the rear room of the fourth floor of the building of the L'Espanayes, Dupin identifies the spring for the first window, which is nailed shut. Examining the intact nail of that first window, he deduces what the Prefect and his men were not able to deduce—that if there is a corresponding spring for the second window (as there is), then the nail of that second window must be somehow different. Dupin's critical inference and his testing of it constitute the center of "The Murders in the Rue Morgue":

> "There *must* [Poe's emphasis] be something wrong," I said, "about the nail." I touched it; and the head, with about a quarter of an inch of the shank, came off in my fingers. The rest of the shank was in the gimlet-hole, where it had been broken off. The fracture was an old one (for its edges were incrusted with rust), and had apparently been accomplished by the blow of a hammer, which had partially imbedded, in the top of the bottom sash, the head portion of the nail. I now carefully replaced this head portion in the indentation whence I had taken it, *and the resemblance to a perfect nail was complete*—the fissure was invisible. Pressing the spring, *I* gently *raised the sash* for a few inches; the head went up with it, remaining firm in its bed. *I closed the window, and the semblance of the whole nail was again perfect.*
>   The *riddle*, so far, was now *unriddled*. (*Collected Works* 2:553)

Thus, Dupin realizes at the framed center of the story (concerning the second window "frame" [2:552], which frames the ourang-outang, the sailor, and Dupin) that the seemingly whole nail is actually broken. And this center is itself symmetrical; the statement "*the resemblance to a perfect nail was complete*" and the later one "*the semblance of the whole nail was again perfect*" frame the raising and the lowering of the window—the action that confirms the solution to the first locked-room mystery. Furthermore, the symmetry is underscored by the phrases "inc*rust*ed with *rust*" (discussed by Henri Justin in "An Impossible Aesthetics") and "*riddle...unriddled*." (We may even have a literary antecedent for the nail " 'incrusted with rust' " near the center of "Rue Morgue"—the "barrel" of Rip's "old firelock" "encrusted with rust" near the center of Washington Irving's "Rip Van Winkle" [*The Sketch Book* 35].)

The doubleness of the center (and of the story) is reinforced by a pattern first noted by John T. Irwin—the translation of the word "nail" is the French "clou"—and so, the "clou" is the "clew."[4] A French pun may be found in "The Purloined Letter," as well (as has also been noted in the scholarship): Dupin's use of "'a seal formed of bread'" (*Collected Works* 3:992) suggests "du pain," or the detective himself, "Dupin."[5] We may recall, in this regard, that in Walsh's *Sketches*, André Dupin, Poe's model for his detective, is said to have indulged in punning.[6] Elsewhere Poe objected to the continual punning of

Thomas Hood, but he added, "A rare pun, rarely appearing, is, to a certain extent, a pleasurable effect... (*Collected Writings* 3:198; see also 2:419–20; for comment, see 4:153–54 and 2:422). He particularly espoused "*unexpectedness*" in a pun (3:198). His own unexpected puns of "clew"/"clou" and "Dupin"/"du pain" are especially appropriate for English language stories set in Paris.

And Poe indulged not only in punning, but also in inverting. It is not just that he inverts expectations, providing as the murderer, in the case of "Rue Morgue," a nonreasoning ape instead of the anticipated reasoning human. He sometimes also inverts language—as in *Pym*, when a biblical prophecy for the peace of Jerusalem (Isaiah 33:20: "stakes" will not be removed, nor "cords" broken") is inverted for an allegorical rendering of the destruction of Jerusalem (the Tsalalians pull on "cords" that are attached to "stakes," causing a landslide). Or we may consider "The Tell-Tale Heart," where Nathaniel Hawthorne's earlier assertion that "I loved the old man [editor Thomas Green Fessenden], because his heart was as transparent as a fountain" becomes the ironic "I loved the old man," who is killed because of his veiled eye, and whose murder is revealed by his tell-tale heart.[7] Accordingly, we may well wonder whether in "Rue Morgue" Poe was inverting the familiar expression for arriving at the right answer, so appropriate for the first modern detective story, "hitting the nail on the head," by describing at his story's center his protagonist's arriving at the right answer by removing the nail's head. (The *Oxford English Dictionary* traces the original expression back to the sixteenth century.)

The critical image of the separated "head" and "shank" of the nail at the story's center is elsewhere underscored by Dupin: both early on, with reference to Madame L'Espanaye—"The head of the deceased... was entirely separated from the body..." (*Collected Works* 2:544; see also 2:557, 567)—and later, with reference to the Prefect, who is ingenious without being analytical, "too cunning to be profound. In his wisdom is no *stamen* [Poe's emphasis]. It is all head and no body..." (2:568). Poe thus intimates what he terms "the affair of the nails"—the central passage around which the rest of the story is built (2:558).

And Poe seems to comment on the center in the center. In the first three versions of the tale (the March 1841 manuscript, the April 1841 *Graham's* version, and the 1843 *Prose Romances* version), Poe's Dupin stated, "...the resemblance to a perfect nail was complete." In the 1845 *Tales* version, and subsequent versions, his detective asserted,

"...the resemblance to a perfect nail was complete—the fissure was invisible." Literally, the "fissure" of the nail was "invisible," but figuratively, the "fissure" of the story—the hinge, the central crease, the place at which the story may fold over on itself—was also invisible. No one, apparently, had noticed it. Ironically, the contemporary readers, like the French police, were "at fault" (*Collected Works* 2:544, 547; see also 553). (Henri Justin terms this invisible fissure "one of the nervous centers of Poe's aesthetics of the impossible.")[8]

Poe's respect for symmetry is nowhere better stated than in his 1848 prose-poem *Eureka*. He writes, "... the sense of the symmetrical is an instinct which may be depended on with an almost blindfold reliance. It is the poetical essence of the Universe—*of the Universe* which, in the supremeness of its symmetry, is but the most sublime of poems."[9] Or, we may add, perhaps, "of tales." The symmetrical structure of "The Murders in the Rue Morgue" is a signature feature of a number of Poe's works. Continued attention to this pattern will certainly yield additional insight into Poe's creativity. But before we see how this is so with regard to the other Dupin tales, we should consider one final feature of the center of "Rue Morgue": the signature itself.

Building on an argument by Arden Reed, David Ketterer has perceptively explored the double "*d*"s of the word "shudder" (the two letters dropped for an anagram of the eponymous name "Usher"). He suggests that the sounded-out letter, "de" and its reverse, "ed," may be inverted, and that "*Ed-de*...is the micro-*crypt*-ogram encoded in the word *shudder*"—that is "Eddy, or Eddie, the diminutive form of Edgar by which our author was familiarly known."[10] The frequency of the double "*d*"s in Poe argues for Ketterer's surmise. I have noted, in particular, the occurrence of the double "*d*"s at the center of Poe works: in "The Man of the Crowd ("As the night *deepened*, so *deepened* to me..." [*Collected Works* 2:510; emphasis added] and in "A Tale of the Ragged Mountains" ("'You arose and *descended* into the city.' 'I arose...as you say, and *descended* into the city'" [3:946; emphasis added]).[11] Furthermore, at the center of "The Murders in the Rue Morgue" appear the words "ri*dd*le" and "unri*dd*led"—I take the double "*d*"s to signify "Eddy." And I should add that the word "imbedded" seems suggestive of the author's identity, as well. That is, to take Ketterer's point a step further, "imbedded" in the word "imbedded" are the words "I'm Eddy."[12]

That Poe's stories sometimes feature his signature at their centers invites a biographical interpretation of these works—one they often receive.[13] And it is especially fitting in "Rue Morgue" since, according to the newspaper, one of the deponents about the mysterious murder is a laundress named *"Pauline Dubourg* [Poe's emphasis]" (*Collected Works* 2:538): young Edgar took classes in London with the Dubourg sisters.[14] But in the case of the Dupin tales, there is another biographical concern that, I will argue, seems to unite these works— one discernible with consideration of the prompting sources for the three works. This point is discussed in chapter V.

Let us return, for now, to formal considerations of the Dupin tales. The symmetrical pattern we have found in "The Murders in the Rue Morgue" will reappear, with interesting differences, in "The Mystery of Marie Rogêt" and "The Purloined Letter."

"The Mystery of Marie Rogêt" is unlike the other two Dupin stories in that it tries to solve a mysterious contemporary murder. The risk to Poe in writing "Marie Rogêt" was considerable since new evidence might arise that would challenge his solution—as, indeed, it did, in the form of a reported deathbed confession regarding a botched abortion. In accordance with this new explanation, Poe made modifications in the 1845 *Tales* version of the story, away from the single-murderer theory that he had offered in the serial publication.[15] Furthermore, "Marie Rogêt" is unlike the former and latter Dupin stories in that it is longer and more ponderous. Yet, notably, in both the 1842/43 version and the 1845 version, "Marie Rogêt" shares with "Rue Morgue" and "The Purloined Letter" a symmetrical form framing a significant midpoint.

We again proceed from the outside in. (Emphasis is my own, except where it is identified as both mine and Poe's.) Encouraging our close attention is Dupin's own: the narrator speaks of Dupin's reading newspapers about Marie Rogêt "with what seemed to me a minuteness altogether objectless" (*Collected Works* 3:753), echoing the narrator's describing Dupin's examining the Rue Morgue house and neighborhood "with a minuteness of attention for which I could see no possible object" (2:546). And encouraging our expectation for the symmetry of the work are two early terms, "half-credence" and "half-credences" (3:723).

We find in the epigraph and the first two paragraphs, concerning the correspondence between the story of Mary Rogers and that of Marie Rogêt, such language as "'ideal series of events which run *parallel* with the real ones,'" "the doctrine of chance, or, as it is technically termed, *the Calculus of Probabilities*," "a series of scarcely intelligible *coincidences*" (dual emphasis), and "the late murder of

MARY CECILIA ROGERS" (*Collected Works* 3:723–24). We find in the
ultimate and penultimate paragraphs of the tale, again concerning
the correspondences between the tales of Mary and Marie, such
language as "...I speak of these things only as of *coincidences*," "the
fate of the unhappy *Mary Cecilia Rogers*," "...there has existed a *parallel* in the contemplation of whose wonderful exactitude the reason
becomes embarrassed," and "*the* very *Calculus of Probabilities* to which
I have referred" (3:772–73). T. O. Mabbott observed the repetition
of the phrase "Calculus of Probabilities" (3:774 n. 2), but clearly this
repetition is part of a larger pattern. The first pair of framing corresponding passages is evident and invites our identification of the subsequent pairs. We can readily note seven additional pairs of framing
corresponding passages.

The second pair of the framing passages involves Poe's narrator's
stating somewhat after the beginning, "In the proclamation setting
forth this *reward, a full pardon* was promised to any accomplice who
should come forward in evidence against his fellow..." (*Collected
Works* 3:727), and Dupin's mentioning somewhat before the end, "the
circumstances of large *reward* offered, and *full pardon* to any King's
evidence" (3:768). The first half of the third pair involves the narrator's statement, drawn from newspaper accounts about Marie's
clothing, that "*In the outer garment, a slip, about a foot wide, had been
torn upward from the bottom hem to the waist....It was wound three times
around the waist, and secured by a sort of hitch in the back*" (3:730). The
second half of the pair involves Dupin's quoting the relevant passage
from a newspaper that "...*in the outer garment* of the corpse when
found, '*a slip, about a foot wide, had been torn upward from the bottom
hem to the waist, wound three times round the waist, and secured by a sort
of hitch in the back*'" (3:765).

Subsequently, relying on "important information" that "reached
the police," the narrator states of the scene of the suspected murder, "*The earth was trampled, the bushes were broken, and there was every
evidence of a struggle*" (*Collected Works* 3:734); Dupin later completes
this fourth pair of framing corresponding passages, reordering the
elements: "'*There was evidence,*' it is said, '*of a struggle; and the earth was
trampled, the bushes were broken*'" (3:762). Also, the narrator states that
inside the "*close thicket*" "*were three or four large stones, forming a* kind
of *seat, with a back and footstool. On the upper stone lay a white petticoat*;
*on the second a silk scarf. A parasol, gloves, and a pocket-handkerchief
were* also here found. *The handkerchief bore the name 'Marie Rogêt'*"
(3:734). And Dupin offers the corresponding half of the fifth pair

of corresponding passages; he states that inside the *"dense" "thicket"* *"were three extraordinary stones, forming a seat with a back and footstool"* (final eight words, dual emphasis). And he adds, *"On the upper stone lay a white petticoat; on the second a silk scarf;* scattered around, *were a parasol, gloves, and a pocket-handkerchief bearing the name, 'Marie Rogêt'"* (3:761; dual emphasis for "'upper'" and "'second'"). Associated with the two halves of this ample frame is a lengthy passage after its first half, from the newspaper *Le Soleil*, including mention of a mildewed parasol (3:735) and a lengthy passage after its second half, involving Dupin's quoting the same passage from *Le Soleil*, including mention of the mildewed parasol (3:759).[16]

Now we quickly approach the center. In the first half of the sixth pair of framing corresponding passages, Dupin states, *"The question of identity is* not even approached..." (*Collected Works* 3:744); in the second half, he asserts "...*the question of identity was* readily determined..." (3:751). Closing in on that center, we find two questions offered by the narrator of Dupin—the seventh pair of framing corresponding passages: *"And what...do you think of the opinion of Le Commerciel?"* (3:748), and *"And what are we to think...of the article in Le Soleil?"* (3:750). And the eighth and final pair of these parallel passages comprises Dupin's references to "some *gang of low ruffians*" (3:749) and "the *lowest class of ruffians*" (3:750).

These eight pairs of corresponding passages frame the significant midpoint of "The Mystery of Marie Rogêt"—a passage in which Dupin speaks of the parallel implicitly contended for by a newspaper writer between his pattern of walking in the city and that of Marie Rogêt. The central passage warrants lengthy quotation. (Emphasis is my own, except where an exception is noted.)

And, knowing the extent of his [the *Le Commercial* writer's] *personal acquaintance with others, and of others with him*, he compares his notoriety with that of the perfumery-girl, finds no great difference between them, and reaches at once the conclusion that she, in her walks, would be equally liable to recognition with himself in his. This could only be the case were her walks of the same unvarying, methodical character, and within the same *species* [Poe's emphasis] of limited region as are his own. He passes to and fro, at regular intervals, within a confined periphery, abounding in individuals who are led to observation of his person through interest in the kindred nature of his occupation with their own. But the walks of Marie may, in general, be supposed discursive. In this particular instance, it will be understood *as most probable, that she proceeded upon a route* of more than average diversity from her accustomed ones. The parallel which we imagine to have existed in the mind of Le Commerciel would only be sustained in the event of the two individuals' traversing the whole city. In this case, granting the *personal acquaintances* to be *equal*, the chances would be also equal that an *equal* number of *personal rencounters* would be made. For my own part, I should hold it not only as possible, but *as very far more than probable, that Marie* might have *proceeded*, at any given period, *by any one of the many routes* between her own residence and that of her aunt, without meeting a single individual *whom she knew, or by whom she was known.* In viewing this question in its full and proper light, we must hold steadily in mind the great disproportion between the *personal acquaintances* of even the most noted individual in Paris, and the entire population of Paris itself. (*Collected Works* 3:749–50)

The symmetry in the center of "Marie Rogêt" is apparent: the language *"personal acquaintance," "with others, and of others with him," "as most probable, that she proceeded upon a route," "personal acquaintances,"* and *"equal"* reflects *"equal," "personal rencounters," "as very far more than probable, that Marie* might have *proceeded...by any one of the many routes," "whom she knew, or by whom she was known,"* and *"personal acquaintances."* The central sentence, featuring two of the aforementioned pairs of corresponding language, is, "In this case [if the newspaper writer and Marie walked across the entire city, which they did not], granting the *personal acquaintances* to be *equal*, the chances would be also equal that an *equal* number of *personal rencounters* would be made." The repeated word "equal" is not applicable to the subject at hand—the different walks that the writer and Marie took. However, it is applicable to the parallel stories of Mary Rogers and Marie Rogêt. And it is also clearly applicable to the form of the story—this sentence appears precisely between the two equal halves of "The Mystery of Marie Rogêt."

Using a mixture of common sense, scientific information, a broad (and close) reading of newspapers, and identification with others' thinking, Dupin works to solve the mystery. With this knowledge and approximation of knowledge, he calculates likelihoods. They range from the extremely probable to the extremely improbable. He offers "a wager of one thousand to one" that the Deluc boys would seat themselves in the "natural throne" in the thicket (*Collected Works* 3:761). He states that "In ninety-nine chances from the hundred" he would follow the decision of the public (3:757). He states that "The chances are ten to one . . . " that the naval officer who had once eloped with Marie Rogêt would suggest elopement again, rather than that another man would suggest elopement for the first time (3:754). (The odds were originally "ten thousand to one" [3:754n].) Toward the end of the story, Poe maintains that throwing sixes with dice is just as likely if one had just thrown them twice as if one had not (3:773). He then shifts to the least likely occurrences. A thorn's tearing off a piece from a garment is "the rarest of accidents" (3:762). Ruffians' accidentally leaving incriminating articles behind in the thicket is "almost impossible" (3:764). Having left these articles in the thicket for longer than a week is "little less than miraculous" (3:760). One gang of ruffians committing at nearly the same time the same crime as another gang of ruffians would be "a miracle indeed" (3:757).

With his assorted methodologies and his recurring estimate of probabilities, Dupin determines, in the original publication of the story, that Marie Rogêt was killed by the naval officer. Later, with the appearance of the reported confession, Poe modified the language of his mystery in the 1845 *Tales* to leave room for the possibility of an unsuccessful abortion. Regardless of his later assertion—"[t]he 'naval officer' who committed the murder (or rather the accidental death arising from an attempt at abortion) *confessed* it; and the whole matter is now well understood..." (*Letters* 2:641)—Poe did not resolve the matter; as T. O. Mabbott noted, "...he did not solve the mystery" (*Complete Works* 3:722). Indeed, the mystery has never been definitively solved.

And Poe does offer problematic logic, as when Dupin argues against inferences based upon the past (*Collected Works* 3:752), yet discusses the walks of the newspaper writer and Marie based upon their past (3:749–50) and determines the guilt of the naval officer in 1841 based upon his past with Marie in 1838 (3:754–55). And the narrator writes against the importance of examining detail (3:774), yet Dupin investigates the detail of the newspapers with great care (3:753). Poe even later admitted that at the close of his tale he offered "mystification" (*Letters* 2:640).[17]

However, if "The Mystery of Marie Rogêt" is not, as Richard P. Benton has argued, "a masterpiece of detective fiction," it is also not, as J. Gerald Kennedy has maintained, "that forgettable experiment in forensic narrative" either.[18] Although T. O. Mabbott stated that "Marie Rogêt" "enjoy[s] a higher reputation among general readers than it deserves" (*Collected Works* 3:715), he defended the tale by stating that Poe did successfully challenge three contemporary views: "...he demolished the gang theory, he cleared John Anderson [Mary's employer], and he regarded the delayed discovery of the dead girl's clothes as contrived…" (3:722). I would like to defend the tale with one additional point: the presence of a hitherto-unremarked symmetry and significant midpoint suggest that with "The Mystery of Marie Rogêt" Poe provided further evidence of his literary craftsmanship.

A final word on "Marie Rogêt" is inevitably biographical. Looking for the double "*d*"s in the central passage, we find them: "proceeded" and "proceeded." (We may be reminded of the two appearances of the word "deepened" at the center of "The Man of the Crowd" and of the word "descended" at the center of "A Tale of the Ragged Mountains.") And we should not be surprised to read about a corpse "imbedded" in "the soft mud or ooze" (*Collected Works* 3:742). Apparently, "Eddy" is present here, too.

But for now, let us turn to the last Dupin story—the one that Poe termed "perhaps, the best of my tales of ratiocination" (*Letters* 1:450)—"The Purloined Letter."

The form of this tale also involves symmetry, immediately suggested by the narrator's reference to his enjoying "the *twofold* [emphasis added] luxury of meditation and a meerschaum" (*Collected Works* 3:974). We are reminded of this phrase by Dupin's later mention of the "folded" and "refolded" letter (3:992).

Like "The Murders in the Rue Morgue," "The Purloined Letter" offers the unexpected—in the former, the murderer is an orangutan; in the latter, the document is hidden in plain sight. However, the careful scrutiny in "Rue Morgue" and "Marie Rogêt" is not significantly praised in "The Purloined Letter." Attention to detail in "The Purloined Letter" is represented by the Prefect and his men; attention to the intellect of the opponent, the Minister D——, is represented by Dupin. Dupin infers that the minister realizes he must outwit the police by hiding the letter in the open. It is identification that is key to Dupin's approach. We have seen identification before to a more limited degree in the Dupin tales—the detective imagines the thoughts of the French sailor in "The Murders in the Rue Morgue" (*Collected Works* 2:561–62) and those of the writer for *Le Commercial* and Marie Rogêt and the murderer in "The Mystery of Marie Rogêt" (2:749; 756; 764–65, 771).[19] Identification is the primary method of detection in "The Purloined Letter" because in that tale alone Dupin is challenged by an intellect approaching or equaling his own.

To illustrate the hiddenness of the obvious, Dupin discusses a game involving finding the names on a map: "A novice in the game generally seeks to embarrass his opponents by giving them the most minutely lettered names; but the adept selects such words as stretch, in large characters, from one end of the chart to the other" (*Collected Works* 3:989). With Dupin's example we have a suggestion of the critical approach taken here—reading closely for the symmetry that stretches from one end of the story to the other. We work to be "the adept"—as Umberto Eco has said, "...the model reader is the one who plays your game."[20]

There are eight pairs of corresponding language framing the center of "The Purloined Letter." (And, again, emphasis is my own except where otherwise noted.) Near the beginning, the narrator states, that "Dupin now *arose*...but *sat down* again" (*Collected Works* 3:975); near the end, Dupin states, with regard to climbing, that "...it is far more easy to *get up* than to *come down*" (3:993). Subsequently, the Prefect comments that "...*it* [the letter] still *remains in his* [the Minister's] *possession*" and "...the paper gives its holder a certain *power* ..." (3:976); toward the end, before his remark about climbing, Dupin declares, "...the Minister has had her [the Queen] in his *power*" and "...*the letter is* not *in his* [the Minister's] *possession*..." (3:993). Next come the two thefts: "...*he* [the Minister] *takes* also from the table *the letter* to which he had no claim" (3:977) and "...*I* [Dupin] stepped to the card-rack, *took the letter*..." (3:992). In both thefts, another letter is substituted for the much-sought one.

The fourth pair of corresponding language involves a variety of comments about the Minister. Elements in the first half include the Prefect's stating, "...I have investigated every *nook*...[where] the paper can be *concealed*," Dupin's referring to "affairs at *court*" and "those *intrigues* in which [Minister] D—— is known to be involved," the narrator's speaking of "[the letter] concealed...elsewhere than *upon* his own *premises*" and concluding "...*the paper* is clearly then *upon the premises*," and Dupin's adding "D——...must *have anticipated these waylayings*..." (*Collected Works* 3:978–79). Those elements in the second half include Dupin's asserting, "I knew him as a *courtier*, too, and as a bold *intriguant* [dual emphasis]," "*He* could not *have* failed *to anticipate*...he did not fail *to anticipate—the waylayings*..." "...*the letter was* not *upon the premises*," and the Minister despised "all the ordinary *nooks* [dual emphasis] of *concealment*" (3:988).

Working forward and backward, closer to the center of the story, we find the Prefect stating that Minister D—— is "Not *altogether* [Poe's emphasis] a *fool*...but then he's a *poet*, which I take to be only one remove from a *fool*" (*Collected Works* 3:979) and Dupin declaring, "All *fools* are *poets*; this the Prefect *feels* [Poe's emphasis]; and he is merely guilty of a *non distributio medii* [Poe's emphasis] in thence inferring that all *poets* are *fools*" (3:986). The latter passage in its chiastic structure reinforces the symmetry of the narrative.[21]

Then we come to the sixth pair of corresponding language. The first half involves Dupin's telling the Prefect, "…you *probed* the beds and the bed-clothes…" and the Prefect's trying to reassure Dupin, "We *divided* its [the house's] entire *surface* into compartments, which we numbered…; then we *scrutinized* each individual *square inch* throughout the premises, including the two houses immediately adjoining, *with the microscope*…" (*Collected Works* 3:980). The second half involves Dupin's questioning the Prefect's technique: "What is all this boring, and *probing*, and sounding, and *scrutinizing with the microscope*, and *dividing* the *surface* of the building into registered *square inches*…" (3:985).

And finally we come to the seventh and eighth pairs of corresponding language. Mention in the first half of the "*reward*" which is "*prodigious*" (*Collected Works* 3:980) is matched by mention in the second half of the "*extraordinary reward*" (3:985). Furthermore, a reference slightly later in the first half to "the most *accurate admeasurement*" (3:981) parallels that slightly earlier in the second half to "the *accuracy* with which the opponent's intellect is *admeasured*" (3:985).

We arrive, then, at the center. Not surprisingly, the exchanges at the beginning and the end of the story—those involving the precious letter and its relatively worthless replacement—frame an exchange at the center—that of the precious letter for a check.[22] Poe writes:

> "In that case [if you are willing to pay fifty thousand francs for the letter]," replied Dupin, opening a drawer, and producing a check-book, "you may as well *fill* me *up a check for the amount mentioned*. When you have *signed* it, I will *hand* you the letter."
> I was astounded. The Prefect appeared absolutely thunder-stricken. For some minutes he remained speechless and motionless, looking incredulously at my friend with open mouth, and eyes that seemed starting from their sockets; then, apparently recovering himself in some measure, he seized a pen, and after several pauses and vacant stares, finally *filled up* and *signed a check for fifty thousand francs*, and *handed* it across the table to Dupin. The latter examined it carefully and deposited it in his pocket-book; then, unlocking an *escritoire* [Poe's *underscoring*], took thence a letter and gave it to the Prefect. (*Collected Works* 3:983)

The careful repetition at the center is evident: *"fill...up," "a check for the amount mentioned," "signed,"* and *"hand"* followed by *"filled up," "signed," "a check for fifty thousand francs,"* and *"handed."* This is where "The Purloined Letter" folds over on itself.

Looking for the double *"d"*s, we notice at the center of the symmetrical phrasing the word "astoun*ded*." And the pattern of double *d*s is underscored with the subsequent exchange between Dupin and the narrator:

> "...I felt entire confidence in his [the Prefect's] having made a satisfactory investigation—so far as his labors exten*ded*."
> "So far as his labors exten*ded*?" said I. (*Collected Works* 3:983)

"Eddy" is plainly at the center here, too. We may recall the anticipation early on, "the curling *eddies* of smoke" and "the two houses *immediately* adjoining" (3:974, 980).[23]

And then Dupin explains the inadequacy of the Prefect's approach—an exhaustive search not informed by an accurate gauging of the acuity of Minister D—— —as opposed to the validity of his own approach, informed by an astute identification with his canny opponent. In part to illustrate the value of identification, Dupin offers a story demonstrating a schoolboy's skill in guessing even and odd.[24] This story, it turns out, contains the *mise en abime* for the entire work.

Tracked backward by Bruce Krajewski as far as Cicero's *De Finibus*,[25] the game of even and odd is described with care by Dupin in "The Purloined Letter." The cunning schoolboy is able to win "all the marbles of the school" by correctly estimating the intelligence of his opponent. His first opponent is "an arrant simpleton," and when the schoolboy loses with his initial guess of "odd," he judges that his opponent will shift from an even number of marbles to an odd number, so "...he guesses odd and wins." However, his second opponent is "a simpleton a degree above the first." (Poe's gradations of intelligence are familiar—in "Letter to B——" he refers to both "the fool" and "the fool's neighbor, who is a step higher on the Andes of the mind" [*Essays and Reviews* 5].) With this second, slightly more intelligent opponent, the schoolboy guesses "odd" and loses, and then calculates that his opponent, who had begun by holding an even number of marbles, would think to make the obvious shift to an odd number, but then would reconsider and decide to hold an even number. Dupin concludes, "...he [the schoolboy] guesses even, and wins" (*Collected Works* 3:984).

The narrator understands that the principle behind the schoolboy's success is "identification"; Dupin confirms this and goes on to explain that this identification was facilitated by the schoolboy's assuming the expression of his opponent. Mabbott readily notes the immediate source for this technique in Horace Binney Wallace's *Stanley* (*Collected Works* 3:994–95, n. 12).[26] But what remains to be noted is the formal importance of the game of even and odd for "The Purloined Letter." We must again try to be "the adept"—the one who wins the map game by selecting "such words as stretch, in large characters, from one end of the chart to the other"—Poe's "model reader," who plays his game.

The schoolboy's guesses with the slightly more intelligent "simpleton" are first "odd" and then "even." These two answers constitute an essential feature of the hidden structure of the tale. In the first half of the work, Poe's uses the word "odd" five times (and never the word "even"). (Emphasis is again my own, except as otherwise indicated.) The Prefect responds to Dupin, "That is another of your *odd* notions." The narrator comments, "...the Prefect...had a fashion of calling every thing '*odd*' that was beyond his comprehension, and thus lived amid an absolute legion of '*odd*ities.'" The Prefect says, "...I thought Dupin would like to hear the details of it [the theft of the letter], because it is so excessively *odd* [dual emphasis]." And Dupin responds, "Simple and *odd*" (*Collected Works* 3:975).

In the second half of the work, after the description of the game of even and odd, Poe uses the word "even" three times (and never the word "odd"). Dupin states, "The great error [of mathematical reasoning] lies in supposing that *even* the truths of what is called *pure* [Poe's emphasis] algebra, are abstract or general truths" (*Collected Works* 3:987). (The word "even" does not appear in the *Stanley* source passage.)[27] To hide from the minister his roving gaze so that he may search for the missing letter, Dupin states, "To be *even* with him, I complained of my weak eyes, and lamented the necessity of the spectacles..." (3:990). He then observes the letter: "It was thrust carelessly, and *even* as it seemed, contemptuously, into one of the upper divisions of the rack" (3:991).

"'From one end of the chart to the other'" stretch two words—the word "odd" (in the beginning) and the word "even" (toward the end). Hidden in plain sight are the two answers of the schoolboy to the second opponent, he who is slightly more intelligent than the first. These answers encapsulate the form of the work. We may infer that the clever schoolboy is analogous to Poe, and that the "simpleton a degree above the first," who nonetheless loses, is analogous to Poe's slightly better readers—that is, to us! And yet although we implicitly lose in the game of marbles, we win in the game of fiction. For we have found Poe's design; we have played his game.

A revealing *mise en abime* may be found elsewhere in Poe's oeuvre. The best example is the native chief Too-wit standing midway between infinitely reflecting facing mirrors in the hold of the *Jane Guy* in Poe's novel *The Narrative of Arthur Gordon Pym*. Pym states, "...I was afraid he would expire upon the spot" (*Collected Writings* 1:169). Poe thus offers in miniature the structure of the narrative: Augustus Barnard (who represents Poe's brother Henry) dies midway (in the central chapter) between the coded infinitely reflecting facing mirrors (the ship the *Penguin* in the first and last chapters, which, like the bird, has "the spirit of reflection" [1:153]). Through the infinite reflection of the death of Augustus, Poe represents his *"Mournful and Never-ending Remembrance"* (*Complete Works* 14:208) of the death of this brother.[28] The use of *mise en abime* is characteristic of Poe. It clarifies the unity of a work and offers a satisfying aesthetic self-consciousness.

And there is another game to consider in "The Purloined Letter" in addition to the map game and the even-odd game: the card game. The game of whist is discussed at length in "The Murders in the Rue Morgue"; "Beyond doubt," the narrator says, "there is nothing of a similar nature so greatly tasking the faculty of analysis." And he adds, "The necessary knowledge is that of *what* to observe" (*Collected Works* 2:529–30). Shawn Rosenheim rightly argues that "'The Purloined Letter' emerges, in some sense, from this discussion of cards in 'The Murders in the Rue Morgue': in it, king, queen, and Minister play out the drama of the face cards...."[29] We should observe, however, that in his discussion of whist in "Rue Morgue," the narrator speaks of counting the cards not only "honor by honor," but also "trump by trump" (2:530). And here we may again see Poe winning the game.

Most readers first reading "The Purloined Letter," trying to anticipate Dupin's solution to the mystery of the letter's whereabouts, do not anticipate that the letter is hidden in plain sight. So, Dupin outwits not only the minister, but also his reader. His description of the otherwise unrecognized "hiding place" is key to understanding Poe's elaboration of the card trope. Dupin states, "At length my eyes, in going the circuit of the room, fell upon a *trump*ery fillagree *card*-rack of pasteboard, that hung dangling by a dirty blue ribbon from a little brass knob just beneath the middle of the mantel-piece"

(*Collected Works* 3:990–91; emphasis added). The location of the valuable letter—unexpectedly and brilliantly in the open—is Poe's "*trump…card.*" And, notably, playing cards are often made of "pasteboard" and sometimes feature on their backs a "fillagree" [or "filigree"] design. And so again, Poe wins. But even as, in recognizing our defeat at Poe's hands in the story of the game of even and odd, we win by recognizing his design, so again, in realizing our loss to Poe at the game of whist, we triumph by understanding his fulfillment of his figure. Even as Dupin recognizes the hiding place in plain sight, we may recognize the significance of that hiding place—also in plain sight.[30]

And then there is the word "card-rack" (*Collected Works* 3:990, 992, 993). Poe was Assistant Editor of *Burton's Gentleman's Magazine* when a filler item, "A Literary Curiosity," was published in the February 1840 issue, a slight piece, following Poe's "Peter Pendulum, the Business Man," which concerned a sentence comprising seven palindromic Latin words, "ODO TENET MULUM, MADIDAM MAPPAM TENET ANNA." Poe was still Assistant Editor of *Burton's* when a piece titled "Palindromes," in the "Omniana" series, was published in the May 1840 issue; this work offered two palindromic words ("*madam*" and "*eye*"), a palindromic line ("Lewd did I live, and evil I did dwell"), and a riddling poem suggesting five palindromic words (Mum, Anna, Deed, Anana, and Minim), all five of which form an acrostic for a sixth palindromic word (Madam). Some scholars have suggested that Poe provided the comments on the palindromes—even wrote the poem. However, T. O. Mabbott, who had assigned the "Omniana" to Poe, later changed his mind.[31] Yet whatever attribution we accept, we can be sure that as Assistant Editor, Poe knew both "A Literary Curiosity" and "Palindromes." It is very difficult to conceive that four years later he would not have recognized that his key word "card-rack" was itself a near-palindrome. He must have been aware that the word was nearly identical backward and forward. And as such, it suggests Poe's tale itself.

The formal richness of "The Purloined Letter"—including the use of the game involving the map, the game of even and odd, and the game of whist, and a near-palindromic key word—probably helped lead Poe to consider the work "perhaps, the best of my tales of ratiocination" (*Letters* 1:450). There is a remarkable blend of complexity and control that is, for the reader, both admirable and pleasurable.

Still, we should also see "The Purloined Letter" as resembling "The Murders in the Rue Morgue" and "The Mystery of Marie Rogêt" with regard to its symmetrical phrasing and significant midpoint. The tales' centers are particularly memorable: the opening and closing of the window in "Rue Morgue," the nonparallel walks in "Marie Rogêt," and the exchange of the letter for the check in "The Purloined Letter." Each center is a satisfying reversal of its context: an open window at the center of a locked-room mystery, illusory parallelism at the center of a tale based on parallelism, and the purchase of the much-sought letter at the center of a tale about its repeated theft. And all three centers seem to suggest the stillness of the center. (The emphasis that follows is my own.) Dupin mentions at the center of "Rue Morgue" "the head [of the nail]...*remaining firm* in its bed" (*Collected Works* 2:553); he advises at the center of "Marie Rogêt" that "...we must *hold* [a thought] *steadily* in mind..." (3:750); and the narrator writes of the stunned Prefect at the center of "The Purloined Letter," "...he *remained* speechless and *motionless*..." (3:983). Here we have calm, equilibrium. It should be added that all three centers feature Poe's signature, "Eddy." In their careful structuring, the three Dupin tales clearly appeal to "considerations analogous with those which are the essence of sculptural taste" (*Complete Works* 10:120). Other tales by Poe also appeal to such considerations, and future scholarship should attend to them.

In his May 1842 review of Nathaniel Hawthorne's *Twice-Told Tales*, Poe elaborates his theory of the desirability of a "single *effect*," a "preconceived effect," in the tale (*Complete Works* 11:108; see also 13:153 and 14:194). He adds that "...Truth is often, and in very great degree, the aim of the tale. Some of the finest tales are tales of ratiocination" (11:109). Certainly the Dupin tales work out the truth of the mystery and thereby prompt a compelling effect: the amazement of the reader. Yet although Poe writes that "...Beauty can be better treated in the poem" (11:109), he does admit Truth and Passion in the poem, with "proper subservience" and enveiling (see the 1846 essay "The Philosophy of Composition; 14:198). So he would similarly admit Beauty in the tale. And there is a beauty to the subtly shaped Dupin tales—one properly subservient and enveiled—the consideration of which may be thought of as a secondary effect: an aesthetic satisfaction that quietly complements the intellectual one.

In light of the evident form of the three Dupin tales—corresponding passages framing a significant center—we may be able to respond to a provocative comment by Mary Douglas in *Thinking in Circles* regarding "ring structures":

> I have no example as yet of detective fiction that conforms exactly to the rules of ring structures. But this digression on the rules of

detective fiction [including the twenty rules of S. S. Van Dine]
convinces me that there is no reason why there should not be one.
Some detective stories are structurally nowhere near rings, some are
almost rings, and there may well be true ring forms to be found. (79)

What would those "true ring forms" offer? According to Douglas, the
seven characteristics for "long ring compositions" are (1). *"Exposition
or prologue"*; (2) *"Split into two halves"*; (3) *"Parallel sections"* (on either
side of the center or "mid-turn"); (4) *"Indicators to mark individual
sections"*; (5) *"Central loading"* (at "a well-marked turning point");
(6) *"Rings within rings"*; and (7) *"Closure at two levels"* (a verbal and
thematic return, circle-like, to the beginning at the ending) (35–38).
As short works, the Dupin tales need not possess "indicators to
mark individual sections" or "rings within rings." But they do clearly
possess the other five elements.

It would seem that Poe's Dupin tales do feature the "true ring
forms" whose existence Douglas suspected in some detective fiction.
Accordingly, these tales may be linked not only with other works in
the detective fiction genre that they began, but also with works, from
The Iliad and the Bible forward, that offer the "true ring forms" that
Douglas describes.[32] Close reading may indeed have far-reaching
implications. And hermeneutic circles may yield literary ones.

We may at this point continue to explore the Dupin tales,
proceeding from this close reading to a thorough identification with
Poe as a reader. A Philadelphia newspaper—then several New York
City newspapers—then an obscure book about British royalty—will
prove key to our genetic analyses.

CHAPTER II

"THE MURDERS IN THE RUE MORGUE" AND *THE PHILADELPHIA SATURDAY NEWS*

C riticism of "The Murders in the Rue Morgue" has varied widely, from the early psychoanalytic (e.g., Marie Bonaparte on the tale's latent sexual content) and the historicist (for instance, Burton R. Pollin on the tale's divergences from early nineteenth-century Paris) to studies of gender (e.g., Judith Fetterley on the tale's focus on violence against women) and those of race (e.g., Elise Lemire on the tale's concern with miscegenation).[1] Potentially useful for all these approaches, and others as well—and vitally illuminating in its own right—is a greater recognition of Poe's reading and his transformation of it. And so we follow Dupin's interest in "things external to the game."

The narrator of "The Murders in the Rue Morgue" asserts, "There are few persons who have not, at some period of their lives, amused themselves in retracing the steps by which particular conclusions of their own minds have been attained" (*Collected Works* 2:535). He thus comments on Dupin's retracing his own thoughts, the "*analysis*" (2:527n) that anticipates Dupin's retracing the actions that led to the mysterious murders. Similarly, scholars have long striven to retrace the steps by which Poe composed this classic tale and thus engendered a genre. Killis Campbell, considering Poe's acknowledged reliance on "newspaper accounts" for "The Mystery of Marie Rogêt," inferred, "The plot of his companion story, 'The Murders in the Rue Morgue,' was also in every likelihood drawn from newspaper accounts...."[2] The present chapter will bear out Campbell's inference and will elaborate its important interpretive implications. But first, we should review briefly the scholarship on the sources and potential sources for "Rue Morgue."

T. O. Mabbott has provided a useful overview in his edition's headnote to the tale, drawing on relevant scholarship. He mentions a source for Dupin's inductive method in Voltaire's *Zadig* (1747). He identifies several possible sources for Poe's murderous orangutan—an 1834 story of a thieving baboon, later stories of a shaving monkey, and an account of a murderous orangutan in Sir Walter Scott's *Count Robert of Paris* (1831). He also refers to two potentially related stories by J. S. LeFanu (one about a locked room, the other mentioning "a long lock of coarse sooty hair") and a third such story by J. C. Mangan (about associative thinking). Mabbott notes the source for Dupin's initial and middle name in C. Auguste Dubouchet, an acquaintance of Poe's who was being considered for a position as a French teacher in 1840. And regarding the model for Dupin, he writes, "The person Poe had in mind was almost surely André-Marie-Jean-Jacques Dupin (1783–1865), a French politician" who appears in Robert M. Walsh's translation *Sketches of Living Characters of France* (1841), which Poe reviewed. Mabbott provides in his notes additional information on possible source passages, including a discussion of the idea of men having "windows in their bosoms," in Horace Binney Wallace's novel *Stanley* (1838); a description of a murdered elderly woman in her apartment in "Doctor D'Arsac" in the 1838–39 *Burton's Gentleman's Magazine* series "Unpublished Passages in the Life of Vidocq"; a commentary regarding indirect vision in Sir David Brewster's *Letters on Natural Magic* (1832); and a treatment of the orangutan in Thomas Wyatt's *A Synopsis of Natural History* (1839).[3]

Since Mabbott's edition, new sources and potential sources proposed for the orangutan of "Rue Morgue" have included the 1823 *Blackwood's* tale "A Chapter on Goblins," a folktale motif, a yet-to-be-determined jest-book that offers a shaving monkey story drawn ultimately from the 1583 *A Mirror of Mirth*, works by George and Frederick Cuvier, a piece on the orangutan in the 1835 *Saturday Evening Post*, another in the 1836 *American Magazine of Useful and Entertaining Knowledge*, and yet another in the 1839 *Pennsylvania Inquirer*. George Long's *Hoyle* has been suggested as a source for information regarding whist. And autobiographical details of the work have been noted and proposed.[4]

Of particular interest is the 1828 novel *Pelham*, by Edward Bulwer-Lytton (1803–1873), as a source for "Rue Morgue." Stuart and Susan Levine note the appearance in both Bulwer's novel and Poe's tale of mention of Rousseau's *La Nouvelle Héloïse* (with regard to the statement *"de nier ce qui est, et d'expliquer ce qui n'est pas"*), reference to Crébillon, and the use of the Faubourg St.-Germain.[5] To these parallels may be added the phrases *"au troisième"* and *"Jardin des Plantes."*

Notable, too, is that Bulwer comically presented a monkey attacking a landlady even as Poe's orangutan attacked Madame L'Espanaye. Unquestionably, Bulwer's *Pelham* is a source for Poe's first detective story, one that helped Poe—who had never been to France—elaborate a French setting and character. It is a notable irony that Poe's French face had, in part, a British origin. And we may wonder if Poe's notorious eponymous street, added late to his manuscript, may also owe a debt to Bulwer's novel: previous to the attack, Pelham dines with his friends (and the monkey) at a restaurant in "Rue Mont Orgueil" (*"Rue Mont Orgue*il"?).[6]

This compendium should be expanded to include an important series of pieces that appeared in May-December 1838 in a long-neglected newspaper, *The Philadelphia Saturday News and Literary Gazette*. They came to my attention in a series of archival investigations, from the Nantucket Atheneum to the Library of Congress. These pieces, I would argue, were a part of the prompt for the writing of "The Murders in the Rue Morgue"; they are the "newspaper accounts" that Campbell long ago anticipated. Recognition of these newspaper sources will enhance our understanding of the first of Poe's Dupin tales.

The *Saturday News* came into being when publisher Charles W. Alexander "transferred his interest" in the *Gentleman's Vade Mecum: Or the Sporting Dramatic Companion* to Louis A. Godey, Joseph C. Neal, and Morton McMichael.[7] Godey was publisher of the new, more sizable, weekly paper—which ran from 2 July 1836 through 5 January 1839—and Neal and McMichael were editors. At the time, Godey was already publisher of *The Lady's Book*, where he had featured Poe's short story "The Visionary" (later revised as "The Assignation") in the January 1834 issue.[8] Neal, former editor of the *Vade Mecum*, was editor of the *Pennsylvanian* (a newspaper from which Poe drew a positive notice of the monthly that he edited, the *Southern Literary Messenger*, for the supplement to the January 1836 issue).[9] McMichael, Alderman of Spring Garden, had been editor of the *Saturday Evening Post*, and then, from 1831 to 1835, of the Philadelphia *Saturday Courier*. In 1831, he, Alexander, and other Philadelphia literati had judged the *Courier*'s short story contest, one to which Poe had submitted his work. Although the contest committee did not select any of Poe's stories as the winning entry, editor McMichael did publish five of Poe's tales in the *Courier* in 1832: "Metzengerstein," "The Duke De L'Omelette," "A Tale of Jerusalem," "A Decided Loss," and "The Bargain Lost."[10]

The *Saturday News* was a large newspaper—it comprised four pages, each of which measured 26–1/4 inches by 20 inches and featured eight columns.[11] The paper was published every Saturday; a yearly subscription cost two dollars. Editorial offices were located at 100 Walnut Street (later at 211 Chesnut Street).[12] According to its editors, the *Saturday News* would be "an agreeable and instructive miscellany—a medium through which a large amount of choice literature may be obtained for a trifling equivalent—a vehicle for independent criticism...."[13] These goals did not go unmet. The *Saturday News* evidently proved "agreeable"—by November 1836, Godey and his editors could assert that "...the subscription list has increased with a constancy and rapidity never equalled in this city..."; by March 1838, they laid claim to fifteen thousand subscribers—impressive even if adjusted for editorial enthusiasm.[14] The *Saturday News* typically featured, on page one, an excerpt from a British annual or periodical—"choice literature," perhaps written by Theodore Hook or Frederick Marryat—and, on pages two, three, and four, the news of the day (sometimes reprinted, often with an eye toward the novel, the strange, the amusing); theater, book, and journal reviews; and additional literary items. Neal's "City Worthies" sketches were a staple of the *Saturday News*; other pieces were contributed by such Philadelphia writers as Robert Montgomery Bird, Richard Penn Smith, Robert T. Conrad, and William E. Burton. Among the most celebrated American writers whose works were reprinted in the *Saturday News* were Washington Irving, Ralph Waldo Emerson, and Oliver Wendell Holmes.[15]

The "independent criticism" of Neal and McMichael also distinguished the *Saturday News*; the editors reviewed a variety of theatrical performances, and book and journal publications with clarity and force. They regularly reviewed the *Southern Literary Messenger*, often praising the strength of Poe's criticism, but acknowledging toward the end of his tenure his occasional harshness. A summative comment may be representative: "We are sorry to lose Mr. Poe, who, although occasionally severe in his strictures, and sometimes, perhaps a little unjust, generally exhibited a boldness and independence, which entitled him to much commendation."[16] Significantly, Neal and McMichael reprinted Poe's poem "The City of Sin" in their review of the August 1836 issue of the *Messenger*, and probably it was McMichael who wrote the very favorable appraisal of Poe's novel *The Narrative of Arthur Gordon Pym* (1838): "From the casual glance at different pages, which we have been enabled to give, we perceive that it abounds in the wild and wonderful, and it is apparently written with great ability."[17]

Poe knew of the *Saturday News* from its beginning—as editor of the *Southern Literary Messenger*, he reprinted in a supplement to the July 1836 issue a favorable review of the magazine that had appeared in the first issue of the newspaper.[18] It is certain that Poe, an assiduous reader of newspapers, would have continued to read the *Saturday News*, especially since the editors clearly esteemed his work. And Godey and McMichael had published his fiction early on. Poe had particular regard for McMichael; he would come to write of him, "...we have the highest respect for the judgment of Mr. McMichael" (*Complete Works* 15:256; see also 15:224).[19]

Furthermore, the *Saturday News* would have been eminently accessible to Poe. As editor of the *Messenger* from December 1835 through January 1837, Poe would have received the paper in exchange; as a resident of Philadelphia from early 1838 on, Poe would readily have obtained the paper in the city. Notably, from early 1838 through 4 September 1838, Poe lived at 202 Mulberry (or Arch) Street, just a few blocks from 211 Chesnut Street, the office of the *Saturday News*. His new residence at Sixteenth Street and Locust was still within walking distance of that office.[20]

During the early part of his residence in Philadelphia, 1838—the last months of the publication of the *Saturday News*—Poe would find in this newspaper not only the aforementioned encomium for his recent fiction *The Narrative of Arthur Gordon Pym*, but also news items that would prove important for his imagining "The Murders in the Rue Morgue." Poe may have found details here for others of his works of fiction: the "liquid ruby" wine of "An Octogenary, Fifty Years Since" for the "ruby colored fluid" in "Ligeia" (*Collected Works* 2:325); the bear and man grappling, rolling together "over the edge of a precipice" in "Bear Story" for the bear that "hung over the precipice" and attacked a man in "Julius Rodman" (*Collected Writings* 1:579); and the ancestral estate featuring a lake and a great mansion with a library, old pictures, and an "Usher" who takes the invited stranger, the narrator, down to the cellar, from "Life of an English Nobleman" for similar elements of setting and plot in "The Fall of the House of Usher" (*Collected Works* 2:397–417).[21] But the 1838 issues of the *Saturday News* would prove most suggestive for Poe's first detective story.

The first of the *Saturday News* pieces that would be suggestive for "The Murders in the Rue Morgue," titled simply "Orang Outang," was published on 26 May 1838. Since Poe and his family had moved to Philadelphia in early 1838, he would very likely have encountered this *Saturday News* piece when it appeared, and well before reading the *Pennsylvania Inquirer* item "An Ourang Outang," published on 1 July 1839 (and really concerning a chimpanzee).[22] With regard to the aforementioned earlier plausible sources for Poe's orangutan, none would have been as immediate for Poe as the *Saturday News* article. Notable correspondences are apparent. This piece, in part quoting from a *Penny Magazine* item about a remarkable orangutan in the London Zoo, offers, like "The Murders in the Rue Morgue," an orangutan of characteristic "prodigious" strength (*Collected Works* 2:559) that recovers from its voyage from Borneo, attempts to break out of its confinement, and, excited, engages in "*unusual* activity" (2:555), including dragging a heavy piece of furniture across the floor (2:564–67). And while the London Zoo orangutan repeatedly crosses its "latticed enclosure," Poe's orangutan grasps a "latticed" shutter to enter Madame L'Espanaye's room (2:554, 565). These common details are provocative, but, of course, not indicative that Poe would have conceived of "The Murders in the Rue Morgue" after reading this item—in fact, he probably did not fully imagine the work until 1839, after the *Saturday News* had ceased publication. As will be seen, Poe would have read all the relevant *Saturday News* pieces before elaborating the plot of the tale.

In 1839, he would probably have remembered details of this *Saturday News* article for elements of "Rue Morgue" and, in light of the correspondences noted here, reread "Orang Outang" in a saved clipping or in a file copy of the 26 May 1838 issue of the *Saturday News*, owned, borrowed, or at least consulted by him. That Poe would very likely have owned newspaper files in 1839 is suggested by the testimony of bookseller William Gowans, who lodged with Poe in New York City in 1837: "Poe...had a library made up of newspapers, magazines bound and unbound, with what books had been presented to him...."[23] That Poe would have consulted newspaper files in 1839 is intimated by his February 1840 review of Henry Wadsworth Longfellow's book of poetry, *Voices of the Night*, in which Poe mentions "looking over a file of newspapers, not long ago..." (*Complete Works* 10:72).

Critically, Poe's transmutation of the *Saturday News* "orang outang" into the murderous orangutan of the Rue Morgue would have been significantly assisted by a subsequent *Saturday News* piece, one concerning the murderous behavior of a human, Edward Coleman. The story, titled "Deliberate Murder in Broadway, at Midday," appeared in the 4 August 1838 issue of the newspaper *adjacent to* the McMichael review of *Pym*. Poe would not have missed it. We should recall, in this regard, that the story of the actual wreck of the *Ariel*—the initial prompt for Poe's *Pym*—appeared in the *Norfolk Herald adjacent to* a review of a recent issue of his *Southern Literary Messenger*.[24]

According to this *Saturday News* piece, Edward Coleman, a black man, suspected his wife Ann of infidelity—perhaps with good reason—and, when walking with her down Broadway near Walker Street, opposite Jollie's Music Store, at approximately 11 a.m. on Saturday, 28 July 1838, he slit her throat with a razor. The article offers relevant background information on the couple, an account of Coleman's arrest, and a description of his effort to appear insane while in prison. This grim story would have intrigued Poe. In view of his recent stay in New York City, he would have been familiar with the site of the murder—when in New York City, he would probably have passed it while walking or riding between his Sixth Avenue home or Carmine Street home and William Gowans's lower Broadway bookshop or the City Hotel.[25] Furthermore, judging from Poe's fiction—especially "The Tell-Tale Heart" and "The Black Cat" (*Collected Works* 3: 792–97, 849–59)—and his reportorial piece "The Trial of James Wood," Poe would have been fascinated by the themes of murder and insanity.[26]

The important correspondences between the *Saturday News* piece on Coleman's murder of his wife and Poe's tale of an orangutan's murder of two women involve distinctly similar language. The newspaper story characterizes Coleman's act as an "atrocious murder"; Poe's story refers to the orangutan's act as "a murder so singularly atrocious" (*Collected Works* 2:557). The news story states that Coleman murdered his wife by "nearly severing her head from her body with a razor," and later reasserts that Coleman's razor "nearly severed her head from her body"; Poe's work states of the razor-flourishing orangutan, "With one determined sweep of its muscular arm it nearly severed her head from her body" (2:566–67).[27] Tellingly, the pronouns "its" and "it" were, in the earliest versions of Poe's story, "his" and "he" (2:567n). The *Saturday News* piece refers to Coleman's then "dropping her [his dead wife] upon the pavement"; Poe's tale relates that the orangutan "hurled [the body of Madame L'Espanaye] through the window headlong" (2:567) to "the stone pavement" (2:557). Finally, the *Saturday News* piece asserts that, feigning insanity in prison (on the advice of his counsel, it is implied), Coleman responded to questions with answers "of the most *outre* kind"; Poe's story remarks on "the *outré* character of its [the mystery's] features" (2:547) and the *"excessively outré"* manner in which the younger L'Espanaye's body was disposed of (2:557).

These clear language parallels strongly suggest that Poe adapted this *Saturday News* account of the Coleman murder for "The Murders in the Rue Morgue." Another language parallel suggests that Poe also adapted the newspaper's follow-up story for his tale: a piece in the 11 August 1838 issue, titled "Examination of Coleman," mentions the murder weapon, "the razor, upon the blade and handle of which there was a great quantity of congealed blood";[28] Poe's tale mentions the murder weapon, "a razor, besmeared with blood" (*Collected Works* 2:537). The notable closeness of the verbal correspondences cited tends to lead to the broadening of an earlier view—in all likelihood, Poe not only remembered the salient *Saturday News* pieces in 1839, as he conceived his tale, but also reread these pieces (including the Coleman items) in clippings or in a file of the newspaper that was available to him.

Poe's conflation of the murderous Edward Coleman and the orangutan of the London Zoo in "Rue Morgue" leads to an important effect—the crime becomes even more sensational and appears insoluble, requiring the discernment of the gifted detective whom Poe wished to introduce. In this regard, we should recall the October 1845 *Aristidean* review of Poe's *Tales*, which Mabbott thought that Thomas Dunn English had written after conversation with Poe (*Collected Works* 2:525). Although the evidence reveals that the "incidents" for "Rue Morgue" were not "purely imaginary," the story may well have been composed with the climax in mind—thus, it was "written backwards." And Poe may well have begun thinking about his tale by "imagining a deed committed by such a creature, or in such a manner, as would most effectually mislead inquiry. Then he applies analysis to the investigation."[29]

Imagining an orangutan as the killer does "effectually mislead inquiry"—it defies expectation and obviates concern with human motive. Yet despite its purpose—which leads to the highlighting of the brilliance of Dupin—the association of African American and orangutan is unarguably racist. A characteristic late twentieth-century or early twenty-first-century American sensibility is particularly offended by this linking. However, a typical early or mid-nineteenth-century American sensibility was very likely less sensitive to this linking, and Poe, sharing elements of this sensibility, may have shared the insensitivity. Terence Whalen ably articulates what he terms Poe's "average racism."[30] "Average racism" in 1841 would surely have involved race-related fears that the orangutan's attack on two white women would have suggested, including slave rebellion and miscegenation. The racial thematics of "Rue Morgue" have been well studied,[31] and they warrant continued examination and discussion. By way of intimation, I should note that by making the aforementioned association in "Rue Morgue," Poe again transmuted an item from the *Saturday News*—an article in a later issue, to be mentioned hereafter, which explicitly relates a black man and an orangutan.[32]

The 18 August 1838 issue of the *Saturday News* offered no further information on the Coleman murder, but it did include "Life of an English Nobleman," the very probable "Usher" source, as well as an untitled piece next to it concerning a French woman, Mademoiselle Mars, whose former servant had robbed her, tried to rob her again, and was believed to have intended to stab her to death. The police searched her house and discovered the culprit. The piece refers to the thief's likely object, "the iron box containing her jewelry," suggestive of the "small iron safe," "the iron chest" of the L'Espanayes, which contained "some papers" and had probably contained Madame L'Espanaye's two bags of gold francs, and other valuables (*Collected Works* 2:537–38; 566).[33] In imagining the scene beheld by the orangutan as it swung into the bedroom of the L'Espanayes—an older woman and a younger one positioned near this iron chest in the middle of the room—Poe may well have drawn from this untitled piece and a later important *Saturday News* piece, to be discussed.

The issues of the *Saturday News* of late August and early September 1838 provided Poe with little material, but the issue of 15 September recalled the "wild and wonderful" in *Pym* in a humorous comment on the circulation of *The Lady's Book*: "We dare not mention what is the present circulation of this work, lest we should be suspected to be of the Arthur Gordon Pym school."[34] This issue featured, too, a piece whose title, "Horrid Murders," resembles the title of the first newspaper story quoted in "Rue Morgue," "EXTRAORDINARY MURDERS" (*Collected Works* 2:537). However, while the *Saturday News* piece includes a series of testimonies, as does the later piece from Poe's "Gazette des Tribunaux" (2:538–44), the testimonies here are markedly different from those in "Rue Morgue." It is the following issue of the *Saturday News*, that of 22 September 1838, which offered Poe a vitally useful piece, elements of which he came to combine with elements of the orangutan story and the Coleman story for "The Murders in the Rue Morgue." The brief item is titled "A Mischievous Ape."[35]

The story relates the escape of a "large ape or baboon" on Elizabeth Street in New York City; its venturing through the window of a house and causing havoc within; and its later attacking two small boys in the yard. Again, important correspondences between a *Saturday News* piece and "Rue Morgue" are apparent. The ape in the *Saturday News* piece escaped from a "stable"; Dupin asserted near the tale's close that the orangutan was at "a livery stable" (*Collected Works* 2:563). The Elizabeth Street ape opened a window in a house and "entered the parlor"; the Rue Morgue ape swung through an open window in a house and "entered the room" (2:565). Once chased out of the house, the ape in this news story "seized hold of the hair of a child" and "nearly took his scalp off"; Poe's orangutan "seized Madame L'Espanaye by the hair" (2:566) and tore her hair out "by the roots," revealing "the flesh of the scalp" (2:557). The "mischievous ape" "scratched and bit a boy severely in the leg and thigh"; the murderous ape caused "severe scratches" on the face of Mademoiselle L'Espanaye (2:538; see also 2:543), whose tongue had been "partially bitten through" (2:543).

These correspondences suggest that when Poe came to imagine "The Murders in the Rue Morgue" in 1839, he fashioned details pertaining to his orangutan not only from the May 1838 *Saturday News* piece on the London Zoo's orangutan and the August 1838 *Saturday News* pieces on the Coleman murder, but also from this September 1838 *Saturday News* piece on the fugitive ape. The closeness of the correspondences again suggests that Poe not only recalled the story, but also reread it. Most noteworthy about his transmutation of specifics of this piece is his focus on the horror and his heightening of it—a process Poe referred to as "the fearful coloured into the horrible" (*Letters* 1:84). The tendency toward the horrible in Poe's writing led Horace Greeley's *New-Yorker* to refer to Poe's tale as "of deep but repulsive interest."[36] Yet for some readers, the vivid horror of "Rue Morgue" heightens both the mystery and the satisfactoriness of its solution.

The October and November 1838 issues of the *Saturday News* included no major stories that Poe adapted for "Rue Morgue"; they did, though, offer interesting minor items: two pieces concerning a Parisian morgue, a reprint of a story from the *"Gazette des Tribunaux"* (the newspaper from which Dupin and his friend first learned of the Rue Morgue murders in later versions of the tale), two accounts of a husband's murder of his wife, and a brief report of the trial and conviction of Edward Coleman for "willful murder."[37] Issues of the

Saturday News for December 1838, however—among the last of the newspaper's run—featured pieces crucial to Poe's imagining his first detective story.

The *Saturday News* of 1 December 1838 reported that Edward Coleman would be executed on 12 January 1839; in a column adjacent to this story is a review of the December 1838 issue of Poe's former journal, the *Southern Literary Messenger*, and, below that review, a story titled "Deaths in New York."[38] According to this piece, two unknown black women, living in a house at the corner of 34th Street and Third Avenue in New York City, died from suffocation caused by smoke from their lit charcoal furnace.[39] Details of the story anticipate details of "Rue Morgue." These women, "aged about 40 and 17," died in their "small upper room," whose door had to be broken in; the L'Espanayes, a mother ("the old lady" [*Collected Works* 2:539, 547, 567]) and daughter ("the young lady," "the girl" [2:543, 567]), were murdered in "the upper part of the house," a fourth-story room whose door had to be forced open (2:537). Significantly, the two New York women had placed their charcoal furnace "in the middle of the room" and had lain down to sleep on either side of it; the L'Espanayes had "wheeled" their "iron chest" "into the middle of the room" and had seated themselves in front of it (2:566). The evident parallels suggest that Poe employed elements of this story for the scene encountered by the orangutan in "Rue Morgue." The "iron chest" in "Rue Morgue" that was substituted for the charcoal furnace of "Deaths in New York" may have been prompted, in part, by "the iron box containing...jewelry" in the untitled 18 August *Saturday News* piece ["Mdlle. Mars"] concerning the French woman and the servant-turned-thief. It seems probable that Poe not only remembered these two items, but also reread them before he developed his short story.

Poe's apparent synthesis of these items is effective. His borrowing the alluring "iron box" from the untitled piece to replace the quotidian furnace of "Deaths in New York" allows his tale to become even more mysterious; his borrowing the two women from "Deaths in New York" to replace the one French woman in the untitled piece and his transforming the 40-year-old into a "childish" "old lady" (*Collected Works* 2:539) permit the murders to become even more dreadful. Both Poe's selection of details and his transmutation of them seem astute.

One additional detail from the 1 December 1838 issue of the *Saturday News* warrants mention. An article titled simply "A Story," from the *New York American*, states that a young Indian dancer at the Court in Paris "had…produced, by her singular dress, strange exploits and antelope lightness of movement, the extraordinary sensation that every one is eager to experience now at the *Theatre des Varietes.*" The Théâtre des Variétés—"a place of light entertainment," according to T. O. Mabbott (*Collected Works* 2:570)—is the theater recommended by Dupin for the cobbler-turned-actor Chantilly, who had failed at tragedy: "'He is a very little fellow, that's true, and would do better for the *Théâtre des Variétés*'" (2:534; see also 537). Poe would have encountered this name, as well, in an 1832 *New-York Mirror* piece by N. P. Willis (2:668); however, the appearance of the name in the *Saturday News* of 1 December 1838 was a timely one, and probably the immediate prompt for Poe's using the name in his literary production of "extraordinary sensation."

The next week's issue of the *Saturday News* reprinted the short item on Coleman's sentencing and offered in an adjacent column a victim's narrative, "Escape of the Bear from the Liverpool Zoological Garden." This account in the 8 December issue may be a minor source for "Rue Morgue"; it mentions a nearby "man with a basket of nuts for sale," calling to mind the "fruiterer, carrying upon his head a large basket of apples" (*Collected Works* 2:534), and it details the bear's biting "completely through" the victim's left arm, an incident possibly related to the orangutan's attack and Mademoiselle L'Espanaye's "partially bitten through" tongue (2:543). The more important story in this issue, however, appearing below the story of the escaped bear, is titled "Mahometan Worship."[40]

This piece depicts the coming together of different races and nationalities at an unnamed mosque for Ramadan prayers. The sounds of the service—"a sort of scream," a "shrill and piercing" "voice," "a low murmur"—find their correspondences in "Rue Morgue" in "The screams…of the old lady" (*Collected Works* 2:566–67), the "shrill voice" of the orangutan (2:540–43, 549, 550, 555), and the murmuring of the narrator (2:536), but it is a brief characterization of the worshipers' appearance that deserves particular attention. The writer refers to "The Turk in magnificent apparel, squatted beside the squalid, half-naked Biskari; the pale Moor, with noble mien, by the hideous Negro with ourang-outang face.…" With that last, obviously racist phrase, the possibility of the conflation of black man and orangutan is made explicit. Had the synthesis not already occurred to Poe, it is suggested here; had it already struck him, it is reinforced here. That last phrase brings together the *Saturday News* orangutan story and escaped-ape story with its Edward Coleman stories and furnishes

Poe with a key to the "Rue Morgue" mystery: the bestial murderer may be a murderous beast. And with that key, Poe could "effectually mislead inquiry."[41]

While the *Saturday News* of 15 December 1838 offered Poe little for his imaginative transformation, the issue of 22 December 1838 featured both "Apparent Death," a piece concerning burial alive that anticipates elements of Poe's story "The Premature Burial," and "Appalling Accident," a piece concerning a man who fell from a building and whose face was "horribly mutilated"—a phrase that anticipates the identical phrase in "Rue Morgue": the body of Madame L'Espanaye, which was thrown from a building, was "horribly mutilated" (*Collected Works* 2:543).[42] The penultimate issue of the *Saturday News*, that of 29 December 1838, featured the newspaper's last source for "Rue Morgue": "Humorous Adventure—Picking Up a Madman."[43]

This allegedly comical piece concerns the unusual behavior of an insane man, one Abbot, who had been given lodging at a Boston hotel by a "good Samaritan." Again, the language employed resonates notably with that of "Rue Morgue." While a Thanksgiving dance and various parties are taking place, Abbot appears as "a wild-looking object, holding on the window shutters outside of the house, and peering into the room." He is later said to have been "swinging upon the window shutters during the night." This language is close to that of Dupin when he speculates that the murderer "might have swung the shutter" and "swung himself into the room" of the L'Espanayes (*Collected Works* 2:555), and similar, too, to that of the French sailor when he admits that the orangutan "grasped the shutter" and "swung itself [originally 'himself']" into the room (2:565). Abbot's "peering into the room" corresponds significantly with the orangutan owner's obtaining "a glimpse of the interior of the room" as he held on to the lightning-rod outside the L'Espanayes' window (2:566). The *Saturday News* piece later refers to Abbot as "grinning like a yellow monkey," a phrase that would probably have invited Poe's imaginative assimilation of this man to his orangutan. The correspondences presented suggest that Poe adapted this *Saturday News* piece for "Rue Morgue"; a further correspondence tends to corroborate this view. In "Humorous Adventure—Picking Up a Madman," it is revealed that Abbot "had recently escaped from an insane Hospital";[44] in "Rue Morgue," the narrator responds to Dupin's analysis of the evidence by stating, "A madman...has done this deed—some raving maniac, escaped from a neighboring *Maison de Santé*" (2:558). Dupin's reply is very curious—he says, "In some respects...your idea is not irrelevant" (2:558). The parallels noted suggest that the narrator's idea is "not irrelevant" because it covertly acknowledges one of the *Saturday News* sources for "Rue Morgue." This reading is strengthened by the fact that no other relevance for the narrator's comment is apparent. It would seem that with this passage, "The Murders in the Rue Morgue" intimates its own origins.

Perhaps it is not surprising, then, that numerous passages in "Rue Morgue" concern newspapers. The narrator refers often to newspapers that he and Dupin read—once to the *"Musée"* (*Collected Works* 2:536), five times to the "Gazette des Tribunaux" (2:537, 538, 544, 546, 547), and twice to "Le Monde" (2:547, 560). He quotes two news stories about the Rue Morgue murders from the "Gazette des Tribunaux"— one of them composed of five paragraphs (2:537–38), the other of seventeen paragraphs (2:538–44); he also quotes Dupin's paragraph-long advertisement in "Le Monde" (2:560–61). This newspaper material constitutes approximately one-fifth of Poe's tale. Particularly salient is Dupin's visit to the office of "Le Monde" since Poe lived close to the office of the *Saturday News* through 4 September 1838, and could readily visit even after his move.

The significance of newspapers in "The Murders in the Rue Morgue" arguably reflects their significance in Poe's imagining this tale—a significance that seems hinted not only in the narrator's remark about an escaped madman, but also in his earlier remarks about the game of whist—remarks that his later narrative illustrates. Identifying what is necessary for "proficiency in whist," the narrator cites "a comprehension of *all* the sources whence legitimate advantage may be derived," "The...knowledge...of *what* to observe," and (as I have noted) the acceptance of "deductions from things external to the game" (*Collected Works* 2:529–30). The narrator's remarks apply well to "proficiency in whist," to proficiency in detection, and, markedly, to proficiency in reading about detection. After all, comprehension of the *Saturday News* "sources"—clearly "external to the game"—does offer considerable "legitimate advantage" in understanding Poe's creation of a genre.

We may even come to wonder if Poe alludes to his arranging these *Saturday News* sources when his narrator reveals that at the critical moment that the orangutan entered the L'Espanayes' apartment, mother and daughter were "arranging some papers" (*Collected Works* 2:566)—elsewhere termed "a few old letters, and other papers of little consequence" (2:538). We may recall that in "The Purloined

Letter," it was a letter of apparent "worthlessness" (3:991) that was the much-sought treasure.

Even as "Rue Morgue" reveals Dupin's analysis of the mystery of the murders, it subtly invites analysis of the mystery of its creation. In early versions of the tale, Poe's narrator characterizes analysis as "the capacity for resolving thought into its elements" (*Collected Works* 2:527n) and thus aptly introduces Dupin's coming resolution of the narrator's thought into its elements (2:534–37), Dupin's "retracing the steps" (2:535) of the narrator's cogitations. Applied to reading a story, analysis would seem to be the capacity for resolving a work of literature into its sources, "retracing the steps" of its making. Resolution—analysis—clarifies its converse (according to Poe)—creation (2:527n). By unimagining "Rue Morgue," we may approach Poe's imagining. Poe's tale ultimately celebrates the double process of creation and resolution, of imagining and unimagining, of writing and the "kindred art" (*Complete Works* 11:108) of reading. And as the tale honors this double process, it honors, too, the brotherhood of writer and reader. Furthermore, it appears to anticipate—perhaps prepare the way for—the irradiation and return of Matter and Spirit in *Eureka*. Indeed, Poe's enigmatic cosmological prose-poem may be interpretable, at least in part, as an allegory of writing and reading.

Resolving "Rue Morgue" into its elements—the *Saturday News* sources, the "newspaper accounts" that Killis Campbell once posited—does not challenge Poe's originality: Poe wrote in June 1845, "To originate is carefully, patiently, and understandingly to combine" (*Collected Writings* 3:137). And he acknowledged in January 1840, "The wildest and most vigorous effort of the mind cannot stand the test of...analysis" (*Complete Works* 10:62; see also *Collected Writings* 3:16). To undo Poe's combination is therefore not to undo his reputation. And, it should be added, reliance on newspapers for the writing of fiction has long been a respectable practice among American writers—Herman Melville's reliance on newspapers for his own literary imaginings is a good case in point.[45] It is on the quality of its combination that a literary work may be judged. In this regard, Poe wrote of Imagination in January 1845, "Even out of deformities it fabricates that *Beauty* which is at once its sole object and its inevitable test" (*Collected Writings* 3:17; see also 2:369). Out of the *Saturday News* stories—many horrific and therefore classifiable as "deformities"—Poe fabricated a story that does possess beauty. The deformities are combined harmoniously, seemingly seamlessly, and with great novelty and economy. A unity of effect—a sense of wonder at Dupin's acuity—is evident, and the unity of theme—the doubleness of creation and resolution—is skillfully reflected in the story's unity of design, a symmetry of event and language, with a carefully elaborated center (as discussed in chapter I). If, as Poe suggests in January 1840, "a *creation* of intellect" is akin to a griffin— both seem new but are made up of already-existing parts (*Complete Works* 10:62; *Collected Works* 3:16)—then perhaps "The Murders in the Rue Morgue" may be termed one of the finest specimens of griffin that Poe ever imagined.

In the 29 December 1838 issue of the *Saturday News*—the same in which "Humorous Adventure" appeared—Louis Godey announced the cessation of the *Saturday News* for causes "that need not be mentioned." He referred only to the "other pursuits" of the proprietors, "avocations... of a higher and more important character." In the subsequent and final issue, that of 5 January 1839, Godey stated that the *Saturday News* will not be discontinued but rather "will be issued by Mr. Samuel C. Atkinson, jointly with the Saturday Evening Post." Thus ended the career of *The Philadelphia Saturday News and Literary Gazette*.[46]

On 12 January 1839, Edward Coleman was executed in New York City.[47] In June 1839, Poe became Assistant Editor of *Burton's Gentleman's Magazine*. William E. Burton held a dinner party for him— one attended by, among others, Louis A. Godey, Joseph C. Neal, and Morton McMichael.[48] In September of the year, Neal praised Poe's "The Fall of the House of Usher" in the *Pennsylvanian*; in December, he favorably reviewed there Poe's *Tales of the Grotesque and Arabesque*.[49] According to the present reading, at some time or times during this year, Poe reread issues of the recently absorbed *Saturday News* and, relying on a number of its stories, conceived and began to elaborate "The Murders in the Rue Morgue." It is possible that Poe was able to reread these issues in a file he owned or borrowed, or in one he could examine at the office of the newspaper that had bought the *Saturday News*, the *Saturday Evening Post*—edited, and soon owned, by Poe's associate, and future employer and publisher of his work, George R. Graham.[50] Of particular note in this regard is the fact that, in 1839, one of those who contributed to the *Post* and may have helped edit that paper was Poe's friend Lambert Wilmer.[51]

The *Saturday News*-"Rue Morgue" connection may be briefly recapitulated. The "hideous Negro with ourang-outang face" in the *Saturday News* piece "Mahometan Worship" suggested or reinforced the idea of the synthesis of *Saturday News* stories concerning an

orangutan and an ape—"Orang Outang" and "A Mischievous Ape"—
with the paper's stories concerning a black man's murder of his wife—
"Deliberate Murder in Broadway, at Midday" and "Examination of
Coleman." A *Saturday News* piece concerning an insane man swinging from window shutters and looking into a room, "Humorous
Adventure—Picking Up a Madman," provided Poe with details for
the activity of his orangutan and its owner. A *Saturday News* story
about an older woman and a younger one who suffocated when they
slept near a charcoal furnace in the middle of their room—"Deaths
in New York"—led to the scene that Poe's orangutan encountered
on entering the fourth floor window: an older woman and a younger
one seated near an "iron chest" in the middle of the room. The chest
might have been suggested by the "iron box" in the untitled *Saturday
News* piece about the French woman and the servant-turned-thief;
some language regarding the L'Espanayes might have been offered
in *Saturday News* items "Appalling Accident" and "Escape of the
Bear from the Liverpool Zoological Garden." Additional important details were probably supplied by such *Saturday News* pieces as
"Horrid Murders" (an item offering a title close to that of one of Poe's
newspaper stories), ["The New Caspar Hauser"] (a reprint from the
"Gazette des Tribuneaux"), and "A Story" (an account featuring "the
Theatre des Varietes").

In 1840, Poe would very likely have continued to reshape these
Saturday News items for "Rue Morgue." Pertinently, in January
of that year, Morton McMichael lauded Poe's *Tales* in *The Lady's
Book*.[52] In September 1840, Poe received a letter concerning the
terms for a possible position as a French teacher for "M[onsieur]
C. Auguste Dubouchet, a gentleman of your acquaintance."[53] Poe
borrowed the initial and middle name for his detective, and cou-
pled them, most probably, with the surname of the jurist André-
Marie-Jean-Jacques Dupin, about whom Poe would have read in
R. M. Walsh's aforementioned 1841 translation, the volume *Sketches
of Conspicuous Living Characters of France* (which Poe reviewed in
the same issue of *Graham's Magazine* in which "Rue Morgue" first
appeared). Notably, Dupin's writings are characterized in Walsh's
volume as offering an "abundance of facts and logical deduction"
and revealing their author to be "a perfect living encyclopedia";
furthermore, Dupin is termed "the greatest redresser of wrongs
in the world."[54] Dated "Philadelphia March, 1841," "The Murders
in the Rue Morgue" appeared in March in the April 1841 issue of
Graham's Magazine.[55]

Some of the readers of Philadelphia's *Graham's Magazine* in 1841 would surely have been readers of the *Philadelphia Saturday News* in 1838. Yet there is no evidence that anyone recognized the *Saturday News* stories—"things external to the game"—in Poe's story. Perhaps these readers are well described in Poe's narrator's mention of "men...[who] find themselves upon the brink of remembrance, without being able, in the end, to remember" (*Collected Works* 2:555). However, memory lost is not necessarily irrecoverable, even 170 years later. We need only consult the famous epigraph to Poe's tale for confirmation: "What song the Syrens sang, or what name Achilles assumed when he hid himself among women, although puzzling questions, are not beyond *all* conjecture" (2:527).

CHAPTER III

"THE MYSTERY OF MARIE ROGÊT" AND "VARIOUS NEWSPAPER FILES"

"The Mystery of Marie Rogêt" was Poe's effort to solve the actual mystery of Mary Rogers, "the beautiful cigar girl" who had disappeared from her Manhattan home in October 1838, returned, and then disappeared again in July 1841, her body found in the river near Hoboken, New Jersey. The Mary Rogers case was a great sensation at the time, and Poe followed it from Philadelphia by reading newspapers (see *Collected Works* 3:723n)— especially New York City newspapers. For his second Dupin tale, Poe naturally set the events again in Paris. And he employed excerpts from the newspapers as either foils or prompts for Dupin's solution. In the first printing (in Snowden's *Ladies' Companion* of November and December 1842 and February 1843), Dupin contended for a "secret lover," a "naval officer" as guilty of the murder (Mabbott 3:754–55; see also 768), rather than her fiancé St. Eustache (Daniel C. Payne), her rejected suitor Beauvais (Alfred Crommelin), her acquaintance Mennais (Joseph W. Morse), or a gang. However, to accommodate a reported death-bed account that pointed elsewhere, Poe modified language in the revised version of "Marie Rogêt" in the 1845 *Tales* so that Dupin also allowed for the possibility of a botched abortion.

"Marie Rogêt" has elicited fewer scholarly analyses than "Rue Morgue" or "The Purloined Letter," but there is still a range of approaches, from the early psychoanalytic (e.g., again, Marie Bonaparte on the latent sexual content by way of Mary Rogers as Poe's Virginia) to cultural studies (e.g., Amy Gilman Srebnick on the Mary Rogers case as a lens for studying sexuality and pre-Civil War urban life).[1] Not surprisingly, since "Marie Rogêt" explicitly responds to contemporary journalistic accounts, significant scholarship has developed related to sources and potential sources. This scholarship warrants a brief review here.

For his 1941 article "Poe and the Mystery of Mary Rogers," William K. Wimsatt Jr. read the ten newspapers that Poe mentioned in his notes (in the 1845 version of the tale) for the period July to September or October 1841—the *Brother Jonathan*, the *Commercial Advertiser*, the *Morning Courier and New York Enquirer*, the *Express*, the *Herald*, the *Journal of Commerce*, the *Sunday Mercury*, the *Evening Post*, and the *Standard* (all of New York), and the *Saturday Evening Post* (of Philadelphia)—and he named nine types of sources and their newspaper locations. Much of the detail, he notes, is in one newspaper, the *Brother Jonathan*. He also considers Poe's various arguments in "Marie Rogêt"—against such published views as that Mary Rogers was still alive and that a gang murdered her, for example, and for the naval officer theory. Furthermore, Wimsatt discusses Poe's revisions for the 1845 version of the tale and speculates on who that naval officer—supposedly named "Spencer"—might have been.[2] T. O. Mabbott wrote of Wimsatt's essay," "It is rarely necessary to go back of this synoptic article…" (*Collected Works* 3:716n). We may be tempted to accept this judgment, but some "things external to the game" might still be missed.

John Walsh, in his 1968 book *Poe the Detective*, offers newspaper accounts of the Mary Rogers story from the aforementioned papers (especially the *Herald*), employing, too, detail from the *Atlas*, the *Sun*, the *Times and Commercial Intelligencer*, the *Sunday News*, the *Advocate of Moral Reform*, and the Newark *Daily Advertiser*. He offers general comment, stating that "…Poe adds nothing important, and for the most part only rephrases the arguments, pro and con, that had overflowed the newspaper columns." He does relate the second of six extracts to the *Herald* (as Wimsatt had done), but he argues that the sixth and final extract, about a rudderless boat, "was invented." He also argues (unconvincingly) for Poe's supposed travel to New Jersey in connection with Mary Rogers, and he discusses the modified passages and the mysterious Spencer.[3]

Raymond Paul read newspapers from October 1838, from July through December 1841 (including the *Evening Tattler* and the *Times and Evening Star*), and from November through December 1842. His glib, breezy 1971 book—*Who Murdered Mary Rogers?*—dismisses Poe's solution, considers the original tale a hoax, disputes the abortion explanation for Mary Rogers' death, and imaginatively renders his own solution: a "temporarily deranged" Daniel C. Payne choked Mary Rogers to death.[4]

T. O. Mabbott offers in his edition of Poe's works a full headnote and copious annotations. He mentions in the headnote the invitation to "analysis" in the *Saturday Evening Post* and states, "Poe went to work, using especially the material in the New York weekly *Brother Jonathan* and the New York *Evening Post*" (*Collected Works* 3:717). Mabbott provides in his notes great detail regarding specific newspaper sources, including selected quotations. He discusses the *Brother Jonathan* most frequently (in 36 of the 122 notes) and also mentions the daily complement to this weekly, the *Evening Tattler.* Tracing back three of the six extracts, he concurs with Walsh regarding the sixth (as he had already done in his introduction to *Poe the Detective*)—Poe made it up (3:783–84). Like the studies of Wimsatt and Walsh, Mabbott's work is also "fundamental to any serious consideration of the tale" (3:716n).

Laura Saltz, in her 1995 essay "'Horrible to Relate!': Recovering the Body of Marie Rogêt," discusses contemporary newspapers, especially with regard to their treatment of abortion. The aforementioned Amy Gilman Srebnick, in her 1995 book *The Mysterious Death of Mary Rogers*, finds "[m]ost useful" the reports in the *Herald*, the *Tribune*, the *Commercial Advertiser*, the *Brother Jonathan*, the *Evening Post*, and *The Morning Courier and the New York Enquirer*. However, her reading in these newspapers doesn't especially illuminate Poe's tale. She argues that Dupin is mad; that perhaps Mary Rogers had an affair with a man named Spencer and died of an abortion; and that Poe is attacking William Attree, reporter for the New York *Herald*, whom he intimated at the end of "The Purloined Letter" with his reference to Atreus. And Daniel Stashower in his 2006 book *The Beautiful Cigar Girl* reviews the Mary Rogers case and Poe's handling of it, accepting its mysteries as finally unresolvable. Notably, he too considers Dupin's sixth extract as "fabricated for the occasion of the story."[5]

Among these studies of "Marie Rogêt," those by Wimsatt, Walsh, and Mabbott are especially revealing. We might be inclined to conclude that, for scholarly consideration of "Marie Roget," Poe's newspaper world is exhausted. Yet identification with Poe as a reader directs us back there nonetheless. Renewed attention to that newspaper world yields a greater understanding of its importance for Poe's composition of "Marie Rogêt." In particular, attention to the *New York Times and Evening Star* leads to the hitherto-unknown source for Dupin's sixth newspaper extract; examination of the *New York Herald* leads to the relevant 1835 novel by Theodore S. Fay (1807–98), *Norman Leslie*, and its historical basis, the 1799 murder of Gulielma Sands; and consideration of the *Brother Jonathan* leads to Poe's related literary conflict with editor H. Hastings Weld (1811–88).

Dupin's sixth newspaper extract concerns "an empty boat" that was recovered. This was the boat from which, Dupin states, the murderer must have cast the body of Marie Rogêt (*Collected Works* 3:771). The extract reads:

> On Monday, one of the bargemen connected with the revenue ser-
> vice, saw an empty boat floating down the Seine. Sails were lying in
> the bottom of the boat. The bargeman towed it under the barge office.
> The next morning it was taken from thence, without the knowledge
> of any of the officers. The rudder is now at the barge office. (3:754)

Poe attributes this extract to "*Le Diligence*," and his note identifies this imaginary Parisian newspaper as the New York *Standard* (3:754). Mabbott acknowledges that examination of the *Standard* did not yield the source (3:784), but he also cites Wimsatt's statement, "Since the [foot]notes in which Poe supplies the names of the papers would seem to have been prepared especially for the 1845 version, and very likely from memory, the remarkable thing is not that some of the references cannot be found but that so many can be" (3:783). Yet (as previously indicated) Mabbott adds regarding this sixth extract, "I believe this incident to be Poe's invention" (3:784).

But this incident was not Poe's invention—it was fact. The source for the sixth extract was not the *Standard*, but the *Star*—the *New York Times and Evening Star*. Perhaps Poe misremembered the newspaper's name. Alternatively, perhaps he wished to avoid possible confusion with his French name for the *Brother Jonathan*—"L'Etoile" (*Collected Works* 3:731). In any case, a letter to the editor in the issue of 26 August 1841 reads, in part:

> On the Monday morning, at sunrise, following the day Miss Rogers
> was supposed to have been murdered, one of the bargemen connected
> with the U. S. revenue service saw a boat floating down the North
> river, without any person in it. He immediately put out for it, and
> towed it under the barge office. The sails were lying in the boat. The
> boat has since been taken from thence, (but before the murder was
> known) without the knowledge of any of the officers connected with
> the establishment. The *rudder* is now at the barge office, and the boat,
> it is supposed, could be identified by the officer who picked her up: it
> may give some clue to the perpetrator of so daring an outrage.[6]

The sixth extract *was* drawn from a newspaper, as Poe's narrator states (3:753). Poe adapted the original slightly by eliminating the designation of "U. S." for the "revenue service," by changing the North River (the Hudson between lower Manhattan and New Jersey) to the Seine for the sake of his Parisian setting, by eliminating the specific Mary Rogers references to emphasize Dupin's making the connections, and by inverting two sentences. But Poe's version is still exceptionally close to the newspaper piece.

And the attraction of that newspaper piece is clear: its details and other related newspaper details prompted Dupin's solution to the mystery. We may recall his summary of the evidence, leading to the conclusion that a naval officer was the murderer:

> This associate is of a swarthy complexion. This complexion, the "hitch" in the bandage and the "sailor's knot," with which the bonnet-ribbon is tied, point to a seaman. His companionship with the deceased, a gay, but not an abject young girl, designates him as above the grade of the common sailor. Here the well written and urgent communications to the journals are much in the way of corroboration. The circumstance of the first elopement, as mentioned by Le Mercurie, tends to blend the idea of this seaman with that of the "naval officer" who is first known to have led the unfortunate into crime. (*Collected Works* 3:768–69)

Remarkably, Dupin is adducing actual details from real newspapers in "The Mystery of Marie Roget" to lead him to the supposed murderer, a naval officer, even as he had adduced details that Poe had presumably imagined (including a "ribbon" with a "knot") in "The Murders in the Rue Morgue" to lead him to the man who owned the murderous orangutan, a sailor (2:561).

This naval officer would have known how to handle the boat. And, considering the story from "*Le Diligence*" (the *Times and Evening Star*), Poe adds a more pointed connection:

> The rudder *of a sailboat* would not have been abandoned, without inquiry, by one altogether at ease in heart. And here let me pause to insinuate a question. There was no *advertisement* of the picking up of this boat. It was silently taken to the barge-office, and as silently removed. But its owner or employer—how *happened* he, at so early a period as Tuesday morning, to be informed, without the agency of advertisement, of the locality of the boat taken up on Monday, unless we imagine some connexion with the *navy*—some personal permanent connexion leading to cognizance of its minute interests—its petty local news?" (*Collected Works* 3:770)

Moreover, Poe imagines the guilty naval officer's response to learning about the securing of his boat:

> In the morning, the wretch is stricken with unutterable horror at finding that the boat has been picked up and detained at a locality which he is in the daily habit of frequenting—at a locality, perhaps, which his duty compels him to frequent. The next night, *without daring to ask for the rudder*, he removes it. (3:771)

Clearly, Dupin's final newspaper extract is significant; in fact, the detective declares it critical to solving the mystery:

> Now *where* is that rudderless boat? Let it be one of our first purposes to discover. With the first glimpse we obtain of it, the dawn of our success shall begin. This boat shall guide us, with a rapidity which will surprise even ourselves, to him who employed it in the midnight of the fatal Sabbath. Corroboration will rise upon corroboration, and the murderer will be traced. (3:771)

The newly found original of Dupin's sixth and final newspaper extract confirms the validity of the narrator's presentation, highlights the cohesiveness of the newspaper stories that led Dupin to his solution, and clarifies further Poe's method of adapting his sources. And it demonstrates anew that examination of newspapers published at the time of the Mary Rogers story will be rewarded.

Beyond this new source, a relevant novel, Theodore S. Fay's *Norman Leslie*, and its historical basis, the murder of Gulielma Sands, merit attention. We may be guided by contemporary associations with the Mary Rogers case in the New York newspapers.

In the month after the death of Mary Rogers, several notorious previous murders were remembered. One of these was the murder of Captain Joseph White of Salem on 6 April 1830, for which Daniel Webster had successfully and memorably prosecuted John Francis Knapp. On 14 August 1841, a writer for the *Journal of Commerce* (signing only "H."), prompted by "[t]he late murder of Mary C. Rogers," recalled the White murder. This writer quoted three paragraphs from Webster's speech to warn that "murder will out" and to encourage anyone with knowledge of the circumstances of the murder to come forward. On 21 August, H. Hastings Weld, in the *Brother Jonathan*, quoted two of the same three paragraphs. And on 26 August 1841, the *New York Herald* cited the White murder to reassure readers that a mysterious murder may indeed be solved.[7] Another murder noted was that of Ellen Jewett, a New York City prostitute who had been hatcheted to death on 10 April 1836. The accused, Richard Robinson, had been acquitted. This murder was mentioned in a piece in the *Journal of Commerce*, and the *Journal of Commerce* item was reprinted in the *New York Herald* of 14 August 1841.[8]

But earlier newspaper associations with the Mary Rogers case were those involving the 1835 novel *Norman Leslie*, by Theodore S. Fay, and the novel's factual source, the 22 December 1799 murder in New York City of Gulielma (or Julianna) Sands.

On 3 August 1841, in only its third article on the death of Mary Rogers, "The Late Murder of a Young Girl at Hoboken," the *Herald* opined, "Nothing of so horrible and brutal a nature has occurred since the murder of Miss Sands, which murder formed the basis of the story of Norman Leslie." (Notably, for its subsequent sentences on Mary Rogers's 1838 disappearance, this same article has already been cited as a source for Poe by Wimsatt and Mabbott [*Collected Works* 3:783].)[9] A week later, in "The Murdered Mary Rogers," the *Herald* restated its association: "Nothing has yet been found out definitely in relation to this murder; which was even a far more horrible affair than the murder of Miss Sands."[10] Finally, on 30 August 1841, the *Herald* introduced a letter about the Sands-Rogers connection ("The Mary Roger's [*sic*] Mystery"), stating, "The whole country is beginning to feel an interest in the brutal violation and murder of Mary Rogers. Read the following." The letter itself appears thus:

Philadelphia, Aug. 27, 1841

MR. BENNETT:—

The mystery which yet surrounds the terrible case of Miss Rogers, excites in this community, intense anxiety—the effects [efforts?] by your police to discover the authors of this "murder most foul" are properly estimated, and do receive merited commendation.

It has been intimated in your paper of yesterday, that by persevering efforts the villians [*sic*] will eventually be brought to punishment, and it is to be hoped that perseverence [*sic*] will be unremitted.

Whether you have any recollection or knowledge of a case somewhat similar, which occurred in New York, very many years ago, I do not know. It was that of a certain Levi Weeks (whose brother, a most estimable man, was then the owner of the City Hotel). Levi was charged with the abduction and murder of a Miss Sands, who was taken from her sister's house in Greenwick [*sic*] street, conveyed by her lover, to whom she was engaged to be married, on a cold winter night, and in a then lonely street, thrown into a well of large size owned by the

Manhatten [*sic*] Company. Being missed, she was sought for and there found, with marks of violence on her person, showing great resistence [*sic*], and proving the strong efforts made to preserve herself—her lacerated fingers, etc.

Now, Sir, the circumstance excited an intense concern, as does the case of Miss Rogers. So great was the rush to see the body, that it was deemed proper to place it in the public street, where many thousands looked upon it—among them the writer of this.

Weeks was arrested—circumstances were extremely strong against him, and although acquitted by the Jury, public feeling was such that he left your city and never returned to it—he died a vagabond.

Cadwallader D. Colden was then the Attorney General, and among the witnesses who were introduced for the defendant, was one individual, whose name I do not now recollect, who was one of the fatal sleighing party. Mr. Colden was extremely close in his examination of that man, and was impressed with a belief that he was the actual murderer.

Some time afterwards the witness was indicted for committing a forgery—and it was most remarkable that, in that trial, [circumstances] were developed which induced Mr. Colden to say, "that is the murderer of Miss Sands."

It would therefore seem, that despite of all the machinations of the Devil and his imp, that by a wise Providence "murder will out."

I refer you to the documents of that day, and think you may make a good moral use of the facts.

Yours, W. C.[11]

Before proceeding to "Miss Sands," we should comment on Fay's novel. The linking of Mary Rogers and *Norman Leslie* is appropriate since this work concerns the apparent murder of a beautiful young girl, Rosalie Romain, in New York City. Poe, who had so thoroughly attacked the book in his December 1835 *Southern Literary Messenger* review (*Complete Works* 8:51–62; *Collected Writings* 5:60–62), would certainly have recalled it. He referred, in his plot summary, to "Miss Romain—whose disappearance has already created much excitement," and he mentioned "a hat and feathers" thrown in a stream and Rosalie's "handkerchief" placed "in a wood" (*Complete Works* 8:56; *Collected Writings* 5:61).[12]

We should here recall Dupin's reference, in "Marie Rogêt," to "the guilty authors" of "communications" to an evening newspaper blaming "*a gang*" (*Collected Works* 3:761; see also 3:770, and the fifth extract, 3:753–54) and his later reference to communications "sent to the morning newspaper" "insisting so vehemently upon the guilt of

Mennais [Joseph W. Morse]" (3:770; see the fourth extract, 3:753). Dupin thus implies that the actual murderer made false accusations. *Norman Leslie* is apposite again, given Clairmont's "singular and artful malice" during his testimony and his later cry as he "rescued" Flora, "Ho! *Leslie the murderer!*"[13] Poe referred in his notorious review to Clairmont's "directing of public suspicion against Mr. Leslie as the murderer of Miss Romain" (*Complete Works* 8:56; *Collected Writings* 5:61). *Norman Leslie* has an affinity with "The Mystery of Marie Rogêt," and perhaps Poe was drawing from the novel, especially with regard to false accusations by the guilty.

Poe stated in his review of *Norman Leslie*, "In the Preface Mr. Fay informs us that the most important features of his story are founded on fact..." (*Complete Works* 8:52; *Collected Writings* 5:60). But there has been no evidence that Poe knew that fact. However, the cited pieces from the *Herald* make clear that if Poe had not already known the work's origins in the murder of Gulielma Sands, he would have come to know them. Furthermore, the letter from "W. C." makes evident the parallel between the accusation of the innocent Levi Weeks for the murder of his fiancée, a horrific event that was a great sensation in its day, and the accusation of the innocent Daniel C. Payne for the murder of his fiancée, another horrific event, a great sensation in Poe's day. These elements are characteristic of Poe's "Marie Rogêt." (Daniel C. Payne is the innocent "Jacques St. Eustache" [*Collected Works* 3:729].) What is remarkable, especially at this early point in the investigation of the Mary Rogers case (30 August 1841), is the implied possibility that someone who gave testimony may have been the guilty man.

Referred to what "W. C." refers to as "the documents of that day," we may find William Coleman's *Report of the Trial of Levi Weeks,* James Hardie's *An Impartial Account of the Trial of Mr. Levi Weeks,* and David Longworth's *A Brief Narrative of the Trial for the Bloody and Mysterious Murder.* (The prosecutor was Cadwallader D. Colden; the defense attorneys were Brockholst Livingston, Alexander Hamilton, and Aaron Burr.) The witness who seemed guilty (actually a witness for the prosecution) was Richard David Croucher, who was later tried for another crime and found guilty of rape, then again of fraud, and was subsequently executed in England. The interesting point about Croucher, in this context, is that four witnesses testified that he had tried to persuade people that Levi Weeks was guilty of the murder.[14]

Croucher was the original for Theodore S. Fay's Clairmont. And reading the letter from "W. C." in the *New York Herald*, Poe would have been reminded of the link between *Norman Leslie* and the Mary

Rogers case, and would also have learned (if he did not know it already) of the link between the Gulielma Sands case and the Mary Rogers case. Reading of a guilty man's blaming an innocent man for the murder of a beautiful young woman in the 1835 novel and learning of a similar occurrence reported in the 1800 trial, Poe may have concluded that the actual letters to the newspaper editors against a gang and against Joseph W. Morse might be his guilty naval officer's false accusations. These accusations provide tension and drama and furnish a means of identifying the man whom Poe specified—by way of the correspondences between the handwriting in the accusing letters and that of the suspected naval officer (see *Collected Works* 3:770).

Even as contemporary newspapers helped Poe turn to 1838 (for Mary Rogers's first disappearance) to help determine what happened in 1841 (for Mary Rogers's second disappearance), they also helped him turn to 1835 (*Norman Leslie*) and 1799 and 1800 (the murder of Gulielma Sands and the trial of Levi Weeks). Studying the immediate newspaper context for the story of Mary Rogers, we also find literary and historical antecedents.

Continued exploration of Poe's newspaper world inevitably involves the oft-mentioned *Brother Jonathan*. Mabbott notes, specifically, "Much of the history of the Rogers' case is to be found in . . . one issue of the weekly"—that of 28 August 1841 (*Collected Works* 3:778). That issue featured three editorials from the related daily newspaper, the *Evening Tattler*: "Is Mary C. Rogers Murdered?" "Further Remarks on the Rogers Case," and "More Remarks upon the 'Murder Case.'" These pieces would have been written by the principal editor, whom Poe names in the 1845 version of his tale: "H. Hastings Weld, Esq." (3:731n).[15] Poe may also have punnishly hinted at H. Hastings Weld in the 1842/43 version: "But L'Etoile [the *Brother Jonathan*] was again overhasty" (3:733); "He [the editor of L'Etoile/the *Brother Jonathan*] is accordingly in haste . . ." (3:744).

The *Brother Jonathan* editorials argue that the body found in the river was not that of Mary Rogers. Arguments include that the body ascended to the surface of the water in too short a time, that Alfred Crommelin's (the failed suitor's) observations of the body revealed no irrefutable correspondences with the actual Mary Rogers, that the seeming indifference of her family suggested that they knew that the body was not hers, and that Crommelin may have been in some way at fault.

However, other newspapers disagreed with the *Brother Jonathan*. Wimsatt declared that they "united in a chorus of dissent" from Weld's editorials, and he cited six of those that objected. Of these, the

Commercial Advertiser (termed by Poe "Le Moniteur" [*Collected Works* 3:740]) offered examples of drowned bodies that rose in three or four days, asserted that the clothing on the body was positively identified as Mary's, and noted that "... no other young woman but Miss Rogers has disappeared in an unaccountable manner." The *Herald* (termed by Poe "Le Mercurie" [3:753]) was blunt: "As to the story told that Mary Rodgers [*sic*] is still alive—it is base and foolish."[16]

And the editorial view of the *Evening Tattler* and the *Brother Jonathan*, that Mary Rogers was still alive, provoked more than just dissent. The *Evening Tattler* of 24 August 1841 and the *Brother Jonathan* of 28 August 1841 stated, at the end of "Further Remarks on the Rogers Case," "The remarks made upon this subject in yesterday's Tattler will be found republished upon the last page of this day's paper—the supply of copies of the Tattler having been unequal to the demand." So the first of the three editorials prompted a greater-than-usual readership. Furthermore, the *Sunday Times* furnished in its 29 August 1841 poem, "News of the Week," the following verse reflecting public interest in the editorials of the *Evening Tattler*:

> Dame Rumor says—the Tattler too—
> That Mary Rogers—Mary Rogers,
> Still walks this world, amongst its crew
> Of living lodgers!—living lodgers!
> And hence, that now to seek, 'tis vain
> Her murd'rers further—murd'rers further:
> Because—at least on her, 'tis plain
> They did no murther—did no murther.
> But still a slaughtered girl was found
> In Hudson lying—Hudson lying;
> Whose blood is yet from out the ground
> For vengeance crying!—vengeance crying!

And the 4 September *Evening Tattler* provided dramatic evidence of its story's considerable effect:

QUITE A MOB, and not a little excitement, was produced in Broadway on Thursday afternoon by the appearance there of a young lady who bore, or was supposed by many to bear, so strong a resemblance to the mysteriously disappearing Miss Rogers, that they took her for that renowned young lady: and the ice once broken by some of those who believed she was the veritable Mary, by addressing her and questioning her as to her disappearance and hiding place, a large and eagerly curious crowd soon surrounded her. The young lady was released from her troublesome predicament by a passing friend.[17]

Poe appears to have been correct when he wrote that the one suggestion of the journalists "which attracted the most notice, was the idea that Marie Rogêt still lived—that the corpse found in the Seine was that of some other unfortunate" (*Collected Works* 3:731). Poe offers his analysis of the appeal of the idea through Dupin, his intellectual stand-in: "...it is the mingled epigram and melodrame of the idea, that Marie Rogêt still lives, rather than any true plausibility in this idea, which have suggested it to L'Etoile, and secured it a favorable reception with the public" (3:738)

And through Dupin, Poe refutes several of Weld's arguments, contending that the length of time for a body to rise to the water's surface is "indeterminate" (*Collected Works* 3:743), that Beauvais's (Crommelin's) observations of the body indicate impressive correspondences with the living Mary Rogêt (3:745–47), and that Beauvais is not at fault beyond "*romantic busybodyism*" (3:747–48). Poe's narrator had earlier asserted that the family's indifference was only apparent (3:732–33).

The arguments that Poe presents in "Marie Rogêt" reflect his disagreement with Weld's arguments about Mary Rogers—Poe's view was that the corpse was indeed that of "the beautiful cigar girl." But with regard to one Poe passage, another consideration is relevant. Poe's Dupin states, regarding Beauvais's conviction that the body was Marie's, "The editor of L'Etoile had no right to be offended at M. Beauvais' unreasoning belief" (*Collected Works* 3:748). Yet nowhere in the three *Brother Jonathan* editorials does Weld state that he was offended—rather, having asserted, "He [Crommelin (Beauvais)] admits our facts, but disputes our inferences," the editor admits his fear that his surmise of a cover-up regarding the actual Mary Rogers may be "uncharitable" ("Further Remarks").

Of course, Poe may have been inferring or imagining Weld's having been offended. But a likelier possibility presents itself: Poe knew well that one of his own book reviews had recently offended Weld. And Poe, in turn, had been displeased with Weld's editorial response.

It is true that Poe's narrator writes that L'Etoile is "a paper conducted, in general, with much ability" (*Collected Works* 3:731), but he also offers many negative comments. The critical literary battle involved Seba Smith's (1792–1868; a.k.a Jack Downing's) narrative poem *Powhatan*.

Weld reviewed this Harper and Brothers book in the *Brother Jonathan* of 1 May 1841. His opinion was a high one—he writes, in part:

> This work is an honor to American Literature. We say it, uninfluenced by personal partiality for the author, much as we esteem him as a man; and we say it too without being insensible to its occasional inaccuracies of rythm [*sic*] and accent. These very little faults are to us, however, but evidences of the spirit in which the author wrote—the true spirit of narrative—the true spirit in which a poem of this kind should be indited.... We trust that the public taste of Mr. Smith's countrymen may be vindicated by a call for a large edition of this work. If not; they don't deserve to have their history and the traditions of their country sung—that's all.[18]

Poe may not have seen this assessment; he wrote in his review of *Powhatan* in the July 1841 issue of *Graham's Magazine*, "What few notices we have seen of this poem speak of it as the production of *Mrs.* Seba Smith [Elizabeth Oakes Smith (1806–93)]" (*Complete Works* 10:162). On the other hand, perhaps Poe had seen Weld's response and was trying to avoid a too-direct disagreement. Certainly the *Brother Jonathan* would have been readily available to Poe in Philadelphia. The newspaper reported in November 1839 that it "can always be had on the day of publication, at the Philadelphia arcade." And a Philadelphia correspondent for the *Brother Jonathan* reported in June 1840—after mentioning that a "young gentleman" (Poe) had left *Burton's Gentleman's Magazine* to start his own magazine— that "[i]n my walks through the streets, I often observe the familiar visage of 'Brother Jonathan';—I should say that he is unrivalled among the weeklies in the estimation of our citizens."[19]

Whether he had seen Weld's review or not, Poe was clearly contemptuous in his own review of Smith's work. Early on in his July 1841 treatment of *Powhatan*, he asserted, "In truth, a more absurdly *flat* affair—for flat is the only epithet which applies in this case—was never before paraded to the world with so grotesque an air of bombast and assumption" (*Complete Works* 10:163). After describing the contents mockingly, he declared, "It is very difficult to keep one's countenance when reviewing such a *work* as this; but we will do our best, for the truth's sake, and put on as serious a face as the case will admit" (10:165).

"The leading fault of 'Powhatan,' then, is precisely what its author supposes to be its principle merit," Poe argued—its fidelity to historical detail. And then Poe "the tomahawk man" raised his weapon:

> The truth is, Mr. Downing has never dreamed of any artistic *arrangement* of his facts. He has gone straight forward like a blind horse, and turned neither to the one side nor to the other, for fear of stumbling. But he gets them all in, every one of them—the facts we mean. Powhatan never did anything in his life, we are sure, that Mr. Downing has not given in his poem. He begins at the beginning, and goes on steadily to the end, painting away at his story, just as a sign-painter at a sign; beginning at the left-hand side of his board, and plastering through to the right. But he has omitted one very ingenious trick of the sign-painter. He has forgotten to write under the portrait,—"this is a pig," and thus there is some danger of mistaking it for an opossum.

Poe commented on the foregoing, "But we are growing scurrilous, in spite of our promise, and must put on a sober visage once more" (*Complete Works* 10:165).

Poe failed to forbear. His final paragraph opens, "The simple truth is, Mr. Downing never committed a greater mistake in his life than when he fancied himself a poet, even in the ninety-ninth degree. We doubt whether he could distinctly state the difference between an epic and an epigram." He continued slashing, "And it will not do for him to appeal from the critic to the *common* readers, because we assure him that his book is a very *un*common book. We never saw any one so uncommonly bad, nor one about whose parturition so uncommon a fuss has been made, so little to the satisfaction of common sense." And he continued his attack, "Your poem is a curiosity, Mr. Jack Downing; your 'Metrical Romance' is not worth a single half sheet of the pasteboard upon which it is printed" (*Complete Works* 10:166–67). He closed with a final stroke:

> But we wish, before parting, to ask you one question. What *do* you mean by that motto from Sir Philip Sidney upon the title-page? "He cometh to you with a tale that holdeth children from play, and old men from the chimney-corner." What do you mean by it, we say? Either you cannot intend to apply it to the "*tale*" of Powhatan, or else all the "old men" in your particular neighbourhood must be *very* old men; and all the "little children" a set of dunder-headed little ignoramuses. (10:167)

Weld responded quickly and angrily in his 26 July 1841 notice in the *Brother Jonathan* of the July 1841 issue of *Graham's Magazine*. He begins, "Of the literary contents we care not to speak, for having read the notices of new books in the number, we could not be answerable for the consequences." And he continues, more pointedly:

> Of one thing we can assure the publishers, however; and that is that there is not a single paper in the Magazine, which could not be made twice as ridiculous as some MacGrawler has striven to make a poem which he professes to review. A more capricious, unjust, and ridiculous affair, purporting to be a review, we never happened upon than is the notice of Powhatan, in Graham's Magazine.
>
> The correspondents of the work behave better than the critic; and the volume opens well.

A "MacGrawler," we should note, is an epithet of severe opprobrium, drawn from the character Peter MacGrawler in Bulwer-Lytton's novel *Paul Clifford*—the unscrupulous editor of the "Asinaeum," who believes that "...criticism...may be divided into three branches, viz: 'to tickle, to slash, and to plaster.'"[20] It is, of course, Poe's slashing that provokes Weld.

Poe offered his response to Weld's comments at the end of a personal letter to the editor of 14 August 1841. First published in *The Dial* as "An Unpublished Letter of Poe," this letter was said there to be "characteristically Poesque in its elaborate courtesy and in the touch of temper at the end." And the author of *The Dial*'s introduction to the letter infers, accurately, "Presumably Mr. Weld had been attacking Poe for some of his critical articles."[21] Poe begins by explaining that he will soon be writing on "American Autography"; he proposes to include Weld and asks his assistance:

> My object in addressing you now is to request that you would favor me with your own Autograph, in a reply to this letter. I would be greatly obliged to you, also, could you make it convenient to give me a brief summary of your literary career. (*Letters* 1:303)

He also asks if Weld has—and would be willing to provide for an engraving—"the Autographs of Sprague, Hoffman, Dawes, Bancroft, Emerson, Whittier, R. A. Locke, and Stephens, the traveller" (*Letters* 1:303).

And then Poe closes with salient reference to Weld's recent comments in the *Brother Jonathan*:

> Should you grow weary, at any time, of abusing me in the "Jonathan" for speaking what no man knows to be truth better than yourself,

it would give me sincere pleasure to cultivate the friendship of the
author of "Corrected Proofs." In the meantime, I am

Very respy. Yours,
Edgar A. Poe. (*Letters* 1:303)

Poe makes an overture to Weld, but not without critiquing his
critique. Implicitly, Poe is suggesting that the editor of the *Brother
Jonathan* should not have responded as he had regarding the July 1841
Graham's Magazine, for he understood all too well the validity of the
charges against Seba Smith's *Powhatan*.[22]

The Poe-Weld conflict of July/August 1841 should be considered as
we think about Poe's treatment of Weld's editorials in the 28 August
1841 *Brother Jonathan* in "The Mystery of Marie Rogêt." When Poe's
Dupin states "The editor of L'Etoile [the *Brother Jonathan*] had no
right to be offended at M. Beauvais' unreasoning belief" (*Collected
Works* 3:748), Poe appears to be allowing his own faulting of Weld's
review of his own review to inflect his faulting of Weld's editorial.
That is, if we may rephrase Dupin's statement, the editor of the
Brother Jonathan had no right to be offended at Mr. Poe's censure
of *Powhatan*, inferior a work as he knows it to be. There was no
bad behavior, no "capricious, unjust, and ridiculous affair," only
"truth"—as "no man...knows better than yourself." Dupin's response
to the editorial from L'Etoile seems a partial displacement of Poe's
response to Weld's judgment of the *Powhatan* review. We may imagine Poe using Dupin's words against Weld: "...it is difficult to suppose the reasoner in earnest" (3:746).

Before Weld received Poe's letter, he offered, in a review of the
August 1841 *Graham's Magazine*, a lightly mocking comment on Poe's
second angelic dialogue, "The Colloquoy of Monos and Una,"[23] but
then provided in an *Evening Tattler* review of the September 1841 issue
words of praise: "A superior number—of which we shall give the reader
proof in next week's issue of the Jonathan. Mr. Poe has a very good
story, illustrating the folly of one's betting his own head against any
thing." The story was the jeu d'esprit "Never Bet Your Head. A Moral
Tale," also known as "Never Bet the Devil Your Head." Weld proved
that the September 1841 *Graham's Magazine* was superior by reprinting
"Never Bet Your Head" in the *Brother Jonathan* of 4 September 1841.[24]

Poe's inclusion of two autobiographical quotations in his Weld
piece in the December 1841 "A Chapter on Autography" (*Collected
Works* 15:229) suggests that Weld had written to Poe—possibly providing not only his own autograph, but also the autographs of others.

However, Weld did eventually advert to the sensitive issue of Poe's critical severity. In a review of the April 1842 *Graham's Magazine*, he maintained, "...Mr. Poe shows in his literary judgments much discrimination, and not quite so much hypercriticism as is usual with him. His standards are apt to be 'frical' to use a Yankeeism, and his literary code is entirely too much after the precedent of Draco." And in a review of the October 1842 *Graham's Magazine*, Weld returned to his lament in his response to Poe's *Powhatan* review: "We are very sorry to find a very unjust attack by Mr. Poe upon Mr. [Rufus] Dawes's [1803–59] poetry in the number.... [W]hatever may be the faults of Mr. Dawes's verse, that poem is not yet written which could not be picked to pieces in the same style that Mr. Poe has done this."

Poe continued his respectful tone toward Weld in "A Chapter on Autography" (*Complete Works* 15:229)—perhaps in part owing to Weld's responsiveness to Poe's letter, and perhaps also owing to some interference by publisher George R. Graham. Poe admitted to F. W. Thomas, "I was weak enough to permit Graham to modify my opinions (or at least their expression) in many of the notices" (*Letters* 1:325). He writes:

> Mr. Weld is well known as the present working editor of the New York "Tattler" and "Brother Jonathan." His attention was accidentally directed to literature about ten years ago, after a minority, to use his own words, "spent at sea, in a store, in a machine shop, and in a printing-office." He is now, we believe, about thirty-one years of age. His deficiency of what is termed regular education would scarcely be gleaned from his editorials, which, in general, are unusually well written. His "Corrected Proofs" is a work which does him high credit, and which has been extensively circulated, although "printed at odd times by himself, when he had nothing else to do."
>
> His MS. resembles that of Mr. Joseph C. Neal in many respects, but is less open and less legible. His signature is altogether much better than his general chirography. (*Complete Works* 15:229)

The qualification regarding the "well written" editorials—"in general"—finds its way into "Marie Roget" in that, as mentioned, "L'Etoile" (the *Brother Jonathan*) is said to have been "conducted, in general, with much ability" (*Collected Works* 3:731). Poe's refutation of the *Brother Jonathan* editorials on Mary Rogers constitute his eventual elaboration on that qualification.

Poe also treated Seba Smith in his "A Chapter on Autography" (the November 1841 installment). Although he did not back down with regard to his low opinion of Seba Smith's *Powhatan*, he expressed it with a much milder tone (again, perhaps owing to the interference of George Graham): "Mr. S. is also the author of several poems; among others, of 'Powhatan, a Metrical Romance,' which we do not very particularly admire." He explains the work with reference to Smith's backwoods hero, Major Jack Downing: "The fact is that 'The Major' is not *all* a creation; at least one-half of his character actually exists in the bosom of his originator. It was the Jack Downing half that composed 'Powhatan'" (*Complete Works* 15:200).

It may have been Weld's return to public admonishment of Poe in his review of the April 1842 *Graham's Magazine*—"...his literary code is entirely too much after the precedent of Draco"—that freed Poe to go on the attack in "The Mystery of Marie Rogêt" (which he finished by 4 June 1842 [*Collected Works* 3:718]). And he was free there, too, from the unwelcome revisions of George R. Graham. Of course, Poe genuinely disagreed with Weld's three editorials in the *Brother Jonathan* of 28 August 1841. But he also had an issue with Weld himself because of his hostile comments on Poe's criticism. So despite initial praise of "L'Etoile" in "Marie Rogêt" (3:731), through Dupin Poe soon alleges the "zeal" of the editor (3:738), asserts that a paragraph of his is "a tissue of inconsequence and incoherence" (3:743), and contends that L'Etoile is "obviously disingenuous" (3:745) and that it possesses a "pertinacity in error" (3:746). Arguably, Weld's offended response to Poe's review of *Powhatan* informed Dupin's mention of the editor's offended response to Beauvais. Or we may say that when Weld ventured upon insult—the reviewer is a "MacGrawler," author of a "capricious, unjust, and ridiculous affair, purporting to be a review," hypercritical and Draconian—Poe vowed revenge. With his subtle attack in "The Mystery of Marie Rogêt," Poe deftly immured H. Hastings Weld.[25]

Certainly the obscurity into which *Powhatan* has fallen suggests that, though Poe's tone was caustic, his judgment was correct. And a reading of *Powhatan* confirms Poe's judgment.

On 4 June 1842, Poe wrote queries to George Roberts (1807–1860) of the Boston *Times and Notion* and Joseph Even Snodgrass (1813–80) of the *Baltimore Saturday Visiter* regarding publication of his "just completed" work, "The Mystery of Marie Rogêt" (*Letters* 1:337–42). (A third letter to this purpose, to T. W. White [1788–1843] and Matthew F. Maury of Richmond's *Southern Literary Messenger*, may also have been written [1:339n].) To Roberts, Poe writes, "For reasons, however, which I need not specify, I am desirous of having this tale printed in Boston..." (1:338); to Snodgrass, he states, "For reasons which I may mention to you hereafter, I am desirous of publishing it [the tale] *in Baltimore*" (1:340). (Presumably his preference to White and Maury was Richmond.) What is clear is that Poe did not initially wish to publish "The Mystery of Marie Rogêt" in New York or Philadelphia. Perhaps, given his critical comments in that tale on the editor of "L'Etoile," Poe thought his chances were better at a distance from Weld's journalistic world in New York or that of Weld's friends in Philadelphia. (He did eventually publish the tale in New York.)

So it *was* "necessary to go back of [Wimsatt's] synoptic article." Returning to Poe's newspaper world to understand "The Mystery of Marie Rogêt," we find a new source, a new literary/historical background, and a new and pertinent literary conflict. And it was identification with Poe as a reader that guided us back there—that is the rudder to which we should continue to hold.

CHAPTER IV

"THE PURLOINED LETTER" AND *DEATH-BED CONFESSIONS*

A s has been observed, a supposed death-bed confession led to Poe's modifying his second Dupin tale. Ironically—and perhaps satisfyingly—Poe made another supposed death-bed confession the basis for his third Dupin tale.[1] But we get ahead of ourselves.

"The Purloined Letter" has prompted an extensive critical response, including the celebrated and elaborate commentary from early psychoanalysis (Marie Bonaparte) to French theory (Jacques Lacan, Jacques Derrida, Barbara Johnson), which will be revisited in chapter V.[2] And there are many other critical responses, ranging from the treatment of affinity (e.g., J. P. Telotte on "The Purloined Letter" and the film *Casablanca*) and that of influence (e.g., Elizabeth Sweeney on "The Purloined Letter" and Arthur Conan Doyle's short story "A Scandal in Bohemia" and Vladimir Nabokov's novel *The Real Life of Sebastion Knight*) to the study of the "numerical/geometrical" (John T. Irwin on the relationship of "The Purloined Letter" to Jorge Luis Borges's short story "Death and the Compass") and that of the topological (Paul Harris on space and knowledge in "The Purloined Letter").[3] Of special note here of the myriad responses are those concerning the tale's origins.

With regard to "The Purloined Letter," T. O. Mabbott wrote, "No exact source for Poe's plot has been pointed out..." (*Collected Works* 3:972). Definite and possible sources for particular passages, however, have been identified. Early on, Mabbott himself stated that "Cyrano de Bergerac mentions that Campanella used the method Poe describes [assuming another's expression] to determine the thought of his inquisitors." Subsequently, George Egon Hatvary specified Poe's immediate source, Horace Binney Wallace's 1838 novel *Stanley*, for both Dupin's recommending that to infer another's thoughts one must take on that person's expression and for his faulting mathematics as a basis for nonmathematical truths. S. L. Varnado posited Edmund Burke's *Philosophical Inquiry* (1757) for the same passage on adopting another's expression. In the Harvard edition, Mabbott mentions De Bergerac and Burke and quotes the critical passage from Wallace (3:994–95). He also cites as the original for the anecdote about Dr. Abernethy a similar tale about Sir Isaac Pennington appearing in a book that Poe reviewed, *Nuts to Crack* (1835) (3:994), and he mentions Wallace's *Stanley* for the passage on the limits of mathematics (acknowledging a book list of J. J. Cohane) (3:995–96). Furthermore, Mabbott traces Latin allusions ("*facilis descensus Averni*" and "*monstrum horrendum*") at the tale's close to Vergil's *Aeneid* (3:996, 997). Burton Pollin cites *Stanley* as a source for Dupin's remark on "a *non distributio medii*" (*Collected Writings* 3:986). And Bruce Krajewski relates the game of even and odd to Cicero's *De Finibus*.[4]

To pursue further the origins of "The Purloined Letter," we should consult the beginning of "The Philosophy of Composition," where Poe wrote of his "commencing [to write a story] with the consideration of an *effect*," as opposed to "the usual mode of constructing a story." With regard to the latter, he wrote, "Either history affords a thesis—or one is suggested by an incident of the day—or, at best, the author sets himself to work in the combination of striking events to form merely the basis of his narrative . . ." (*Complete Works* 14:193–94). Undoubtedly, Poe sought an effect in his Dupin stories—one of amazement. But his comments on "the usual mode of constructing a story" are relevant to these stories, as well. Clearly, "The Murders in the Rue Morgue" and "The Mystery of Marie Rogêt" were "suggested by an incident of the day." By contrast, "The Purloined Letter," because of its royal intrigue, hints that perhaps here "history afford[ed] a thesis." Identification with Poe as a reader leads to a search for the historical source.

There has been a repeated claim in scholarship, probably suggested by the Parisian setting of "The Purloined Letter," that the "personage of most exalted station" (*Collected Works* 3:976), who would be compromised by the release of "the purloined letter," was the Queen of France. Marie Bonaparte stated this, Martin Priestman and Heta Pyrhönen agreed, and John T. Irwin added, "Given that [Henri-Joseph] Gisquet [the model for Poe's Prefect] was prefect from 1831 to 1836, the French king and queen in the tale would then be Louis Philippe and his queen Maria Amelia."[5] Mabbott disagreed with Bonaparte, asserting "Although some of the ideas [in 'The Purloined Letter'] are from books in which Poe was interested, and some of the characters are based on real people, it goes without saying that the real Queen of France, Marie Amélie, was not portrayed" (3:973). Richard P. Benton called into question Mabbott's assertion, but not convincingly.[6]

What does not go without saying is that the "personage of most exalted station" in Poe's tale *was* based on a British princess— Caroline, the Princess of Wales (1768–1821). Furthermore, the source for a key portion of Poe's plot—the theft of "the purloined letter"—is *The Death-Bed Confessions of the Late Countess of Guernsey, to Lady Anne H******** ([1822]). "The Purloined Letter," an American classic set in France, is based on a political intrigue that took place in Britain. It is clear that for Poe, as he wrote in 1836, "... *the world* is the true theatre of the biblical histrio..." (*Complete Works* 8:277; see also 11:2; *Collected Writings* 5:164).

A sketch of the life of Princess Caroline will be helpful here. She was born in Brunswick, Germany, on 17 May 1768. Her father was Hereditary Prince Charles William Ferdinand; her mother was Duchess Charlotte, sister of King George III. The king's son George, Prince of Wales (whose marriage to a Catholic woman had been annulled), agreed to wed his cousin Caroline because their marriage would lead to Parliament's resolving his financial difficulties. On 8 April 1795, Caroline and George married, and they had one daughter, Charlotte. However, Caroline and George quickly came to repulse one another, and they lived separate lives, taking lovers. In 1806, a government effort to prove Caroline's infidelity—known as "the Delicate Investigation"—was foiled: some of the charges—including one accusation that Caroline had had an illegitimate child—were false, and Caroline threatened to have the resulting report published and to charge her husband with infidelity, as well. The report was printed as "The Book," but not distributed. The precipitating conflict between Caroline and George would, of course, reemerge.[7]

On 5 February 1811, George was made Prince Regent because his father, King George III, had gone mad. The Prince Regent insisted on limiting his estranged wife's access to their daughter Charlotte. In response, ambitious adviser Henry Brougham (1778–1868) wrote a letter for Caroline to the Queen; this letter and the Queen's response were published in December 1812. Then, in January 1813, Brougham wrote a letter for Caroline to the Prince Regent, defending her reputation ("There is a point beyond which a guiltless woman cannot with safety carry her forbearance...") and arguing against her separation from her daughter ("To see myself cut off from one of the very few domestic enjoyments left me—certainly the only one upon which I set any value—the society of my child—involves me in such misery, as I well know your Royal Highness never could inflict upon me, if you were aware of its bitterness"). On 10 February 1813, after George failed to respond to the letter, it was published in the *Morning Chronicle*, increasing the public's support for the princess. Novelist Jane Austen (1775–1817) wrote, "I suppose all the World is sitting in Judgement upon the Princess of Wales's Letter. Poor woman, I shall support her as long as I can, because she *is* a Woman, & because I hate her Husband.…" The Princess's celebrated letter, which so provoked the Prince Regent, became known, ironically, as "The Regent's Valentine."[8]

To escape what she considered mistreatment and to gain greater freedom, Princess Caroline sailed from England on 8 August 1814. She traveled to Italy, where she had a love affair with Bartolomeo Pergami, whom she promoted from courier to baron. In England, her daughter Charlotte married Prince Leopold, but their child was stillborn, and Charlotte died soon thereafter. A new government inquiry into Caroline's infidelity was conducted; the Milan Commission relied on information provided by spies. Caroline traveled through Europe and intimated that she would return to England to face her enemies. Then, on 29 January 1820, King George III died. The Prince Regent therefore became King George IV, and Princess Caroline was now the Queen.[9]

On 5 June 1820, Queen Caroline and her retinue landed at Dover and traveled to Canterbury, to great popular acclaim. On 6 June, she proceeded on to London, with crowds welcoming her. A Secret Committee met to determine the government's response, and on 17 August 1820, the trial of Queen Caroline began in the House of Lords. By 10 November the trial concluded, and although many thought that she was guilty of infidelity, the questionable evidence, the public sympathy, and the effective advocacy of Henry Brougham yielded an acquittal. However, Caroline's triumph was short-lived. On 19 July 1821, she was prevented from attending the coronation of King George IV and from being crowned herself. And on 7 August, she died, of a digestive ailment.[10]

Edgar Allan Poe would have heard of Caroline early on, and certainly by 1820 (when he was eleven years old), after George III died and Prince George became King and Princess Caroline Queen. He was then attending Manor House School in Stoke Newington, near London, where his foster parents, John and Frances Allan, lived.

(The family had traveled to London from Richmond, Virginia, in the summer of 1815 so that John Allan might expand his business. Poe would later draw on his experience at the Manor House School for his short story "William Wilson" [1839].) John Allan predicted accurately, in a letter of 1 February, that George IV "will never allow her [the Queen Consort] to be crowned"[11] — clearly he understood the tension between king and queen, and perhaps he would have discussed such a matter with his family. By this time, Allan's business was going badly, and he decided to return to Virginia. In early June, the family traveled to Liverpool for the voyage back. They arrived in Liverpool on 8 June, two days after Caroline's arrival in London, and John Allan wrote sympathetically of the Queen on 9 June: "The arrival of the Queen produced an unexpected sensation few thought she would return, but the bold & courageous manner by which she effected it has induced a vast number to think her not guilty. She was received with immense acclamations & the Populace displaced her horses drew her past Carlton House & thence to Alderman Wood's House, South Audley St. The Same day the King made a Communication to the House of Lords charging her with High Treason a certain offense being committed by the Queen is High Treason (adul[ter]y)."[12] Edgar would surely have heard about Caroline's dramatic return—from his foster father and others, and from the British newspapers, as well. The *Liverpool Mercury* of 9 June 1820, for example, which featured a listing for the vessel that the Allans would soon take back to the United States, the *Martha* ("coppered and copper-fastened," like the *Penguin* of *Pym* [*Collected Writings* 1:62]), featured also a favorable piece titled "Arrival of the Queen of England."[13]

The Allans set sail from Liverpool on the *Martha* on 16 June 1820. We may reasonably conjecture that the uncertain fate of the Queen would have been a topic of conversation among the ship's passengers. The vessel docked in New York City on 21 July 1820, and the Allan family arrived along with the remarkable news of the Queen's dramatic return. The *New-York Spectator* mentioned on page two, under "ARRIVED LAST EVENING," "Mr. John Allan and lady, E. Allen [*sic*], Miss Valentine of Richmond," and it featured on pages one and two, under "Late and Important from England and the Continent," three columns summarizing reports from London and Liverpool newspapers on Queen Caroline. These columns began, "ENGLAND has been thrown into great ferment and agitation by the sudden arrival of the Queen."[14] The Queen's return was the great story on both sides of the Atlantic. Perhaps the Allans—including Edgar—would have told and retold the latest news about Caroline from their time in England to those whom they met in New York City (where they stayed for a week) and others in Richmond.

As an adult, Poe occasionally mentioned Queen Caroline and King George IV. He briefly reviewed *Continuation of the Diary Illustrative of the Times of George IV* for the September 1839 issue of *Burton's Gentleman's Magazine*. Referring to the earlier volumes, *Diary Illustrative of the Times of George IV*, Poe wrote, "It may even be questioned whether, with some reservation, Queen Caroline is not here truly depicted; and we should by no means wonder if the work were hereafter gravely referred to as affording the clearest light in respect to her character."¹⁵ Poe evidently took here a balanced view of Caroline, characteristic of the *Diary* (as the preface to *Continuation* asserts) and of *Continuation* itself. In contrast, he elsewhere took a wholly negative view of George IV. Poe referred to him in the March 1842 issue of *Graham's Magazine*, in a review of Harry Lorrequer's *Charles O'Malley*, as "that filthy compound of all that is bestial—that lazar-house of all moral corruption," "this reprobate" (*Complete Works* 11:97–98).¹⁶ In light of these strong comments, although Poe must have come to recognize that Caroline was flawed, he clearly would have been a partisan of hers against her oppressive husband.

We can be sure that the American public, through British and American newspapers and magazines of the time, would have become aware of the royal melodrama, but we might well wonder whether Caroline would have endured in the American memory many years after she died. An 1841 review of *Speeches of Henry Lord Brougham* in the *New York Commercial Advertiser* and the *New York Spectator* helps to clarify the matter: "Who that read with almost breathless interest the memorable trial of Queen Caroline, twenty-one years ago, will not be eager to revive the history by a perusal of Brougham's mighty speeches in behalf of that singular and most unfortunate woman, as revised in the maturity of his years by his own hand?" Long aware of the story of Caroline and George, Poe would also have known that the sad and sensational story lingered in the popular imagination. The prompt to his making literary use of this story would have been a remarkable defense of Caroline and George, the slender volume *Death-Bed Confessions*. This work purports to provide the account of the guilt-ridden Countess of Guernsey [Jersey] (1753–1821), who repeatedly diminishes the culpability of the royal couple, blaming her own deceit and manipulativeness for their difficulties.

The history of the publication of *Death-Bed Confessions* is noteworthy. On 31 March 1822, serial publication of "The Death-Bed Confessions of the Right Hon The Countess of *Guernsey*. Addressed to Lady Anne H*******" began in a weekly newspaper, *Bell's Life in London, and Sporting Chronicle*.[17] Editor and proprietor Robert Bell introduced the work by vouching for its authenticity but refusing to explain his possession of the manuscript. Regarding its authorship, he stated that "... the substance of them [the *Confessions*] is most decidedly correct, having been communicated by the party to whom alone these facts were disclosed by the dying Countess [i.e., communicated by Lady Anne Hamilton (1766–1846) as disclosed by Frances Twysden, Countess of Jersey]." (Later writers attribute the work variously to Lady Hamilton; to Mrs. Olivia Serres [who referred to herself as Princess Olive of Cumberland] (1772–1834); to Mrs. Olivia Serres with the assistance of Lady Hamilton; and to the Shakespeare forger William Henry Ireland [1777–1835].)[18] Bell stated that the work presents the king and queen "in a far more amiable point of view than the fiends of Party would desire" since it reveals that "... the basest passions that ever influenced the human breast [those of the Countess of Jersey], were in constant action to excite in noble minds [those of Caroline and George] unjust suspicion and malignant jealousy...." The sensational serial ran in *Bell's Life in London* through 16 June 1822. It was reprinted elsewhere, including, "with some omissions" (owing to occasional uncertainty about authenticity), in London's *Independent Observer* (soon to be the *Sunday Times*) from 7 April through 18 August 1822.[19]

On 9 June 1822, Robert Bell announced in *Bell's Life in London*, "The numerous applications we have received for the 'Death-Bed Confessions of the late Countess of Guernsey,' in a detached form, have induced us to prepare a complete Work under that title, the publication of which will be shortly announced in the newspapers" ("Notices to Correspondents"). At the end of the final installment, on 16 June 1822, Bell added that "... the 'Confessions' will tomorrow be published..."—"*eighty pages*" for "*one shilling and sixpence*" ([Editor's Final Note]). He advertised the book in *Bell's Life in London* on 23 June 1822; the publisher was W. R. Macdonald.[20] Macdonald soon had competition from John Fairburn, who published the book for one shilling; Bell warned, "As part of this Work [*Death-Bed Confessions*] has been pirated by one Fairburn, and published as *complete*, we deem it necessary to caution the Public against Imposture; this being the only genuine and authorised Edition" ([Advertisement for *Death-Bed*

Confessions, with Warning]). Bell later termed Fairburn "the greatest literary thief in London" ("Literary Hoaxing").[21] Fairburn had purloined what would come to be a vital source for "The Purloined Letter."

Other editions of *Death-Bed Confessions* that appeared in London in 1822 were published by Jones and Company and Dean and Munday. Also, the work was reprinted not only in British newspapers, but in American newspapers, as well.[22] And a Philadelphia edition of *Death-Bed Confessions*—termed "the first American from the first British edition"—was published in 1822 by James E. Moore. (I will rely on this American edition as the likeliest for Poe to have encountered in early 1840s Philadelphia or 1844 New York City.[23] Page numbers will be provided parenthetically.)

The parallels between *Death-Bed Confessions* and "The Purloined Letter" are evident in language, character, and plot. The subtitle of *Death-Bed Confessions* includes the phrase "*the Most Illustrious Personages in the Kingdom,*" and the introduction refers to Princess Caroline (later Queen) and Prince George (later King) as "the most exalted personages" and "*two most illustrious personages*" (vii, ix).[24] Poe's Prefect, describing to Dupin the theft of a letter from "the royal apartments," refers to the Queen opaquely as "the illustrious personage" and the King as "the other exalted personage" (*Collected Works* 3:976–77). In *Death-Bed Confessions*, the princess's private letter to the Prince Regent was read and "laid...aside" by a minister, and then, a supposed "friend of the princess," who was seeking a salary increase from the ministers, "procured the original letter from the secretary's desk" and had it published in the newspapers (72–73). In "The Purloined Letter," the Queen, who has received a compromising letter, presumably from her lover, is forced by the King's sudden appearance "to place it, open as it was, upon a table," and Minister D——, who "fathoms [the Queen's] secret" "takes...from the table the letter to which he had no claim" (3:977). In *Death-Bed Confessions*, the thief thereby gains position; in "The Purloined Letter," Minister D—— thereby gains power. Finally, and critically, in *Death-Bed Confessions*, "The man in office [the thief] met that day his *confreres* at——, and, after dinner, amused them with an account of the purloined letter" (74). And in "The Purloined Letter," the missing document, so honored in the title, is also referred to twice in the text as "the purloined letter" (3:982, 986).[25]

The clear parallels permit a greater understanding of how "history"—or at least one version of "history"—"afford[ed] a thesis" to Poe and of how he transformed that thesis in his writing "The Purloined Letter." The source passage in *Death-Bed Confessions* is a version of the story of "the Regent's Valentine." Here, an ambitious man steals the Princess's private letter to her husband in order to pass it to the newspapers and to satisfy thereby the ministers of the Prince Regent, who seek a greater distance between George and Caroline. The publication of the letter angers the Prince and provides the desired distance; the thief, "[t]he man in office," wins promotion and becomes "from that day... an active agent against the princess" (73). This story fits well in the narrative of *Death-Bed Confessions* for it casts blame on neither the Prince nor the Princess.

Yet it must be added that the story in *Death-Bed Confessions* is at variance with historical scholarship. Evidently, there was no theft. Henry Brougham wrote the letter to the Prince Regent for Princess Caroline, and she signed it. He provided the letter to the *Morning Chronicle*, with Caroline's support.[26] Brougham's authorship of the letter could have been known to Poe from *Diary Illustrative of the Times of George IV*.[27]

Still, it is possible that "[t]he man in office" who conveyed the letter to the newspaper in *Death-Bed Confessions* had some affinity with Lord Brougham, who wrote the letter and then conveyed it to the newspaper. Although Brougham did not become "an active agent against the princess," he was, Flora Fraser observes, a "political opportunist *par excellence*," "a man with no fixed principles."[28] And Poe seems to have recognized Brougham's mixed nature: he wrote in his September 1839 review of Brougham's *Historical Sketches*, "...his [Brougham's] known deficiencies, as well as his known capacities, are precisely those of a chivalrous heart, no less than of a gigantic understanding."[29] And he stated in his March 1842 review of Brougham's *Critical and Miscellaneous Writings*, "An intellect of unusual capacity, goaded into diseased action by passions nearly ferocious, enabled him to astonish the world..." (*Complete Works* 11:98–99; see also *Collected Writings* 2:545). Moreover, Poe's description of Minister D——in "The Purloined Letter" comports with Lord Brougham. Minister D——'s ambition is plain in the Prefect's comment, allusive to *Macbeth* (1.7.46): "...[the minister] dares all things, those unbecoming as well as those becoming a man" (*Collected Works* 3:976). Minister D——'s political involvement is manifest in Dupin's referring to "The present peculiar condition of affairs at court, and especially of those intrigues in which D——is known to be involved..." (3:978) and in his stating, "I knew him as a courtier, too, and as a bold *intriguant"* (3:988). Of course, Brougham was no blackmailer—and he eventually served as Caroline's counsel during her trial. But elements of his character were shared by Minister D——.

Evidence suggesting that Poe was thinking of Brougham as he wrote of the Minister D——is a parallel between a portion of an extract by Brougham that Poe quoted in his July 1839 *Burton's Gentleman's Magazine* review of *Sketches of Public Characters, Discourses, and Essays* and a well-known passage in "The Purloined Letter."[30] (Emphasis in the following parallels is my own, except where otherwise indicated.)

The relevant passage in "The Purloined Letter" about the Minister D——is based partly on a line in Wallace's novel *Stanley*: "He has reached the conclusion that all good books are unpopular, and by a very harmless *non distributio medii* [Wallace's emphasis], resolved therefrom that all unpopular books, like his own, are good."[31] Yet the passage from "The Purloined Letter" is also based partly on the end of the following portion of an extract by Brougham that Poe included in his review:

> A celebrated physician having said, somewhat more flippantly than beseemed the gravity of his cloth, "Oh, you know Sir William [Scott (1778–1868)], after forty a man is always either a *fool* or a *physician!*" "May'nt *he be both*, Doctor?" was the arch rejoinder....[32]

Poe offers a conversation between Dupin and the narrator about the Minister D——, drawing partly on the Brougham passage he had quoted in 1839,

> "... the remote source of his [the Prefect's] defeat lies in the supposition that the Minister is a *fool*, because he has acquired renown as a *poet*. All *fools* are *poets*; this the Prefect *feels* [Poe's emphasis]; and he is merely guilty of a *non distributio medii* [Poe's emphasis] in thence inferring that all *poets* are *fools*."
>
> "But is this really the poet?" I asked.... He is a mathematician, and no poet."
>
> "You are mistaken; I know him well; *he is both*." (*Collected Works* 3:986)

Poe's evident adaptation of the language of the Brougham extract for the conversation between Dupin and the narrator about the Minister tends to support a connection between Henry Brougham and Minister D——. It should be added that Henry Brougham had an accomplished brother—as the Minister did. And Henry Brougham had attainments in both math and letters.[33]

We inferred that Poe was making use of Henry Brougham in "The Purloined Letter" because he was clearly relying on *Death-Bed Confessions*, a work in which an aide (like Brougham) took a letter from the Princess and had it published in a newspaper. The allusion in "The Purloined Letter" to a Brougham passage that Poe had quoted earlier appears to bear out our inference.

Poe borrowed a "striking event"—according to *Death-Bed Confessions*, the purloining of Princess Caroline's letter—and he modified it. The Princess's letter to her husband, protesting her innocence and her separation from Princess Charlotte—perhaps considered too specific, too complicated—became, for Poe, a letter from the Queen's lover to the Queen. Furthermore, since there was no mystery for Dupin to solve if the letter were published in the newspaper—as in *Death-Bed Confessions*, as in fact—Poe had to have "the purloined letter" hidden—but hidden by the thief (Minister D——, the Brougham character) in plain sight, where the Prefect and his men could not find it.

And it is possible that other details from the Regency period (1811–20)—details not elaborated in *Death-Bed Confessions*—found their way into "The Purloined Letter." For example, through Dupin, Poe mentions Vienna (*Collected Works* 3:993), suggesting the 1815 Congress of Vienna; he describes a hired agent firing "among a crowd of women and children," provoking "a series of fearful screams, and the shoutings of a mob" (3:992), recalling the infamous 1819 Peterloo massacre;[34] and he refers to "[t]he good people of Paris" (3:992), intimating the good people of England, who so ardently supported Caroline throughout, and most dramatically on her return in 1820 (as Poe would have known). Even as he borrowed from his time in England for "William Wilson," Poe seems to have done so again for "The Purloined Letter."

But it was primarily through *Death-Bed Confessions*—one of the "things external to the game"—that "history" "afford[ed] a thesis" to Poe. He then transformed it, as noted, for the core of his plot about "the purloined letter" and blended with it other elements—the master detective C. Auguste Dupin; detail from other British works, such as Wallace's *Stanley* and Brougham's *Sketches of Public Characters* (for the dialogue of Dupin and the narrator) and Gooch's *Nuts To Crack* (for Dupin's tale of Dr. Abernethy); as well as language from the works of Vergil and Cicero, Shakespeare and Crébillon. Once again, we may clarify Poe's "creation" through "resolution," "analysis." And it is identification with Poe as a reader that is key.

Relevant here is Poe's stating, as aforementioned, "...at best, the author sets himself to work in the combination of striking events to form merely the basis of his narrative...." Poe reworked aspects of his sources for "the basis of his narrative," artfully bringing the whole together through powerful characterization, compelling argument, and engaging language. He also provided a subtle but discernible form, as elaborated in chapter I. The autobiographical implications of "The Purloined Letter"—related to those of the two other Dupin stories—now warrant fuller discussion.

CHAPTER V

AUTOBIOGRAPHICAL CONSIDERATIONS OF THE DUPIN TALES

Poe's signature at the centers of "The Murders in the Rue Morgue," "The Mystery of Marie Roget," and "The Purloined Letter" encourages us to pursue the autobiographical in these tales. And Poe would probably approve of our quest. He wrote favorably of Francis Lieber's translation of Barthold Niebuhr's (1776–1831) "Essay on the Allegory in the First Canto of Dante" (*Complete Works* 8:163–64; see also *Collected Writings* 5:96), the key assertion of which is, "...everything must be explained by his [Dante's] life, and the peculiarities connected therewith."[1] Poe himself inferred the personal in the literary, as when he wrote in a review of Friedrich de la Motte Fouqué's (1777–1843) 1811 novel *Undine* in the September 1839 issue of *Burton's Gentleman's Magazine*, "From internal evidence afforded by the book itself, we gather that the author has deeply suffered from the ills of an ill-assorted marriage..." (*Complete Works* 10:35–36; see also 16:48–49 and *Collected Writings* 2:197). A telling comment in Poe's "Literati" essay on Margaret Fuller is relevant here: "The supposition that the book of an author is a thing apart from the author's self, is, I think, ill-founded" (*Complete Works* 15:81). *The Narrative of Arthur Gordon Pym*, a memorial to his brother Henry and his mother Eliza, is one compelling example of the closeness of Poe's writing to his self.[2]

To try to determine the autobiographical thematic of the Dupin tales, we must step back from our close examination of each tale to consider all three tales at once. Poe might have presented Dupin and his inductive acuity with regard to a variety of mysteries, but he chose the three he chose. For the first of these tales, he selected a story about Edward Coleman, who murdered his wife Ann because he believed that she had committed adultery. For his second Dupin tale, he chose a story about the beautiful cigar girl Mary Rogers, who had earlier disappeared under questionable circumstances and then disappeared again and mysteriously died. And for his third Dupin tale, Poe employed a story involving Princess Caroline, who was repeatedly suspected and accused of adultery. I would argue that all three Dupin tales have one critical element in common: a woman's uncertain reputation. This "deviation from the plane of the ordinary" merits our attention.

The relevant crux in Poe biography is the abandonment of his family by Poe's father David by late 1809 and the birth of Poe's sister Rosalie in December 1810. According to Kenneth Silverman, "The widow of Charles Ellis, who had known the Allans [Poe's foster parents] well, reportedly said that 'Mrs. Poe's husband had deserted her so long before her death, as to cast a doubt upon Rosalie's birth.'" In light of this, Silverman asserts, "The lapse of a year between David Poe's disappearance and Rosalie's birth stirred rumors in Richmond that she was Eliza's child not by David but by a lover."[3] And John Allan confirmed the doubt, the rumors, writing in a letter to Edgar's older brother Henry about Rosalie, "At least She is half your Sister & God forbid my dear Henry that We should visit upon the living the Errors & frailties of the dead."[4]

Poe wrote indirectly of his love for his mother in an October/November 1829 letter to John Neal, "... there can be no tie more strong than that of brother for brother—it is not so much that they love one another, as that they both love the same parent..." (*Letters* 1:47). And he wrote more directly of this love in a 1 December 1835 letter to Beverly Tucker: "In speaking of my mother you have touched a string to which my heart fully responds" (1:116). He wrote admiringly of his mother's theatrical achievement in a 19 July 1845 *Broadway Journal* article: "The writer of this article is himself the son of an actress—has invariably made it his boast—and no earl was ever prouder of his earldom than he of the descent from a woman who, although well-born, hesitated not to consecrate to the drama her brief career of genius and of beauty" (*Complete Works* 12:186; *Collected Writings* 3:176). And he spoke fondly of his mother to Marie Louise Shew Houghton, who wrote to John Ingram in a letter of 16 May 1875, "... he [Edgar] told me himself privately that he owed to his Mother 'every good gift of his intellect, & his heart.'"[5] He may have disbelieved or tried to disbelieve or at least tried to ignore his mother's rumored intimacy with a lover after his father left the family. Yet throughout his "prolonged mourning" for his mother Eliza,[6] Poe could not have utterly repressed the remembered questions.

Revealingly, Marie Louise Shew Houghton (d. 1877), in whom Poe had confided in his later years, recalled that he clearly suffered from his own guilt: "...it was the regret of his life, that he had not vindicated his mother to the world, as pure, as angelic and altogether lovely, as any woman could be on earth."[7]

"The regret of his life"—this is very strong language. In light of the connection in the three Dupin tales with a woman's uncertain reputation, it may well be that Poe created Dupin—who solves mysteries and assigns guilt—in order, by analogy, to solve the ultimate mystery of Rosalie's birth and to face his own guilt. "The Raven," as we know from "The Philosophy of Composition," concerned Poe's *"Mournful and Never-ending Remembrance"* (*Complete Works* 14:208); the Dupin tales may concern his Mournful and Never-ending Remorse.

Poe touches on the matter of a woman's uncertain reputation on occasion in his criticism. For example, with regard to Nathaniel William Wraxall's (1751–1831) *Posthumous Memoirs of His Own Time*, Poe wrote in the October 1836 issue of the *Southern Literary Messenger* about "...the queen's [Marie Antoinette's] evident innocence in this singular robbery" and the fact that nonetheless "...a numerous class of Parisians either believed or affected to believe her implicated in the guilt of the whole transaction" (*Complete Works* 9:183). More pointedly, he wrote in a review of Bulwer's novel *Night and Morning* in the April 1841 issue of *Graham's Magazine* (in which "The Murders in the Rue Morgue" appeared) about the effort of son Philip "to demonstrate the marriage [of his parents] and redeem the good name of his mother" (10:115–16). Poe tried to distance himself from Bulwer's plot, terming it "absurdly commonplace" (10:116), but this epithet seems a defensive one. Regarding a woman's acknowledged guilt, we may recall Castiglione's assertion regarding Lalage in Poe's verse drama *Politian*, "Never in woman's breast enthroned sat / A purer heart! If ever woman fell / With an excuse for falling it was she!" (*Collected Works* 1:254).[8]

It seems fitting then to consider here the autobiographical detail in the Dupin tales with a particular attention to the theme of a woman's possible guilt.

That "The Murders in the Rue Morgue" has autobiographical elements is clear, from the name C. Auguste Dupin, drawn from Poe's "acquaintance" C. Auguste Dubouchet, to the name *"Pauline Dubourg"* (*Collected Works* 2:538), borrowed from Poe's teachers in London. Kenneth Silverman mentions a number of these elements.[9] The double *"d"*s of "The riddle, so far, was now unriddled" (2:553) recall "Eddy," as do the three instances of the word "imbedded" (2:553, 559, 567).

Early psychoanalytic critic Marie Bonaparte (1882–1962)[10] carefully considered the autobiographical elements of "The Murders in the Rue Morgue"—she began from a different starting point than mine, but came to a similar conclusion. She assumed that as an infant Poe observed his mother having sex: "In Poe's case, there seems every reason to believe he did, in fact, observe the *primal scene*."[11] Bonaparte inferred that this scene involved his mother and her illicit partner, the father of Rosalie. She argued that the orangutan is Poe's unconscious rendering of that partner and that its cutting Madame L'Espanaye's throat and choking Mademoiselle L'Espanaye and stuffing her up the chimney represent Poe's unconscious representation of this partner's making love to his mother and impregnating her.[12]

I begin with the interrelationship of Poe's reading the *Saturday News* and his private revelation to Marie Louise Shew Houghton (neither of which would have been known to Bonaparte). Poe read of Edward Coleman cutting the throat of his wife Ann, who, the angry husband believed—"not without cause," according to acquaintances—had been unfaithful. Poe purposefully transformed Coleman into the angry orangutan cutting the throat of Madame L'Espanaye (Coleman and the orangutan "nearly severed her head from her body") and choking Mademoiselle L'Espanaye—the L'Espanayes are literally innocent, but they replace the betraying woman. The singular violence after the murders—the throwing of Madame L'Espanaye to the street and the pushing of her daughter up the chimney—offered Dupin evidence of the nonhuman nature of the murderer. Poe, I would argue, was reworking the Coleman story, in part, to represent covertly allegations against his mother and to suggest his own guilt for not defending her. The orangutan represents not his mother's lover, but those who talked of that lover, impugning Eliza Poe, assassinating her reputation.

Bonaparte's approach is more generic, less close to Poe's demonstrable actual feelings and experience. And the primal scene does seem, as Richard Wilbur terms it, a "dreary idea."[13] And Bonaparte's approach does not accord sufficient artistry to Poe's writing since she sees much of his work as unconscious.

Yet Bonaparte nonetheless perceptively concludes:

> We already know, however, that Elizabeth Arnold's pregnancy with
> Rosalie gave rise to much suspicion. Who, demanded gossip, had put

her in that condition; a question John Allan was to repeat with cruel insistence? And, in fact, it seems to be just this problem which Poe, in his turn, sets in *The Murders in the Rue Morgue*, that first of our modern detective novels. Dupin, venerable ancestor of Sherlock Holmes and the whole race of detectives was possibly merely created to solve, for Poe's unconscious, the riddle of who was his sister's father?[14]

Especially given the motive for murder in Poe's Edward Coleman source, the riddle of Rosalie's father does seem at work in the tale. I would underscore, though, given Poe's admission to Marie Louise Shew Houghton, that Poe felt guilt about not defending his mother's reputation. And I wonder if perhaps Poe was conscious of shadowing forth his guilt—his not having vindicated the accused mysteriously pregnant Eliza Poe.

How did Poe deal with his remorse? He created his own therapist, another version of himself, the highly ratiocinative C. Auguste Dupin, who, though unable to solve the actual problem, could solve a substitute problem and thus restore to Poe a greater measure of control, a greater sense of balance.

Richard Wilbur is right when he describes "a recurrent plot in Poe": "...a woman's love or honor is the ground of contention between two men, one of them lofty-minded and the other base or brutish." In "Rue Morgue," I would argue, the "woman's...honor" is that of the L'Espanayes—who suggest his mother—and the "lofty-minded" and the "base or brutish" are Dupin and the orangutan—Poe's intellectual ideal and his mother's unopposed detractors. The "redemptive principle," if not the L'Espanayes, may well be the art that permitted Poe to try to forgive himself.[15]

Like "The Murders in the Rue Morgue," "The Mystery of Marie Roget" also offers autobiographical elements. The undercurrent concerning H. Hastings Weld reflects Poe's hitherto neglected literary battle. The central terms "proceeded" (*Collected Works* 3:749) suggest, according to David Ketterer's argument, "Eddy." And the word "imbedded" (3:742) reinforces the self-referentiality. Marie Bonaparte shifted her argument for this tale; she alleged that the work concerns the "'rape' of [Poe's] child-wife, Virginia."[16] I will focus on Poe's text, Poe's reading, and Poe's confession to Marie Louise Shew Houghton regarding his guilt about not protecting his mother's reputation.

Marie Rogêt had a public role—she was the *grisette* at a perfumery, even as Mary Rogers had been the "cigar-girl" (*Collected Works* 3:725–26). (Likewise, Eliza Poe had been a well-known actress.)[17]

Three years earlier, Marie had disappeared from her perfumery and a week later had reappeared "with a somewhat saddened air." Poe refers to her earlier disappearance as "her previous notoriety" (3:726) and later mentions her "old *amour*" (3:754). Dupin includes, among his six extracts, two extracts that refer to Marie's earlier vanishing (3:753). Similarly, in one newspaper, Mary "[a]bout a year since" "was published as having fled with a young man" and in another "was missing from Anderson's store, three years ago, for two weeks.... she was then seduced by an officer of the U. S. Navy...."[18] Although "[t]he medical testimony [regarding Marie Rogêt] spoke confidently of the virtuous character of the deceased" (3:730) (as did that of Mary Rogers),[19] Poe acknowledges L'Etoile's implied "charge against her [Marie's] chastity" (3:733; see also "Is Mary C. Rogers Murdered?") and refers to Marie as "young, beautiful and notorious" (3:757). Dupin twice speaks of Marie's "secret lover" (3:755) and later of "a lover, or at least... an intimate and secret associate of the deceased" (3:768). The uncertain reputation of Marie Rogêt and Mary Rogers resonates with that of Ann Coleman, and, critically, with that of Eliza Poe. I believe that the same dynamic at work in "Rue Morgue" is present in "Marie Rogêt."

The imagined murderer would again seem to represent those who spoke against Poe's mother Eliza—those whose insinuations Poe did not refute—leading to "the regret of his life." (The fact that the probable cause of Marie's/Mary's death was an abortion gone wrong [which had been suggested in the newspapers early on] eliminates, of course, a purposeful malice. But it does confirm, from a nineteenth-century perspective, the young woman's damaged reputation.)[20]

Again Dupin solves, or tries to solve, a substitute problem—this time, who killed Mary Rogers? Bringing reason to bear through his detective, Poe tries to diminish the anguish that is beyond reason—his sorrow for not having "vindicated his mother."

The link between "Rue Morgue" and "Marie Rogêt"—that of a woman's compromised reputation—extends to the third and final Dupin tale, "The Purloined Letter." On the level of source figures, Princess Caroline is the latest incarnation of Ann Coleman and Mary Rogers. What is different about this tale, however, is that, through Dupin, Poe moves beyond guilt to the defense that he wished he had actually offered.

And "The Purloined Letter" has evident autobiographical elements. We need only recall the double "*d*"s of the central words "astounded" and "extended" (*Collected Works* 3:983), "the curling eddies of smoke" (3:974), and "the two houses immediately adjoining" (3:980). And there is more. Let us turn briefly to psychoanalytic criticism.

Marie Bonaparte is only partly successful in her discussion of "The Purloined Letter." She rightly recognizes a family dynamic, but her Freudian preoccupation with anatomy seems problematic. Yes, it is fair enough to see the King and Queen as David and Eliza Poe, and the struggles between Dupin and Minister D—— as an Oedipal struggle between Poe and John Allan (or between Poe and both John Allan and Eliza's secret lover). Yet to characterize that struggle as an effort "to seize possession, not of the mother herself, but of a part; namely, her penis" seems an ideological forcing, one that is ultimately reductive.[21]

The famous responses of Jacques Lacan, Jacques Derrida, and Barbara Johnson are clever and perhaps admirable for a certain kind of discourse. But with regard to Poe and his tale, they do not satisfy. Lacan sees the two thefts as emblematic of the primal scene, exemplifying a repetition compulsion. Dismissing the matter of "guilt and blame," he first compares "the purloined letter" to "an immense female body," but then, noting the letter's position "between the cheeks of the fireplace," links it not to a female body, but to a female body part.[22] Picking up from Lacan, Derrida sees the letter "on the immense body of a woman, between the 'legs' of the fireplace," but he quarrels with Lacan for neglecting the narrator, Poe's other texts, the difference between "above" and "beneath," and the critical doubling. And he questions the similarity between Lacan's work and Bonaparte's.[23] Barbara Johnson amusingly critiques both Lacan and Derrida and admits at her essay's close, "And the true otherness of the purloined letter of literature has perhaps still in no way been accounted for."[24]

We have come a long way from Poe's principle of identification. It may be that the work of these critics, if unworthy of Dupin, is worthy of the Prefect. Reconsideration of *The Purloined Poe* may suggest that it is time to purloin Poe back.[25] I would return our attention to Poe's reading—specifically, his reading of the theft of "the purloined letter" from Princess Caroline in *Death-Bed Confessions*. Recalling Caroline's actual adulterous relationships and Poe's sense of guilt for not having defended his mother, whose reputation had been compromised, we may come closer to the autobiographical import of "The Purloined Letter."

Whereas in "The Murders in the Rue Morgue" and "The Mystery of Marie Roget" Poe reworked accounts of women of uncertain reputation in part to intimate his guilt—and to recover order through Monsieur Dupin's disentangling—in "The Purloined Letter" he not only reworked an account of another such woman and again recovered order through Dupin's analysis, but also diminished his guilt through Dupin's protecting the compromised woman. With the power of identification (illustrated by the schoolboy whose guesses of "odd" and "even" subtly structure the entire tale), Dupin finds "the purloined letter" and returns it to the threatened Queen. And he asserts, "For eighteen months the Minister has had her in his power. She has now him in hers..." (*Complete Works* 3:993). Through Dupin, Poe has rescued his Caroline figure from his Brougham figure; indeed, he has rescued his mother; she can no longer be maligned by John Allan.

We know that Poe considered "The Purloined Letter" to be "perhaps, the best of my tales of ratiocination" (*Letters* 1:450), and certainly its formal complexity would have contributed to this judgment. But I think it was his private victory that was more important. In this last of the Dupin stories, though he was not able to prove his mother innocent, he could, through Dupin, prevent someone else from proving her guilty.

No writer, Poe once stated, could write a book titled "My Heart Laid Bare" (*Complete Works* 16:128; *Collected Writings* 2:322–23), but he came very close to writing a novel that deserved such a title—*The Narrative of Arthur Gordon Pym*—and to writing a story that deserved it as well—"The Purloined Letter." Through Dupin—who identifies himself as "a partisan of the lady concerned" (*Collected Works* 3:993)— Poe stood up for an "illustrious personage" in his own life. In this tale, at least, he would not allow his mother to be seen as less than "as pure, as angelic and altogether lovely, as any woman could be on earth." And perhaps, through his brilliant art in "The Purloined Letter," Poe was able to diminish, even slightly, "the regret of his life." It may be that he did not write another Dupin tale after "The Purloined Letter" not because he had given up on the detective fiction genre but because he determined that he could not write a greater one, or a more personally satisfying one.

Reading E. L. Doctorow on Poe, one wonders about claims that Poe was "a hack writer," not "a major poet," perhaps not even "a minor poet," and so on. However, the claim that warrants particular mention here is that "We would still have Poe if he had never written a detective story. But we would not have him without his dead women and rotting manses and vengeful maniacs." Needless to say, there are gothic elements in Poe's detective stories. But, more importantly, Poe had several strengths that would sustain a major literary reputation, no one dominating the others. Responding to Evert A. Duyckinck's (1816–78) selection for the 1845 *Tales*—which favored the ratiocinative—Poe wrote, "Were all my tales now before me in a large volume and as the composition of another—the merit which would principally arrest my attention would be the wide *diversity and* variety" (*Letters* 1:596). The greatness of Poe's achievement in the tale of terror does not obscure or diminish the greatness of his achievement in creating the modern detective story. Indeed, the two achievements may illuminate one another. Poe is certainly not "the boy next door"—but he may well have the apartment above us—as well as the one below.[26]

W. H. Auden has written, "The interest in the detective story is the dialectic of innocence and guilt." The purpose of reading a detective story is the recovery of "a state of innocence"; the prompt is "the feeling of guilt." John Cawelti states, "... [the detective] uses his powers not to threaten but to uphold the reader's self-esteem by proving the guilt of a specific individual rather than exposing some general guilt in which the reader might be implicated." He adds, "Poe's Dupin stories explored the terms in which the secret depths might be brought under control and the sense of hidden guilt and insecurity overcome.... [the detective] demonstrated that there was not after all a secret guilt. Instead, he proves that it was someone else all along."[27] It is true that it was "someone else"—the orangutan in "The Murders in the Rue Morgue," the sailor in "The Mystery of Marie Rogêt" (or the implied abortionist in the later version of the tale), and the Minister D— in "The Purloined Letter." Yet, as I have argued, there is still a "secret guilt" that unites these stories. First, there is the guilt or alleged guilt of the woman, evident in the selected source characters, whether mentioned (Mary Rogers in "Marie Rogêt") or hidden (Ann Coleman in "Rue Morgue," Princess Caroline in "The Purloined Letter"), and in Eliza Poe. Second, there is Poe's own guilt for not having "vindicated his mother." According to this reading, it was "the regret of his life" that led Poe to create Dupin and the detective story. The genre emerged from suffering. And its purpose was redemption.

CONCLUSION

With Dupin's blended methodology as our guide, we have worked to solve the Dupin mysteries. We have studied the verbal patterning of the three Dupin stories and recognized consistently a symmetrical structure with a significant midpoint. Furthermore, for "The Murders in the Rue Morgue," we have found Poe reshaping stories of murder and madness from *The Philadelphia Saturday News*. For "The Mystery of Marie Rogêt," we have found him reworking an account of an empty boat from the *New York Star* and incorporating for that tale both literary/historical precedent offered in the *New York Herald* and professional animus prompted by a review in the *Brother Jonathan*. For "The Purloined Letter," we have found him refashioning an incident involving the theft of a letter from a princess, as described in an 1822 volume, *Death-Bed Confessions*. And we have identified a woman of uncertain reputation as critical to important sources for the Dupin tales and have interpreted the three tales as suggestive of the uncertain reputation of his mother and his guilt for inadequately defending her reputation.

Poe consistently wrote for two audiences, the many and the few, and his Dupin tales illustrate his usual doubleness of purpose. For the many, he offered an intriguing mystery and the brilliant hero who could solve it, a combination so compelling that it initiated a genre. For the few, he offered formal complexity, creative transformation, and autobiographical revelation, features so subtle that no one of them has been fully appreciated. But surely Poe's private satisfaction was considerable. And our satisfaction—in Poe's artistry and in our learning from his detective to read Poe—is great, as well.

The interpretation offered here invites new consideration of links from the Dupin tales both backward and forward. We may make brief forays.

Oedipus may be considered an early detective—through a series of interrogations, he discovers the cause of the plague in Thebes—his own having unknowingly killed his father and slept with his mother. Hamlet may be considered another early detective—through the performance of a play that he skillfully modified, he proves the validity of the ghost's accusation that his uncle had murdered his father.[1] In both cases, there is a woman of problematic reputation—Oedipus's mother Jocasta and Hamlet's mother Gertrude (who married and slept with her husband's murderer). And the guilt of the son—Oedipus for parricide and incest, Hamlet for irresolution—is profound. But despite affinities, these works starkly contrast with the Dupin tales. Poe's detective has no guilt. And whereas Oedipus and Hamlet suffer their tragic fates, Dupin suffers none—and he seems to help his creator endure his. Clearly, *Oedipus Rex* and *Hamlet*, both of which involve crucial detection, offer the reader and the viewer a powerful catharsis; "The Purloined Letter," by contrast, offers its author—and implicitly its reader—a second chance.

Roger Chillingworth in Nathaniel Hawthorne's novel *The Scarlet Letter* is another detective, discovering the secret guilt of the minister, Arthur Dimmesdale. And Hester Prynne is the noble woman of compromised reputation. I have argued elsewhere that Hawthorne transformed Poe's "The Tell-Tale Heart" for Chapter 10 of *The Scarlet Letter*;[2] future scholarship might well investigate parallels between Poe's Dupin tales and Hawthorne's novel, paying particular attention to Nina Baym's assertion that the "bridal pregnancy" of Hawthorne's mother may have contributed to his imagining the story of Hester Prynne.[3]

And then there is Sherlock Holmes. What is particularly interesting here is Arthur Conan Doyle's empowering of women in tales influenced by Poe. The May 1887 story "A Scandal in Bohemia" is a work with plain indebtedness to "The Purloined Letter" (as Elizabeth Sweeney has noted).[4] It concerns a royal figure blackmailed with evidence of indiscretion (a photo, in this case), as well as waylayings and ransacking, a disturbance caused by the detective's confederates, and a triumphal substitution for the hidden evidence. Yet it is not a woman of uncertain reputation who is at risk here—rather, it is a man, threatened with exposure by his former lover, Irene Adler, a woman whom Holmes clearly admires. Given the subtext in the Dupin tales of Poe's guilt for not sufficiently defending his mother's reputation, Doyle's reworking of "The Purloined Letter" here is all the more remarkable—there is significant regard in "A Scandal in Bohemia" for a woman who tries to use her former intimacy with another to her advantage.

And the empowering of women is also apparent in Doyle's January 1899 Sherlock Holmes story "The Adventure of Charles Augustus Milverton." Here we have a work with allusions to "The Raven"—a nighttime visitor taps at the door of a study that includes a bust of

Athena—and to "The Purloined Letter"—women are blackmailed with evidence of previous compromising behavior. However, in this work, a woman is not always helpless. Indeed, one of the women whose past has been revealed—to disastrous consequences—arranges to meet the man who had revealed it (she is the unnamed nighttime visitor) and shoots him to death. Holmes then protects the woman, believing her actions to be warranted. So the compromised woman achieves an uncompromising revenge.[5]

In Poe's sources for the Dupin tales, the woman of uncertain reputation is either killed (Ann Colemen, Mary Rogers) or betrayed (Princess Caroline). And we see such fates for the women in the Dupin tales themselves. But in these two Poe-influenced works by Poe's most famous heir, the woman with a previous liaison takes the initiative and takes control. The empowering of women in the detective story has continued through the twentieth century and into the twenty-first century—women have become detectives—and authors.[6]

These brief forays suggest the promise of the continued recontextualizing of the Dupin tales in literary history by way of the reading presented here. I would like to close now by returning to the matter of Poe's reputation.

Certainly the present work confirms the strong positive judgments about the Dupin tales provided by Doyle, T. S. Eliot, and Jorge Luis Borges. But how does this work relate to our sense of Poe in general? We might turn to Louis D. Rubin Jr.'s thoughtful assessment. Considering Poe's personal and professional struggles, his literary craftsmanship, and his addressing (and sometimes anticipating) the darker concerns of human existence, Rubin considers Poe a hero.[7] I would not disagree. But I would add something here. Poe offers in the Dupin tales a great delight and an engaging challenge. And he offers, too, through his brilliant detective/teacher, a guide as to how to meet that challenge. Furthermore, he shares with his readers, in the course of these tales, intimations of his own private sorrow and his attempt to overcome it. He is not remote, but, rather, subtly confiding. Poe is no doubt a hero—but perhaps, especially in light of his extraordinary Dupin tales, we may also consider him a friend.

Notes

Introduction

1. See Borges 23; Conan Doyle, *Through the Magic Door* 117–18; and Eliot 5:362 . For discussion of Borges and Poe, see Bennett and Irwin, *The Mystery to a Solution*. For discussion of Doyle and Poe, see Sweeney. Although Sherlock Holmes termed Dupin "a very inferior fellow" (*The New Annotated Sherlock Holmes* 3:42), Doyle held Dupin in high esteem. And he complained when the distinction was not noted and respected: "As the creator I've praised to satiety / Poe's Monsieur Dupin, his skill and variety, / And have admitted that in my detective work, / I owe to my model a deal of selective work. / But is it not on the verge of inanity / To put down to me my creation's crude vanity?" (See Fisher, "Verses on Poe and Arthur Conan Doyle.") For comment on Eliot and Poe, see Osowski.

2. See Gribben (re Twain) 17; Chesterton 106; Van Doren Stein 228; Sayers, "Introduction" 18; Benton, "The Mystery of Marie Rogêt: A Defense" 149, 151; Queen, "Introduction" ix; and Mabbott, "Introduction," *Selected Poetry and Prose of Poe* 3.

3. For an examination of hard-boiled detective fiction, see Irwin, *Unless the Threat of Death Is behind Them*. For assessment of the metaphysical detective story, see Merivale and Sweeney. For reference works on detective fiction in general, see Herbert and Murphy.

4. Referring to "Rue Morgue," Poe wrote in 1842, "Its *theme* was the exercise of ingenuity in the detection of a murderer" (*Letters* 1:337; see also 1:340). He added, regarding "Marie Rogêt," "My main object...is an analysis of the true principles which should direct inquiry in similar cases" (1:338; see also 1:340). He observed, in 1846, that "people think them [the Dupin tales] more ingenious than they are"—for example, people take Dupin's ingenuity for his own—but he precedes this by clarifying, "I do not mean to say that they are not ingenious" (1:595). Burton R. Pollin considers Poe's aforementioned self-deprecatory remark "disingenuous" ("Poe's 'Murders in the Rue Morgue'" 237). J. Lasley Dameron effectively argues that Dupin is "a major hero in American literature" ("Poe's Auguste Dupin" 160).

5. Levinson 560. The author identifies two types of "new formalism"—the "activist new formalism" (growing out of New Historicism) and "normative new formalism" (a nonideological approach) (559).
6. See Cantalupo 79.
7. Cantalupo 79.
8. See Ingram 1:183.
9. For recent examples, see Victor A. Doyno on Mark Twain; my own work on Hawthorne (*Threads*); and Tom Quirk, in *Nothing Abstract*, on a variety of American authors, from Edgar Allan Poe to Tony Hillerman. See also Barbour and Quirk, *Writing the American Classics* and *Biographies of Books*.
10. For a thoughtful study of "intertext" and "source study," see "Sources, Influences, and Intertexts" in Quirk's *Nothing Abstract* (13–31). For the cited quotation, see Barbour and Quirk, "Introduction" to *Writing the American Classics* xii.
11. Reynolds's "reconstructive criticism" combines "formalist criticism" and "extrinsic approaches" (562). Employing this approach, Reynolds examines the origins of nineteenth-century canonical American literature in the popular literature of its time.

I   Formal Considerations of the Dupin Tales

1. For a related critical comment, see a passage on plot in Poe's 1843 treatment of James Fenimore Cooper's novel *Wyandotté* (*Complete Works* 11:209–10).
2. For the symmetry of *Pym*, see my "Introduction" xx–xxiii; "Explanatory Notes" 224–25, 231–32, 239–41, 242–43. For the structure of "The Tell-Tale Heart," see my *Threads* 107.
3. See Wilbur 136. The symmetry of the tale is also discussed by Henri Justin in "The Fold Is the Thing" (30) and "An Impossible Aesthetics." I am happy to add that Maureen Bollier, a former student at Penn State DuBois, wrote a paper on symmetry in "Rue Morgue" in 1987.
4. See Irwin, *The Mystery to a Solution* 196–97. Irwin explores further the presence of the myth of Theseus in "Rue Morgue." Justin mentions the "clou"/"clew" pun in "An Impossible Aesthetics."
5. For an early mention of the French translation for the phrase "of bread," "du pain," and its pun, "Dupin," see Bloom 24. For a discussion of the pun in Poe, see Zimmerman 291–92.
6. See R. M. Walsh 211.
7. For the inversion of the biblical passage in *Pym*, see my introduction to the Penguin edition of Poe's novel (xxv). For the inversion of Hawthorne's tribute to Fessenden in "The Tell-Tale Heart," see my *Threads* 28.
8. For a selection of reviews of "The Murders in the Rue Morgue," consult the index in Walker 414. For Justin's comment, see "An

Impossible Aesthetics." For the fold in Poe in general, see Justin, "The Fold Is the Thing."

9. See *Edgar Allan Poe—Eureka* 96.

10. See Ketterer 197.

11. See Kopley, *Threads* 157 n. 23.

12. Two other instances of the word "imbedded" occur in "Rue Morgue." Describing the orangutan, Poe's Dupin states, "Each finger has retained—possibly until the death of the victim—the fearful grasp by which it originally *imbedded* itself" (*Collected Works* 2:559; emphasis added). And the sailor states of the orangutan, "Gnashing its teeth, and flashing fire from its eyes, it flew upon the body of the girl, and *imbedded* its fearful talons in her throat..." (2:567; emphasis added). The word appears also in six other Poe works: "The Duc de L'Omelette" (2:36v), "William Wilson" (2:428), "The Mystery of Marie Rogêt" (3:742), "[Preface to] Marginalia" (3:1115), "The Cask of Amontillado" (3:1259), and "Landor's Cottage" (3:1337). (These instances were gathered from Pollin's *Word Index* 172.) Notably, the word "imbedded" in "Landor's Cottage" had initially been (in a text not used in the edition) "embedded" (3:1337n). The words "embed," "embedded," and "imbed" are not listed in the *Word Index* (112, 172).

13. For commentary on biographical criticism of Poe's works, see Peeples 41–53.

14. For the Dubourg sisters as Poe's teachers, see Thomas and Jackson 29–30, 32, 33–34. Several biographical details in "Rue Morgue" are suggested by Kenneth Silverman 173.

15. For commentary about the reported confession regarding the botched abortion and Poe's modification of "The Mystery of Marie Rogêt" to accommodate the new view, see Wimsatt, "Poe and the Mystery of Mary Rogers" 242–46; Walsh 52–73; Paul 93–121; and Srebnick 29–32.

16. We may note, in passing, parallel passages that don't precisely fit in the noted sequence of pairs of corresponding framing passages. The testimony of Madame Deluc regarding "a gang of miscreants," eating and drinking without paying and then following a young man and a girl and crossing the river, appears twice in "Marie Rogêt" (*Collected Works* 3:735, 767).

17. Scholars have previously objected to other aspects of Poe's logic in "Marie Rogêt." See, for example, William K. Wimsatt Jr. (236–37), on Poe's arguing that one gang's crime against a young woman precludes that gang's (or another gang's) similar crime against another young woman at a similar time and place (*Collected Works* 3:757–58).

18. For the Benton assessment, see 151. For the Kennedy appraisal, see 120. For other negative critiques of the story, see Ketterer 245–48 and Irwin 323–29.

19. Srebnick praises Poe's skill in identifying with Marie Rogêt by imagining her thoughts: "Marie quite literally comes alive, not as the destroyed subject of reanimation but as a living being, as Poe endows Marie with a voice, as well as agency" (131). For discussion of Poe's "speaking in another person's character" ("dialogismus"), see Zimmerman 181.

20. For Eco's comment, see Basbanes 226.

21. Poe's chiasmus regarding poets and fools is a transformation of a passage by Lord Brougham (*Sketches of Public Characters*) and another, involving chiasmus, by Horace Binney Wallace (*Stanley*). This point is elaborated in chapter IV. We see Poe again reworking Wallace's chiasmus in "A Chapter of Suggestions," published a few months after "The Purloined Letter": "*All* men of genius have their detractors; but it is merely a *non distributio medii* to argue, thence, that all men who have their detractors are men of genius" (*Complete Works* 14:189). For Poe's reliance on other passages from Wallace's novel *Stanley* for "The Purloined Letter," see George Egon Hatvary, "Poe's Borrowings" 370–71 and *Horace Binney Wallace* 67–68. For consideration of chiasmus in Poe, see my own "Hawthorne's Transplanting" 235, and *The Threads of "The Scarlet Letter"* 107, as well as Zimmerman 164–66.

22. Ross Chambers noted years ago that "At the midpoint of the tale... in return for the Prefect's check, Dupin hands over the letter" (67), but he did not observe the symmetry of language.

23. For comment on "curling eddies of smoke," see Ketterer, "'Shudder': A Signature *Crypt*-ogram in 'The Fall of the House of Usher'" 202.

24. Mary E. Phillips provides a passage by R. M. Hogg linking the marbles game in "The Purloined Letter" to one familiar in Irvine, Scotland (2:931–32). However, Hogg mentions a game involving guessing the number of marbles in two hands rather than determining whether an odd or even number of marbles is held in one hand. The rhyme he cites focuses on which hand holds the marbles. It is possible that Poe drew his even-odd game from his boyhood stay in Irvine in 1815, but the evidence is insufficient for us to ascertain this with certainty.

25. For the reference to Cicero, see Krajewski 25. For Poe on Cicero, see most critically his comments on Charles Anthon's edition of the orations (*Complete Works* 9:266–68; 16:103; see also *Collected Writings* 5:358; 2:279).

26. For additional observation of the correspondence between this passage from "The Purloined Letter" and Wallace's *Stanley* regarding assuming another's expression, see Hatvary, "Poe's Borrowings" 370 and *Horace Binney Wallace* 67. S. L. Varnado (also mentioned by Mabbott [*Collected Works* 3:994]) suggests Edmund Burke's *A Philosophical Inquiry* as an alternative source for the passage.

27. To check the *Stanley* source passage, see *Collected Works* 3:995–96; Hatvary, "Poe's Borrowings" 370–71 or *Horace Binney Wallace* 67–68;

or the Wallace work itself (1:206–8). The shift from the source corresponds to Poe's adding a second mirror to the one mirror in his Benjamin Morrell source, *A Narrative of Four Voyages.* See Kopley, "The Hidden Journey of *Arthur Gordon Pym*" 31, and the Introduction to the Penguin *Pym* xxi.

28. For the *mise en abime* in *Pym*, see my essay "The Hidden Journey of *Arthur Gordon Pym*" 30–32 and my Introduction to the Penguin *Pym* xx–xxi.

29. For the comment on cards in "Rue Morgue" and "The Purloined Letter," see Rosenheim 29.

30. LeRoy Lad Panek discusses Hoyle as an influence on Poe in "Rue Morgue," but cites the 1821 New York volume published by George Long. Perhaps a more likely one would be the 1838 Philadelphia volume published by Thomas, Cowperthwait. Other canonical works that involve a significant playing-card motif include Alexander Pope's *The Rape of the Lock* and Lewis Carroll's *Alice's Adventures in Wonderland.*

31. T. O. Mabbott attributed "A Literary Curiosity" and "Palindromes" to Poe, with the solution for the riddling poem, in "Palindromes (and Poe)." An earlier version of the poem, titled "Enigma," had appeared in 1827. J. H. Whitty included the 1840 poem as Poe's (146; see also 287). Killis Campbell seemed to accept the brief introduction to the poem in "Palindromes" as Poe's, remained noncommital on the attribution of the poem itself, and printed the 1827 version (199 200). William Doyle Hull II gives the "Omniana" section, including "Palindromes," to Poe (272–73), and Thomas and Jackson give it to Poe, as well (294). T. O. Mabbott had reprinted the 1827 poem in his Introduction to the 1941 facsimile of *Tamerlane and Other Poems* but had stated, "...the authorship is doubtful..." (li). He became convinced of Poe's authorship of the poem, as evidenced by his 1946 piece (see also Brigham 67), but later changed his mind, arguing in the Poe edition that Poe's authorship of "Omniana" "now seems most improbable." He added, "The amusing poems (on palindromes) can be removed from the canon" (*Collected Works* 1:504).

32. Interestingly, Douglass attributes the nonrecognition of the ring structure in literature to the postmodern preference for open-endedness (142–48).

II   "The Murders in the Rue Morgue" and *The Philadelphia Saturday News*

1. See Bonaparte 427–57; Pollin, "Poe's 'Murders in the Rue Morgue'"; Fetterley 154–58; and Lemire, especially 188–200.

2. Campbell 165n. Campbell mentions a possible source for "Rue Morgue" suggested in the *Washington Post* of 3 October 1912, but that unfound, undated, unattributed "source" is termed by Mabbott "an

absurd hoax" (*Collected Works* 2:524). Still, Campbell's initial hypothesis regarding the debt of "Rue Morgue" to newspapers is a valid one.

3. For Mabbott's comments, see *Collected Works* 2: 521–26, 569–74. E. D. Forgues, Brander Matthews, and Mozelle S. Allen wrote about *Zadig*, W. F. Waller discussed the thieving baboon, and John Robert Moore considered the Scott novel. The stories of LeFanu and Mangan were brought up by Patrick Diskin. Mention of C. Auguste Dubouchet was made by W. T. Bandy. Howard Haycraft referred to André-Marie-Jean-Jacques Dupin and his brother François Charles Pierre Dupin (22–25); see also John T. Irwin, "Reading Poe's Mind." Buford Jones and Kent Ljungquist propose that Poe would have known of André-Marie-Jean-Jacques Dupin before he read the Walsh volume, citing satirical treatment of the famed lawyer in the 1821 newspaper *John Bull*. (For a focus on Charles Dupin, see Harrison; for confirmation that Poe's model was André, see Pollin, "Poe's 'Murders in the Rue Morgue,'" 239, 255–56.) Mabbott credits J. J. Cohane with mentioning the Wallace text, I. V. K. Ousby with citing "Unpublished Passages," and W. K. Wimsatt Jr. with examining the Brewster work. For more on Wallace, see Hatvary; for more on Vidocq, see Quinn 310–11; for more on Brewster, see Pollin ("'MS Found in a Bottle'"), Shear, and Brody.

4. For "A Chapter on Goblins," see Fisher, "Poe, Blackwoods, and 'The Murders in the Rue Morgue.'" For the folktale motif, see Doyle. The jest-book is suggested by Stewart, and the Cuviers' works by Mitchell. For mention of treatment of the orangutan in the *Saturday Evening Post*, see Dameron, "More Analogues and Resources"; for discussion of the account of the animal in *American Magazine of Useful and Entertaining Knowledge*, see Dameron, "Six More Analogues and Resources for Poe"; for consideration of the orangutan (actually a chimpanzee) in the *Pennsylvania Inquirer*, see Thomas and Jackson 265, as well as Thomas 50–51. The chimp was also treated in the *Philadelphia Gazette* and the *Weekly Spirit of the Times* (Thomas 57–59). For a discussion of the significance of *Hoyle* in "Rue Morgue," see Panek. For the noting and proposing of autobiographical details, see Silverman 173. Further consideration of the autobiographical implications of "The Murders in the Rue Morgue" will be offered in chapter V.

5. See Levine 153. For earlier comments on Poe and Bulwer's *Pelham*, see Pattee 128, and Thompson, "The Nose—Further Speculation on the Sources and Meaning of Poe's 'Lionizing'" and "Poe's Readings of *Pelham*: Another Source for 'Tintinnabulation' and Other Piquant Expressions." See also Richard P. Benton's response to the former Thompson piece ("Reply to Professor Thompson"). Heather Worthington focuses on the character Pelham as a detective (57–58). A useful recent study of Poe and Bulwer is Burton R. Pollin's "Bulwer-Lytton's Influence on Poe's Works and Ideas."

Poe's opinion of Bulwer changed: in the February 1836 issue of the *Southern Literary Messenger*, reviewing *Rienzi, The Last of the Tribunes*, Poe considered Bulwer the novelist "unsurpassed by any writer living or dead" (*Collected Writings* 5:121), but in the April 1841 issue of *Graham's Magazine* (which featured "Rue Morgue"), Poe negatively reviewed *Night and Morning: A Novel*, emphatically asserting that Bulwer was *"shallow,"* and unfavorably comparing him with Scott and Dickens (*Complete Works* 10:131–32). Despite his diminished estimation of Bulwer, Poe continued to transform elements of Bulwer's writing for his own writing. In light of Dupin's criticizing Vidocq (and the "Parisian police") by saying, "Truth is not always in a well" (*Collected Works* 2:545), it is interesting to note that Poe wrote in "Literary Small Talk" in 1839, "Bulwer, in my opinion, wants the true vigour of intellect which would prompt him to seek, and enable him to seize truth upon the surface of things. He images her forever in the well" (*Complete Works* 14:91). (For Mabbott on Poe's use of "truth in a well," see 2:332, 572; for Ridgely on the same, see *Collected Writings* 5:132–33.)

I first encountered Poe's borrowings for "Rue Morgue" from Bulwer's *Pelham* when I examined the markings of Palmer C. Holt in an edition of Bulwer's novels. I am pleased to acknowledge the Palmer C. Holt Collection in Manuscripts, Archives, and Special Collections, Washington State University Libraries, Pullman, Washington. I have spoken and published on Poe's other borrowings from *Pelham* in "Poe's Taking of *Pelham* 1-2-3-4-5-6."

6. For the 1828 second edition of *Pelham*, available in a 1972 scholarly edition, the pagination of significant language is as follows: monkey attack (81–82), *"au troisième"* (32, 84), *"Faubourg St. Germain"* (41), *"Crébillon"*/ *"Crébillon's"*/ *"Crébillon"* (46, 87, 99), *"Jardin des Plantes"* (72, 86, 97, 117), *"de nier ce qui est, et d'expliquer ce qui n'est pas"* (94), and "Rue Mont Orgueil" (79, 111). For "The Murders in the Rue Morgue," the pagination is as follows: orangutan attack (*Collected Works* 2:564–68), *"au troisième"* (2:561), "Faubourg St. Germain"/*"Faubourg St. Germain"* (2:532, 561), "Crébillon's" (2:534), *"Jardin des Plantes"* (2:568), *"de nier ce qui est, et d'expliquer ce qui n'est pas"* (2:568), and "Rue Morgue" (2:527, 537, 542, 546, 563, 566). For studies of the manuscript of "The Murders in the Rue Morgue," see Boll and Asarch.

7. Godey, Neal, and McMichael, "A Card." For background on Charles W. Alexander, see Brigham.

8. For information on Godey, see Stearns and Sewell. For information on *Godey's Lady's Book*, see Bulsterbaum. Godey publicized the *Saturday News* in *The Lady's Book*; see especially "To the Patrons of the Lady's Book," "A Publishing Month," and "The Philadelphia Saturday News and Literary Gazette." For a brief discussion of Godey and McMichael as publishers, see Hoffman.

9. McClure. See also McMichael's essay "Joseph C. Neal" and two more recent essays, David E. E. Sloane's "Joseph C. Neal" and this writer's "Neal, Joseph C[lay]." For Poe's inclusion of the *Pennsylvanian*'s critique of the *Messenger* in the January 1836 issue of his periodical, see the January 1836 "Supplement."

10. For early works concerning Morton McMichael, see John W. Forney, *Memorial Address* and "Morton McMichael, and Many Other Pennsylvania Men"; Mordell; and Baugh. For a more recent sketch, see Gillette Jr. See also Hoffman for Godey and McMichael as publishers. For details regarding the *Courier*'s short story contest and the newspaper's publication of Poe's early tales, consult Thomas and Jackson 120–28 and Varner iii–iv. Also worth consulting is Thomas's dissertation, "Poe in Philadelphia, 1838–1844."

11. These measurements were taken from the first page of the first issue of the *Saturday News*, that of 2 July 1836, which is bound (MWA). The *Saturday News* of 26 November 1836, the "mammoth" issue, featured eight pages (P); the issue of 7 January 1837 offered a two-page "Gems and Flowers" supplement (MWA).

12. The address of the *Saturday News* is first given as 100 Walnut Street in an advertisement in the 2 July 1836 issue, "The Philadelphia Saturday News and Literary Gazette." The office of the *Saturday News* was evidently also that of the *Lady's Book*—see "[Newspaper Exchange]." The relocation of the *Saturday News* to 211 Chesnut Street is first noted in an announcement in the 29 July 1837 issue, "REMOVAL."

13. Neal and McMichael, "Salutatory." Godey may also have had a hand in writing this piece.

14. See Godey, Neal, and McMichael, "To Our Patrons" and "[Advertisement for the *Saturday News*]" 10 March 1838. For additional commentary regarding the newspaper's circulation, see Godey, Neal, and McMichael, "[Advertisement for the *Saturday News*]," 7 January 1837, and "[Note to Subscribers]." The former item declares, "In every state of the Union, and throughout the Canadas, its [the newspaper's] circulation is wide and constantly increasing..."; the latter reports, "Such has been the increase of our city lists that the routes have had to be new modelled, and four additional carriers employed."

15. An excerpt from Irving's *Astoria* appeared in the *Saturday News* of 15 October 1836. (An anonymous and dark reimagining of Irving's "Rip Van Winkle," "Hans Swartz—A Marvelous Tale of Mamakating Hollow," was published in the *Saturday News* of 8 September 1838.) A passage from Emerson's speech on Bonaparte was featured in the 6 October 1838 issue, as was Holmes's poem, "The September Gale."

16. The *Saturday News* reviews of the *Messenger* are not readily attributable to only one of the two editors; therefore, these reviews are attributed to both. Although Neal and McMichael apparently enjoyed some "assistance" (according to Godey, Neal, and McMichael, "[Advertisement for the *Saturday News*]," 7 January 1837), that assistance and its sources are not identified or identifiable; consequently, the double attribution remains. Neal and McMichael reviewed issues of the *Messenger* for June, July, August, September, October, and November 1836, and the issue of January 1837. The quoted assessment of Poe's criticism may be found in their review of that last issue. They also offered their perspective on Poe's criticism in "The 'Southern Literary Messenger' and 'The Pickwick Papers.'" It is not clear whether Neal and McMichael recognized Poe's hand in the review of J. L. Stephens's *Incidents of Travel in Egypt, Arabia Petraea, and the Holy Land* that appeared in the second issue of the *New York Review* (*Complete Works* 10:1–25), early issues of which the two editors commented on favorably.

17. I assign the review of *Pym* to McMichael because the phrase "wild and wonderful" that appears there also appears in McMichael's January 1840 review of Poe's *Tales of the Grotesque and Arabesque* (in *Godey's Lady's Book*): Poe is said to have produced "some of the most vivid scenes of the wild and wonderful which can be found in English literature." The phrase "wild and wonderful" is again applied to Poe's work in Thomas Cottrell Clarke's 22 July 1843 review of *Prose Romances* (in the *Saturday Museum*). Curiously, Henry T. Tuckerman, whom Poe identified as "an insufferably tedious and dull" writer (*Complete Works* 15:217), commented in 1863 that the story of *Moby-Dick* is "wild and wonderful enough without being interwoven with such a thorough, scientific, and economical treatise on the whale..." (Melville 730).

18. For the *Messenger* reprinting of the *Saturday News* review of the June 1836 issue of the *Messenger*, see Neal and McMichael, "From the Philadelphia Saturday News." The editors reveal their familiarity with the *Messenger* from the magazine's beginning, August 1834, in this review's first sentence: "This magazine, from its commencement, has been an especial favorite with us; but it is not so well known at the North as its merits deserve."

19. For Poe's positive view of McMichael's prose and poetry (in "Autography," in *Graham's Magazine* of December 1841), see *Complete Works* 15:224. McMichael referred to Poe's "genius" both in his review of the *Tales* (Thomas and Jackson 285; Walker 129) and in conversation (Phillips 1:771). Poe wrote in "Autography" of December 1841 of Godey, "No man has warmer friends or fewer enemies" (*Complete Works* 15:218); however, his own regard for Godey was modulated

(*Letters* 2:648) and his assessment of parlor-focused magazines slight (1:333, 432). In "Autography" of November 1841, Poe offered a low opinion of Neal's *Charcoal Sketches*, but a higher one of Neal's editorial work and political writing (*Complete Works* 15:199–200). In a later elaboration of the faults of *Charcoal Sketches*, Poe termed Neal "unquestionably *small potatoes*" (*Doings of Gotham* 104).

20. According to Dwight Thomas and David K. Jackson, it was "early in 1838" that Poe and his wife and mother-in-law moved from New York City to Philadelphia (247; see also 248). For Poe's Mulberry Street residence, see Thomas and Jackson 248. For his next Philadelphia residence, see 255. See also the "Poe-Plan of Philadelphia," front endpaper of the second volume of the Phillips biography.

21. "Life of an English Nobleman" in the *Saturday News* is taken from a somewhat longer essay by the same title, which appeared in the *Boston Daily Evening Transcript*.

22. "Orang Outang" also preceded the New York *Evening Tattler*'s mock review of the imaginary novel *The Ourang-Outang*, "NOTICE OF THE LATEST NEW NOVEL," published on 9 July 1839.

23. Gowans's comment, which first appeared in his Catalogue 27 (1869), is quoted in Stoddard 26. For a related "Marginalia" item, see *Collected Writings* 2:201–2. We may readily attribute Poe's ownership of newspapers to their small cost and great literary usefulness. For Poe's later review of a book published by Gowans, see 3:249.

24. "Deliberate Murder" was drawn from a New York City newspaper or New York City newspapers; related pieces include "Jealousy and Murder," "Atrocious Murder," and "The Murder in Broadway." Although Poe would not have overlooked the Coleman murder piece adjacent to McMichael's review of *Pym* in the *Saturday News* as he read or reread this local newspaper, he might well have missed, or read more cursorily, New York coverage of the story. For Poe's reshaping for *Pym* a newspaper article appearing next to a review of the *Southern Literary Messenger*, see Kopley, "Introduction" ix–x and "The '*Very* Profound Under-current'" 143–45.

25. William Gowans lived with Poe and his family at Sixth Avenue and Waverly Place in 1837; at the time, his bookshop was at the Long Room, 169 Broadway (near Cortlandt). (See Phillips 1:549–61). Hervey Allen wrote that "Poe was much in his bookstore browsing among the volumes..." (2:411). The site of the Coleman murder—opposite Jollie's Music Store, 385 Broadway, between White and Walker Streets—was en route from either the Sixth Avenue or Carmine Street residence of Poe to the bookshop. (See Phillips, "Poe-Plan of New York City," rear endpaper of the second volume.) A few blocks south of the Long Room was the City Hotel (Broadway between Thames and Cedar Streets), where Poe attended a

Booksellers Dinner on 30 March 1837. (See Phillips 1:557–58; Thomas and Jackson 243; and Silverman 130). An advertising poster for Jollie's Music Store circa 1845 probably closely approximates the store's appearance in 1838 (Black 3, 98). It is interesting to add that four blocks south of Jollie's Music Store was John Anderson's tobacco shop (321 Broadway, below Anthony), where Mary C. Rogers, the model for Marie Rogêt, was employed in 1838 (Walsh 9–14, 82).

26. See Brigham 63–64.

27. Ian V. K. Ousby notes that in "Doctor D'Arsac" (in the series "Unpublished Passages in the Life of Vidocq, the French Minister of Police"), the old woman is found "with her throat cut so as almost to sever the head from the body," and he relates this to the passage in "Rue Morgue" in which the old lady is found "with her throat so entirely cut that, upon an attempt to raise her, the head fell off, and rolled to some distance." However, as noted, the Coleman story's phrase "nearly severed her head from her body" is identical with the phrase in Poe's later description

28. The *Saturday News* piece "Examination of Coleman" was taken from "Examination of Edward Coleman, the Murderer," which had appeared in New York City newspapers. Doubtless the *Saturday News* of Philadelphia—so readily available and friendly to Poe—was the newspaper in which he read of Coleman's examination. Legal documents concerning the Coleman murder have been preserved— the Coroner's report regarding the body of Ann Coleman (28 July 1838), the transcripts of eyewitness testimony and of the interrogation of Coleman (31 July 1838), and the indictment of Coleman (13 August 1838) are in the Municipal Archives of New York City. According to the Coroner's report, the murder took place "In Broadway near No 388"; the eyewitness from this address was one Walter T. Smith.

29. See Walker 196–97. While Walker gives the review to English and Poe (192), G. R. Thompson gives it entirely to Poe in *Edgar Allan Poe—Essays and Reviews* 1502. Yet, like Mabbott, Thomas and Jackson give the review to English (574). William Henry Gravely Jr. states that "English later acknowledged the authorship of the longer review [the October 1845 review of Poe's *Tales* in his *Aristidean*]." In Gravely's judgment, "a considerable degree of collaboration may have occurred," but, given locutions such as "if we mistake not" and "by-the-by," "the actual phrasing was English's own" (499–500; see also 469–70). I would add that in light of Poe's having termed "The Purloined Letter" in July 1844 "the best of my tales of ratiocination" (*Letters* 1:450), it seems highly unlikely that he would write in October 1845, "There is much made of nothing in 'The Purloined Letter'.... We like it less than the others, of the same class. It has not their continuous and absorbing interest." (See Thompson, *Edgar Allan Poe—Essays*

and Reviews 872. Walker omits the paragraph in which this passage appears.)

30. See Whalen, "Average Racism," or chapter V of *Edgar Allan Poe and the Masses* (111–46). Notably, Whalen effectively disproves the Rosenthal attribution to Poe of the Paulding/Drayton review (which tries to justify slavery), showing the author to be Beverly Tucker (113–21). See also Ridgely and *Collected Writings* 5:153–54.

31. For treatment of "The Murders in the Rue Morgue" and slave rebellion, see Rowe 99, Person 218–21, and White. For discussion of that tale and interracial sex, see Levin 141, Nygaard 251, Rowe 99, and Lemire. For consideration of Dupin's reasoning and racial views, see Barrett. For discussion of race and crime in "Rue Morgue," see Harrowitz.

32. Relevantly, Poe's classic tale may be related to Richard Wright's classic, *Native Son*. Linda Prior has cogently discussed Richard Wright's "ironic inversion" of the tale in his 1940 novel. She concludes, "Poe's murderer,... an ape, is assumed by the authorities to be a man; Wright's murderer, a man, is assumed to be an ape." Perhaps Wright had this inversion in mind when he wrote in the essay that introduced *Native Son* that he had employed "imaginative terms... known and acceptable to a common body of readers" (xlii). If so, then an "ironic inversion" of creative process may be noted as well: Poe modified details from a well-known news story about a murderous black man for his tale of a murderous ape; Wright modified details from Poe's well-known story of a murderous ape for his novel about a murderous black man. The influence of the *Saturday News* story on Poe may be recalled when one considers the striking conclusion of Wright's essay: "...if Poe were alive, he would not have to invent horror; horror would invent him" (li). Doubtless Richard Wright was correct about Poe in 1940, but the pieces on the Coleman murder—and other *Saturday News* pieces concerning similarly appalling events—suggest that horror also helped to invent Poe in 1838. Wright relied on newspaper accounts, too; significantly, one of the vital newspaper pieces concerning the black murderer Robert Nixon stated, "These killings were accomplished with a ferocity suggestive of Poe's 'Murders in the Rue Morgue'—the work of a giant ape" (qtd. in Kinnamon). See also McCall 70 and Gross 23.

33. See ["Mdlle. Mars" (*sic*)]. Poe's phrase "the iron chest"—originally "the iron-chest" (*Collected Works* 2:566n)—is common enough, yet its use as a play title warrants mention. "The Iron Chest," a 1796 play written by George Colman the Younger, was one in which Poe's mother Eliza Poe had performed in Boston in November 1806. See Quinn 713 and Smith 141. The play was based on William Godwin's novel *Caleb Williams*. For Poe's high estimate of Godwin and his writing, see Pollin, "Godwin and Poe." Pollin mentions Godwin in

the context of "Rue Morgue" in "Poe's 'The Murders in the Rue Morgue': The Ingenious Web Unravelled" 241. Perhaps "the iron box containing her jewelry" in the *Saturday News* piece on Mademoiselle Mars recalled to Poe the play, or the novel, or both, for the play featured a trunk of jewels supposedly from the iron chest, and the novel featured a box of jewels supposedly from a locked trunk. Perhaps, too, the repeated name Coleman in the *Saturday News* reinforced for Poe the George Colman connection. Interestingly, even as "Rue Morgue" reveals that the chest contained papers, Colman's play revealed that the trunk contained a paper—a confession of murder (2:122–23)—and Godwin's novel speculated that the trunk contained such a document (315).

34. For the comment on the "Arthur Gordon Pym school," see "The Lady's Book," probably by Neal and McMichael (but possibly by McMichael alone).

35. "A Mischievous Ape" was probably drawn from the *New York Evening Star*, 17 September 1838: [2] (NHi) or the *New York Morning Herald*, 18 September 1838: [2] (NHi). It was reprinted in as distant a newspaper as the *Nantucket Inquirer*, 26 September 1838: [2] (Nantucket Atheneum). Clearly, the newspaper in which Poe would most probably have encountered the piece was the *Saturday News*.

36. For the Greeley comment, see Thomas and Jackson 321.

37. For the morgue stories, see "Education at the Morgue" and "M. Perrin, of the Morgue." For the reprint from *Gazette des Tribuneaux*, see "The New Caspar Hauser." For the accounts of a husband's murder of his wife, see "A Scene of Horror and Murder" and "Baltimore County Court." For the report of Coleman's conviction, see "Conviction for Murder." It should be noted that while the *Saturday News* credits "The New Caspar Hauser" to the "*Gazette des Tribuneaux*," Poe refers to the "Gazette des Tribunaux" (*Collected Works* 2:537). In the 1845 *Tales*, the latter spelling of the name replaced "Le Tribunal" (2:537n). Poe might have remembered the name from the *Saturday News*, reread the item in a file of the newspaper, or encountered the name again in another publication. It might be added that a piece anticipating Poe's "A Descent into the Maelström" appeared in the 6 October 1838 *Saturday News* next to the morgue pieces: "The Maelstrom Whirlpool."

38. For Coleman's sentence, see ["Coleman...has been sentenced"]. For accounts related to "Deaths in New York," see "The Danger of Carbonic Acid Gas" and "Deaths from Charcoal."

39. The verdict of the Coroner's Jury of "Death from suffocation" for both women is documented in two Coroner's reports of 26 November 1838 held by the Municipal Archives of New York City. Witnesses' accounts of the discovery of the fire and its victims accompany these reports. See Legal Documents.

40. The essay from which this piece is drawn is "Algiers in the Spring of 1837." For the section excerpted in the *Saturday News*, see 167–68.
41. Noting an earlier association of orangutan and black men, Joan Dayan writes, "Poe had no doubt read that most severe of colonial historians, Edward Long [author of *History of Jamaica*]...." There is no evidence that Poe read this 1774 work, although he may have. In any case, the association made in the 8 December 1838 *Saturday News* piece "Mahometan Worship" would have been more immediate for Poe as he began to think about writing "The Murders in the Rue Morgue."
42. "Apparent Death" is credited to the *Liverpool Mercury*. "Appalling Accident" is credited to "*The Times*," presumably *The New York Times and Commercial Intelligencer.*
43. "Humorous Adventure" is credited to the *Boston Morning Herald*; I have not yet found the issue of this newspaper in which this story appeared.
44. The "insane Hospital" may have been the McLean Asylum for the Insane in Charlestown.
45. See Bergmann, Sattelmeyer and Barbour, and Sealts. Twain scholars may be interested to know that the *Saturday News* published a story on the wreck of the ship *Walter Scott* ("The Walter Scott" 17 November 1838: [2] (NHi). Perhaps Missouri newspapers also ran this story, and young Samuel Clemens then heard about the wreck or, in subsequent years, read about it. This story may well have contributed to Twain's conceiving chapters XII and XIII of *Adventures of Huckleberry Finn*, which concern the wreck of a ship named *Walter Scott.*
46. These announcements are respectively titled "To the Subscribers to the Saturday News" and "To the Subscribers to the 'Saturday News.'"
47. For reports of the death of Coleman, see "Last of the Murderer, Coleman" and "Execution of Coleman."
48. For Poe's new position on *Burton's* and the dinner party in his honor, see Thomas and Jackson 262–63. See also Silverman 143–44.
49. For Neal's review of "Usher," see Thomas and Jackson 267–68. For his review of *Tales of the Grotesque and Arabesque*, see Thomas and Jackson 279–80 or Walker 122.
50. For mention of the absorption of the *Saturday News* by the *Saturday Evening Post*, see Thomas 33–34. For a sketch of George R. Graham, see Pratte.
51. For Wilmer's association with the *Saturday Evening Post*, see Wilmer, *Our Press Gang* 40. See also Mabbott, "Introduction" x.
52. For the McMichael review, which speaks of Poe's "rare and various abilities" and "his genius," see Thomas and Jackson 285 or Walker 129.
53. W. T. Bandy presents and discusses the letter about C. Auguste Dubouchet. Mabbott demurs from Bandy's view that Poe combined

the first syllable of Dubouchet with the second syllable of the last name of Poe's correspondent, Maupin (*Collected Works* 2:524n).

54. For the quotations about Dupin, see Walsh 224.
55. The manuscript of Poe's tale is in the Richard Gimbel Collection of the Free Library of Philadelphia. There is also a published facsimile of this manuscript.

III "The Mystery of Marie Rogêt" and "Various Newspaper Files"

1. For Bonaparte on "Marie Rogêt," see 448–51. For Srebnick's discussion of her interpretive approaches, see xiv–xv.
2. For the list of newspapers that Wimsatt consulted, see "Poe and the Mystery of Mary Rogers" 231n; for the nine types of sources and their newspaper locations, see 231–33.
3. For Poe's adding "nothing important" to the newspaper reports, see Walsh, *Poe the Detective* 42. For Walsh's treatment of the newspaper extracts, see 43–46. Notably, Mabbott, in his introduction to *Poe the Detective*, states his agreement with Walsh regarding the sixth extract: "…I am in complete agreement with Mr. Walsh that the whole account of the lost boat found adrift (which is not essential to Poe's proposed solution) is the author's invention" (3). And Leon Howard cited Walsh's view: "…no actual newspaper item pointing to the clue of a missing rowboat has been discovered. John Walsh, whose *Poe the Detective* is a comprehensive study of the story and its background, believes the item to be a fabrication" (3).
4. Paul lists the newspapers he consulted; see *Who Murdered Mary Rogers?* 185. For his tale of Payne's choking Mary Rogers, see 164–65.
5. For Saltz's discussion of abortion and the newspapers, see "(Horrible to Relate!)" 244–47. Srebnick identifies the "[m]ost useful" newspapers; see 167. For the latter, see, regarding Dupin's madness, 118–19; regarding the combination of affair and abortion, 193; and regarding Attree as Atreus, 123–24. Stashower concludes with a passage from Poe's "The Man of the Crowd" on "mysteries which will not suffer themselves to be revealed" (308). For his treatment of the sixth extract as created by Poe, see 243, 270.
6. See Letter, *New York Times and Evening Star*. The letter begins, "Mr. Editor: As any information which will serve to throw the least light into the whole dark mystery of the murder of Miss Rogers may be of benefit to the Police, you can make such use of the following as your judgment shall dictate." For brief commentary on this newspaper, edited by Mordecai Manuel Noah (1785–1851), see Fox 94. Poe and Noah shared a mutual respect: in November 1841, Poe wrote of

Noah, "...no man has more friends or fewer enemies" (*Complete Works* 15:207), and in February 1847, Noah testified "that Poe is of good character" (Thomas and Jackson 688). For Poe's probably transforming "A Lecture on Lecturing" from the 11 March 1829 issue of Noah's *New-York Enquirer* for the comic tale "Diddling," see Ljungquist, "'Raising the Wind': Earlier Precedents" and "'Raising More Wind': Another Source for Poe's 'Diddling' and Its Possible Folio Club Context."

7. For the three cited pieces, making the link between the Mary Rogers murder and the murder of Joseph White, see "H." "Murder," *Journal of Commerce*; [H. Hastings Weld], "The Hoboken Tragedy," *Brother Jonathan*; and "The Mary Rodgers [*sic*] Mystery," *New York Herald*. Mabbott mentions the *Brother Jonathan* piece in his discussion of "The Tell-Tale Heart" (3:790n), a story for which the Webster speech was a source. I suggest that Hawthorne would have recognized this source for "The Tell-Tale Heart" (*Threads* 24–25).
8. For the *New York Herald* reprinting of the *Journal of Commerce* piece mentioning Ellen Jewett, see "Administration of Justice in New York." For a fuller depiction of the Jewett murder, see Patricia Cline Cohen, *The Murder of Helen Jewett*. Remarkably, Jewett read *Norman Leslie* and saw the play based on the novel (Cohen 123, 249–50, 360).
9. For the Wimsatt reference to this article, see "Poe and the Mystery of Mary Rogers" 240n.
10. The 10 August 1841 *New York Herald* reference to the Sands case was picked up by the 15 August 1841 *Sunday Mercury* in "The Hoboken Murder—Further Particulars."
11. The reference to "your paper of yesterday" would indicate the *Herald* of 26 August 1841; the relevant article is the already-cited "The Mary Rodgers [*sic*] Mystery," which mentions the White murder.
12. For scholarly treatment of Poe and *Norman Leslie*, see Moss 38–84 and Pollin, "Poe's Mystification."
13. See Fay 1:212 and 2:32. Poe praised Fay's rendering of Clairmont's pushing aside Norman Leslie to "save" Flora ("One incident is tolerably managed..."; see *Complete Works* 8:59; *Collected Writings* 5:62).
14. The Kleiger account is a modern presentation of the Coleman account. For Joseph Watkins on Croucher's accusing Weeks, see Kleiger 128, Coleman 74, and Hardie 27. For David Forest on Croucher's blaming Weeks, see Kleiger 140, Coleman 80–81, and Hardie 79–80. William Dustan testifies to Croucher's speaking against Weeks; see Kleiger 142–43, Coleman 82, and Hardie 80. And Hugh McDougall similarly testifies; see Kleiger 144–45, Coleman 82–83, and Hardie 80–81.
15. The *Evening Tattler* was not, at this time, edited by Benjamin H. Day (1810–89), as Raymond Paul asserts—see 36, 51, 178. (See also Stashower 127, 156, 158, 160, 180, 182, 197, 203, 205, 225.) The town

editor was H. Hastings Weld, and the country editor was N. P. Willis (1806–67). According to Louis H. Fox's information on the *Brother Jonathan* (21), Benjamin H. Day became publisher in 1850. (See also Mott 226–27.) For the *Evening Tattler*, see Fox 104. Weld, who had edited the New York *Sun*, became the editor of the New York *Morning Dispatch* in April 1839. When the *Dispatch* joined J. Gregg Wilson's *Brother Jonathan* in February 1840 (after Rufus Wilmot Griswold and Park Benjamin had left), Weld became editor of the mammoth newspaper and of its daily companion, the *Evening Tattler*. N. P. Willis joined as the country editor in May 1840 and left in October 1841. The *Evening Tattler* was sold in November 1841; Weld continued with the *Brother Jonathan* (which became available in quarto form) for another year, until he moved to Philadelphia in November 1842 to edit the *United States Saturday Post*. For Weld's beginning with the *Morning Dispatch*, see ["The Morning Dispatch"]. For the union of the *Dispatch* and the *Brother Jonathan*, see "Enlargement" and "The Union." For the break of Benjamin and Griswold with the *Evening Tattler* and the *Brother Jonathan*, see Benjamin and Griswold, "NEW DAILY PAPER." Willis's joining the *Brother Jonathan* is announced in "The Brother Jonathan." Willis's departure is reported in the *Brother Jonathan* in "Our Weekly Gossip" of 30 October 1841. The sale of the *Evening Tattler* is announced in the *Brother Jonathan* in "Our Weekly Gossip" of 27 November 1841. Charles J. Peterson states in an 11 November 1842 letter to John Tomlin, included in the Dwight Thomas dissertation, "We have got Weld for the Post, a journal we have never had time properly to edit, and he will make it a great weekly, or I mistake his character" (460). Weld's coming to the *Post* is anticipated in "Announcement" of 5 November 1842; his first editorial comment is made in "Our Weekly Chat" of 12 November 1842. For further information on Weld, see the obituary "Death of Dr. H. Hastings Weld," the entry in *Appleton's*, and Charles Frederick Robinson's entry for him in *Weld Collections*. For analysis of Poe's relationship to a later mammoth weekly newspaper from New York City, the *Saturday Emporium*, see Ljungquist, "'Mastadons of the Press.'"

16. Regarding Wimsatt's assertion about "a chorus of dissent" and his list of dissenting newspapers (which included also the *Evening Express*, the *Courier and Enquirer*, the *Journal of Commerce*, and the *Sunday Mercury*), see "Poe and the Mystery of Mary Rogers" 235, 235n. For the response of the *Commercial Advertiser*, see "The Case of Miss Rogers." Poe noted that the editor of this newspaper was Colonel [William Leete] Stone (Mabbott 3:740; see also Fox 27–28; Mott 181, 308. For Poe on Stone, see especially *Complete Works* 8:279–80, 9:24–33, 47–48, and 15:177–78, 213–14. See also *Collected Writings* 5:165, 215–18, 219). For the response of the *Herald*, see "The

Mary Rodgers [*sic*] Mystery." The editor of the *Herald* was James Gordon Bennett (Fox 52–54; Mott 229–38).

17. For information on the *Sunday Times*, see Fox 103. I have not yet found ["QUITE A MOB"] in the *Brother Jonathan*.

18. For an earlier positive review of Seba Smith by Weld, see "Letters of John Smith, with Pictures to Match."

19. See "Publisher's Department," appearing in the *Brother Jonathan* on 30 November 1839, and the letter to the editors, appearing on 13 June 1840. The *Brother Jonathan* had evidently enjoyed considerable success in Boston, too. In November 1839, the Boston *Morning Herald* reported selling nearly all of its five thousand copies of a double-sized issue. See "MAMMOTH SHEET!!"

20. For MacGrawler on criticism, see 1:41–42. *Paul Clifford* is the book that begins with the line made famous by Snoopy of *Peanuts*, and then by The Bulwer-Lytton Fiction Contest, "It was a dark and stormy night...." The *Brother Jonathan*'s country editor, N. P. Willis, would not have responded so severely to his friend Poe. And, notably, little more than two years earlier, Weld had accused Willis himself of a "MacGrawler critique." See "Mr. Willis and Mr. Paulding."

21. For the introductory comments, see "An Unpublished Letter of Poe" 32. The writer who introduced Poe's letter to Weld is not known. The letter is said to be "the property of Mrs. A. H. Heulings [Helen Sarah Weld Heulings (1839–1919)], daughter of the late Rev. Hastings Weld..." (32). According to the relevant note in *Letters*, "The present location of the MS is unknown" (1:304). (See also 2:1201.)

22. The phrase "what no man knows to be truth better than yourself" anticipates a phrase that Poe uses in his later writing about his lecture "Poets and Poetry of America": "...I took occasion to speak what I know to be the truth...that [American editors had] been engaged for many years in a system of indiscriminate laudation of American books..." (*Collected Writings* 3:35).

23. The 14 August 1841 issue of the *Brother Jonathan*, which includes the review of the August 1841 *Graham's Magazine*, includes, as well, a piece on Mary Rogers, "The Hoboken Tragedy." For Mabbott's references to the 14 August 1841 Mary Rogers material, see 3:774–77. Weld refers in his review of the August 1841 issue of *Graham's Magazine* to one of "some very pleasant articles," "a learned affair by Mr. Poe—which we shall buy a German sausage, to eat while we read, if we can only borrow Dominie Sampson's spectacles, and Bombastes Furioso's boots to complete our equipment for the task." Dominie Sampson was a comical scholar (in a novel by Sir Walter Scott [1771–1832], *Guy Mannering*), and obtaining Bombastes Furioso's boots, hanging from a tree, constituted the meeting of a challenge (in a play by William Barnes Rhodes [1772–1826], *Bombastes*

Furioso; A Burlesque Tragic Opera, in One Act). (For the introduction of Sampson in *Guy Mannering*, see Scott 11; for Sampson's joy in books, see 109–10; for his bibliophilic reward, see 353. For the challenge of the boots in *Bombastes Furioso*, see Rhodes 34–40.) Weld's comments here seem more humorous than antagonistic.

24. The 4 September 1841 issue of the *Brother Jonathan*, which features "Never Bet Your Head," also features several stories about Mary Rogers. For Mabbott's references to these stories, see 3:775, 777–78, 779, 782, 784–85, and 786. "Never Bet Your Head" also appeared in *Jonathan's Miscellany* (*Letters* 1:304n).

25. For Poe's hostility to Thomas Dunn English (1819–1902) informing his classic tale of immurement, "The Cask of Amontillado," see *Collected Works* 3:1252–53. For a fuller discussion of Poe's revenge in that tale, allusive to English's novel *1844*, see Rust. For an account of the Poe-English conflict, see Moss, *Poe's Major Conflict*.

IV   "The Purloined Letter" and *Death-Bed Confessions*

1. That Mary Rogers died during an abortion was contended in a supposed death-bed confession by Mrs. Frederica Loss in November 1842 (*Collected Works* 3:719; see also Wimsatt, "Poe and the Mystery of Mary Rogers" 245–46, and Walsh 53–58). Notably, when he wrote "The Purloined Letter," Poe had recently written memorable fictional confessions, "The Tell-Tale Heart" and "The Black Cat."

2. For a sympathetic consideration of the psychoanalytic/theoretical treatments of "The Purloined Letter," see Peeples 51–61.

3. See Terlotte 360–62, 364–65, 366; Sweeney's "Purloined Letters: Poe, Doyle, Nabokov" and "Postscript to a Purloined Letter"; Irwin, *The Mystery to a Solution* 30–42; and Harris, especially 23–30.

4. For the early Mabbott note about Cyrano de Bergerac, see "Notes" 424. For Hatvary on the Wallace sources, see "Horace Binney Wallace" 138–39, "Poe's Borrowings" 370–71, and *Horace Binney Wallace* 67–68. For Pollin on Wallace's phrase *"non distributio medii,"* see *Collected Writings* 2:271. For Varnado on Burke, see "The Case of the Sublime Purloin." And for Krajewski on the game of even and odd in Cicero, see "Simple Hermeneutics of 'The Purloined Letter'" 25–26.

5. To review the characterization of the threatened female royal in "The Purloined Letter" as the French Queen, consult Bonaparte 483, Priestman 53, Pyrhönen 74, and Irwin, "Reading Poe's Mind" 191 and *The Mystery to a Solution* 342–43.

6. See Benton, "The Dupin MSS." 111.

7. The account presented here of the life of Princess Caroline is drawn from Flora Fraser's excellent biography, *The Unruly Queen: The Life of*

Queen Caroline. That book may be consulted for her birth and parentage (9–10), the prince's early marriage and its annulment (33–37, 39–41), the agreement to marry and Prince George's motive (43), the wedding itself (59–60), the birth of Charlotte (74–75), the prince and princess's living separately (98), Caroline's affairs in the early years of their marriage (119, 124–25, 128, 135–36), George's affairs (64, 77, 119), and "The Delicate Investigation" (166–92).

8. For this early period of the Regency, see Fraser 220–35. For the full "Regent's Valentine," see "Letter of the Princess of Wales to the Prince Regent" (attributed to Caroline but actually by Lord Brougham) or [Bury], *Diary Illustrative of the Times of George the Fourth* 1:218–26. For Jane Austen's comment, see *Jane Austen's Letters to Her Sister Cassandra and Others* 504.

9. Consult Fraser for Caroline's leaving England (250–51), her taking on Pergami as her lover (256, 284), the marriage of Charlotte and Leopold (290–91), the birth of Charlotte's stillborn child and her death (297), the proceedings of the Milan Commission (293–321), Caroline's threatening to return to England (326), and the death of King George III (340).

10. Check Fraser for Caroline's landing at Dover and journey to Canterbury and London, (363–68), the beginning of the Secret Committee (396–97), the trial itself (413–44), the deterrence of Queen Caroline from the coronation (1–8), and her death (460–61).

11. See John Allan, letter to Charles Ellis, 1 February 1820. (I am glad to acknowledge the Ellis & Allan Papers, Rare Book and Special Collections, Library of Congress.) For a previously published version of John Allan's prescient comment, see Phillips 1:170.

12. See John Allan, letter to Charles Ellis, 9 June 1820. (I am pleased to acknowledge the Ellis & Allan Papers, Rare Book and Special Collections, Library of Congress.) For a previously published version of this quotation, see Quinn 80.

13. See ["The Well-Known American Ship MARTHA"], "Arrival of the Queen of England," and "The Queen."

14. For further detail on the voyage of the *Martha,* see Thomas and Jackson 44–46. This detail includes mention in *The New-York Daily Advertiser* of the arrival of the Allans and additional information in the *Richmond Compiler* drawn from the *New York Commercial Advertiser.* The semiweekly version of the *Commercial Advertiser* was the *New-York Spectator.* See Fox 91.

15. To identify the review of *Continuation of the Diary Illustrative of the Times of George IV* as Poe's, see his letter to Joseph E. Snodgrass of 11 September 1839, stating, as Assistant Editor, with regard to the September issue, "[All the criticisms in the Mag: are mine] *with the exception of the 3 first*" (*Letters* 1:190). (The review of *Continuation* was not one of the three first.) Poe also wrote to Philip P. Cooke, on

21 September, "The critiques, such as they are [earlier termed "not worth your notice"], are all mine in the July No—& all mine in the Aug and Sep. with the exception of the 3 first in each—which are by Burton" (1:194). Poe also published in the September 1839 issue of *Burton's* his classic tale "The Fall of the House of Usher."

16. With a sardonic tone, Poe wrote in February 1836 that Morris Mattson's Paul Ulric stated that his father was made a Baronet "for merely picking up and carrying home his Majesty George the Fourth, whom Mr. U. assures us upon his word of honor, his father found lying beastly drunk, one fine day, in some gutter, in some particular thoroughfare of London" (*Complete Works* 8:180; *Collected Writings* 5:107). Poe's negative view of King George IV was anticipated by Charles Lamb in a well-known 1812 poem about the Prince Regent, "The Triumph of the Whale." Melville includes six lines for his "Extracts" in *Moby-Dick* (xxiv). For commentary, see Rogers. For an 1827 poem by Lamb, expressing his compassion for Queen Caroline, see "Lines Suggested by a Sight of Waltham Cross."

It is possible that Poe was satirizing King George IV in the 1827 tale "Epimanes," later titled "Four Beasts in One; The Homo-Cameleopard." George IV and Charles X (of France) had each been given a "cameleopard" (giraffe) in 1827 by the Egyptian Pasha. Mabbott speculates on Poe's having heard about or seen political cartoons concerning Charles X and the giraffe (*Collected Works* 2:118). Poe may have seen others of George IV and the giraffe. For two of these cartoons, see Baker 132–33. Mabbott considered the name "*George*" appearing in the devil's wallet in Poe's 1835 tale "Bon-Bon" (2:112) to signify George IV (2:117). He also believed that Poe may have been noting the same person when he referred to "That sad little rake, the Prince of Wales" (2:180) in the 1845 version of "Lionizing" (2:185). And Mabbott wrote that "The king [in the 1849 tale 'Hop-Frog'] reminds one a little of George IV, who indulged in coarse practical jokes" (3:1354).

17. For background on the newspaper, see *Bell's Life in London, and Sporting Chronicle*. See also "*Journals* Exploiting the Goodwill of the Name 'Bell'" 29–30.

18. The various attributions for *Death-Bed Confessions* appeared in an exchange in *Notes and Queries*. William J. Thoms, in "The Serres Scandal," gave *Death-Bed Confessions* to Lady Anne Hamilton, citing Miss C. E. Cary. James Henry Dixon responded in a February 1875 piece, "The Death-Bed Confessions of the Countess of Guernsey," stating that the book was the work of W. H. Ireland and citing the authority of "[a]n intelligent old bookseller in London." Thoms replied, reasserting Lady Hamilton's authorship, but allowing that Lady Hamilton may have supplied information to Mrs. Olivia Serres, who actually wrote the work. Dixon, in an April 1875 piece,

also titled "The Death-Bed Confessions of the Countess of Guernsey," restated his attribution to Ireland, whom he termed the "factotum" of publisher John Fairburn. Edward Solly joined the fray three years later in another piece titled "The Death-Bed Confessions of the Countess of Guernsey," stating that the Fairburn edition was "only a reprint" of the Jones edition. Finally, one "Calcuttensis," in "Mrs. Olivia Wilmot Serres: The 'Princess Olive of Cumberland,'" argued that if Mrs. Serres wrote other works for Lady Anne Hamilton (as he believed she did), then she may well have written *Death-Bed Confessions*. It is relevant to add that the *Dictionary of Anonymous and Pseudonymous English Literature* (written by Samuel Halkett and John Laing, and enlarged by James Kennedy, W. A. Smith, and A. F. Johnson) lists *The Secret History of the Court of England* as "[By Mrs. Olive Wilmot Serres]" and adds "Wrongly attributed to Lady Anne Hamilton" (5:211). Ireland seems an unlikely attribution. Either Anne Hamilton, or Olivia Serres, or Anne Hamilton in collaboration with Olivia Serres seems the more probable attribution for *Death-Bed Confessions*. Interestingly, Robert Bell asserted that the "Confessions" "*were not* intended *by a* certain party *to have seen the light; but, falling into our hands, we deemed it but justice* to ALL *parties that they should do so*" ("Notice to Correspondents," 11 August 1822).

19. Over the course of the run of "Death-Bed Confessions" in *Bell's Life in London*, the newspaper featured a number of related items, several of which may be mentioned here. Shortly after the installments began, the editor complained that four newspapers had "pillaged" an "article" from *Bell's* that had taken "great expence and trouble"— presumably the first installment of the series ("Notice to Correspondents [14 April 1822]"). (The editor may well have had in mind, as one of these newspapers, the *Independent Observer*.) Three weeks later, the editor acknowledged the great demand for the last five numbers of his newspaper—those containing installments of "Death-Bed Confessions" (Editor's Note). Also in this issue, he featured a letter from "A. H." (presumably Lady Anne Hamilton) introducing "The Real Cause of the Queen's Death Stated" and "The Letter," the Queen's final letter to the King ("To the Editor of Bell's Life in London," "The Real Cause of the Queen's Death Stated," and "The Letter" [possibly written by William Cobbett (1763–1835)—see Fulford—but attributed to the Queen]). And on 2 June 1822, the editor vigorously defended his newspaper against claims that its circulation was small (it was actually "not less than 2,000") and "Death-Bed Confessions" against allegations that the work was drawn from Thomas Ashe's novel *The Spirit of the Book* (1811) ("A Reply to the Impudent Coxcomb"). See "The Death-Bed Confessions" in the *Independent Observer* for the installment dates of the series reprinted in that newspaper. The reference to "some

omissions" occurs in the prefatory note for the first installment, 7 April 1822.

20. During 1822, Robert Bell advertised *Death-Bed Confessions* in a first, second, and third edition. Advertisements for the book began to appear elsewhere, as well, including *The Times* (of London), *John Bull*, *The Real John Bull*, the *Literary Chronicle*, and the *Morning Chronicle*. (See various entries for [Advertisement for *Death-Bed Confessions*].) The book's publication was announced in the July 1822 issue of *Blackwood's Edinburgh Magazine* ("Monthly List" 119). (The Macdonald edition of *Death-Bed Confessions* is rare; a copy of the second edition is held by the Huntington Library [RLG].)

21. Bell also wrote that Fairburn was well known as the "'*Broadway literary pilferer*'" and characterized him as "an impudent, literary pander to the basest passions of the multitude," "this hoaxing EMPEROR OF GRUB STREET," and "a periodical plunderer." According to Bell, Fairburn not only stole from the series appearing in *Bell's Life in London*, but also "purloined from the *Pamphlet* published by W. R. Macdonald . . ." ("Literary Hoaxing"). We may speculate that Bell's "Notice to Correspondents [27 July 1822]" alludes to the competition with Fairburn in its reference to "The 'Battle of the Books'" and to Lady Anne Hamilton in a comment on "Lady H*******" and an envelope to be "unsealed" when "her Ladyship's agent commissions us to do so." Early advertisements for Fairburn's edition of *Death-Bed Confessions* may be found in *The Real John Bull*, the *Literary Chronicle*, and the *Morning Chronicle*. In the 14 September 1822 issue of the *Literary Chronicle*, the Fairburn edition advertisement is on the same page as a comment in a *Bell's Life in London* advertisement with regard to all editions of *Death-Bed Confessions* not published by Macdonald: "*All other Publications of this Work are imperfect Piracies*" ("ROYAL CORRESPONDENCE!!!").

22. One American newspaper that reprinted "Death-Bed Confessions" was the *New-Hampshire Patriot and State Gazette*.

23. Later American editions of *Death-Bed Confessions* were published by Dougherty in Frederick, Maryland (1823) and F. Adancourt in Troy, New York (1826). For further information, see WorldCat.

24. It is of note that Princess Caroline's letter to the queen and the queen's response were published in the newspaper in December 1812 as "Illustrious Personages" (see Fraser 229). For William Cobbett's use of the phrase "*Illustrious Personage*" to refer to Princess Caroline in 1806, see Mulvihill 243.

25. Minor correspondences exist, as well. Though they may be coincidental, they are nonetheless worth noting. *Death-Bed Confessions* includes the Countess of Jersey's "so diabolical a plan" (35), a "seal" of an "olive-branch" (53), mention of "two brothers" who examine a home when its owner is away (70), an anonymous

correspondent's owning an "escrutoire" (89), and the queen's appearing as "a lunatic" (92). "The Purloined Letter" includes Dupin's quoting from Crébillon "Un dessein si funeste" ("So baleful a plan") (*Collected Works* 3:993, 997), "a seal formed of bread" (3:992), mention of "two brothers" (3:986), the Prefect's examining a home when its owner is away (3:978), Dupin's owning an *"escritoire"* (3:983), and a man's appearing "as a lunatic" (3:992). It should be noted that in the first half of the nineteenth century there were instances of the appearance of the phrase "purloined letter" in other contexts. See the 1817 "Letter Stealing" (regarding Mordecai M. Noah [1785–1851]), the March 1831 ["An Able Extract"] (regarding an accusation against Andrew Jackson [1767–1845]), and the November 1844 "Jackson and Adams" (regarding an accusation by Andrew Jackson). However, the theft, from a desk, of "the purloined letter" belonging to a female royal makes clear that *Death-Bed Confessions* is the critical source for Poe's "The Purloined Letter." It is interesting to observe that Poe used the phrase "purloining letters" (regarding a theft from a post office) in his 30 May 1835 letter to Thomas W. White (*Letters* 1:88).

26. For the scholarly account, see New 93–94. See also Hibbert 40–41, Erickson 109, and David 341.
27. See [Bury], *Diary Illustrative of the Times of George the Fourth* 1:187–88, 192.
28. See Fraser 235, 323.
29. That the September 1839 *Burton's Gentleman's Magazine* review of Brougham's *Historical Sketches of Statesmen* is Poe's is evident from his aforementioned 11 September 1839 letter to Joseph Evans Snodgrass and his 21 September 1839 letter to Philip P. Cooke. See note 15 and *Letters* 1:190, 194. The review of *Historical Sketches* is the fifth in the September number.
30. The 21 September 1839 letter from Poe to Cooke indicates that the July 1839 *Burton's Gentleman's Magazine* review of *Sketches of Public Characters* is Poe's (see note 15 and *Letters* 1:194). The review of *Sketches of Public Characters* is the eighth in the July number. Poe also wrote the review of *Opinions of Lord Brougham* in the October 1839 issue of *Burton's Gentleman's Magazine*: he wrote to Joseph E. Snodgrass on 7 October 1839, "In the Octo. no: all the criticisms are mine…" (*Letters* 1:197).
31. See Wallace, *Stanley* 1:132–33.
32. For the original from which Poe was drawing, see Brougham, *Sketches of Public Characters* 1:193. A related line in Poe's 1835 tale "Lion-izing" (*Collected Works* 2:175) is, of course, not indebted to the later *Stanley* or *Sketches of Public Characters*.
33. For commentary on Henry Brougham's brother James, see Fraser 307, 318–21, 323, 330–32, 428, 430. For Henry Brougham's background

in mathematics and letters, see "Brougham and Vaux, Henry Peter Brougham." In his review of *Opinions of Lord Brougham...*, Poe praises the "Memoir of Lord Brougham," which mentions Henry Brougham's brother James, as well as Henry Brougham's article on geometry and his writing for the *Edinburgh Review* (6–8).

34. The Peterloo massacre took place on 16 August 1819, a response to the perceived threat of reformers at the Manchester Meeting. Flora Fraser writes, "Forty yeoman cavalry broke into the tightly packed crowd, estimated later at some 60,000 strong, and including women and children" (334). Eleven people died. Understandably, for a while, this event took precedence over Caroline's planned return from Europe. See Fraser 333–37.

V Autobiographical Considerations of the Dupin Tales

1. See Lieber 190–91.
2. See my introduction to the Penguin edition of *The Narrative of Arthur Gordon Pym*, xx–xxiii.
3. For the discussion of Eliza Poe and the birth of Rosalie, as well as cited quotations, see Silverman 7–9, 452. For the statement of Charles Ellis's widow, see also Phillips 1:219.
4. See Quinn 89. For a brief study of Poe's sister, see Miller, "Poe's Sister Rosalie."
5. See Houghton 140.
6. See Silverman 78.
7. See Houghton 140.
8. Lalage was based on the seduced and abandoned Ann Cooke of the infamous "Kentucky Tragedy" (*Collected Works* 1:242–45, 288–91). For a full treatment of this sensational story, see Bruce.
9. See Silverman 173.
10. For a biography of Bonaparte, see Bertin's *Marie Bonaparte: A Life*.
11. See Bonaparte 446.
12. See Bonaparte 451–56.
13. See Wilbur, "The Poe Mystery Case" 137.
14. See Bonaparte 455.
15. See Wilbur, "The Poe Mystery Case" 133, 137.
16. Consult Bonaparte 451.
17. Regarding Eliza Poe's theatrical career, see Smith.
18. See "Supposed Murder," *New York Sun*; "The Late Murder of a Young Girl at Hoboken," *New York Herald*.
19. According to "The Murder of Mary Rogers—Examination of Dr. Cook before His Honor the Mayor, and the Coroner, Dr. Archer," "...[Mary Rogers] had evidently been a person of chastity and

correct habits...." Earlier testimony by Alfred Crommelin had spoken of her "irreproachable character for chastity and veracity." See "Murder of Mary Rogers at Hoboken."

20. The 14 August 1841 article in the *New York Express*, "The Murder of Miss Rogers," reported one of the rumors about Mary Rogers (then dismissed it): "that between the deceased and the young man who boarded in the house an improper intimacy had subsisted, and that fear of exposure and shame had induced her to take refuge in one of those places, where infamous practices are known to be used, and where as our readers are aware, life has before been sacrificed." A 19 August 1841 piece in the *New York Herald*, "Shocking," presented Horace Greeley's similar view (then attacked it): "... I have a suspicion that her death was not the result of malice or outrage, but of some of the infernal practices to procure *abortion*, for which our city has for some years been notorious." For a focus on the Mary Rogers case and abortion, see Srebnick and Saltz. For related work, see Wimsatt, Worthen, Walsh, Paul, and Stashower.

21. See Bonaparte 483–84.
22. See Lacan 30, 45, 48.
23. See Derrida 184, 179, 189, 202–3, 187.
24. See Johnson 250.
25. *The Purloined Poe*, which features Lacan, Derrida, Johnson, and others, was edited by John P. Muller and William J. Richardson and published in 1988. J. Albert Robbins had commented earlier, "As one would expect with Lacan and Derrida, the object is not to clarify 'The Purloined Letter' but to use it as a laboratory specimen for their psycholinguistic discourse" (44).
26. For the noted claims, see Doctorow 11–12. For the comment on the detective story, see Doctorow 14.
27. The Auden quotations may be found in "The Guilty Vicarage" 147, 158; the Cawelti quotation is in *Adventure, Mystery, and Romance*, 95, 104. See also MacDonald 180.

Conclusion

1. Oedipus and Hamlet are discussed in terms of the history of detective fiction by Tony Magistrale and Sidney Poger in *Poe's Children* (2–3).
2. See "A Tale by Poe" in *The Threads of "The Scarlet Letter"* (22–35).
3. See Baym, "Nathaniel Hawthorne and His Mother."
4. See "Purloined Letters" 216–22.

5. For the Sherlock Holmes stories, I consulted *The New Annotated Sherlock Holmes*. For "A Scandal in Bohemia," see 1:5–40; for "The Adventure of Charles Augustus Milverton," see 2:1006–32.
6. See, for example, Walton and Jones, *Detective Agency*.
7. See Rubin Jr. "Edgar Allan Poe: A Study in Heroism" 63–65. For a compelling evaluation of Poe's having explored human horror, see Hirsch, "'Postmodern' or Post-Auschwitz: The Case of Poe."

WORKS CITED

A. H. [Anne Hamilton?]. "The Real Cause of the Queen's Death Stated." *Bell's Life in London and Sporting Chronicle* 5 May 1822: 73.

["An Able Article"]. *Baltimore Patriot* 23 March 1832: [2].

"Administration of Justice in New York." *New York Herald* 14 August 1841: [2].

[Advertisement for *Death-Bed Confessions*]. *Bell's Life in London and Sporting Chronicle* 23 June 1822: 135.

[Advertisement for *Death-Bed Confessions*]. *John Bull* 23 June 1822: 639.

[Advertisement for *Death-Bed Confessions*]. *Literary Chronicle* 15 June 1822: 383; 22 June 1822: 400; Third Edition, 5 October 1822: 637.

[Advertisement for *Death-Bed Confessions*]. *Morning Chronicle* 17 June 1822: 2.

[Advertisement for *Death-Bed Confessions*]. *The Real John Bull* 23 June 1822: 606. British Library, Colindale.

[Advertisement for *Death Bed Confessions*]. *The Times* (of London) 17 June 1822: [5]; Third Edition 12 September 1822: [1] and 5 October 1822: [1]. British Library, Colindale.

[Advertisement for *Death-Bed Confessions*, with Warning]. *Bell's Life in London and Sporting Chronicle* 21 July 1822: 168; rpt., for Second Edition, 28 July 1822: 176, 4 August 1822: 184; rpt. for Second Edition with Fairburn's name deleted, 11 August 1822: 192, 18 August 1822: 197, 25 August 1822: 208; rpt. for Third Edition with Fairburn's name deleted, 13 October 1822: 264, 20 October 1822: 272, 10 November 1822: 296.

[Advertisement for Fairburn Edition of *Death-Bed Confessions*]. *Literary Chronicle* 24 August 1822: 542; 14 September 1822: 590; Twentieth Edition 12 October 1822: 654; 9 November 1822: 718.

[Advertisement for Fairburn Edition of *Death-Bed Confessions*]. *Morning Chronicle* 28 June 1822: 2.

[Advertisement Fairburn Edition of *Death-Bed Confessions*]. *The Real John Bull* 23 June 1822: 606. British Library, Colindale.

"Algiers in the Spring of 1837." *The New Monthly Magazine and Humorist* October 1838: 166–77; rpt. 6 May: 76.

Allan, John. Letter to Charles Ellis. 1 February 1820. Ellis & Allan Papers. Manuscripts Division. Library of Congress.

——. Letter to Charles Ellis. 9 June 1820. Ellis & Allan Papers. Manuscripts Division. Library of Congress.

Allen, Hervey. *Israfel: The Life and Times of Edgar Allan Poe.* 2 Vols. New York: George H. Doran, 1926.

Allen, Mozelle S. "Poe's Debt to Voltaire." *University of Texas Studies in English* 15 (1925): 63–75.

"Announcement." *United States Saturday Post* 5 November 1842: [2] (MWA).

"Appalling Accident." *The Philadelphia Saturday News* 22 December 1838: [2] (DLC).

"Apparent Death." *The Philadelphia Saturday News* 22 December 1838: [2] (DLC).

"Arrival of the Queen of England." *Liverpool Mercury* 9 June 1820: 415–16.

"ARRIVED LAST EVENING." *New-York Spectator* 25 July 1820: [2] (MWA).

Asarch, Joel Kenneth. "A Telling Tale: Poe's Revisions in 'The Murders in the Rue Morgue.'" *Poe at Work: Seven Textual Studies.* Ed. Benjamin Franklin Fisher IV. Baltimore: Poe Society, 1978. 83–90.

"Atrocious Murder." *New York Morning Herald* 30 July 1838: 2 (NHi).

Auden, W. H. "The Guilty Vicarage." *The Dyer's Hand and Other Essays.* London: Faber and Faber, 1963. 146–58; rpt. Winks, 15–24.

Austen, Jane. *Jane Austen's Letters to Her Sister Cassandra and Others.* Second Edition. Ed. R. W. Chapman. Oxford: Oxford University Press, 1979.

Baker, Kenneth. *George IV: A Life in Caricature.* London: Thames & Hudson, 2005.

"Baltimore County Court." *The Philadelphia Saturday News* 24 November 1838: 3 (NHi).

Bandy, W. T. "Who Was Monsieur Dupin?" *PMLA* 79 (1964): 509–10.

Barbour, James, and Tom Quirk. Eds. *Biographies of Books: The Compositional Histories of Notable American Writings.* Columbia: University of Missouri Press, 1996.

——. "Introduction." Barbour and Quirk, *Writing the American Classics* ix–xiv.

——, eds. *Writing the American Classics.* Chapel Hill: University of North Carolina Press, 1990.

Barrett, Lindon. "Presence of Mind: Detection and Racialization in 'The Murders in the Rue Morgue.'" Kennedy and Weissberg, 157–76.

Basbanes, Nicholas A. *Patience & Fortitude: Wherein a Colorful Cast of Determined Book Collectors, Dealers, and Librarians Go about the Quixotic Task of Preserving a Legacy.* New York: HarperCollins, 2001.

Baugh, Albert C. "McMichael, Morton." *Dictionary of American Biography* (1933).

Baym, Nina. "Nathaniel Hawthorne and His Mother: A Biographical Speculation." *American Literature* 54 (1982): 1–27.

"Bear Story." *The Philadelphia Saturday News* 23 June 1838: [4] (NHi).

[Bell, Robert]. [Editor's Final Note]. *Bell's Life in London and Sporting Chronicle* 16 June 1822: 121.

——. [Editor's Note]. *Bell's Life in London and Sporting Chronicle* 5 May 1822: 73.

——. "Introduction, by the Editor" [to "The Death-Bed Confessions of the Right Hon the Countess of Guernsey. Addressed to Lady

Anne H******"]. *Bell's Life in London and Sporting Chronicle* 31 March 1822: 33.

———. "Literary Hoaxing." *Bell's Life in London and Sporting Chronicle* 13 October 1822: 264.

———. "Note to Correspondents [28 July 1822]." *Bell's Life in London and Sporting Chronicle* 28 July 1822: 172.

———. "Notice to Correspondents [14 April 1822]." *Bell's Life in London and Sporting Chronicle* 14 April 1822: 52; rpt. 15 April 1822: 56.

———. "Notice to Correspondents [11 August 1822]." *Bell's Life in London and Sporting Chronicle* 11 August 1822: 188.

———. "Notices to Correspondents [9 June 1822]." *Bell's Life in London and Sporting Chronicle* 9 June 1822: 116.

———. "A Reply to the Impudent Coxcomb, Styling Himself 'Bob Logic,' and a True Exposé of Certain Matters at Issue between Him and Us." *Bell's Life in London and Sporting Chronicle* 2 June 1822: 195.

"Bell's Life in London, and Sporting Chronicle." *The Waterloo Directory of English Newspapers and Periodicals 1800–1900.* Waterloo, Ontario, Canada: North Waterloo Academic Press, 2003. 2: 132–34.

Benjamin, Park, and Rufus W. Griswold. "NEW DAILY PAPER." *Morning Dispatch* 12 October 1839: [3] (MWA).

Bennett, Maurice J. "The Detective Fiction of Poe and Borges." *Comparative Literature* 35 (1983): 262–75.

Benton, Richard P. "The Dupin MSS. As 'Contes À Clef,' Mathematics, and Imaginative Creation." Ramakrishna, 109–25.

———. "The Mystery of Marie Rogêt—A Defense." *Studies in Short Fiction* 6 (1969): 144–51.

———. "Reply to Professor Thompson." *Studies in Short Fiction* 6 (1968): 97.

Bergmann, Johannes Dietrich. "'Bartleby' and *The Lawyer's Story*." *American Literature* 47 (1975): 432–36.

———. "The Original Confidence Man." *American Literature* 21 (1969): 560–77.

Bertin, Celia. *Marie Bonaparte: A Life.* 1982. New Haven: Yale University Press, 1987.

Black, Mary. *American Advertising Posters of the Nineteenth Century.* New York: Dover, 1976.

Bloom, Clive. "Capitalising on Poe's Detective: The Dollars and Sense of Nineteenth-Century Detective Fiction." *Nineteenth-Century Suspense.* Ed. Clive Bloom, Brian Docherty, Jane Gibb, and Keith Shand. New York: St. Martin's, 1988. 14–25.

Boll, Ernest. "The Manuscript of 'The Murders in the Rue Morgue' and Poe's Revisions." *Modern Philology* 40 (1943): 302–15.

Bonaparte, Marie. *The Life and Works of Edgar Allan Poe: A Psycho-Analytic Interpretation.* Foreword by Sigmund Freud. Trans. John Rodker. London: Imago, 1949.

Borges, Jorge Luis, in collab. with Esther Zemborain de Torres. *An Introduction to American Literature.* Trans. and ed. L. Clark Keating and Robert O. Evans. 1971. New York: Schocken Books, 1973.

Brigham, Clarence S. *Edgar Allan Poe's Contributions to Alexander's Weekly Messenger*. Worcester, MA: American Antiquarian Society, 1943.

Brody, Selma B. "Poe's Use of Brewster's *Letters on Natural Magic*." *English Language Notes* 27 (1989): 50–54.

"The Brother Jonathan." *Brother Jonathan* 16 May 1840: [2] (MWA).

Brougham, Henry Lord. *Sketches of Public Characters, Discourses and Essays. To Which Is Added a Dissertation on the Eloquence of the Ancients*. 2 vols. Philadelphia: Carey & Hart, 1839.

"Brougham and Vaux, Henry Peter Brougham." *Encyclopedia Britannica*. Eleventh Edition (1910–11).

Bruce, Dickson D. Jr. *The Kentucky Tragedy: A Story of Conflict and Change in Antebellum America*. Baton Rouge: Louisiana State University Press, 2006.

Bulsterbaum, Allison. "Godey's Lady's Book." *American Literary Magazines: The Eighteenth and Nineteenth Centuries*. Ed. Edward E. Chielens. Westport, CT: Greenwood Press, 1986. 144–50.

Bulwer-Lytton, Edward. *Bulwer's Novels*. New York: George Routledge and Sons, n.d. With markings by Palmer C. Holt. Palmer C. Holt Collection. Manuscripts, Archives, and Special Collections. Washington State University Libraries, Pullman, Washington.

———. *Paul Clifford*. 2 vols. New York: J. & J. Harper, 1830 (PSt).

———. *Pelham or the Adventures of a Gentleman*. Ed. Jerome J. McGann. Second Edition, 1828. Lincoln: University of Nebraska Press, 1972.

[Bury, Lady Charlotte]. *Diary Illustrative of the Times of George the Fourth, Interspersed with Original Letters from the Late Queen Caroline, and from Various Other Distinguished Persons*. 2 vols. London: Henry Colburn, 1838.

Calcuttensis. "Mrs. Olivia Wilmot Serres: The 'Princess Olive of Cumberland.'" *Notes and Queries* Sixth Serres 4 (27 August 1881): 164–65.

Campbell, Killis. *The Mind of Poe and Other Studies*. Cambridge, MA: Harvard University Press, 1933.

Cantalupo, Barbara. "Interview with Richard Wilbur (May 2003)." *The Edgar Allan Poe Review* 4:1 (2003): 68–85.

Caroline, Princess [actually Lord Brougham]. "Letter of the Princess of Wales to the Prince Regent." *Morning Chronicle* 10 February 1813: [2].

Caroline, Queen [?]. "The Letter." *Bell's Life in London and Sporting Chronicle* 5 May 1822: 73 and 12 May 1822: 81.

Carroll, Lewis. *The Annotated Alice—The Definitive Edition*. Introduction and Notes by Martin Gardner. New York: W. W. Norton, 2000.

"The Case of Miss Rogers." New York *Commercial Advertiser* 25 August 1841: [2].

Cawelti, John G. *Adventure, Mystery, and Romance: Formula Stories as Art and Popular Culture*. Chicago: University of Chicago Press, 1976.

Chambers, Ross. *Story and Situation: Narrative Seduction and the Power of Fiction*. Foreword by Wlad Gozdich. Minneapolis: University of Minneapolis Press, 1984.

Chesterton, G. K. "The Best Detective Story." *Detection Medley.* Ed. John Rhode. London: Hutchinson, 1939. 106–7.

Clarke, Thomas Cottrell. Review of *Prose Romances* [by Edgar Allan Poe]. Thomas and Jackson 429; Walker, 131.

Cohen, Patricia Cline. *The Murder of Helen Jewett: The Life and Death of a Prostitute in Nineteenth-Century New York.* New York: Alfred A. Knopf, 1998.

["Coleman…has been sentenced"]. *The Philadelphia Saturday News* 1 December 1838: [2] (NHi); rpt. *The Philadelphia Saturday News* 8 December 1838: [4] (DLC).

Coleman, William. *Report of the Trial of Levi Weeks, on an Indictment for the Murder of Gulielma Sands on Monday the Thirty-First Day of March and Tuesday the First Day of April, 1800. Taken in Short Hand by the Clerk of the Court.* New York: John Furman, 1800.

Colman, George, the Younger. "The Iron Chest: A Play; in Three Acts." *The Plays of George Colman the Younger.* Ed. Peter A. Tasch. New York: Garland, 1981. 2: i–xxiii, 1–127.

"Conviction for Murder." *The Philadelphia Saturday News* 24 November 1838: [2] (NHi).

Dameron, J. Lasley. "More Analogues and Resources for Poe's Fiction and Poems." *University of Mississippi Studies in English* 10 (1992): 154–66.

———. "Poe's Auguste Dupin." *No Fairer Land: Studies in Southern Literature before 1900.* Ed. J. Lasley Dameron and James W. Mathews. Troy, NY: Whitson, 1986. 159–71.

———. "Six More Analogues and Resources for Poe." *Poe Studies* 31 (1998): 36.

"The Danger of Carbonic Acid Gas." *New York Morning Herald* 27 November 1838: [2] (NIIi).

David, Saul. *Prince of Pleasure: The Prince of Wales and the Making of the Regency.* New York: Atlantic Monthly Press, 1998.

Dayan, Joan. "Romance and Race." *The Columbia History of the American Novel.* Ed. Emory Elliott. New York: Columbia University Press, 1991. 89–109.

"Death of Dr. H. Hastings Weld." *Philadelphia Public Ledger* 28 August 1888. Clipping from the Weld Collection of the Historical Society of Moorestown, New Jersey.

"The Death-Bed Confessions of Lady Guernsey [American Reprinting]." *New Hampshire Patriot & State Gazette* 28 July 1823: [1]; 4 August 1823: [1]; 11 August 1823: [1]; 18 August 1823: [1]. (The "Queen's Last Letter to the King" follows on 25 August 1823: [1].)

Death-Bed Confessions of the Late Countess of Guernsey, to Lady Anne H*******; Developing a Series of Mysterious Transactions Connected with the Most Illustrious Personages in the Kingdom: To Which Are Added, the Q----'s Last Letter to the K----, Written a Few Days before her M------'s Death, and Other

Authentic Documents, Never before Published. London: John Fairburn [1822].

Death-Bed Confessions of the Late Countess of Guernsey, to Lady Anne Hamilton, Developing a Series of Mysterious Transactions Connected with the Most Illustrious Personages in the Kingdom: To Which Are Added, the Queen's Last Letter to the King, Written a Few Days before Her Majesty's Death, and Other Authentic Documents, Never before Published. "First American from the First London Edition." Philadelphia: James E. Moore, 1822.

"The Death-Bed Confessions of the Right Hon the Countess of *Guernsey.* Addressed to Lady Anne H******." *Bell's Life in London, and Sporting Chronicle* 31 March 1822: 33; rpt. 1 April 1822: 36; 7 April 1822: 41; rpt. 8 April 1822: 44; 14 April 1822: 49; rpt. 15 April 1822: 52; 21 April 1822: 57; rpt. 22 April 1822: 60; 28 April 1822: 65; rpt. 29 April 1822: 66; 5 May 1822: 73; rpt. 6 May 1822; 12 May 1822: 81; 19 May 1822: 89; 26 May 1822: 97; 2 June 1822: 105–6; 9 June 1822: 113; 16 June 1822: 121.

"The Death-Bed Confessions of the Right Hon. The Countess of Guernsey. Addressed to Lady Anne H******." *Independent Observer* 7 April 1822: 430; 14 April 1822: 435; 21 April 1822: 446; 28 April 1822: 454; 5 May 1822: 462–63; 12 May 1822: 471; 19 May 1822: 473; 2 June 1822: 494; 16 June 1822: 510; 21 July 1822: 549; 18 August 1822: 578 (British Library, Colindale).

"Deaths from Charcoal." *New York Evening Star* 27 November 1838: [2] (NHi).

"Deaths in New York." *The Philadelphia Saturday News* 1 December 1838: [2] (NHi).

"Deliberate Murder in Broadway, at Midday." *The Philadelphia Saturday News* 4 August 1838: [2] (P).

Derrida, Jacques. "The Purveyor of Truth." Muller and Richardson, 173–212.

Diskin, Patrick. "Poe, LeFanu, and the Sealed Room Mystery." *Notes and Queries* n.s. 13 (1966): 337–39.

Dixon, James Henry. "The Death-Bed Confessions of the Countess of Guernsey." *Notes and Queries* Fifth Series 3 (20 February 1875): 153.

———. "The Death-Bed Confessions of the Countess of Guernsey." *Notes and Queries* Fifth Series 3 (17 April 1875): 318.

Doctorow, E. L. "E. A. Poe." *Creationists: Selected Essays, 1993–2006.* New York: Random House, 2006. 11–20.

Douglas, Mary. *Thinking in Circles: An Essay on Ring Composition.* New Haven: Yale University Press, 2007.

Doyle, Arthur Conan. *The New Annotated Sherlock Holmes.* 3 vols. Ed. Leslie S. Klinger. New York: W. W. Norton, 2005.

———. *Through the Magic Door.* New York: McClure, 1908.

Doyle, Charles Clay. "The Imitating Monkey: A Folklore Motif in Poe." *North Carolina Folklore Journal* 23 (1975): 89–91.

Doyno, Victor A. *Writing "Huck Finn": Mark Twain's Creative Process.* Philadelphia: University of Pennsylvania Press, 1991.

"Education at the Morgue." *The Philadelphia Saturday News* 6 October 1838: [4] (DLC). Rpt. from John Sanderson's *The American in Paris*.

Eliot, T. S. *The Criterion 1922–1939*. 18 vols. 1922–39. London: Faber and Faber, 1967.

Emerson, Ralph Waldo. "Emerson's Oration." *The Philadelphia Saturday News* 6 October 1838: [4] (DLC).

"Enlargement." New York *Evening Tattler* 15 February 1840: [2] (MWA).

Erickson, Carolly. *Our Tempestuous Day: A History of Regency England*. New York: William Morrow, 1986.

"Escape of the Bear from the Liverpool Zoological Garden." *The Philadelphia Saturday News* 8 December 1838: [4] (DLC).

"The Examination of Coleman." *The Philadelphia Saturday News* 11 August 1838: [2] (P).

"Examination of Coleman, the Murderer." *The New York Times and Commercial Intelligencer, for the Country* 31 July 1838: [4] (WHi); rpt. *The Times and Commercial Intelligencer* (of New York) 1 August 1838: [2] (NHi).

"Execution of Coleman." *New York Evening Star* 14 January 1839: [2] (NHi).

Fay, Theodore S. *Norman Leslie: A Tale of the Present Times*. 2 vols. New York: Harper and Brothers, 1835.

Fetterley, Judith. "Reading about Reading: 'A Jury of Her Peers,' 'The Murders in the Rue Morgue,' and 'The Yellow Wallpaper.'" *Gender and Reading: Essays on Readers, Texts, and Contexts*. Ed. Elizabeth A. Flynn and Patrocinio P. Schweickart. Baltimore: Johns Hopkins University Press, 1986. 147–64.

Fisher, Benjamin Franklin IV. "Poe, Blackwood's, and 'The Murders in the Rue Morgue.'" *American Notes and Queries* 12 (1974): 109–11.

———. "Verses on Poe and Arthur Conan Doyle." *PSA Newsletter* 25:1 (1997): 1–2.

Forgues, E. D. "Les Contes d'Edgar Poe." *Revue des Deux Mondes* 5 (15 October 1846): 341–66.

Forney, John W. *Memorial Address Upon the Character and Public Services of Morton McMichael, as Editor, Public Officer, and Citizen*. Philadelphia: Sherman, 1879.

———. "Morton McMichael, and Many Other Pennsylvania Men." *Anecdotes of Public Men*. 2 vols. New York: Harper and Brothers, 1873–81. 2:115–22.

Fox, Louis H. *New York City Newspapers, 1820–1850: A Bibliography*. The Papers of the Bibliographical Society of America 21:1–2 (1928). 1–294.

Fraser, Flora. *The Unruly Queen: The Life of Queen Caroline*. Berkeley: University of California Press, 1996.

Fulford, Tim. "Cobbett, Coleridge, and the Queen Caroline Affair." *Studies in Romanticism* 37 (1998): 523–43.

Fusco, Richard. "Poe's Revisions of 'The Mystery of Marie Rogêt'—A Hoax?" *Poe at Work: Seven Textual Studies*. Ed. Benjamin Franklin Fisher IV. Baltimore: Edgar Allan Poe Society, 1978. 91–99.

Galt, John. "Editor's Preface." *Continuation of the Diary Illustrative of the Times of George IV*. Ed. John Galt. 2 vols. Philadelphia: Lea and Blanchard, 1839. iii–vi.

Gillette, Howard Jr. "McMichael, Morton." *Biographical Dictionary of American Mayors, 1820–1880—Big City Mayors*. Ed. Melvin G. Holli and Peter d'A Jones. Westport, CT: Greenwood Press, 1981. 237–38.

Godey, Louis A. "The Philadelphia Saturday News and Literary Gazette." *The Lady's Book* January 1837: 48.

———. "A Publishing Month." *The Lady's Book* July 1836: 46.

———. "To the Patrons of the Lady's Book." *The Lady's Book* June 1836: 283.

———. "To the Subscribers to the Saturday News." *The Philadelphia Saturday News* 29 December 1838: [2] (NHi).

———. "*To the Subscribers to the 'Saturday News.*'" *The Philadelphia Saturday News* 5 January 1839: [3] (NHi).

Godey, Louis A., Joseph C. Neal, and Morton McMichael. "[Advertisement for the *Saturday News*]." *The Philadelphia Saturday News* 7 January 1837: [2] (MWA).

———. "[Advertisement for the *Saturday News*]." *The Philadelphia Saturday News* 10 March 1838: [4] (DLC).

———. "A Card." *The Philadelphia Saturday News* 2 July 1836: [2] (MWA).

———. "[Newspaper Exchange]." *The Philadelphia Saturday News* 1 April 1837: [2] (MWA).

———. "[Note to Subscribers]." *The Philadelphia Saturday News* 11 February 1837: [2] (MWA).

———. "REMOVAL." *The Philadelphia Saturday News* 29 July 1837: [2] (DLC).

———. "To Our Patrons." *The Philadelphia Saturday News* 26 November 1836: [4] (P).

Godwin, William. *Caleb Williams*. Ed. David McCracken. London: Oxford University Press, 1970.

Gravely, William Henry Jr. "The Early Political and Literary Career of Thomas Dunn English." Diss. University of Virginia, 1953.

Gribben, Alan. "'That Pair of Spiritual Derelicts': The Poe-Twain Relationship." *Poe Studies* 18 (1985): 17–21.

Gross, Seymour. "*Native Son* and 'The Murders in the Rue Morgue': An Addendum." *Poe Studies* 8 (1975): 23.

"H." "Murder." *Journal of Commerce* 14 August 1841: 2 (NN).

"Hans Swartz—A Marvelous Tale of Mamakating Hollow." *The Philadelphia Saturday News* 8 September 1838: [4] (DLC).

Hardie, James. *An Impartial Account of the Trial of Mr. Levi Weeks, for the Supposed Murder of Miss Julianna Elmore Sands, at a Court Held in the City of New York*. New York: N. McFarlane, 31 March 1800.

Harris, Paul A. "Poe-etic Mathematics: Detecting Topology in 'The Purloined Letter.'" *Poe Studies* 36 (2003): 18–31.

Harrison, Michael. "Dupin: The Reality behind the Fiction." *The Exploits of the Chevalier Dupin.* Sauk City: Mycroft & Moran, 1968. 3–14.

Harrowitz, Nancy A. "Criminality and Poe's Orangutan: The Question of Race in Detection." *Agonistics: Arenas of Creative Contest.* Ed. Janet Lungstrum and Elizabeth Sauer. Albany: State University of New York Press, 1997. 177–95.

Hatvary, George E. *Horace Binney Wallace.* Boston: Twayne, 1977.

——. "Horace Binney Wallace: A Study in Self-Destruction." *Princeton University Library Chronicle* 25 (1964): 137–49.

——. "Poe's Borrowings from H. B. Wallace." *American Literature* 38 (1966): 365–72.

Haycraft, Howard. *Murder for Pleasure: The Life and Times of the Detective Story.* New York: D. Appleton-Century, 1941.

Heartman, Charles F., and James R. Canny. Comps. *A Bibliography of First Printings of the Writings of Edgar Allan Poe.* Revised Edition. Hattiesburg, MS: Book Farm, 1943.

Herbert, Rosemary. *Whodunit? A Who's Who in Crime & Mystery Writing.* New York: Oxford University Press, 2003.

Hibbert, Christopher. *George IV: Regent and King 1811–1830.* New York: Harper & Row, 1973.

Hirsch, David H. "'Postmodern' or Post-Auschwitz: The Case of Poe." *Poe's "Pym": Critical Explorations.* Ed. Richard Kopley. Durham: Duke University Press, 1992. 141–50; rpt. in David H. Hirsch, *The Deconstruction of Literature: Criticism after Auschwitz.* Hanover, NH: University Press of New England, 1991. 244–54.

"The Hoboken Murder—Further Particulars." *Sunday Mercury* 15 August 1841: [1] (MWA).

Hoffman, Elizabeth. "Godey and McMichael."*American Literary Publishing Houses, 1638–1899* (Part 1: A–M). Ed. Peter Dzwonkoski. Detroit: Gale, 1986. 178.

Holmes, Oliver Wendell. "The September Gale." *The Philadelphia Saturday News* 6 October 1838: [1] (DLC).

"Horrid Murders." *The Philadelphia Saturday News* 15 September 1838: [3] (DLC).

Houghton, Marie Louise Shew. "To John Ingram." 16 May [18]75. Letter 39 of *Building Poe Biography.* Ed. John Carl Miller. Baton Rouge: Louisiana State University Press, 1977. 136–41.

Howard, Leon. "Poe's *Eureka*: The Detective Story That Failed." *Mystery & Detection Annual 1972.* Beverly Hills: Donald Adams, 1972. 1–14.

Hoyle's Improved Edition of the Rules for Playing Fashionable Games.... Philadelphia: Thomas, Cowperthwait, 1838.

Hull, William Doyle, II. "A Canon of the Critical Works of Edgar Allan Poe with a Study of Poe as Editor and Reviewer." Diss. University of Virginia, 1941.

"Humorous Adventure—Picking Up a Madman." *The Philadelphia Saturday News* 29 December 1838: [4] (NHi).

Ingram, John H. *Edgar Allan Poe: His Life, Letters, and Opinions.* 2 vols. London: John Hogg, 1880.

"Inquests at Hoboken." *New York Herald* 31 July 1841: [2].

Irving, Washington. Excerpt from *Astoria. The Philadelphia Saturday News.* 15 October 1836: [2–3] (MWA).

———. *The Sketch Book of Geoffrey Crayon, Gent.* Ed. Haskell Springer. Boston: Twayne, 1978. Vol. 8 of *The Complete Works of Washington Irving.* Ed. Richard Dilworth Rust.

Irwin, John T. *The Mystery to a Solution: Poe, Borges, and the Analytic Detective Story.* Baltimore: Johns Hopkins University Press, 1993.

———. "Reading Poe's Mind: Politics, Mathematics, and the Association of Ideas in 'The Murders in the Rue Morgue.'" *American Literary History* 4 (1992): 187–206.

———. *Unless the Threat of Death Is behind Them: Hard-Boiled Fiction and Film Noir.* Baltimore: Johns Hopkins University Press, 2006.

"Jackson and Adams—Letter from Gen. Jackson." *New-Hampshire Patriot and State Gazette* 21 November 1844: [1].

"Jealousy and Murder." *The Times and Commercial Intelligencer* 30 July 1838: [2] (NHi).

Johnson, Barbara. "The Frame of Reference: Poe, Lacan, Derrida." Muller and Richardson, 213–51.

Jones, Buford, and Kent Ljungquist. "Monsieur Dupin: Further Details on the Reality behind the Legend." *Southern Literary Journal* 9 (1976): 70–77.

Jordan, Cynthia S. *Second Stories: The Politics of Language, Form, and Gender in Early American Fictions.* Chapel Hill: University of North Carolina Press, 1989.

"*Journals* Exploiting the Goodwill of the Name 'Bell.'" *A Catalogue of Books Newspapers &c. Printed by John Bell b. 1745 d. 1831 of "The British Library," "The Morning Post," "Bell's Weekly Messenger," &c. and by John Browne Bell b. 1779 d. 1855 Son of the Above: Founder of "Bell's New Weekly Messenger," "The News of the World," Etc.* London: n.p., 1931. 29–34.

Justin, Henri. "The Fold Is the Thing: Poe Criticism in France in the Last Five Years." *Poe Studies* 16 (1983): 25–31.

———. "An Impossible Aesthetics or an Aesthetics of the Impossible?" In "Poe Writing/Writing Poe." Ed. Richard Kopley and Jana Argersinger. To be published by AMS Press.

Kennedy, J. Gerald. *Poe, Death, and the Life of Writing.* New Haven, CT: Yale University Press, 1987.

Kennedy, J. Gerald, and Liliane Weissberg, eds. *Romancing the Shadow: Poe and Race.* New York: Oxford University Press, 2001.

Kennedy, J., W. A. Smith, and A. F. Johnson. *Dictionary of Anonymous and Pseudonymous English Literature.* New and Enlarged Edition. 9 vols.

(Original authors, Samuel Halkett and John Laing). London: Oliver and Boyd, 1929.

Ketterer, David. *The Rationale of Deception in Poe*. Baton Rouge: Louisiana State University Press, 1979.

——. "'Shudder': A Signature *Crypt*-ogram in 'The Fall of the House of Usher.'" *Resources for American Literary Study* 25 (1999): 192–205.

Kinnamon, Keneth. *The Emergence of Richard Wright—A Study in Literature and Society*. Urbana: University of Illinois Press, 1972.

Kleiger, Estelle Fox. *The Trial of Levi Weeks or the Manhattan Well Mystery*. Chicago: Academy Chicago, 1989.

Kopley, Richard. "Hawthorne's Transplanting and Transforming 'The Tell-Tale Heart.'" *Studies in American Fiction* 23 (1995): 231–41.

——. "The Hidden Journey of *Arthur Gordon Pym*." *Studies in the American Renaissance 1982*. Ed. Joel Myerson. Charlottesville: University Press of Virginia, 1982. 29–51.

——. "Introduction" and "Explanatory Notes." *The Narrative of Arthur Gordon Pym*. By Edgar Allan Poe. New York: Penguin Books, 1999. ix–xxix; 223–45.

——. "Neal, Joseph C[lay]." *Encyclopedia of American Literature*. General Editor Steven R. Serafin. Associate Editor Alfred Bendixen. New York: Continuum, 1999. 814–15.

——. "Poe's Taking of *Pelham* 1-2-3-4-5-6." Transatlanticism in American Literature: Emerson, Hawthorne, and Poe. 13–16 July 2006. Oxford, England: *Poe Studies* 41 (2008): 109–16.

——. *The Threads of "The Scarlet Letter": A Study of Hawthorne's Transformative Art*. Newark: University of Delaware Press, 2003.

——. "The '*Very* Profound Under-current' of *Arthur Gordon Pym*." *Studies in the American Renaissance 1987*. Ed. Joel Myerson. Charlottesville: University Press of Virginia, 1987.

Krajewski, Bruce. "Simple Hermeneutics of 'The Purloined Letter.'" *Traveling with Hermes*. Amherst: University of Massachusetts Press, 1992. 7–30.

Lacan, Jacques. "Seminar on 'The Purloined Letter.'" Muller and Richardson, 28–54.

Lamb, Charles. "Lines Suggested by a Sight of Waltham Cross." Charles Lamb and Mary Lamb. 4: 121.

——. "The Triumph of the Whale." Charles Lamb and Mary Lamb. 4: 116–18.

Lamb, Charles, and Mary Lamb. *The Works of Charles and Mary Lamb*. 1903–5. 6 vols. London: Methuen, 1912.

"Last of the Murderer, Coleman." *New York Morning Herald* 14 January 1839: [2] (NHi).

"Late and Important from England and the Continent." *New-York Spectator* 25 July 1820: [1–2] (MWA).

"The Late Murder of a Young Girl at Hoboken." *New York Herald* 3 August 1841: 2.

Legal Documents, Edward Coleman Case. 28 July–13 August 1838. Municipal Archives, New York City.

Lemay, J. A. Leo. "The Psychology of 'The Murders in the Rue Morgue.'" *American Literature* 54 (1982): 165–88.

Lemire, Elise. "'The Murders in the Rue Morgue': Amalgamation Discourses and the Race Riots of 1838 in Poe's Philadelphia." Kennedy and Weissberg, 177–204.

Letter. *Brother Jonathan* 13 June 1840: [2–3] (MWA).

Letter. *New York Times and Evening Star* 26 August 1841: [2] (NHi).

"Letter Stealing." *New-York Columbian* 20 November 1817: [2].

Levin, Harry. *The Power of Blackness: Hawthorne, Poe, Melville.* New York: Alfred A. Knopf, 1958.

Levine, Stuart and Susan, eds. *The Short Fiction of Edgar Allan Poe: An Annotated Edition.* 1976. Urbana: University of Illinois Press, 1990.

Levinson, Marjorie. "What Is New Formalism?" *PMLA* 122:2 (2007): 558–69.

Lieber, Francis. *Reminiscences of an Intercourse with Mr. Niebuhr the Historian, during a Residence with Him in Rome, in the Years 1822 and 1823.* Philadelphia: Carey, Lea and Blanchard, 1835.

"Life of an English Nobleman." *Boston Daily Evening Transcript* 26 October 1837: [2] and 27 October 1837: [2] (PSt).

"Life of an English Nobleman." *The Philadelphia Saturday News* 18 August 1838: [4] (DLC).

"A Literary Curiosity." *Burton's Gentleman's Magazine* February 1840: 89.

Ljungquist, Kent P. "'Mastodons of the Press': Poe, the Mammoth Weeklies, and the Case of the *Saturday Emporium.*" *Masques, Mysteries, and Mastodons: A Poe Miscellany.* Ed. Benjamin F. Fisher. Baltimore: Edgar Allan Poe Society, 2006. 77–101.

———. "'Raising the Wind': Earlier Precedents." *Poe Studies* 27:1–2 (1994): 42.

———. "'Raising More Wind': Another Source for Poe's 'Diddling' and Its Possible Folio Club Context." Ramakrishna, 53–62.

Longworth, David. *A Brief Narrative of the Trial for the Bloody and Mysterious Murder of the Unfortunate Young Woman, in the Famous Manhattan Well. Taken in Short Hand by a Gentleman of the Bar.* New York: 1800.

"M. Perrin, of the Morgue." *The Philadelphia Saturday News* 6 October 1838: [4] (DLC). Rpt. from John Sanderson's *The American in Paris.*

Mabbott, Thomas Ollive. Introduction. *Merlin*, by Lambert A. Wilmer. 1941; rpt. Darby, PA: Folcroft Library Editions, 1973. v–xiii.

———. Introduction. *Selected Poetry and Prose of Edgar Allan Poe.* New York: Modern Library, 1951. v–xiv.

———. Introduction. *Tamerlane and Other Poems*, by Edgar Allan Poe. New York: Columbia University Press, 1941. v–lxvi.

——. "Notes." *Selected Poetry and Prose of Poe.* New York: Modern Library, 1951. 406–27.

——. "Palindromes (and Edgar Poe)." *Notes and Queries* 191 (30 November 1946): 238–39.

MacDonald, Ross. "The Writer as Detective Hero." Winks, 179–87.

"The Maelstrom Whirlpool." *The Philadelphia Saturday News* 6 October 1838: [4] (NHi).

Magistrale, Tony, and Sidney Poger. *Poe's Children: Connections between Tales of Terror and Detection.* New York: Peter Lang, 1999.

"Mahometan Worship." *The Philadelphia Saturday News* 8 December 1838: [4] (DLC).

"MAMMOTH SHEET." Boston *Morning Herald*; rpt. *Brother Jonathan* 2 November 1839: [2] (MWA).

"The Mary Rodgers [*sic*] Mystery." *New York Herald* 26 August 1841: [2].

"The Mary Roger's [*sic*] Mystery." *New York Herald* 30 August 1841: [2].

Matthews, Brander. "Poe and the Detective Story," *Scribner's* (September 1907). 287–93.

McCall, Dan. *The Example of Richard Wright.* New York: Harcourt, Brace, & World, 1969.

McClure, N. E. "Neal, Joseph Clay." *Dictionary of American Biography* (1934).

McMichael, Morton. "Joseph C. Neal." *Graham's Magazine* February 1844: 49–52.

——. Review of *The Narrative of Arthur Gordon Pym* [by Edgar Allan Poe]. *The Philadelphia Saturday News* 4 August 1838: [2] (P).

——. Review of *Tales of the Grotesque and Arabesque* [by Edgar Allan Poe]. Thomas and Jackson 285; I. M. Walker 129.

["Mdlle. Mars" (*sic*)]. *The Philadelphia Saturday News* 18 August 1838: [4] (DLC).

Melville, Herman. *Moby-Dick or the Whale.* Ed. Harrison Hayford, Hershel Parker, and G. Thomas Tanselle. Volume Six of the Northwestern-Newberry Edition of *The Writings of Herman Melville.* Evanston and Chicago: Northwestern University Press and the Newberry Library, 1988.

"Memoir of Lord Brougham." *Opinions of Lord Brougham, on Politics, Theology, Law, Science, Education, Literature, etc., etc. as Exhibited in His Parliamentary and Legal Speeches and Miscellaneous Writings.* 2 vols. Philadelphia: Lea and Blanchard, 1839. 1: 5–32.

Merivale, Patricia, and Susan Elizabeth Sweeney, eds. *Detecting Texts: The Metaphysical Detective Story from Poe to Postmodernism.* Philadelphia: University of Pennsylvania Press, 1999.

Miller, John C. "Poe's Sister Rosalie." *Tennessee Studies in Literature* 8 (1963): 107–17.

"A Mischievous Ape." *The Philadelphia Saturday News* 22 September 1838: [2] (NHi).

Mitchell, Robert W. "The Natural History of Poe's Orangutan." *Poe Studies* 31 (1998): 32–34.

"Monthly List of New Publications." *Blackwood's Edinburgh Magazine* July 1822: 117–25.

Moore, John Robert. "Poe, Scott, and 'The Murders in the Rue Morgue.'" *American Literature* 8 (1936): 52–58.

Mordell, Albert, ed. *In Re "Morton McMichael."* Privately printed, 1921.

["The Morning Dispatch"]. *Rhode-Island Republican* 30 April 1839: 2. From *Early American Newspapers*, Series I.

Moss, Sidney P. *Poe's Literary Battles: The Critic in the Context of His Literary Milieu.* Durham, NC: Duke University Press, 1963.

Mott, Frank Luther. *American Journalism: A History of Newspapers in the United States through 250 Years 1690 to 1940.* New York: Macmillan, 1941.

Muller, John P., and William J. Richardson, eds. *The Purloined Poe: Lacan, Derrida, and Psychoanalytic Reading.* Baltimore: Johns Hopkins University Press, 1988.

Mulvihill, James. "Publicizing Royal Scandal: Nathaniel Jefferys and the 'Delicate Investigation' (1806)." *Nineteenth-Century Contexts* 26 (2004): 237–56.

"The Murder at Hoboken." Philadelphia *Public Ledger* 4 August 1841: 2 (DLC).

"The Murder in Broadway." *New York Evening Star* 30 July 1838: [2] (NHi).

"Murder of Mary Rogers at Hoboken." *New York Herald* 6 August 1841: 2.

"The Murder of Mary Rogers—Examination of Dr. Cook before His Honor the Mayor, and the Coroner, Dr. Archer." *New York Herald* 17 August 1841: 2.

"The Murder of Miss Rogers." *New York Express* 14 August 1841: 2 (NHi).

"The Murder of Miss Rogers at Hoboken." *New York Herald* 2 August 1841: [2].

"The Murdered Mary Rogers." *New York Herald* 10 August 1841: [2].

Murphy, Bruce F. *The Encyclopedia of Murder and Mystery.* 1999. New York: Palgrave, 2001.

Neal, Joseph C. and Morton McMichael. "The Lady's Book." *The Philadelphia Saturday News* 15 September 1838: [2] (DLC).

———. Review of *The New York Review* (January 1838), *The Philadelphia Saturday News*, 13 January 1838: [2] (P).

———. Review of the *Southern Literary Messenger* (June 1836), *The Philadelphia Saturday News* 2 July 1836: [3] (MWA); rpt. "From the Philadelphia Saturday News," "Supplement," *Southern Literary Messenger* July 1836: 525.

———. Review of the *Southern Literary Messenger* (July 1836), *The Philadelphia Saturday News* 23 July 1836: [3] (MWA).

———. Review of the *Southern Literary Messenger* (August 1836), *The Philadelphia Saturday News* 27 August 1836: [2] (MWA).

———. Review of the *Southern Literary Messenger* (September 1836), *The Philadelphia Saturday News*, 8 October 1836: [3] (MWA).

———. Review of the *Southern Literary Messenger* (October 1836), *The Philadelphia Saturday News*, 26 November 1836: [5] (P).

———. Review of the *Southern Literary Messenger* (November 1836), *The Philadelphia Saturday News*, 24 December 1836: [3] (MWA).

———. Review of the *Southern Literary Messenger* (January 1837), *The Philadelphia Saturday News*, 11 February 1837: [3] (MWA).

———. Review of the *Southern Literary Messenger* (December 1838), *The Philadelphia Saturday News* 1 December 1838: [2] (NHi).

———. "Salutatory." *The Philadelphia Saturday News* 2 July 1836: [2] (MWA).

———. "The 'Southern Literary Messenger' and 'The Pickwick Papers.'" *The Philadelphia Saturday News* 7 October 1837: [2] (P).

["The New Caspar Hauser"]. *The Philadelphia Saturday News* 6 October 1838: [4] (DLC).

New, Chester W. *The Life of Henry Brougham to 1830*. London: Oxford University Press, 1961.

"News of the Week." *Sunday Times* 29 August 1841: 2.

"NOTICE OF THE LATEST NEW NOVEL." New York *Evening Tattler* 9 July 1839: 2 (NN).

Nygaard, Loisa. "Winning the Game: Inductive Reasoning in Poe's 'Murders in the Rue Morgue.'" *Studies in Romanticism* 33 (1994): 223–54.

"An Octogenary, Fifty Years Since." *The Philadelphia Saturday News* 10 March 1838: [4] (DLC).

"Orang Outang." *The Philadelphia Saturday News* 26 May 1838: [4] (P).

Osowski, Judy. "T. S. Eliot on 'Poe the Detective.'" *Poe Newsletter* 3 (1970): 39.

Ousby, Ian V. K. "'The Murders in the Rue Morgue' and 'Doctor D'Arsac': A Poe Source." *Poe Studies* 5 (1972): 52.

"Palindromes." (In "Omniana.") *Burton's Gentleman's Magazine* May 1840: 236.

Panek, LeRoy Lad. "Poe and Long's Hoyle." *Studies in Short Fiction* 16:4 (1979): 344–48.

Pattee, Fred Lewis. *The Development of the American Short Story: An Historical Survey*. New York: Harper and Brothers, 1923.

Paul, Raymond. *Who Murdered Mary Rogers?* Englewood Cliffs, NJ: Prentice-Hall, 1971.

Peeples, Scott. *The Afterlife of Edgar Allan Poe*. Rochester, NY: Camden House, 2004.

Person, Leland. "Poe's Philosophy of Amalgamation: Reading Racism in the Tales." Kennedy and Weissberg, 205–24.

"The Philadelphia Saturday News and Literary Gazette." *The Philadelphia Saturday News* 2 July 1836: [3] (MWA).

Phillips, Mary E. *Edgar Allan Poe—The Man*. 2 vols. Chicago: John C. Winston Company, 1926.

Poe, Edgar Allan. *The Collected Letters of Edgar Allan Poe.* Originally edited by John Ward Ostrom. Revised, corrected, and expanded by Burton R. Pollin and Jeffrey A. Savoye. Third Edition. 2 vols. 1948; New York: Gordian Press, 2008

——. *Collected Works of Edgar Allan Poe.* Ed. Thomas Ollive Mabbott. 3 vols. Cambridge, MA: Harvard University Press, 1969–78.

——. *The Complete Works of Edgar Allan Poe.* Ed. James A. Harrison. 17 vols. New York: T. Y. Crowell, 1902; rpt., New York: AMS Press, 1979.

——. *Doings of Gotham.* Comp. Jacob E. Spannuth. Introduction and comments by T. O. Mabbott. Pottsville, PA: Jacob E. Spannuth, 1929.

——. *Edgar Allan Poe—Essays and Reviews.* Ed. G. R. Thompson. New York: Library of America, 1984.

——. *Edgar Allan Poe—Eureka.* Ed. Stuart Levine and Susan F. Levine. Urbana: University of Illinois Press, 2004.

——. "The Murders in the Rue Morgue." *Graham's Magazine* April 1841: 166–79.

——. *The Murders in the Rue Morgue, Facsimile of the MS in the Drexel Institute.* Philadelphia: George Barrie, 1895.

——. "Never Bet Your Head. A Moral Tale." *Brother Jonathan* 4 September 1841: [1] (MWA).

——. Rev. of *Continuation of the Diary Illustrative of the Times of George IV....* Ed. John Galt. *Burton's Gentleman's Magazine* September 1839: 174.

——. Rev. of *Historical Sketches of Statesmen Who Flourished in the Time of George III,* Second Series, 2 vols., by Henry Lord Brougham. *Burton's Gentleman's Magazine* September 1839: 166–67.

——. Rev. of *Opinions of Lord Brougham on Politics, Theology, Law, Science, Education, Literature, Etc., Etc., as Exhibited in His Parliamentary and Legal Speeches, and Miscellaneous Writings,* 2 vols., by Henry Lord Brougham. *Burton's Gentleman's Magazine* October 1839: 230.

——. Rev. of *Sketches of Conspicuous Living Characters of France.* Trans. R. M. Walsh. *Graham's Magazine* April 1841: 202–3.

——. Rev. of *Sketches of Public Characters, Discourses, and Essays. To Which Is Added a Dissertation on the Eloquence of the Ancients,* by Henry Lord Brougham. *Burton's Gentleman's Magazine* July 1839: 62.

Pollin, Burton R. "Bulwer-Lytton's Influence on Poe's Works and Ideas, Especially for an Author's 'Preconceived Design.'" *The Edgar Allan Poe Review* 1 (2000): 5–12.

——. "Godwin and Poe." *Discoveries in Poe.* Notre Dame: University of Notre Dame Press, 1970. 107–27, 263–68.

——. "'MS Found in a Bottle' and Sir David Brewster's *Letters*: A Source." *Poe Studies* 15 (1982): 40–41.

——. "Poe's 'Murders in the Rue Morgue': The Ingenious Web Unravelled." *Studies in the American Renaissance 1977.* Ed. Joel Myerson. Boston: G. K. Hall, 1977. 235–59.

———. "Poe's Mystification [*sic*]: Its Source in Fay's *Norman Leslie*." *Mississippi Quarterly* 25 (1972): 111–30.

———. Ed. *Word Index to Poe's Fiction*. New York: Gordian Press, 1982.

Pope, Alexander. *The Rape of the Lock and Other Poems*. Ed. Geoffrey Tillotson. Third Edition. London: Methuen, 1962.

Pratte, Alf. "George Rex Graham." *American Magazine Journalists, 1741–1850*. Ed. Sam G. Riley. Detroit: Gale, 1988. 153–58.

Priestman, Martin. *Detective Fiction and Literature: The Figure on the Carpet*. London: Macmillan, 1990.

Prior, Linda T. "A Further Word on Richard Wright's Use of Poe in *Native Son*." *Poe Studies* 5 (1972): 52–53.

Pyrhönen, Heta. *Murder from an Academic Angle: An Introduction to the Study of the Detective Narrative*. Columbia, SC: Camden House, 1994.

"Publisher's Department." *Brother Jonathan* 30 November 1839: [3] (CtY).

"The Queen." *Liverpool Mercury* 9 June 1820: 416.

Queen, Ellery. "Introduction." *The Exploits of Chevalier Dupin*, by Michael Harrison. Sauk City, WI: Mycroft & Moran, 1968. ix–xi.

Quinn, Arthur Hobson. *Edgar Allan Poe: A Critical Biography*. 1941. New York: Cooper Square, 1969.

Quirk, Tom. *Nothing Abstract: Investigations in the American Literary Imagination*. Columbia: University of Missouri Press, 2001.

———. "Sources, Influences, and Intertexts." *Nothing Abstract* 13–31.

["QUITE A MOB"]. New York *Evening Tattler* 4 September 1841: 2.

Ramakrishna, D., ed. *Perspectives on Poe*. New Delhi: APC, 1996.

Rev. of *Speeches of Henry Lord Brougham*. 2 vols. Philadelphia: Lea and Blanchard, 1841. *New York Commercial Advertiser* 18 October 1841: [2]; rpt. from *New York Spectator* 20 October 1841: [1].

Reynolds, David S. *Beneath the American Renaissance: The Subversive Imagination in the Age of Emerson and Melville*. New York: Alfred A. Knopf, 1988.

Rhodes, William Barnes. *Bombastes Furioso; A Burlesque Tragic Opera, in One Act*. London: Bell and Daldy, 1873.

Ridgely, J. V. "The Authorship of the 'Paulding-Drayton Review.'" *PSA Newsletter* 20 (1992): 1–3, 6.

Robbins, J. Albert. "Poe." *American Literary Scholarship an Annual/1979*. Durham: Duke University Press, 1981. 35–46.

Robertson, John W., comp. *Bibliography of the Writings of Edgar A. Poe*. San Francisco: Russian Hill Private Press, 1934.

Robinson, Charles Frederick. "Horatio Hastings Weld." *Weld Collections*. Ann Arbor, MI: n.p., 1938. 179–80.

Rogers, Ben J. "A Pun from Charles Lamb in *Moby Dick*." *ANQ: A Quarterly Journal of Short Articles, Notes, and Reviews* 13 (2000): 41–44.

Rosenheim, Shawn James. *The Cryptographic Imagination: Secret Writing from Edgar Poe to the Internet*. Baltimore, MD: Johns Hopkins University Press, 1997.

Rosenheim, Shawn James, and Stephen Rachman, eds. *The American Face of Edgar Allan Poe*. Baltimore: Johns Hopkins University Press, 1995.

Rosenthal, Bernard. "Poe, Slavery, and the *Southern Literary Messenger*." *Poe Studies* 7 (1974): 29–38.

Rowe, John Carlos. "Edgar Allan Poe's Imperial Fantasy and the American Frontier." Kennedy and Weissberg, 75–105.

"ROYAL CORRESPONDENCE!!!" *Literary Chronicle* 14 September 1822: 590.

Rubin, Louis D. Jr. "Edgar Allan Poe: A Study in Heroism." *The Curious Death of the Novel: Essays in American Literature*. Baton Rouge: Louisiana State University Press, 1967. 47–66.

Rust, Richard. "'Punish with Impunity': Poe, Thomas Dunn English, and 'The Cask of Amontillado.'" *The Edgar Allan Poe Review* 2:2 (2001): 33–52; rpt. in "Poe Writing/Writing Poe," ed. Richard Kopley and Jana Argersinger. To be published by AMS Press.

Saltz, Laura. "'(Horrible to Relate!)': Recovering the Body of Marie Rogêt." Rosenheim and Rachman, 237–67.

Sattelmeyer, Robert, and James Barbour. "The Sources and Genesis of Melville's 'Norfolk Isle and the Chola Widow.'" *American Literature* 50 (1978): 398–417.

Sayers, Dorothy. "Introduction." *The Omnibus of Crime*. 1929. Garden City, NY: Garden City, 1937. 9–47.

"A Scene of Horror and Murder." *The Philadelphia Saturday News* 20 October 1838: [3] (NHi).

Scott, Sir Walter. *Guy Mannering*. Ed. P. D. Garside. Edinburgh: Edinburgh University Press, 1999.

Sealts, Merton M. Jr. *Melville's Reading*. Columbia: University of South Carolina Press, 1988.

Sewell, Edward H. Jr. "Louis A. Godey." *American Magazine Journalists, 1741–1850*. Vol. 73 of *Dictionary of Literary Biography*. Ed. Sam G. Riley. Detroit: Gale, 1988. 139–45.

Shear, Walter. "Poe's Use of an Idea about Perception." *American Notes and Queries* 21 (1983): 134–36.

"Shocking." *New York Herald* 19 August 1841: 2.

Silverman, Kenneth. *Edgar A. Poe: Mournful and Never-Ending Remembrance*. New York: HarperCollins, 1991.

Sloane, David E. E. "Joseph C. Neal." *American Humorists, 1800–1950*. Vol. 2 of *Dictionary of Literary Biography*. Ed. Stanley Trachtenberg. Detroit: Gale, 1982. 344–49.

Smith, Geddeth. *The Brief Career of Eliza Poe*. Rutherford, NJ: Fairleigh Dickinson University Press, 1988.

Solly, Edward. "The Death-Bed Confessions of the Countess of Guernsey." *Notes and Queries* Fifth Series 10 (23 November 1878): 414–15.

Srebnick, Amy Gilman. *The Mysterious Death of Mary Rogers: Sex and Culture in Nineteenth-Century New York*. New York: Oxford University Press, 1995.

Stashower, Daniel. *The Beautiful Cigar Girl: Mary Rogers, Edgar Allan Poe, and the Invention of Murder.* New York: Dutton, 2006.

Stearns, Bertha Monica. "Godey, Louis Antoine." *Dictionary of American Biography* (1931).

Stern, Philip Van Doren. "The Case of the Corpse in the Blind Alley." *Virginia Quarterly Review* 17 (1941): 227–36.

Stewart, E. Kate. "An Early Imitative Ape: A Possible Source for 'The Murders in the Rue Morgue.'" *Poe Studies* 20 (1987): 24.

Stoddard, Roger E. *"Put a Resolute Heart to a Steep Hill": William Gowans, Antiquary and Bookseller.* New York: Book Arts Press, 1990.

"A Story." *The Philadelphia Saturday News* 1 December 1838: [4] (NHi).

"Supposed Murder." *New York Sun* 2 August 1841: 2 (NHi).

Sweeney, S. E. "Purloined Letters: Poe, Doyle, Nabokov." *Russian Literature Triquarterly* 24 (1990): 213–37.

Terlotte, J. P. *"Casablanca* and the Larcenous Film Cult." *Michigan Quarterly Review* 26 (1987): 357–68.

Thomas, Dwight. "Poe in Philadelphia, 1838–1844: A Documentary Record." Diss. University of Pennsylvania, 1978.

Thomas, Dwight, and David K. Jackson. *The Poe Log: A Documentary Life of Edgar Allan Poe 1809–1849.* Boston: G. K. Hall, 1987.

Thompson, G. R. "On the Nose—Further Speculation on the Sources and Meaning of Poe's 'Lionizing.'" *Studies in Short Fiction* 6 (1968): 96.

———. "Poe's Readings of *Pelham*: Another Source for 'Tintinnabulation' and Other Piquant Expressions." *American Literature* 41 (1969): 251–55.

Thoms, William J. "The Death-Bed Confessions of the Countess of Guernsey." *Notes and Queries.* Fifth Series 3 (13 March 1875): 212–13.

———. "The Serres Scandal: The Princess Olive, Miss Cary, Lady Anne Hamilton." *Notes and Queries* Fifth Series 3 (2 January 1875): 5–6.

Twain, Mark. *Adventures of Huckleberry Finn.* Ed. Victor Fischer and Lin Salamo. Berkeley: University of California Press, 2003.

"The Union." *Brother Jonathan* 22 February 1840: [2] (MWA).

"An Unpublished Letter of Poe." *The Dial* 16 January 1908: 32–33.

Varnado, S. L. "The Case of the Sublime Purloin; or Burke's *Inquiry* as the Source of an Anecdote in 'The Purloined Letter.'" *Poe Newsletter* 1 (1968): 27.

Varner, John Grier. *Edgar Allan Poe and the Philadelphia "Saturday Courier."* Charlottesville: University of Virginia, 1933.

Walker, I. M. Ed. *Edgar Allan Poe: The Critical Heritage.* London: Routledge & Kegan Paul, 1986.

[Wallace, Horace Binney.] *Stanley; or the Recollections of a Man of the World.* 2 vols. Philadelphia: Lea and Blanchard, 1838.

Waller, W. F. "Poe's 'Murders in the Rue Morgue.'" *Notes and Queries* 5 (12 May 1894): 366.

Walsh, John. *Poe the Detective: The Curious Circumstances behind "The Mystery of Marie Roget."* New Brunswick, NJ: Rutgers University Press, 1968.

Walsh, R. M., trans. *Sketches of Conspicuous Living Characters of France.* By Louis L. de Loménie. Philadelphia: Lea and Blanchard, 1841.

"The Walter Scott." *The Philadelphia Saturday News* 17 November 1838: [2] (NHi).

Walton, Priscilla L., and Manina Jones. *Detective Agency: Women Rewriting the Hard-Boiled Tradition.* Berkeley: University of California Press, 1999.

"Weld, Horatio Hastings." *Appleton's Cyclopaedia of American Biography.*

[Weld, H. Hastings.] "Further Remarks on the Rogers Case." *Brother Jonathan* 28 August 1841: 3 (MWA); rpt. from New York *Evening Tattler* 24 August 1841: 2 (NN).

——. "The Hoboken Tragedy." *Brother Jonathan* 21 August 1841: 2 (MWA).

——. "Is Mary C. Rogers Murdered?" *Brother Jonathan* 28 August 1841: 2–3 (MWA); rpt. from New York *Evening Tattler* 23 August 1841: 2 (NN); see also New York *Evening Tattler* 24 August 1841: 4 (NN).

——. "Letters of John Smith, with Pictures to Match." *Morning Dispatch* 22 April 1839: [2] (CtY).

——. "More Remarks upon the 'Murder Case.'" *Brother Jonathan* 28 August 1841: 3 (MWA); rpt. from New York *Evening Tattler* 25 August 1841: [2] (NN).

——. "Mr. Willis and Mr. Paulding." *Morning Dispatch* 29 April 1839: [2] (CtY).

——. "Our Weekly Gossip." *Brother Jonathan* 30 October 1841: [2] (MWA).

——. "Our Weekly Gossip." *Brother Jonathan* 27 November 1841: [3] (MWA).

——. "Our Weekly Chat." *United States Saturday Post* 12 November 1842: [2] (MWA).

——. ["QUITE A MOB"]. New York *Evening Tattler* 4 September 1841: [2] (NN).

——. Rev. of *Graham's Magazine* (July 1841). *Brother Jonathan* 26 June 1841: [2] (MWA).

——. Rev. of *Graham's Magazine* (August 1841). *Brother Jonathan* 14 August 1841: [3] (MWA).

——. Rev. of *Graham's Magazine* (April 1842). *Brother Jonathan* (Quarto) 9 April 1842: 409.

——. Rev. of *Graham's Magazine* (October 1842). *Brother Jonathan* (Quarto) 8 October 1842: 168.

——. Rev. of *Graham's Magazine* (September 1841). *Evening Tattler* 26 August 1841: [2] (MWA).

——. Rev. of *Powhatan; a Metrical Romance, in Seven Cantos*, by Seba Smith. *Brother Jonathan* 1 May 1841: [3] (MWA).

["The well-known american ship MARTHA"]. *Liverpool Mercury* 9 June 1820: 412.

Whalen, Terence. "Average Racism: Poe, Slavery, and the Wages of Literary Nationalism." Kennedy and Weissberg, 3–40.

——. *Edgar Allan Poe and the Masses: The Political Economy of Literature in Antebellum America*. Princeton, NJ: Princeton University Press, 1999.

White, Ed. "The Ourang-Outang Situation." *College Literature* 30 (2003): 88–108.

Whitty, J. H. Ed. *The Complete Poems of Edgar Allan Poe*. Boston: Houghton Mifflin, 1911.

Wilbur, Richard. "Poe and the Art of Suggestion." *University of Mississippi Studies in English* ns 3 (1982): 1–13.

——. "The Poe Mystery Case." *Responses—Prose Pieces: 1953–1976*. New York: Harcourt Brace Jovanovich, 1976. 127–38.

Wilmer, Lambert A. *Our Press Gang; or a Complete Exposition of the Corruptions and Crimes of the American Newspapers*. Philadelphia: J. T. Lloyd, 1859.

Wimsatt, William K. Jr. "Mary Rogers, John Anderson, and Others." *American Literature* 21 (1950): 482–84.

——. "Poe and the Chess Automaton." *American Literature* 11 (1939): 138–51.

——. "Poe and the Mystery of Mary Rogers." *PMLA* 56 (1941): 230–48.

Winks, Robin W., ed. *Detective Fiction: A Collection of Critical Essays*. Englewood Cliffs, NJ: Prentice-Hall, 1980.

Worthen, Samuel Copp. "Poe and the Beautiful Cigar Girl." *American Literature* 20 (1948): 305–12.

Worthington, Heather. "Against the Law: Bulwer's Fictions of Crime." *The Subverting Vision of Bulwer Lytton: Bicentenary Reflections*. Ed. Allan Conrad Christensen. Newark: University of Delaware Press, 2004. 54–67.

Wright, Richard. "How 'Bigger' Was Born.'" *Native Son*. New York: Grosset and Dunlap, 1940. xiii–li.

Zimmerman, Brett. *Edgar Allan Poe: Rhetoric and Style*. Montreal and Kingston, Canada: McGill-Queen's University Press, 2005.

THE MURDERS IN THE RUE MORGUE

numbered 5 and 9 are each made up of pieces of paper fastened together. [Through the courtesy of Mr. Howell J. Heaney, Rare Book Librarian, the manuscript has been recently consulted. Scholars should be made aware of the fact that *The Murders in the Rue Morgue facsimile of the MS in the Drexel Institute*, copyright 1895, is reduced in size and has some distortions. This "facsimile" is useful for reference but should not be relied upon.]

In our list of recorded variant readings cancelations in the MS are enclosed in angle brackets, < >; additions are enclosed in arrows, ↑ ↓; and square brackets, [ ], enclose matter lost by mutilation and restored from other texts. The manuscript *(A)* was certainly used in setting up the *Graham's* text *(B)*. See Ernest Boll, "The Manuscript of 'The Murders in the Rue Morgue' and Poe's Revisions," *Modern Philology*, May 1943, for a history of the manuscript and a careful study of Poe's changes.

Translations

La Quotidienne, June 11, 12, 13, 1846, as "Un Meurtre sans exemple dans les fastes de la justice," signed G.B.; *Le Commerce*, October 12, 1846, as "Une sanglante énigme," signed O.N.; *La Démocratie pacifique*, January 31, 1847, as "L'Assassinat de la rue Morgue," by Isabelle Meunier.

THE MURDERS IN THE RUE MORGUE. [E]

What song the Syrens sang, or what name Achilles assumed when he hid himself among women, although puzzling questions, are not beyond *all* conjecture.

Sir Thomas Browne.

The[a] mental features discoursed of as the analytical[a'] are, in themselves, but little susceptible of analysis. We appreciate them

---

Title: The Murders in the Rue <Trianon-Bas> Morgue. *(A)*
Beneath the title, in the same script, is By Edgar A. Poe.
Motto: Omitted (A, B)
In early versions there is an opening paragraph:
    It is not improbable that a few farther steps in phrenological science will lead to a belief in the existence, if not to the actual discovery and location of an organ of *analysis*. If this power (which may be described, although not defined, as the capacity for resolving thought into its elements) be not, in fact, an essential portion of what late philosophers term ideality, then there are indeed many good reasons for supposing it a primitive faculty. That it may be a constituent of ideality is here suggested in opposition to the vulgar dictum (founded ↑ however ↓ upon the

assumptions of grave authority),
<however)> that the calculating and discriminating powers (causality and comparison) are at variance with the imaginative — that the three, in short, can hardly coexist. But, although thus opposed to received opinion, the idea will not appear ill-founded when we observe that the processes of invention or creation are strictly akin with the processes of resolution — the former being nearly, if not absolutely, the latter conversed. *(A, B, C) In the third sentence* however *was transposed in the manuscript (A); in the second sentence* be not *became is not in Prose Romances (C).*
a   It cannot be doubted that the *(A, B, C)*
a'   analytical, *(C, D, E, F) corrected from A, B*

TALES, 1841–1842

only in their effects. We know of them, among other things, that they are always to their possessor, when inordinately possessed, a source of the liveliest enjoyment. As the strong man exults in his physical ability, delighting in such exercises as call his muscles into action,[1] so glories the analyst in that moral activity which *disentangles*. He derives pleasure from even the most trivial occupations bringing his talent into play. He is fond of enigmas, of conundrums, of hieroglyphics; exhibiting in his solutions of each[b] a degree of *acumen*[c] which appears to the ordinary apprehension præternatural.[2] His results, brought about by the very soul and essence of method, have, in truth, the whole air of intuition.

The faculty of re-solution[d] is possibly much invigorated by mathematical study, and especially by that highest branch of it which, unjustly, and merely on account of its retrograde operations, has been called, as if *par excellence,* analysis. Yet to calculate is not in itself to analyse. A chess-player, for example, does the one without effort at the other. It follows that the game of chess, in its effects upon mental character, is greatly misunderstood. I am not now writing a treatise, but simply prefacing a somewhat peculiar narrative by observations very much at random; I will, therefore, take occasion to assert that the higher powers of the reflective intellect are more decidedly and more usefully tasked[e] by the unostentatious game of draughts than by all the elaborate frivolity of chess. In this latter, where the pieces have different and *bizarre*[f] motions, with various and variable values, what[g] is only complex is mistaken (a not unusual error) for what[h] is profound. The *attention* is here called powerfully into play. If it flag for an instant, an oversight is committed, resulting in injury or defeat. The possible moves being not only manifold but involute, the chances of such oversights are multiplied; and in nine cases out of ten it is the more concentrative rather than the more acute player who conquers. In draughts, on the contrary, where the moves are *unique*[i] and have but little variation, the probabilities of inadvertence are dimin-

---

b each and all *(A, B)*	f bizarre *(A, B)*
c acumen *(A, B)*	g that which *(A, B, C)*
d of re-solution/in question *(A, B, C)*	h that which *(A, B, C)*
e taxed *(A, B)*	i unique *(A, B)*

THE MURDERS IN THE RUE MORGUE

ished, and the mere attention being left comparatively unemployed, what advantages are obtained by either party are obtained by superior *acumen*.[j] To be less abstract — Let us suppose a game of draughts where the pieces are reduced to four kings, and where, of course, no oversight is to be expected. It is obvious that here the victory can be decided (the players being at all equal) only by some *recherché*[k] movement, the result of some strong exertion of the intellect. Deprived of ordinary resources, the analyst throws himself into the spirit of his opponent, identifies himself therewith, and not unfrequently sees thus, at a glance, the sole methods (sometimes indeed absurdly simple ones) by which he may seduce into [l]error or hurry into miscalculation.[l]

Whist has long been noted for its influence upon what is[m] termed the calculating power;[n] and men of the highest order of intellect have been known to take an apparently unaccountable delight in it, while eschewing chess as frivolous. Beyond doubt there is nothing of a similar nature so greatly tasking the faculty of analysis. The best chess-player in Christendom *may* be little more than the best player of chess; but proficiency in whist implies capacity for success in all those more important undertakings where mind struggles with mind. When I say proficiency, I mean that perfection in the game which includes a comprehension of *all*[o] the sources whence[p] legitimate advantage may be derived. These are not only manifold but multiform, and lie frequently among recesses of thought altogether inaccessible to the ordinary understanding. To observe attentively is to remember distinctly; and, so far, the concentrative chess-player will do very well at whist; while the rules of Hoyle (themselves based upon the mere mechanism of the game) are sufficiently and generally comprehensible.[3] Thus to have a retentive memory, and to proceed by "the book," are points commonly regarded as the sum total of good playing. But it is in matters beyond the limits of mere rule that[q]

---

j   acumen. *(A, B)*
k   recherché *(A, B)*
l . . . l   miscalculation or hurry into error. *(A, B, C)*
m   are *(A, B)*
n   powers ; *(A, B)*

o   all *(A, B, C)*
p   (whatever be their character) from which *(A, B);* (whatever be their character) whence *(C)*
q   where *(A, B)*

TALES, 1841–1842

the skill of the analyst is evinced. He makes, in silence, a host of observations and inferences. So, perhaps, do his companions; and the difference in the extent of the information obtained$^{q'}$ lies not so much in the validity^{r} of the inference as in the quality of the observation. The necessary knowledge is that of *what* to observe. Our player confines himself not at all; nor, because the game is the object, does he reject deductions^{s} from things external to the game. He examines the countenance of his partner, comparing it carefully with that of each of his opponents. He considers the mode of assorting the cards in each hand; often counting trump by trump, and honor by honor, through the glances bestowed by their holders upon each. He notes every variation of face as the play progresses, gathering a fund of thought from the differences in the expression of certainty, of surprise, of triumph, or of^{t} chagrin. From the manner of gathering up a trick he judges whether the person taking it^{u} can make another in the suit.^{v} He recognises what is^{w} played through feint, by the air with which it is thrown upon the table. A casual or inadvertent word; the accidental dropping or turning of a card,^{x} with the accompanying anxiety or carelessness in regard to its concealment; the counting of the tricks, with the order of their arrangement; embarrassment, hesitation, eagerness or trepidation — all afford, to his apparently intuitive perception, indications of the true state of affairs. The first two or three rounds having been played, he is in full possession of the contents of each hand, and thenceforward puts down his cards with as absolute a precision of purpose as if the rest of the party had turned outward^{y} the faces of their own.[4]

The analytical power should not be confounded with simple ingenuity; for while the analyst is necessarily ingenious, the ingenious man is often remarkably^{z} incapable of analysis.^{a} The con-

---

q′   obtained, *(C, D, E, F)*
corrected from A, B
r   falsity *(A, B, C)*
s   deductions <arising> *(A)*
t   *Omitted in later issues of F*
u   ↑ it ↓ *(A)*
v   *After this:* <Embarrasment,
hesitation, eagerness, or

trepidation.> *(A)*
w   <a card> ↑ what is ↓ *(A)*
x   <anything important,> ↑ a
card, ↓ *(A)*
y   outwards *(A)*
z   utterly *(A, B)*
a   *After this:* I have spoken of this latter
faculty as that of resolving thought

THE MURDERS IN THE RUE MORGUE

structive or combining power, by which ingenuity is usually manifested, and to which the phrenologists (I believe erroneously) have assigned a separate organ, supposing it a primitive faculty, has been so frequently seen in those whose intellect bordered otherwise upon idiocy, as to have attracted general observation among writers on morals. Between ingenuity and the analytic ability there exists a difference far greater, indeed, than that between the fancy and the imagination, but of a character very strictly analogous. It will be found, in fact, that the ingenious are always fanciful, and the *truly*[b] imaginative never otherwise than[c] analytic.

The narrative which follows will appear to the[d] reader somewhat in the light of a commentary upon the propositions just advanced.

Residing in Paris during the spring[e] and part of the summer[f] of 18 — , I there [g]became acquainted[g] with a Monsieur C. Auguste Dupin. This young gentleman was of an excellent – indeed of an illustrious family, but, by a variety of untoward events, had been reduced to such poverty that the[h] energy of his character succumbed beneath[i] it, and he ceased to bestir himself in the world, or to care for the retrieval of his fortunes. By courtesy of his creditors, there still remained in his possession a small remnant of his patrimony; and, upon the income arising from this, he managed, by means of a rigorous[j] economy, to procure the necessaries[k] of life, without troubling himself about its superfluities. Books, indeed, were his sole luxuries, and in Paris these are easily obtained.

[l]Our first meeting was at an obscure library in the Rue Montmartre, where the accident of our both being in search of the same

---

into its elements, and it is only necessary to glance upon this idea to perceive the necessity of the distinction just mentioned. *(A, B, C)*
b <highly> ↑ *truly* ↓ *(A)*
c than profoundly *(A, B, C)*
d the <reflective> *(A)*
e <autumn> ↑ spring ↓ *(A)*
f <winter> ↑ summer ↓ *(A)*

g . . . g contracted an intimacy *(A, B, C)*
h the quondam *(A, B);* the *quondam (C)*
i <before> ↑ beneath ↓ *(A)*
j vigorous *(B) misprint*
k necessaries <, without> *(A)*
l ¶ *inserted before this sentence (A)*

TALES, 1841–1842

very rare and very remarkable volume[l'] brought us into closer communion. We saw each other again and again. I was deeply interested in the little family history which he detailed to me with all that[m] candor[n] which a Frenchman [o]indulges whenever mere[o] self is his[p] theme. I was astonished, too, at the vast extent of his reading; and, above all, I felt[q] my soul enkindled within me by the wild fervor, and[r] the vivid freshness of his imagination. Seeking in Paris the objects I then sought, I felt that the society of such a man would be to me a treasure beyond price; and this feeling I frankly confided to him. It was at length arranged that we should live together during my stay in the city; and as my worldly circumstances were somewhat less embarrassed than his own, I was permitted to be at the expense of renting, and furnishing in a style which suited the rather fantastic gloom of our common temper, a time-eaten and grotesque mansion, long deserted through superstitions into which we did not inquire, and tottering to its fall[5] in a retired and desolate portion of the Faubourg St. Germain.

Had the routine of our life at this place been known to the world, we should have been regarded as madmen — although, perhaps, as madmen of a harmless nature. Our seclusion was perfect. We admitted no visitors.[s] Indeed the locality of our retirement had been carefully kept a secret from my own former associates; and it had been many years since Dupin had ceased to know or be known in Paris. We existed within ourselves alone.

It was a freak of fancy in my friend (for what else shall I call it?) to be enamored of the Night for her own sake; and into this *bizarrerie,* as into all his others, I quietly fell; giving myself up to his wild whims with a perfect[t] *abandon.* The sable divinity would not herself dwell with us always; but we could counterfeit her presence.[6] At the first dawn of the morning we closed all the massy shutters of our old building,[t'] lighting[u] a couple of tapers which,

---

l′ volume, *(C, D, E, F)*
corrected from A, B
m the *changed to* that *(A)*; the *(B, C)*
n candor <of a Frenchman in> *(A)*
o . . . o <only> indulges ↑ only ↓ when *(A)*; indulges only when *(B, C)*
p the *in later issues of F*

q felt <all> *(A)*
r and what I could only term *(A, B, C)*
s visitors whomsoever. *(A, B, C)*
t a perfect/an utter *(A, B)*
t′ building; *(C, D, E, F)*
comma adopted from A, B
u lighted *(F)*

THE MURDERS IN THE RUE MORGUE

strongly perfumed, threw out only the ghastliest and feeblest of rays. By the aid of these we then busied our souls in dreams[7] — reading, writing, or conversing, until warned by the clock of the advent of the true Darkness. Then we sallied forth into the streets, arm in arm, continuing the topics of the day, or roaming far and wide until a late hour, seeking, amid the wild lights and shadows of the populous city, that infinity of mental excitement which quiet observation can[v] afford.

At such times I could not help remarking and admiring (although from his rich ideality I had been prepared to expect it[w]) a peculiar analytic ability in Dupin. He seemed, too, to take an eager delight in its exercise — if not exactly in its display — and did not hesitate[x] to confess the pleasure thus derived. He boasted to me, with a low chuckling laugh, that most men, in respect to himself, wore windows in their bosoms,[8] and was wont to follow up such assertions by direct and very startling proofs of his intimate knowledge of my own. His manner at these moments was frigid and abstract; his eyes were vacant in expression; while his voice, usually a rich tenor, rose into a treble which would have sounded petulantly but for the deliberateness and entire distinctness of the enunciation. Observing him in these moods, I often dwelt meditatively upon the old philosophy of the Bi-Part Soul,[9] and amused myself with the fancy of a double Dupin — the creative and the resolvent.

Let it not be supposed, from what I have just said, that I am detailing any mystery, or penning any romance. What I have described in the Frenchman[x'] was merely[y] the result of an excited, or perhaps of a diseased intelligence. But of the character of his remarks at the periods in question an example will best convey the idea.

We were strolling one night down a long dirty street, in the vicinity of the Palais Royal.[10] Being both, apparently, occupied with thought, neither of us had spoken a syllable for fifteen minutes at least. All at once Dupin broke forth with these words:

---

v   could *(A);* would *(B)*   x'   Frenchman, *(C, D, E, F)*
w   it *omitted (A, B, C)*   *corrected from A, B*
x   hesitute *misprint in later issues of F*   y   but *(A, B, C)*

TALES, 1841–1842

"He is a very little fellow, that's true, and would do better for the *Théâtre*[z] *des Variétés.*"[11]

"There can be no doubt of that," I replied unwittingly, and not at first observing (so much had I been absorbed in reflection) the extraordinary manner in which the speaker had chimed in with my meditations. In an instant afterward[a] I recollected myself, and my astonishment was profound.

"Dupin," said I, gravely, "this is beyond my comprehension. I do not hesitate to say that I am amazed, and can scarcely credit my senses. How was it possible you should know I was thinking of —— ?" Here I paused, to ascertain beyond a doubt whether he really knew of whom I thought.

—— "of Chantilly," said he, "why do you pause? You were remarking to yourself that his diminutive figure unfitted him for tragedy."[12]

This was precisely what had formed the subject of my reflections. Chantilly was a *quondam*[b] cobbler of the Rue St. Denis,[13] who, becoming stage-mad, had attempted the *rôle*[c] of Xerxes, in Crébillon's[d] tragedy so called,[14] and been notoriously Pasquinaded for his pains.

"Tell me, for Heaven's[e] sake," I exclaimed, "the method — if method there is[f] — by which you have been enabled to fathom my soul in this matter." In fact I was even more startled than I would have been willing to express.

"It was the fruiterer," replied my friend, "who brought you to the conclusion that the mender of soles was not of sufficient height for Xerxes *et id genus omne.*"[15]

"The fruiterer! — you astonish me — I know no fruiterer whomsoever."[g]

"The man who ran up against you as we entered the street — it may have been fifteen minutes ago."

I now remembered that, in fact, a fruiterer, carrying upon his head a large basket of apples, had nearly thrown me down, by

---

z	*Théâtre (A)*	d	Crebillon's *(A, B)*
a	afterwards *(A)*	e	God's *(A, B, C)*
b	quondam *(A, B)*	f	be *(A, B, C)*
c	rôle *(A, B)*	g	whatever." *(A)*

THE MURDERS IN THE RUE MORGUE

accident, as we passed from the Rue C —— into the thoroughfare where we[h] stood; but what this had to do with Chantilly I could not possibly understand.

There was not a particle of *charlatanerie*[i] about Dupin. "I will explain," he said, "and that you may comprehend all clearly, we will first retrace the course of your meditations, from the moment in which I spoke to you until that of the *rencontre*[j] with the fruiterer in question. The larger links of the chain run thus — Chantilly, Orion, Dr. Nichol,[k] [16] Epicurus, Stereotomy, the street stones, the fruiterer."

There are few persons who have not, at some period of their lives, amused themselves in retracing the steps by which particular conclusions of their own minds have been attained. The occupation is often full of interest; and he who attempts it for the first time is[l] astonished by the apparently illimitable distance and incoherence between the starting-point and the goal.[17] What, then, must have been my amazement when I heard the Frenchman speak what he had just spoken, and when I could not help acknowledging that he had spoken the truth. He continued:

"We had been talking of horses, if I remember aright, just before leaving the Rue C —— . This was the last subject we discussed. As we crossed into this street, a fruiterer, with a large basket upon his head, brushing quickly past us, thrust you upon a pile of paving-stones collected at a spot where the causeway is undergoing repair. You stepped upon one of the loose fragments, slipped, slightly strained your ankle, appeared vexed or sulky, muttered a few words, turned to look[m] at the pile, and then proceeded in silence. I was not particularly attentive to what you did; but observation has become with me, of late, a species of necessity.

"You kept your eyes upon the ground — glancing, with a petulant expression, at the holes and ruts in the pavement, (so that I saw you were still thinking of the stones,) until we reached the little alley called Lamartine,[18] which has been paved, by way of

---

h we now *(A, B)*
i *charlatânerie (B, C, D, E, F),*
corrected from A
j rencontre *(A, B)*

k Nichols, *(C, D, E, F) corrected*
from A, B
l is <invariably> *(A)*
m look back *(A)*

TALES, 1841–1842

experiment, with the overlapping and riveted blocks.[19] Here your countenance brightened up, and, perceiving your lips move, I could not doubt that you murmured[n] the [o]word 'stereotomy,' a term very affectedly applied to this species of pavement.[o] I knew that you could not [p]say to yourself 'stereotomy' without[p] being brought to think of atomies, and thus of the theories of Epicurus;[20] and since,[q] when we discussed this subject not very long ago, I mentioned to you how singularly, yet with how little notice, the vague guesses of that noble Greek had met with confirmation in the late nebular cosmogony, I felt that you could not avoid casting your eyes upward[r] to the great *nebula*[s] in Orion,[21] and I certainly expected that you would do so. You did look up; and I was now[t] assured that I had correctly followed your steps. But in that bitter *tirade* upon Chantilly, which appeared in yesterday's *'Musée,'* the satirist, making some disgraceful allusions to the cobbler's change of name upon assuming the buskin, quoted a[u] Latin line[v] about which[w] we have often conversed. I mean the line

[x]Perdidit antiquum litera prima sonum[x]

I had told you that this was in reference to Orion, formerly written Urion; and, from certain pungencies connected with this explanation, I was aware that you could not have forgotten it.[22] It was clear, therefore, that you would not fail to combine the two ideas of Orion and Chantilly. That you did combine them I saw by the character of the smile which passed over your lips. You thought of the poor cobbler's immolation. So far, you had been stooping in your gait; but now I saw you draw yourself up to your full height. I was then sure that you reflected upon the diminutive figure of Chantilly. At this point I interrupted your meditations to remark

---

n   murmured to yourself *(A, B, C)*
o . . . o   word stereotomic. You continued the same inaudible murmur, with a knit brow, as is the <habit> ↑ custom ↓ of a man tasking his memory, until I considered that you sought the Greek derivation of the word stereotomy. *(A, B, C)*
p . . . p   find this without *(A, B, C)*
q   as, *(A, B)*

r   upwards *(A)*
s   nebula *(A, B)*
t   was now/now was *(A, B, C)*
u   a very peculiar *(A, B, C)*
v   Latin line/<line> ↑ Latin verse ↓ *(A)*
w   about which/upon whose meaning *(A, B);* upon the meaning of which *(C)*
x . . . x   *Latin italicized (A, B, C)*

THE MURDERS IN THE RUE MORGUE

that as, in fact, he *was* a very little fellow — that Chantilly — he would do better at the *Théâtre des Variétés.*" [y]

Not long after this, we were looking over an evening edition of [z]the "Gazette des Tribunaux,"[z] when the following paragraphs arrested our attention.

"Extraordinary Murders. — This morning, about three o'-clock, the inhabitants of the Quartier St. Roch were aroused from sleep by a succession of terrific shrieks, issuing, apparently, from the fourth story of a house in the Rue Morgue, known to be in the sole occupancy of one Madame L'Espanaye, and her daughter, Mademoiselle Camille L'Espanaye. After some delay, occasioned by a fruitless attempt to procure admission in the usual manner, the gateway was broken in with a crowbar,[a] and eight or ten of the neighbors entered, accompanied by two *gendarmes.*[b] By this time the cries had ceased; but, as the party rushed up the first flight of stairs, two or more rough voices, in angry contention, were distinguished, and[c] seemed to proceed from the upper part of the house. As the second landing was reached, these sounds, also, had ceased, and everything remained perfectly quiet. The party spread themselves, and hurried from room to room. Upon arriving at a large back chamber in the fourth story, (the door of which, being found locked, with the key inside, was forced open,) a spectacle presented itself which struck every one present not less with horror than with astonishment.

"The apartment was in the wildest disorder — the furniture broken and thrown about in all directions. There was only one bedstead; and from this the bed had been removed, and thrown into the middle of the floor. On a chair lay a razor, besmeared with blood. On the hearth were two or three long and thick tresses of grey human hair, also dabbled in blood, and seeming to have been pulled out[d] by the roots. On[e] the floor were found four Napoleons, an ear-ring of topaz, three large silver spoons, three[f] smaller of *métal*[g] *d'Alger,*[23] and two bags, containing nearly four thousand

---

y   Théâtre des Variétés." *(A)*
z . . . z   "Le Tribunal" *(A, B, C)*
a   crow-bar. *(A, B, C)*
b   <gens d'armes.> ↑ *gendarmes.* ↓ *(A)*
c   <proceeding> and *(A)*

d   <up> ↑ out ↓ *(A)*
e   Upon *(A, B, C, D, F)*
f   <and> three *(A)*
g   *metal (A, B)*

TALES, 1841–1842

francs in gold. The drawers of a *bureau*, which stood in one corner, were open, and had been, apparently, rifled, although many articles still remained in them. A small iron safe was discovered under the *bed* (not under the bedstead). It was open, with the key still in the door. It had no contents beyond a few old letters, and other papers of little consequence.

"Of Madame L'Espanaye no traces were here seen; but an unusual quantity of soot being observed in the fire-place, a search was made in the chimney, and (horrible to relate!)[24] the corpse of the daughter, head downward,[h] was dragged therefrom; it having been thus forced up the narrow aperture for a considerable distance.[25] The body was quite warm. Upon examining it, many excoriations were perceived, no doubt occasioned by the violence with which it had been thrust up and disengaged. Upon the face were many severe scratches, and, upon the throat, dark bruises, and deep indentations of finger nails, as if the deceased had been throttled to death.

"After a thorough investigation of every portion of the house, without farther discovery, the party made its way into a small paved yard in the rear of the building, where lay the corpse of the old lady, with her throat so entirely cut that, upon an attempt to raise her, the head fell off.[i] The body, as well as the head, was[j] fearfully mutilated — the former so much so as scarcely to retain any semblance of humanity.

"To this horrible mystery there is not as yet, we believe, the slightest clew."[k]

The next day's paper had these additional particulars.

"*The Tragedy in the Rue Morgue.* Many individuals have been examined in relation to this most extraordinary and frightful affair." [The word *'affaire'* has not yet, in France, that levity of import which it conveys with us,] "but nothing whatever has transpired to throw light upon it. We give below all the material testimony elicited.[26]

"*Pauline Dubourg*, laundress, deposes that she has known both the deceased for three years, having washed for them during that

---

h   downwards, *(A)*
i   off and rolled to some distance. *(A, B)*
j   <were> ↑ was ↓ *(A)*
k   *At first appearance in the MS this word is spelled* clew

THE MURDERS IN THE RUE MORGUE

period. The old lady and her daughter seemed on good terms —
very affectionate towards[1] each other. They were excellent pay.
Could not speak in regard to their mode or means of living. Believed that Madame L. told fortunes for a living. Was reputed to
have money put by. Never met any persons in the house when she
called for the clothes or took them home. Was sure that they had
no servant in employ. There appeared to be no furniture in any
part of the building except in the fourth story.

"*Pierre Moreau,* tobacconist, deposes that he has been in the
habit of selling small quantities of tobacco and snuff to Madame
L'Espanaye for nearly four years. Was born in the neighborhood,
and has always resided there. The deceased and her daughter had
occupied the house in which the corpses were found, for more than
six years. It was formerly occupied by a jeweller, who under-let the
upper rooms to various persons. The house was the property of
Madame L. She became dissatisfied with the abuse of the premises
by her tenant, and moved into them herself, refusing to let any
portion. The old lady was childish. Witness had seen the daughter
some five or six times during the six years. The two lived an exceedingly retired life — were reputed to have money. Had heard
it said among the neighbors that Madame L. told fortunes — did
not believe it. Had never seen any person enter the door except the
old lady and her daughter, a porter once or twice, and a physician
some eight or ten times.

"Many other persons, neighbors, gave evidence to the same
effect. No one was spoken of as frequenting the house. It was not
known whether there were any living connexions of Madame L.
and her daughter. The shutters of the front windows were seldom
opened. Those in the rear were always closed, with the exception
of the large back room, fourth story. The house was a good house
— not very old.

"*Isidore* ᵐ*Musèt, gendarme,*ᵐ deposes that he was called to the
house about three o'clock in the morning, and found some twenty
or thirty persons at the gateway,ⁿ endeavoring to gain admittance.
Forced it open, at length, with a bayonet — not with a crowbar.ᵒ

---

l   toward *(B)*   n   <front door> ↑ gateway, ↓ *(A)*
m . . . m   *Musêt,* gendarme, *(A, B)*   o   crow-bar. *(A, B, C)*

TALES, 1841–1842

Had but little difficulty in getting it open, on account of its being a double or folding gate,[p] and bolted neither at bottom nor top. The shrieks were continued until the gate[q] was forced — and then suddenly ceased. They seemed to be[r] screams of some person (or persons) in great agony — were loud and drawn out, not short and quick. Witness led the way up stairs. Upon reaching the first landing, heard two voices in loud and angry contention — the one a gruff voice, the other much shriller — a very strange voice. Could distinguish some words of the former, which was that of a Frenchman. Was positive that it was not a woman's voice. Could distinguish the words '*sacré*'[s] and '*diable*.' The shrill voice was that of a foreigner. Could not be sure whether it was the voice of a man or of a woman. Could not make out what was said, but believed the language to be Spanish.[t] The state of the room and of the bodies was described by this witness as we described them yesterday.

"*Henri Duval*, a neighbor, and by trade a silver-smith,[u] deposes that he was one of the party who first entered the house. Corroborates the testimony of Musèt[v] in general. As soon as they forced an entrance, they reclosed the door, to keep out the crowd, which collected very fast, notwithstanding the lateness of the hour. The shrill voice, this witness thinks, was that of an Italian. Was certain it was not French. Could not be sure that it was a man's voice. It might have been a woman's. Was not[w] acquainted with the Italian language. Could[x] not distinguish the words, but[y] was convinced by the intonation that the speaker was an Italian. Knew Madame L. and her daughter. Had conversed with both frequently. Was sure that the shrill voice was not that of either of the deceased.

"—— *Odenheimer, restaurateur*.[z] This witness volunteered his testimony. [a]Not speaking French, was examined through an inter-

---

p   <door,> ↑ gate, ↓ *(A)*
q   <door> ↑ gate ↓ *(A)*
r   be the *(A)*
s   '*sacre*' *(A)*
t   *After this:* Might have distinguished some words if he had been acquainted with the Spanish. *(A)*

u   silversmith, *(A)*
v   Musèt *(A)*
w   ↑ not ↓ *(A)*
x   <, and, although he> Could *(A)*
y   ↑ but ↓ *(A)*
z   restaurateur. *(A, B)*
a . . . a   *Inserted (A)*

THE MURDERS IN THE RUE MORGUE

preter.[a] Is a native of Amsterdam. Was passing the house at the time of the shrieks. They lasted for several minutes — probably ten. They were long and loud — very awful and distressing. Was one of those who entered the building. Corroborated the previous evidence in every respect but one. Was sure that the shrill voice was that of a man — of a Frenchman. Could not distinguish the words uttered. They were loud and quick — [b]unequal — spoken[b] apparently in fear as well as in anger. The voice was harsh — not so much shrill as harsh. Could not call it a shrill voice. The gruff voice said repeatedly *'sacré,'*[c] *'diable,'* and once *'mon Dieu.'*

"*Jules Mignaud,* banker, of the firm of Mignaud et Fils, Rue Deloraine. Is the elder Mignaud. Madame L'Espanaye had some property. Had opened an account with his banking house in the spring of the year ——— (eight years previously). Made frequent deposits[d] in small sums. Had checked for nothing until the third day before her death, when she took out in person the sum of 4000 francs. This sum was paid in gold, and a clerk sent home with the money.

"*Adolphe Le Bon,* clerk to[e] Mignaud et Fils, deposes that on the day in question, about noon, he accompanied Madame L'Espanaye to her residence with the 4000 francs, put up in two bags. Upon the door being opened, Mademoiselle L. appeared and took from his hands one of the bags, while the old lady relieved him of the other. He then bowed and departed. Did not see any person in the street at the time. It is a bye-street[f] — very lonely.

"*William Bird,* tailor, deposes that he was one of the party who entered the house. Is an Englishman. Has lived in Paris two years. Was one of the first to ascend the stairs. Heard the voices in contention. The gruff voice was that of a Frenchman. Could make out several words, but cannot now remember all. Heard distinctly *'sacré'*[g] and *'mon Dieu.'* There was a sound at the moment as if of several persons struggling — a scraping and scuffling sound. The shrill voice was very loud — louder than the gruff one. Is sure that

---

b . . . b   unequal — sometimes quick, sometimes deliberate — spoken *(A, B)*
c   *'sacre'* *(A)*
d   deposites *(A, B)*
e   to Messieurs *(A)*
f   bye street *(A, B, C)*
g   *'sacre'* *(A)*

TALES, 1841–1842

it was not the voice of an Englishman. Appeared to be that of a German. Might have been a woman's voice. ^hDoes not understand German.^h

"Four of the above-named witnesses, being recalled, deposed that the door of the chamber in which was found the body of Mademoiselle L.. was locked on the inside when the party reached it. Every thing was perfectly silent — no groans or noises of any kind. Upon forcing the door no person was seen. The windows, both of the back and front room, were down and firmly fastened from within. A door between the two rooms was closed, but not locked. The door leading from the front room into the passage was ⁱlocked, with the key on the inside.ⁱ A small room in the front of the house, on the fourth story, at the head of the passage, was^j open, the door being ajar. This room was crowded with old beds, boxes, and so forth. These were carefully removed and searched. There was not an inch of any portion of the house which was not carefully searched. Sweeps were sent up and down the chimneys. The house was a four story one, with garrets (*mansardes.*)^k A trap-door^l on the roof was nailed down very securely — did not appear to have been opened for years. The time elapsing between the hearing of the voices in contention and the breaking open of^m the room door, was variously stated by the witnesses. Some made it as short as three minutes — some as long as five. The door was opened with difficulty.

"*Alfonzo Garcio,* undertaker, deposesⁿ that he resides in the Rue Morgue.^o Is a native of Spain. Was one of the party who entered the house. Did not proceed up stairs. Is nervous, and was apprehensive of the consequences of agitation. Heard the voices in contention. The gruff voice was that of a Frenchman. Could not distinguish what was said. The shrill voice was that of an Englishman — is sure of this. Does not understand the English language, but judges by the intonation.

---

h . . . h *Inserted (A)*

i . . . i <open — not wide open, but ajar.> ↑ locked with the key on the inside. ↓ *(A)*

j was <also> *(A)*

k ↑ *(mansardes).* ↓ *(A)*

l trap door *(A, B)*

m *Omitted (A)*

n deposed *(A)*

o < — (the street of the murder.)> <↑Trianon. ↓ > ↑ Morgue. ↓ *(A)*

THE MURDERS IN THE RUE MORGUE

[p]"*Alberto Montani,* confectioner, deposes that he was among the first to ascend the stairs. Heard the voices in question. The gruff voice was that of a Frenchman. Distinguished several words. The speaker appeared to be expostulating. Could not make out the words of the shrill voice.[q] Spoke quick and unevenly. Thinks it the voice of a Russian. Corroborates the general testimony. Is an Italian. Never conversed with a native of Russia.[p]

"Several witnesses, recalled, here testified that the chimneys of all the rooms on the fourth story were too narrow to admit the passage of a human being. By 'sweeps' were meant cylindrical[r] sweeping-brushes, such as are employed by those who clean chimneys. These brushes were passed up and down every flue in the house. There is no back passage by which any one could have descended while the party proceeded up stairs. The body of Mademoiselle L'Espanaye was so firmly wedged in the chimney that it could not be got down until four or five of[s] the party united their strength.

"*Paul Dumas,* physician, deposes that he was called to view the bodies about day-break. They were both then[t] lying on the sacking of the bedstead in the chamber where Mademoiselle L. was found. The corpse of the young lady was much bruised and excoriated. The fact that it had been thrust up the chimney would sufficiently account for these appearances. The throat was greatly chafed. There were several deep scratches just below the chin, together with a series of livid spots which were evidently the impression of fingers. The face was fearfully discolored, and the eye-balls protruded. The tongue had been partially bitten through. A large bruise was discovered upon the pit of the stomach, produced, apparently, by the pressure of a knee. In the opinion of M. Dumas, Mademoiselle L'Espanaye had been throttled to death by some person or persons unknown. The corpse of the mother was horribly mutilated. All the bones of the right leg and arm were more or less shattered. The left *tibia*[u] much splintered, as well as all the ribs of the left side. Whole body dreadfully bruised and discolored.

---

p . . . p *Inserted in the margin (A)*
q ↑ voice. ↓ *(A)*
r ↑ cylindrical ↓ *(A)*
s or *(B) misprint*
t both then/then both *(A)*
u tibia *(A, B)*

TALES, 1841–1842

It was not possible to say how the injuries had been inflicted. A heavy club of wood, or a broad bar of iron — a chair — any large, heavy, and obtuse weapon would[v] have produced such results, if wielded by the hands of a very powerful man. No woman could have inflicted the blows with any weapon. The head of the deceased, when seen by witness, was entirely separated from the body, and was also greatly shattered. The throat had evidently been cut with some very sharp instrument — probably with a razor.

"*Alexandre Etienne,* surgeon, was called with M. Dumas to view the bodies. Corroborated the testimony, and the opinions of M. Dumas.

"Nothing farther of importance was elicited, although several other persons were examined. A murder so mysterious, and so perplexing in all its particulars, was never before committed in Paris — if indeed a murder has been committed at all. The police are entirely at fault — an unusual occurrence in affairs of this nature. There is not, however, the shadow of a clew[w] apparent."

The evening edition of the paper stated that the greatest excitement still continued in the Quartier St. Roch[x] — that the premises in question had been carefully re-searched, and fresh examinations of witnesses instituted, but all to no purpose. A postscript, however, mentioned that Adolphe Le Bon had been arrested and imprisoned — although nothing appeared to criminate him, beyond the facts already detailed.

Dupin seemed singularly interested in the progress of this affair — at least so I judged from his manner, for he made no comments.[y] It was only after the announcement that Le Bon had been imprisoned, that he asked me my opinion respecting the murders.[z]

I could merely agree with all Paris in considering them[a] an insoluble mystery.[b] I saw no means by which it would be possible to trace[c] the murderer.

"We must not judge of the means," said Dupin, "by this shell[d]

---

v   could *(A)*
w   clue *(A)*
x   <Rue Trianon> ↑ Quartier St. Roch ↓ *(A)*
y   comments whatever. *(A, B)*
z   the murders./it. *(A, B, C)*

a   it *(A, B, C)*
b   *After this:* <In regard to the perpetrator of the butchery> *(A)*
c   trace <him> *(A)*
d   <*bizarrerie*> ↑ shell ↓ *(A)*

THE MURDERS IN THE RUE MORGUE

of an examination. The Parisian police, so much extolled for *acumen,*[e] are cunning, but no more. There is no method in their proceedings, beyond the method of the moment. [f]They make a vast parade of measures; but, not unfrequently, these are so ill[g] adapted to the objects[h] proposed, as to put us in mind of Monsieur Jourdain's calling for his *robe-de-chambre*[i] — *pour mieux entendre la musique.*[f] [27] The results attained by them are not unfrequently surprising, but, for the most part, are brought about by simple diligence and activity. When these qualities are unavailing, their schemes fail. Vidocq, for example,[j] was a good guesser, and a persevering man.[28] But, without[k] educated thought, he erred continually by the very intensity of his investigations. He impaired his vision by holding the object too close. He might see, perhaps, one or two points with unusual clearness, but in so doing he, necessarily, lost sight of the matter as a whole. Thus there is such a thing as being too profound. Truth is[l] not always[m] in a well. In fact, as regards the more[n] important knowledge, I do believe that she is invariably superficial. The depth lies[o] in the valleys where we seek her, and not[p] upon the mountain-tops[q] where she is found.[29] The modes and sources of this kind of error are well typified in the contemplation of[r] the heavenly bodies. To look at a star by glances — to view it in a side-long[s] way, by turning toward[t] it the exterior portions of the *retina*[u] (more susceptible of feeble impressions of light than the interior), is to behold the star distinctly — is to have the best appreciation of its lustre — a lustre which grows dim just in proportion as we turn our vision *fully* upon it. A greater number of rays actually fall upon the eye in the latter case, but, in the former, there is the more refined capacity for comprehension. By undue profundity we perplex and enfeeble thought; and it is possi-

---

e   acumen, *(A, B)*
f . . . f   *Inserted in right-hand margin (A)*
g   illy *(A, B)*
h   <results> ↑ objects ↓ *(A)*
i   *robe de chambre (A)*
j   ↑ for example ↓ *(A)*
k   without <an> *(A)*
l   <does> ↑ is ↓ *(A)*
m   always <lie> *(A)*

n   <most> ↑ more ↓ *(A)*
o   lies <oftener> *(A)*
p   <than> ↑ and not ↓ *(A)*
q   mountain tops *(A, B)*
r   of <a star> *(A)*
s   side long *(A)*
t   towards *(A)*
u   retina <is to see it distinctly — is> *(A);* retina *(B)*

TALES, 1841–1842

ble to make even Venus herself vanish from the firmament by a scrutiny too sustained, too concentrated, or[v] too direct.[30]

"As for these murders, let us enter into some examinations for ourselves, before we make up an opinion respecting them. An inquiry will afford us amusement," [I thought this an odd term, so applied, but said nothing] "and, besides, Le Bon once rendered me a service for which I am not ungrateful. We will go and see the premises with our own eyes. I know G —— ,[31] the [w]Prefect of Police,[w] and shall have no difficulty in obtaining the necessary permission."

The[x] permission was obtained, and we proceeded at once to the Rue Morgue. This is one of those miserable thoroughfares which intervene between the Rue Richelieu and the Rue St. Roch. It was late in the afternoon when we reached it; as[y] this quarter[z] is at a great distance from that in which we resided. The house was[a] readily found; for there were still many persons gazing up at the closed shutters, with an objectless curiosity, from the opposite side of the way. It was an ordinary[b] Parisian house, with a gateway, on one side of which was a glazed watch-box, with a sliding panel in the window, indicating a *loge de concierge*. Before going in we walked up the street, turned down an alley, and then, again turning, passed in the rear of the building — Dupin, meanwhile, examining the whole neighborhood, as well as the house, with a minuteness of attention for which I could see no possible object.

Retracing our steps, we came again to the front of the dwelling, rang, and, having shown our credentials, were admitted by the agents in charge. We went up stairs — into the chamber where the body of Mademoiselle L'Espanaye had been found, and where both the deceased still lay. The disorders of the room had, as usual, been suffered to exist. I saw nothing beyond what had been stated in the [c]"Gazette des Tribunaux." [c] Dupin scrutinized every thing — not excepting the bodies of the victims. We then went into the other rooms, and into the yard; a *gendarme*[d] accompanying us

---

v   and *(A, B)*
w ...w   *Préfêt de Police, (A, B)*
x   This *(A, B)*
y   it; as/it for *(A, B)*
z   Quartier *(A)*

a   we *(A, B)*
b   ordinary <French hou> *(A)*
c ...c   "Tribunal." *(A, B, C)*
d   gendarme *(A, B)*

THE MURDERS IN THE RUE MORGUE

throughout. The[e] examination occupied us until dark, when we took our departure. [f]On our way home my companion stepped in for a moment at the office of one of the daily papers.[f]

I have said that the whims of my friend were manifold, and that *Je les ménageais:*[g] — for this phrase there is no English equivalent.[32] It was his humor, now, to decline all conversation on the subject of the murder, until[h] about [i]noon the next day.[i] He then asked me, suddenly, if I had observed any thing *peculiar* at the scene of the atrocity.

There was something in his manner of emphasizing the word "peculiar," which caused me to shudder, without knowing why.

"No, nothing *peculiar*," I said; "nothing more, at least, than we both saw stated in the paper."

[j] "The 'Gazette,' " [j] he replied, "has not entered, I fear, into the unusual horror of the thing. But dismiss[k] the idle opinions of this print. It appears to me that this mystery is considered insoluble, for the very reason[l] which should cause it to be regarded as easy of solution — I mean for the *outré* character of its features. The police are confounded by the seeming absence of motive — not for the murder itself — but for the atrocity of the murder. They are [m]puzzled, too, by[m] the seeming impossibility of reconciling the voices heard in contention, with the facts that no one was discovered up stairs but the assassinated Mademoiselle L'Espanaye, and that there were no means of egress without the notice of the party ascending. The wild disorder of the room; the corpse thrust, with the head downward,[n] up the chimney; the frightful mutilation of the body of the old lady; these considerations, with those just mentioned, and others which I need not mention, have sufficed to paralyze the powers, by putting completely at fault the boasted *acumen*,[o] of the government agents. They have fallen into the gross but common[p] error of confounding the unusual with the

---

e   Our *(A, B, C)*
f . . . f   *Inserted in right-hand margin (A)*
g   *menagais: (A, B); ménagais (C, D, E, F)*
h   until after we had taken a bottle of wine together *(A, B, C)*
i . . . i   <midnight.> ↑ noon the next

day. ↓ *(A)*
j . . . j   "Le Tribunal," *(A, B, C)*
k   we will not revert to *(A, B)*
l   reasons *(A)*
m . . . m   puzzled by *(A, B, C)*
n   downwards *(A)*
o   acumen, *(A, B)*
p   ↑ but common ↓ *(A)*

TALES, 1841–1842

abstruse. But it is by these deviations from the[q] plane of the ordinary, that[r] reason feels its way, if at all, in its search for[s] the
true.[33] In investigations such as we are now pursuing, it should not
be so much[t] asked 'what has occurred,' as[u] 'what has occurred that[v]
has never occurred before.' [w] In fact, the facility with which I shall
arrive, or have arrived, at the solution of this mystery, is in [x]the
direct ratio of[x] its apparent insolubility in the eyes of the police."

I stared at the speaker in mute astonishment.[y]

"I am now awaiting," continued he, looking toward[z] the door
of our apartment — "I am now awaiting a person who, although
perhaps not the perpetrator of these butcheries, must have been[a]
in some measure implicated in their perpetration. Of the worst
portion of the crimes committed, it is probable that he is innocent.
I hope that I am right in this supposition; for upon it I build my
expectation of reading the entire riddle. I look for the man here —
in this room — every moment. It is true that he may not arrive; but
the probability is that he will. Should he come, it will be necessary
to detain him. Here are pistols; and we both know how to use
them when[b] occasion demands their use."

I took the pistols, scarcely knowing what I did, or believing
what I heard, while Dupin went on, very much as if in a soliloquy.
I have already spoken of his abstract manner at such times. His
discourse was addressed to myself; but his voice, although by no
means loud, had that intonation which is commonly employed in
speaking to some one at a great distance. His eyes, vacant in expression, regarded only the wall.

"That the voices heard in contention," he said, "by the party
upon the stairs, were not the voices of the women themselves, was
fully proved by the evidence. This relieves us of all doubt upon

---

q the common-place — by these
prominences from the *(A)*
r that <true> *(A)*
s after *(A, B)*
t ↑ so much ↓ *(A)*
u <but> ↑ as ↓ *(A)*
v which *(A, B, C)*
w *After this:* <Just in proportion as
this matter has appeared insoluble to
the police, has been that facility with

which I have arrived at its
solution.> *(A)*
x . . . x an exact ratio with *(A);* exact
ratio with *(B, C)*
y *After this:* He continued. *(A, B, C)*
z towards *(A)*
a ↑ been ↓ *(A)*
b when <the> *(A) deletion is made
in pencil*

THE MURDERS IN THE RUE MORGUE

the question whether the old lady[c] could have first destroyed the daughter, and afterward[d] have committed suicide. I speak of this point chiefly for the sake of method; for the strength of Madame L'Espanaye would have been utterly unequal to the task of thrusting her daughter's corpse up the chimney as it was found; and the nature of the wounds upon her own person entirely preclude the idea of self-destruction. Murder, then, has been committed by some third party; and the voices of this third party were those heard in contention. Let me now advert — not to the whole testimony respecting these voices — but to what was *peculiar*[e] in that testimony. Did you observe any thing peculiar about it?"

I remarked that, while all the witnesses agreed in supposing the gruff voice to be that of a Frenchman, there was much disagreement in regard to the shrill, or, as one individual termed it, the harsh voice.

"That was the evidence itself," said Dupin, "but it was not the peculiarity of the evidence. You have observed nothing distinctive.[f] Yet there *was* something to be observed.[g] The witnesses, as you remark, agreed about the gruff voice; they were here unanimous. But in regard to the shrill voice, the peculiarity is — not that they disagreed — but that, while an Italian, an Englishman, a Spaniard, a Hollander, and a Frenchman attempted to describe it, each one spoke of it as that *of a foreigner*. Each is sure that it was not the voice of one of his own countrymen. Each likens it — not to the voice of an individual of any nation with whose language he is conversant — but the converse. The Frenchman supposes it the voice of a Spaniard, and 'might have distinguished some words *had he been acquainted with the Spanish*.' The Dutchman maintains it[h] to have been that of a Frenchman; but we find it stated that '*not understanding French this witness was examined through an interpreter*.' The Englishman thinks it the voice of a German, and '*does not understand German*.' The Spaniard 'is sure' that it was[i] that of

---

c   ↑ lady ↓ *(A)*
d   afterwards *(A)*
e   peculiar *(A, B)*
f   *After this:* Re-employing my own words I may say that you have pointed out no prominence above the plane of

the ordinary, by which reason may feel her way. *(A, B, C) Except* its way *for* her way *(C)*
g   pointed out. *(A, B, C)*
h   <the voice> ↑ it ↓ *(A)*
i   is *(A, B, C)*

TALES, 1841–1842

an Englishman, but 'judges by the intonation' altogether, *'as he has no knowledge of the English.'* The Italian believes it the voice of a Russian, but *'has never conversed with a native of Russia.'* A second Frenchman differs, moreover, with the first, and is positive that the voice was[j] that of an Italian; but, *not being cognizant of that tongue,* is, like the Spaniard, 'convinced by the intonation.' Now, how strangely unusual must that voice have really been, about which such testimony as this *could* have been elicited[k]! — in whose *tones,* even, denizens of the five great divisions of Europe could recognise nothing familiar! You will say that it might have been the voice of an Asiatic — of an African. Neither Asiatics nor Africans abound in Paris; but, without[l] denying the inference, I will[m] now merely call your attention to three points.[n] The voice is termed by one witness 'harsh rather than shrill.' It is represented by two others to have been 'quick and *unequal.'* No words — no sounds[o] resembling words — were[p] by any witness mentioned as distinguishable.

"I know not," continued Dupin, "what impression I may have made, so far, upon your own understanding; but I do not hesitate to say that legitimate deductions even from this portion of the testimony — the portion respecting the gruff and shrill voices — are in themselves sufficient to engender a suspicion which should[q] give direction to all farther[r] progress in the investigation of the mystery. I said 'legitimate deductions;' but my meaning is not thus fully expressed. I designed to imply that the deductions are[s] the *sole* proper ones, and that the suspicion arises[t] *inevitably* from them as the single result. What the suspicion is, however, I will not say just yet. I merely wish you to bear in mind that, with myself, it was sufficiently forcible to give a definite form — a certain ten-dency — to my inquiries in the chamber.

"Let us now transport ourselves, in fancy, to this[u] chamber.

---

j   is *(A, B, C)*
k   \<given\> ↑ elicited ↓ *(A)*
l   not [*erasure*] ↑ without ↓ *(A)*
m   will just *(A, B, C)*
n   points which have relation to this topic. *(A, B, C)*
o   no sounds/\<nothing\> ↑ no

sounds ↓ *(A)*
p   \<was\> ↑ were ↓ *(A)*
q   should bias, or *(A, B, C)*
r   further *(A)*
s   were *(A, B, C)*
t   arose *(A, B, C)*
u   that *(A, B)*

THE MURDERS IN THE RUE MORGUE

What shall we first seek here? The means of egress employed by the murderers. It is not too much to say that[v] neither of us believe in præternatural events. Madame and Mademoiselle L'Espanaye were not destroyed by spirits. The doers of the[w] deed were material, and escaped materially. Then how? Fortunately, there is but one mode of reasoning upon the[x] point, and that mode *must* lead us to a definite decision. — Let us examine, each by each, the possible means of egress. It is clear that the assassins were in the room where [y]Mademoiselle L'Espanaye was found,[y] or at least in the room adjoining, when the party ascended the stairs. It is then only from these two apartments that we have to seek[z] issues. The police have laid bare the floors, the ceilings, and the masonry of the walls, in every direction. No *secret* issues could have escaped their vigilance. But, not trusting to *their*[a] eyes, I examined with my own. There were, then, *no* secret issues. Both doors leading from the rooms into the passage were securely locked, with the keys inside. Let us turn to the chimneys. These, although of ordinary width for some eight or ten feet above the hearths, will not admit, throughout their extent, the body of a large cat. The impossibility of egress, by[b] means already stated,[c] being thus absolute, we are reduced to the windows. Through those of the front room no one could have escaped without notice from the crowd in the street. The murderers *must* have passed, then, through those of the back room. Now, brought to this conclusion in so unequivocal a manner as we are, it is not our part, as reasoners, to reject it on account of apparent impossibilities. It is only left for us to prove that these apparent[d] 'impossibilities' [e]are, in reality,[e] not such.

"There are two windows in the chamber. One of them is unobstructed by furniture, and is wholly visible. The lower portion of the other is hidden from view by the head of the unwieldy bedstead which is thrust close up against it. The former was found securely fastened from within. It resisted the utmost force of those

---

v   that we *(A, B)*
w   the dark *(A, B, C)*
x   this *(A)*
y . . . y   <the crime was committed,>
↑ Mademoiselle l'Espanaye was found, ↓ *(A)*

z   seek for *(A, B, C)*
a   their *(A, B)*
b   by the *(A)*
c   ↑ stated ↓ *(A)*
d   *Omitted (A, B)*
e . . . e   are *(A, B)*

· 5 5 1 ·

TALES, 1841–1842

who endeavored to raise it. A large gimlet-hole had been pierced in its frame to the left, and a very stout nail was found fitted therein, nearly to the head. Upon examining the other window, a similar nail was seen similarly fitted in it; and a vigorous attempt to raise this sash^e′ failed also. The police were now entirely satisfied that egress had not been^f in these directions. And, *therefore,* it was thought a matter of supererogation to withdraw the nails and open the windows.

"My own examination was somewhat more particular, and was so for the reason I have just given — because here it was, I knew, that all apparent impossibilities *must* be proved to be not such in reality.

"I proceeded to think thus — *à^g posteriori.* The murderers *did* escape from one of these windows. This being so, they could not have re-fastened the sashes from the inside, as they were found fastened; — the consideration which put a stop, through its obviousness, to the scrutiny of the police in this quarter. Yet the sashes *were* fastened. They *must,* then, have the power of fastening themselves. There was no escape from this conclusion. I stepped to the unobstructed casement, withdrew the nail with some difficulty, and attempted to raise the sash. It resisted all my efforts, as I had^h anticipated. A concealed spring must, I now knew, exist; and this corroboration of my idea convinced me that my premises, at least, were correct, however mysterious still appeared the circumstances attending the nails. A careful search soon brought to light the hidden spring. I pressed it, and, satisfied with the discovery, forbore to upraise the sash.

"I now replaced the nail and regarded it attentively. A person passing out through this window might have reclosed it, and the spring would have caught — but the nail could not have been replaced. The conclusion was plain, and again narrowed in the field of my investigations. The assassins *must* have escaped through the other window. Supposing, then, the springs upon each sash to be the same, as was probable, there *must* be found a difference be-

---

e′   sash, *(C, D, E, F)*
corrected from A, B
f   been <made> *(A)*

g   *a (A, B)*
h   ↑ had ↓ *(A)*

THE MURDERS IN THE RUE MORGUE

tween the nails, or at least between the modes of their fixture. Getting upon the sacking of the bedstead, I looked over the head-board minutely at the second casement. Passing my hand[i] down behind the board, I readily discovered and pressed the spring, which was, as I had supposed, identical in character with its neighbor. I now looked at the nail. It was as stout as the other, and apparently fitted in in[j] the same manner — driven in nearly up to the head.

"You will say that I was puzzled; but, if you think so, you must have misunderstood the nature of the inductions. To use a sporting phrase, I had not [k]been once[k] 'at fault.' The scent had never for an instant been lost. There was no flaw in any link of the chain. I had traced[l] the secret to its ultimate result, — and that result was *the nail*. It had, I say, in every respect, the appearance of its fellow in the other window; but this fact was an absolute nullity (conclusive as it might seem to be) when compared with the consideration that here, at this point, terminated the clew.[m] 'There *must* be something wrong,' I said, 'about the[n] nail.' I touched it; and the head, with about a quarter[o] of an inch of the shank, came off in my fingers. The rest of the shank was in the gimlet-hole, where it had been broken off. [p]The fracture was an old one (for its edges were incrusted with rust), and[p] had apparently been accomplished by the blow of a hammer, which had partially imbedded, in the top of the bottom sash, the head portion of the nail. I now carefully replaced this head portion in the indentation whence I had taken it, and the resemblance to a perfect nail was [q]complete — the fissure was invisible.[q] [r]Pressing the spring, I[r] gently raised the sash for a few inches; the head went up with it, remaining firm in its bed. I closed the window, and the semblance of the whole nail was again perfect.

"The riddle, so far, was now unriddled. The assassin[s] had escaped through the window which looked upon the bed. Dropping[s']

---

i   arm *(A)*
j   *Omitted (B, C, D, E, F) restored from manuscript (A)*
k . . . k ↑ been ↓ once <been> *(A)*
l   tracked *(A)*
m   clue. *(A)*
n   this *(A)*

o   a quarter/the eighth *(A, B)*
p . . . p *Written over an erasure in A*
q . . . q complete. *(A, B, C)*
r . . . r I *(A, B)*
s   assassins *(A, B, C)*
s'   Droping *(D, E, F) misprint*

TALES, 1841–1842

of its own accord upon his^t exit (or perhaps purposely closed),^u it had become fastened by the spring; and it was the retention of this spring which had been mistaken by the police for that of the nail, — farther inquiry being thus considered unnecessary.

"The next question is that of the mode of descent. Upon this point I had been^v satisfied in my walk with you around the building. About ^wfive feet and a half^w from the casement in question there runs^x a lightning-rod. From this rod it would have been impossible for any one to reach the window itself, to say nothing of entering it. I observed, however, that the shutters of the fourth story were of the peculiar kind called by Parisian carpenters *ferrades* — a kind rarely employed at the present day, but frequently seen upon very old mansions^y at Lyons and Bourdeaux. They are in the form of an ordinary door, (a single, not a folding door) except that the upper^z half is latticed or worked in open trellis — thus affording an excellent hold for the hands. In the present instance these shutters are fully three feet and a half broad. When we saw them from the rear of the house, they were both about half open — that is to say, they stood off at right angles from the wall. It is probable that the police, as well as myself, examined the back of the tenement; but, if so, in looking at these *ferrades* in the line of their breadth (as they must have done), they did not perceive this great breadth itself, or, at all events, failed to take it into due consideration. In fact, having once satisfied themselves that no egress could have been made in this quarter, they would naturally bestow here a very cursory examination. It was clear to me, however, that the shutter belonging to the window at the head of the bed, would, if swung fully ^aback to the wall,^a reach to within two feet^b of the lightning-rod. It was also evident that, by exertion of a very unusual degree of activity and courage, an entrance into the window,^c from the rod, might have been thus effected. — By reaching to the distance of two^d feet and a half (we now suppose the shutter

---

t their *(A, B, C)*	y <houses> ↑ mansions ↓ *(A)*
u closed by them) *(A, B, C)*	z lower *(A, B, C, D, F)*
v been <sufficiently> *(A)*	a . . . a open, *(A)*
w . . . w <six feet> < ↑ eight ↓ >	b two feet/four feet and a half *(A)*
↑ five feet and a half ↓ *(A)*	c window, <might have> *(A)*
x ran *(A, B)*	d <four> two *(A)*

THE MURDERS IN THE RUE MORGUE

open to its whole extent) a robber might have taken a firm grasp upon the trellis-work. Letting go, then, his hold upon the rod, placing his feet securely[e] against the wall, and springing boldly from it, he might have swung the shutter so as to close it, and, if we imagine the window open at the time, might even have swung himself into the room.

"I wish you to bear especially in mind that I have spoken of a *very* unusual degree of activity as requisite to success in so hazardous and so difficult a feat. It is my design to show you, first, that the thing might possibly have been accomplished: — but, secondly and *chiefly,* I wish to impress upon your understanding the *very extraordinary* — the almost præternatural character of that agility which could have accomplished it.

"You will say, no doubt, using the language of the law, that 'to make out my case,' I should rather undervalue, than insist upon a full estimation of the activity required in this matter. This may be the practice in law, but it is not the usage of reason. My ultimate object is only the truth. My immediate purpose is to lead you to place in juxta-position, that *very unusual* activity of which I have just spoken, with[f] that *very peculiar* shrill (or harsh) and *unequal* voice, about whose nationality[g] no two persons could be found to agree, and in whose utterance no syllabification[h] could be detected."

At these words a vague and half-formed conception of the meaning of Dupin flitted over my mind. I seemed to be upon the verge of comprehension, without power to comprehend — as men, at times, find themselves upon the brink of remembrance, without being able, in the end, to remember. My friend went on with his discourse.[i]

"You will see," he said, "that I have shifted the question from the mode of egress to that of ingress.[j] It was my design to suggest[k] the idea that both were effected in the same manner, at the same point. Let us now revert[l] to the interior of the room. Let us survey

---

e firmly *(A, B)*
f <and> ↑ with ↓ *(A)*
g <language> ↑ nationality ↓ *(A)*
h syllabi ↑ fi ↓ cation *(A)*
i discourse. <for it had now assumed

all the character of such.> *(A)*
j <ingress> *not clear* ingress. *(A)*
k convey *(A, B, C, D, F)*
l revert in fancy *(A, B, C)*

TALES, 1841–1842

the appearances here. The drawers of the bureau, it is said, had been rifled, although many articles of apparel still remained within them. The conclusion here is absurd. It is a mere guess — a very silly one — and no more. How are we to know that the articles found in the drawers were not all these drawers had originally contained? Madame L'Espanaye and her daughter lived an exceedingly retired life — saw no company — seldom went out — had little use for numerous changes of habiliment. Those found were at least of as good quality as any likely to be possessed by these ladies. If a thief had taken any, why did he not take the best — why did he not take all? In a word, why did he abandon four thousand francs in gold to encumber himself with a bundle of linen? The gold *was* abandoned. Nearly the whole sum mentioned by Monsieur Mignaud, the banker, was discovered, in bags, upon the floor. I wish you, therefore, to discard from your thoughts the blundering idea of *motive*,[m] engendered in the brains of the police by that portion of the evidence which speaks of money delivered at the door of the house. Coincidences ten times as remarkable as this (the delivery of the money, and murder committed within three days upon the party receiving it), happen to[n] all of us every hour[o] of our lives, without attracting even[p] momentary notice. Coincidences, in general, are great stumbling-blocks in the way of that class of thinkers who have been educated to know nothing[q] of the theory of probabilities — that theory to which the most glorious objects of human research are indebted for the most glorious of illustration. In the present instance, had the gold been gone, the fact of its delivery three days before would have formed something more than a coincidence. It would have been corroborative of this idea of motive. But, under the real circumstances of the case, if we are to suppose gold the motive of this outrage, we must also imagine the perpetrator so vacillating an idiot as to have abandoned his gold and his motive together.

"Keeping now steadily in mind the points to which I have drawn your attention — that peculiar voice, that unusual agility,

---

m   *motive* <which has been> *(A)*
n   to each and *(A, B)*
o   <day> ↑ hour ↓ *(A)*

p   even a *(A, B, C)*
q   nothing and care less *(A, B, C)*

THE MURDERS IN THE RUE MORGUE

and that startling absence of motive in a murder[r] so singularly atrocious as this — let us glance at the butchery itself. Here is a woman strangled to death by manual strength, and thrust up a chimney, head downward.[s] Ordinary assassins employ no such modes of murder as this. Least of all, do they thus dispose of the murdered. In the manner of thrusting the corpse up the chimney, you will admit that there was something *excessively outré* — something altogether irreconcilable with our common notions of human action, even when we suppose the actors the most depraved of men. Think, too, how great[t] must have been[u] that strength which could have thrust the body *up* such an aperture so forcibly that the united vigor of several persons was found barely sufficient to drag it *down!*

[v]"Turn, now, to other indications of the employment of a vigor most marvellous. On the hearth[w] were thick tresses — very thick tresses — of grey human hair. These had been [x]torn out by the roots.[x] You are aware of the great force necessary in tearing thus from the head even twenty or thirty hairs together. You saw the locks in question as well as myself. Their roots (a hideous sight!) were clotted with fragments of the flesh of the scalp — sure token of the prodigious power[y] which had been exerted in uprooting perhaps half[z] a million of hairs at a time.[34] The throat of the old lady was not merely cut, but the head absolutely severed from the body: the instrument was a mere razor.[a] I wish you also to look[b] at the *brutal*[c] ferocity of these deeds. Of the bruises upon the body of Madame L'Espanaye I do not speak. Monsieur Dumas, and his worthy coadjutor Monsieur Etienne, have pronounced that they were inflicted by some obtuse instrument; and so far these gentlemen are very correct. The obtuse instrument was clearly the stone pavement in the yard, upon which the victim had fallen from the window which looked in upon the bed. This idea, however simple

---

r butchery *(A)*
s downwards. *(A)*
t how great/what *(A, B, C)*
u been the degree of *(A, B, C)*
v *Not a new paragraph in A*
w <sacking of the bedstead>
↑ hearth ↓ *(A)*
x . . . x *torn out by the roots. (A, B, C)*

y ↑ power ↓ *(A)*
z *Omitted (A, B, C)*
a *After this:* Here again we have evidence of that vastness of strength upon which I would fix your attention. *(A, B, C)*
b look, and to look steadily *(A, B, C)*
c brutal *(A)*

TALES, 1841–1842

it may now seem, escaped the police for the same reason that the breadth of the shutters escaped them — because, by the affair of the nails, their perceptions had been hermetically sealed against the possibility of the windows having ever been opened at all.

"If now, in addition to all these things, you have properly reflected upon the odd disorder of the chamber, we have gone so far as to combine the ideas of ᵈan agility astounding, a strength superhuman,ᵈ a ferocity brutal, a butchery without motive, a *grotesquerie*ᵉ in horror absolutely alien from humanity, and a voice foreign in tone to the ears of menᶠ of many nations, and devoid of all distinct or intelligible syllabification. What result, then, has ensued? What impression have I made upon your fancy?"

I ᵍfelt a creeping of the fleshᵍ as Dupin asked me the question. "A madman," I said, "has done this deed — some raving maniac, escaped from a neighboring *Maison de Santé.*"

"In some respects," he replied, "your idea is not irrelevant. But the voices of madmen, even in their wildest paroxysms, are never found to tally with that peculiar voice heard upon the stairs. Madmen are of some nation, and their language, however incoherent in its words, has always the coherence of syllabification. Besides, the hair of a madman is not suchʰ as I now hold in my hand. I disentangled this little tuft from the ⁱrigidly clutched fingersⁱ of Madame L'Espanaye. Tell me what you can make of it."

"Dupin!"ʲ I said, completely unnerved; "this hair is most unusual — this is no *human* hair."

"I have not asserted that it is,"ᵏ said he; "but, before we decideˡ this point, I wish you to glance atᵐ the little sketchⁿ I have here traced upon this paper. It is a *fac-simile*ᵒ drawing of what has been described in one portion of the testimony as 'dark bruises, and deep indentations of finger nails,'ᵖ upon the throat of Mademoiselle

---

d . . . d   a strength superhuman, an agility astounding, *(A, B, C)*
e   grotesquerie *(A)*
f   man *(A) uncertain*
g . . . g   shuddered *(A, B, C)*
h   such hair *(A, B, C)*
i . . . i   among the tresses remaining upon the head *(A, B, C)*

j   "Dupin!"/"Good God," *(A, B, C)*
k   was," *(A, B, C)*
l   decide upon *(A, B)*
m   <your eyes> upon *(A)*
n   sketch which *(B, C)*
o   fac-simile *(A, B, C)*
p   finger-nails' *(A)*

THE MURDERS IN THE RUE MORGUE

L'Espanaye, and in another, (by Messrs.[q] Dumas and Etienne,) as a 'series of livid spots, evidently the impression of fingers.'

"You will perceive," continued my friend, spreading out the paper upon the table before us, "that[r] this drawing gives the idea of a firm and fixed hold. There is no *slipping* apparent. Each finger has retained — possibly until the death of the victim — the fearful grasp by which it originally imbedded itself. Attempt, now, to place all your fingers, at[s] the same time, in the respective[t] impressions as you see them."

I made the attempt in vain.

"We are possibly not giving this matter a fair trial," he said. "The paper is spread out upon a plane surface; but the human throat is cylindrical. Here is a billet of wood, the circumference of which is about that of the throat. Wrap the drawing around it, and try the experiment again."

I did so; but the difficulty was even more obvious than before. "This," I said, "is the mark of no human hand."

[u]"Read now," replied Dupin, "this[u] passage from Cuvier."[35]

It was a minute anatomical and generally descriptive account of the large fulvous[v] Ourang-Outang of the East Indian Islands. The gigantic stature, the prodigious strength and activity,[w] the wild ferocity, and the imitative propensities of these mammalia are sufficiently well known to all. I understood the full horrors[x] of the murder at once.

"The description of the digits," said I, as I made an end of reading, "is in exact accordance with this drawing. I see that no animal but an Ourang-Outang, of the species[y] here mentioned, could have impressed the indentations as you have traced them. This tuft of tawny[z] hair, too,[a] is identical in character with that of the beast of Cuvier. But I cannot possibly comprehend the particulars of this frightful mystery. Besides, there were *two*[b] voices

---

q   Messieurs *(A)*
r   "you will perceive that *(A, B, C)*
s   at one and *(A, B, C)*
t   *Omitted (A, B, C)*
u . . . u   "Assuredly it is not," replied Dupin — "read now this *(A, B, C)*
v   ↑ fulvous ↓ <tawny> *(A)*

w   ↑ and activity, ↓ *(A)*
x   horror *(A)*
y   class *(A)*
z   yellow *(A, B, C)*
a   hair, too,/hair *(A, B)*
b   two *(A, B)*

TALES, 1841–1842

heard in contention, and one of them was unquestionably the voice of a Frenchman."

"True; and you will remember an expression attributed almost unanimously, by the evidence, to this voice, — the expression, *'mon Dieu!'* This, under the circumstances, has been justly characterized by one of the witnesses ᶜ(Montani, the confectioner,)ᶜ as an expression of remonstrance or expostulation. Upon these two words, therefore, I have mainly built my hopes of a full solution of the riddle. A Frenchman was cognizant of the murder. It is possible — ᵈindeed it isᵈ far more than probable — that he was innocent of all participation in the bloody transactions which took place. The Ourang-Outang may have escaped from him. He may have traced it to theᵉ chamber; ᶠbut, under the agitating circumstances which ensued, he could never have re-captured it. It is still at large.ᶠ I will not pursue these guesses — for I have no right to call them moreᵍ — since the shades of reflection upon which they are based are scarcely of sufficient depth to be appreciable by my ownʰ intellect, and since I could not pretend to make them intelligible to the understanding of another.ⁱ We will call them guesses then,ʲ and speak of them as such. If the Frenchman in question isᵏ indeed, as I suppose, innocent of this atrocity, this advertisement, which I left last night, upon our return home, at the office of 'Le Monde,' ˡ(a paper devoted to the shipping interest, and much soughtᵐ by sailors,)ˡ will bring him to our residence."

He handed me a paper, and I read thus:

CAUGHTⁿ — *In the Bois de Boulogne, early in the morning of the — — inst., (the morning of the murder,) a very large, tawny*ᵒ *Ourang-Outang of the Bornese species. The owner, (who is ascertained to be a sailor, belonging to a Maltese vessel,) may have the animal again, upon identifying it satisfactorily, and paying a few*

---

c...c *Omitted (A)*
d...d it is indeed *(A)*
e this *(A, B)*
f...f *Inserted in left-hand margin (A)*
g more than <such> ↑ guesses ↓ *(A);* more than guesses *(B, C)*
h my own/own *(C) misprint*
i another than myself. *(A, B, C)*

j ↑ then, ↓ *(A)*
k be *(A, B)*
l...l *Inserted in right-hand margin (A)*
m sought for *(B, C)*
n <Found> ↑ CAUGHT ↓ *(A)*
o *tawny-colored (A, B, C)*

THE MURDERS IN THE RUE MORGUE

*charges arising from its capture and keeping. Call at No. —— , Rue
——,' Faubourg St. Germain — au troisième.*[p] [36]

"How was it possible," I asked, "that you should know the man
to be a sailor, and belonging to a Maltese vessel?"

"I do *not* know it," said Dupin. "I am not *sure* of it. Here,
however, is a small piece of ribbon, which[q] from its form, and from
its greasy appearance, [r]has evidently been[r] used in tying the hair
in one of[s] those long *queues* of which sailors are so fond. Moreover, this knot is one which few besides sailors can tie, and is peculiar to the Maltese. I picked the ribbon up at the foot of the
lightning-rod. It could not have belonged to either of the deceased.
Now if, after all, I am wrong in my induction from this ribbon, that
the Frenchman was a sailor belonging to a Maltese vessel, still I can
have done no harm in saying[t] what I did in the advertisement. If I
am in error, he will merely suppose that I have been misled by some
circumstance into which he will not take the trouble to inquire.
But if I am right, a great point is gained. Cognizant [u]although innocent of the murder,[u] the Frenchman will naturally hesitate
about replying to the advertisement — about demanding the
Ourang-Outang. He will reason thus: — 'I am innocent; I am poor;
my Ourang-Outang is of great value — to one in my circumstances
a fortune of itself — why should I lose it[v] through idle apprehen-
sions of danger? Here it is, within my grasp. It was found in the
Bois de Boulogne — at a vast distance from the scene of that butchery. How can it ever be suspected that a brute beast should have
done the deed? The police are at fault — they have failed to procure the slightest clew.[w] Should they even trace the animal, it
would be impossible to prove me cognizant of the murder, or to
implicate me in guilt on account of that cognizance. Above all, *I
am known.* The advertiser designates me as the possessor of the
beast. I am not sure to what limit[x] his knowledge may extend.
Should I avoid claiming a property of so great[y] value, which it is

---

p *troisieme. (A, B); troisiême. (C, D, E,
F)*
q which has evidently, *(A, B, C)*
r . . . r been *(A, B, C)*
s ↑ one of ↓ *(A)*
t stating *(A, B, C)*

u . . . u of the murder, although not
guilty, *(A, B, C)*
v <him> ↑ it ↓ *(A)*
w clue. *(A)*
x extent *(A)*
y great a *(A, B, C)*

TALES, 1841–1842

known that I possess, I will render ᶻthe animal at least,ᶻ liable to suspicion. It is not my policy to attract attention ªeither to myself orª to the beast. I will answer the advertisement, get the Ourang-Outang, and keep itᵇ close until this matter has blown over.' "

At this moment we heard a step upon the stairs.

"Be ready," said Dupin, "with your pistols, but neither ᶜuse them nor showᶜ them until at a signal from myself."

The front door of the house had been left open, and the visiter had entered, without ringing,ᵈ and advanced several steps upon the staircase. Now, however, he seemed to hesitate. Presently we heard him descending. Dupin was moving quickly to the door, when we again heard him coming up. He did not turn back a second time, but stepped up with decision,ᵉ and rapped at the door of our chamber.

"Come in," said Dupin, in a cheerful and hearty tone.

A manᶠ entered. He was a sailor, evidently, — a tall, stout, and muscular-looking person,ᵍ with a certain dare-devil expression of countenance, not altogether unprepossessing. His face, greatly sunburnt, was more than half hidden byʰ whisker and *mustachio*.ⁱ He had with himʲ a huge oaken cudgel, but appeared to be otherwise unarmed. He bowed awkwardly, and bade us "good evening," in French accents, which, although somewhat Neufchatel-ish,³⁷ were still sufficiently indicative of a Parisian origin.

"Sit down, my friend,"ᵏ said Dupin. "I suppose you have called about the Ourang-Outang. Upon my word, I almost envy you the possession of him; a remarkably fine, and no doubt a very valuable animal. How old do you suppose him to be?"

The sailor drew a long breath, with the air of a man relieved of some intolerable burden, and then replied, in an assured tone:

"I have no way of telling — but he can't be more than four or five years old. Have you got him here?"

---

z . . . z <the animal> at least ↑ the animal ↓ *(A)*
a . . . a ↑ either to myself or ↓ *(A)*
b <him> ↑ it ↓ *(A)*
c . . . c show them nor use *(B)*
d ringing or rapping, *(A, B, C)*
e with decision,/quickly *(A, B)*

f A man/The visiter *(A, B, C)*
g person,/man *(A, B)*; man, *(C)*
h by a world of *(A, B, C)*
i *mustache.* *(A)*
j *Omitted (A) a slip of the pen*
k freind," *(D, E, F) misprint*

THE MURDERS IN THE RUE MORGUE

"Oh no; we had no conveniences for keeping him here. He is at a livery stable in the Rue Dubourg, just by.[38] You can get him in the morning. Of course you are prepared to identify the property?"[l]

"To be sure I am, sir."

"I shall be sorry to part with him," said Dupin.

"I don't mean that you should be at all this trouble for nothing, sir," said the man. "Couldn't expect it. Am very willing to pay a reward for the finding of the animal — that is to say, any thing[m] in reason."

"Well," replied my friend, "that is all very fair, to be sure. Let me think! — what should I[n] have?[o] Oh! I will tell you. My reward shall be this. You shall give me all the information in your power about these murders[p] in the Rue Morgue."[q]

Dupin said the[r] last words in a very low tone, and very quietly. Just as quietly, too, he walked toward[s] the door, locked it, and put the key in his pocket. He then drew a pistol from [t]his bosom[t] and placed it, without the least flurry, upon the table.

The sailor's face flushed up [u]as if he were struggling with suffocation.[u] He started to his feet and grasped his cudgel; but the next moment he fell back into his seat, trembling violently,[v] and with the[w] countenance of[x] death itself. He spoke not a[y] word. I pitied him from the bottom of my heart.

"My friend," said Dupin, in a kind tone, "you are alarming yourself unnecessarily — you are indeed. We mean you no harm whatever. I pledge you the honor of a gentleman, and of a Frenchman, that we intend you no injury. I perfectly well know that you are innocent of the atrocities in the Rue Morgue.[z] It will not do, however, to deny that you are in some measure implicated in them.

---

l   property." *(A)*

m   thing/reward *(A, B)*

n   should I/reward ought I to *(A, B)*; ought I to *(C)*

o   have. *(A)*

p   these murders/that affair *(A)*; that affair of the murder *(B, C)*

q   <Trianon."> ↑ Morgue." ↓ *(A)*

r   these *(A, B, C)*

s   towards *(A, B, C)*

t . . . t   <his coat pocket> ↑ his bosom ↓ *(A)*

u . . . u   with an ungovernable tide of crimson. *(A, B, C)*

v   convulsively, *(A, B)*

w   a *(A)*

x   as colorless as that of *(A)*

y   a single *(A, B)*

z   <Trianon.> ↑ Morgue. ↓ *(A)*

TALES, 1841–1842

From what I have already said, you must know that I have had means of information about this matter — means of which you could never have dreamed. Now the thing stands thus. You have done nothing which you could have avoided — nothing, certainly, which renders you culpable. You were not even guilty of robbery, when you might have robbed with impunity. You have nothing to conceal. You have no reason for concealment. On the other hand, you are bound by every principle of honor to confess all[a] you know. An innocent man is now imprisoned, charged with that crime of which you can point out the perpetrator."

The sailor had recovered his presence of mind, in a great measure, while Dupin uttered[b] these words; but his original boldness of bearing was all gone.

"So help me God," said he, after a brief pause, "I *will* tell you all[c] I know about[d] this affair; — but I do not expect you to believe one half[e] I say — I would be a[f] fool indeed if I did. Still, I *am* innocent, and I will make a clean breast[g] if I die for it."

[h]What he stated was, in substance, this. He had lately made a voyage to the Indian Archipelago. A [i]party, of which he formed one,[i] landed at Borneo, and passed into the interior on[j] an excursion of pleasure. Himself and a companion had captured the Ourang-Outang. This companion dying, the animal fell into his own exclusive possession. After great trouble, occasioned by the intractable ferocity of his captive during the home voyage, he at length succeeded in lodging it[k] safely at his own residence in Paris, where, not to attract toward[l] himself the unpleasant curiosity of his neighbors, he kept it carefully secluded, until such time as it should recover from a wound in the foot, received from a splinter on board ship. His ultimate design was to sell it.

Returning home from some sailors'[m] frolic on the night, or

---

a   all that *(A, B, C)*
b   [utter]ed *(A) manuscript torn here and later*
c   all that *(A, B, C)*
d   [abo]ut *(A)*
e   half that *(A, B, C)*
f   would [be a] *(A)*
g   [brea]st *(A)*
h   *Before this:* I do not propose to

follow the man in the circumstantial narrative which he now detailed. *(A, B, C)*
i...i   party ↑ of which he formed one ↓ *(A)*
j   upon *(A)*
k   <him> ↑ it ↓ *(A)*
l   towards *(A, B, C)*
m   sailor's *(A)*

THE MURDERS IN THE RUE MORGUE

rather in the morning of the murder, he found the beast[n] occupy-
ing his own bed-room, into which it[o] had broken from a closet adjoining, where it[p] had been, as[q] was thought, securely confined.
Razor[r] in hand, and fully lathered, it[s] was sitting before a looking-
glass, attempting the operation of shaving, in which it[t] had no
doubt previously watched its[u] master through the key-hole[v] of the
closet. Terrified at the sight of so dangerous a weapon in the[w]
possession of an animal so ferocious, and so well able to use it, the
man, for some moments, was at a loss what to do. He had been
accustomed, however, to quiet the creature, even in its fiercest
moods, by the use of a[x] whip, and to this he now resorted. Upon
sight of it, the Ourang-Outang sprang at once through the door of
the chamber, down the stairs, and thence, through a window, un-
fortunately open, into the street.

The Frenchman followed in despair; the ape, razor still in
hand, occasionally stopping to look back and gesticulate at its[y]
pursuer, until the latter had nearly come up with it.[z] It[a] then again
made off. In this manner the chase continued for a long time. The
streets were profoundly quiet, as it was nearly three o'clock in the
morning. In passing down an alley in the rear of the Rue Morgue,[b]
the fugitive's attention was arrested by a light[c] gleaming from the
open window of Madame L'Espanaye's chamber, in the fourth
story of her house. Rushing to the building, it[d] perceived the lightning-rod, clambered up with inconceivable agility, grasped the
shutter, which was thrown fully back against the wall, and, by its
means, swung itself[e] directly upon the headboard[f] of the bed. The
whole feat did not occupy a minute. The shutter was kicked open
again by the Ourang-Outang[g] as it[h] entered the room.

---

n the beast/his prisoner *(A, B, C)*
o he *(A, B, C)*
p he *(A, B, C)*
q as it *(A, B, C)*
r The beast, razor *(A, B, C)*
s *Omitted (A, B, C)*
t he *(A, B, C)*
u his *(A, B, C)*
v key hole *(A)*
w *Omitted (A)*
x a strong wagoner's *(A, B)*

y his *(A, B, C)*
z him. *(A, B, C)*
a He *(A, B, C)*
b Trianon *(A) [Not changed]*
c light (the only one apparent except
those of the town-lamps) *(A, B)*
d he *(A, B, C)*
e himself *(A, B, C)*
f head-board *(A, B, C)*
g ape *(A)*
h he *(A, B, C)*

TALES, 1841–1842

The sailor, in the meantime, was both rejoiced and perplexed. He had strong hopes of now recapturing[i] the brute,[j] as it could scarcely escape from the trap into which it had ventured, except by the rod, where it[k] might be intercepted as it[l] came down. On the other hand, there was much cause for anxiety as to what it[m] might do in the house. This latter reflection urged the man [n]still to follow the fugitive.[n] A lightning-rod is ascended without difficulty, especially by a sailor; but, when he had arrived as high as the window, which lay far to his left, his career was stopped; the most that he could accomplish was to reach over so as to obtain a glimpse of the interior of the room. At this glimpse he nearly fell from his hold[o] through excess of horror. Now it was that those hideous shrieks arose upon the night, which had startled from slumber the inmates of the Rue Morgue.[p] Madame L'Espanaye and her daughter, habited in their night clothes,[q] had apparently been occupied in arranging some papers in the iron chest[r] already mentioned, which had been wheeled into the middle of the room. It was open, and its contents lay beside it on the floor. [s]The victims must have been sitting with their backs toward[s] the window; and, from[t] the time elapsing between the [u]ingress of the beast[v] and the screams,[u] it seems probable that it[w] was not immediately perceived. The flapping-to of the shutter[x] would naturally have been[y] attributed to the wind.

As the sailor looked in, the gigantic animal[z] had seized Madame L'Espanaye by the hair, (which was[a] loose, as she had been combing it,) and was flourishing the razor about her face, in imitation of the motions of a barber. The daughter lay prostrate and motionless; she had swooned. The screams and struggles of the old

---

i   re-capturing *(A)*
j   ape *(A, B, C)*
k   <his master could intercept him>
↑ it ↓ *(A)*
l   <he> ↑ it ↓ *(A)*
m   the brute *(A, B, C)*
n . . . n   <to ascend.> ↑ still to follow the fugitive. ↓ *(A)*
o   hold <in horror> *(A)*
p   Trianon. *(A)* [*Not changed*]
q   night-clothes, *(A)*
r   iron-chest *(A)*

s . . . s   Their backs must have been towards *(A, B, C)*
t   by *(A, B)*
u . . . u   screams and the ingress of the ape, *(A, B)*
v   ape *(C)*
w   he *(A, B, C)*
x   shutter they *(A, B)*
y   *Omitted (A, B)*
z   beast *(A, B, C)*
a   <had> was *(A)*

THE MURDERS IN THE RUE MORGUE

lady (during which the hair was torn from her head) had the effect of changing the probably pacific purposes of the Ourang-Outang into those of[b] wrath. With one determined sweep of its[c] muscular arm it[d] nearly severed her head from her body. The sight of blood inflamed[e] its[f] anger into phrenzy. Gnashing its[g] teeth, and flashing fire from its[h] eyes, it[i] flew upon the body of the girl, and imbedded its[j] fearful talons in her throat, retaining its[k] grasp until she expired. Its[l] wandering and wild glances fell[m] at this moment upon[n] the head of the bed, over which the face[o] of its[p] master, rigid with[q] horror, was[r] just discernible. The fury of the beast, who no doubt bore still in mind the dreaded whip, was instantly converted into fear.[s] Conscious of having deserved punishment, it[t] seemed desirous [u]of concealing[u] its[v] bloody deeds, and skipped about the chamber in an[w] agony of nervous agitation; throwing down and breaking the furniture as it[x] moved, and dragging the bed from the bedstead. In conclusion, it[y] seized first the corpse of the daughter, and thrust it up the chimney, as it was found; then that of the old lady, [z]which it immediately hurled through the window headlong.[z]

As the ape approached the casement[a] with its mutilated burden, the sailor shrank[b] aghast to the rod, and, rather gliding than clambering down it, hurried at once home — dreading the consequences of the butchery, and gladly abandoning, in his terror, all solicitude about the fate of the Ourang-Outang. The words heard by the party upon the staircase were the Frenchman's exclamations of

---

b   of ungovernable *(A, B)*
c   his *(A, B, C)*
d   he *(A, B, C)*
e   enflamed *(A)*
f   his *(A, B, C)*
g   his *(A, B, C)*
h   his *(A, B, C)*
i   he *(A, B, C)*
j   his *(A, B, C)*
k   his *(A, B, C)*
l   His *(A, B, C)*
m   <adverted> ↑ fell ↓ *(A)*
n   <to> ↑ upon ↓ *(A)*
o   the face/those *(A, B)*
p   his *(A, B, C)*

q   rigid with/glazed in *(A, B)*
r   were *(A, B)*
s   dread. *(A, B);* terror. *(C)*
t   he *(A, B, C)*
u . . . u   to conceal *(B)*
v   his *(A, B, C)*
w   an apparent *(A, B, C)*
x   he *(A, B, C)*
y   he *(A, B, C)*
z . . . z   with which he rushed to the window precipitating it immediately therefrom. *(A, B, C)*
a   the casement/him *(A, B, C)*
b   shrunk *(B, C)*

TALES, 1841–1842

horror and affright, commingled with the fiendish jabberings of the brute.

I have scarcely anything to add. The Ourang-Outang must have escaped from the chamber, by the rod, just before the breaking of the door. It^c must have closed the window as it^d passed through it. It^e was subsequently caught by the owner himself, who obtained for it^f a very large sum at the *Jardin des Plantes.*[39] Le Bon was instantly released, upon our narration of the circumstances (with some comments from Dupin) at the *bureau* of the Prefect of^g Police. This functionary, however well disposed to my friend, could not altogether conceal his chagrin at the turn which affairs had taken, and was fain to indulge in a sarcasm or two, about^h the propriety of every person minding his own business.

"Let him talk," said Dupin, who had not thought it necessary to reply. "Let him discourse; it will ease his conscience. I am satisfied with having defeated him in his own castle. ^iNevertheless, that he failed in the solution of this mystery, is by no means that matter for wonder which he supposes it; for,^j in truth, our friend the Prefect is somewhat too cunning to be profound.^i ^kIn his wisdom is no *stamen.*^k It is all head and no body, like the pictures of the Goddess Laverna, — or, at best,^l all head and shoulders, like a codfish.[40] But he is a good creature^m after all. I like him especially for one master stroke^n of cant, by which he has attained his^o reputation for ingenuity.^p I mean the way^q he has *'de nier ce qui est, et d'expliquer ce qui n'est pas.'* " * [41]

---

*Rousseau — Nouvelle Heloise.

---

c   He *(A, B, C)*
d   he *(A, B, C)*
e   He *(A, B, C)*
f   him *(A, B, C)*
g   Prefect of/*chêf de (A); Prefet de (B)*
h   in regard to *(A, B, C)*
i . . . i   In truth, he is too cunning to be acute. *(A, B)*
j   it; for,/it. *Nil sapientiæ odiosius acumine nimio,* is, perhaps, the only line in the puerile and feeble Seneca not absolutely unmeaning; and *(C)*
k . . . k   There is no *stamen* in his

wisdom. *(A, B)*
l   least *(A, B)*
m   fellow, *(A, B)*
n   master-stroke *(A)*
o   that *(A, B, C)*
p   ingenuity./ingenuity which he possesses. *(A, B, C)*
q   way <which> *(A)*
Footnote first appears in C.
Dated at end: Philadelphia, March, 1841. *(B)*

THE MYSTERY OF MARIE ROGET

THE MYSTERY OF MARIE ROGET.* [C]

A SEQUEL TO "THE MURDERS IN THE RUE MORGUE."

Es giebt eine Reihe idealischer Begebenheiten, die der Wirklichkeit parallel lauft. Selten fallen sie zusammen. Menschen und Züfalle modificiren gewöhnlich die idealische Begebenheit, so dass sie unvollkommen erscheint, und ihre Folgen gleichfalls unvollkommen sind. So bei der Reformation; statt des Protestantismus kam das Lutherthum hervor.

There are ideal series of events which run parallel with the real ones. They rarely coincide. Men and circumstances generally modify the ideal train of events, so that it seems imperfect, and its consequences are equally imperfect. Thus with the Reformation; instead of Protestantism came Lutheranism. — Novalis.†

Moralische[a] Ansichten.

There are few persons, even among the calmest thinkers, who have not occasionally been startled into a vague yet thrilling half-credence in the supernatural, by *coincidences* of so seemingly marvellous a character that, as *mere* coincidences, the intellect has been unable to receive them. Such sentiments — for the half-credences of which I speak have never the full force of *thought* —

* On[b] the original publication of "Marie Rogêt," the foot-notes now appended were considered unnecessary; but the lapse of several years since the tragedy upon which the tale is based, renders it expedient to give them, and also to say a few words in explanation of the general design. A young girl, *Mary Cecilia Rogers,* was murdered in the vicinity of New York; and, although her death occasioned an intense and long-enduring excitement, the mystery attending it had remained unsolved at the period when the present paper was written and published (November, 1842). Herein, under pretence of relating the fate of a Parisian *grisette,* the author has followed, in minute detail, the essential, while merely paralleling the inessential facts of the real murder of Mary Rogers. Thus all argument founded upon the fiction is applicable to the truth: and the investigation of the truth was the object.

The "Mystery of Marie Rogêt" was composed at a distance from the scene of the atrocity, and with no other means of investigation than the newspapers afforded. Thus much escaped the writer of which he could have availed himself had he been on[c] the spot, and visited the localities. It may not be improper to record, nevertheless, that the confessions of *two* persons, (one of them the Madame Deluc of the narrative) made, at different periods, long subsequent to the publication, confirmed, in full, not only the general conclusion, but absolutely *all* the chief hypothetical details by which that conclusion was attained.[1]

† The *nom de plume* of Von Hardenburg.

Title: The starred footnote was omitted in A, as were all Poe's other footnotes except that on the motto and that referring to "The Murders in the Rue Morgue"; most are not noticed individually in the variants below.

Motto: gewöhnlich *is misprinted* gewohulich *(A, B, C, D)*.
a   Moral *(A, B, C, D) corrected editorially.*
b   Upon *(B, D)*
c   upon *(B, D)*

TALES: 1843–1844

are[d] seldom thoroughly stifled unless by reference to the doctrine of chance, or, as it is technically termed, the Calculus of Probabilities.[2] Now this Calculus is, in its essence, purely mathematical; and thus we have the anomaly of the most rigidly exact in science applied to the shadow and spirituality of the most intangible in speculation.

The extraordinary details which I am now called upon to make public, will be found to form, as regards sequence of time, the primary branch of a series of scarcely intelligible *coincidences,* whose secondary or concluding branch will be recognized by all readers in the late murder of MARY CECILIA ROGERS, at New York.

When, in an article entitled "The Murders in the Rue Morgue," I endeavored, about a year ago, to depict some very remarkable features in the mental character of my friend, the Chevalier C. Auguste Dupin, it did not occur to me that I should ever resume the subject. This depicting of character constituted my design; and this design was[e] fulfilled in the[f] train of circumstances brought to instance Dupin's idiosyncrasy. I might have adduced other examples, but I[g] should have proven no more. Late events, however, in their surprising development, have startled me into some farther details, which will carry with them the air of extorted confession. Hearing what I have lately heard, it would be indeed strange should I remain[h] silent in regard to what I both heard and saw so long ago.

Upon the winding up of the tragedy involved in the deaths of Madame L'Espanaye and her daughter, the Chevalier dismissed the affair at once from his attention, and relapsed into his old habits of moody[i] reverie. Prone, at all times, to abstraction, I readily fell in with his humor; and, continuing to occupy our chambers in the Faubourg Saint Germain, we gave the Future to the winds, and slumbered tranquilly in the Present, weaving the dull world around us into dreams.

But these dreams were not altogether uninterrupted. It may readily be supposed that the part played by my friend, in the

d	such sentiments are *(A, B, D)*	g	it *(A)*
e	was thoroughly *(A, B, D)*	h	remain longer *(A)*
f	the wild *(A, B, D)*	i	moody and fantastic *(A)*

THE MYSTERY OF MARIE ROGET

drama at the Rue Morgue, had not failed of its impression upon the fancies of the Parisian police. With its emissaries, the name of Dupin had grown into a household word. The simple character of those inductions by which he had disentangled the mystery never having been explained even to the Prefect, or to any other individual than myself, of course it is not surprising that the affair was regarded as[j] little less than miraculous, or that the Chevalier's analytical abilities acquired for him the credit of intuition. His frankness would have led him to disabuse every inquirer of such prejudice; but his indolent humor forbade all farther agitation of[k] a topic whose interest to himself had long ceased. It thus happened that he found himself the cynosure of the policial eyes; and the cases were not few in which attempt was made to engage his services at the Prefecture. [1]One of the most remarkable instances was that[1] of the murder of a young girl named Marie Rogêt.

This event occurred about two years after the atrocity in the Rue Morgue. Marie, whose Christian and family name will at once arrest attention from their resemblance to those of the unfortunate "cigar-girl,"[m] was the only daughter of the widow Estelle Rogêt. The father had died during the child's infancy, and from the period of his death, until within eighteen months before the assassination which forms the subject of our narrative, the mother and daughter had dwelt together in the Rue Pavée Saint Andrée;* Madame there keeping a *pension,* assisted by Marie. Affairs went on thus until the latter had attained her twenty-second year, when her great beauty attracted the notice of a perfumer, who occupied one of the shops in the basement of the Palais Royal, and whose custom lay chiefly among the desperate adventurers infesting that neighborhood. Monsieur Le Blanc† was not unaware of the advantages to be derived from the attendance of the fair Marie in his perfumery;[n] and his liberal proposals were accepted eagerly by

---

* Nassau Street.
† Anderson.

j   *Omitted (A)*
k   on *(A)*
1...1   The only instance, nevertheless, in which such attempt proved

successful, was the instance to which I have already alluded — that *(A)*
m   "segar-girl," *(A)*
n   *parfumerie; (A)*

TALES: 1843–1844

the girl, although[o] with somewhat more of[p] hesitation by Madame.[3]

The anticipations of the shopkeeper were realized, and his rooms soon became notorious through the charms of the sprightly *grisette.* She had been in his employ about a year, when her admirers were thrown into confusion by her sudden disappearance from the shop. Monsieur Le Blanc was unable to account for her absence, and Madame Rogêt was distracted with anxiety and terror. The public papers immediately took up the theme, and the police were upon the point of making serious investigations, when, one fine morning, after the lapse of a week, Marie, in good health, but with a somewhat saddened air, made her re-appearance at her usual counter in the perfumery.[q] All inquiry, except that of a private character, was of course immediately hushed. Monsieur Le Blanc professed total ignorance, as before. Marie, with Madame, replied to all questions, that the last week had been spent at the house of a relation in the country. Thus the affair died away, and was generally forgotten; for the girl, ostensibly to relieve herself from the impertinence of curiosity, soon bade a final adieu to the perfumer, and sought the shelter of her mother's residence in the Rue Pavée Saint Andrée.[4]

It was about three years[r] after this return home, that her friends were alarmed by her sudden disappearance for the second time. Three days elapsed, and nothing was heard of her. On the fourth her corpse was found floating in the Seine,* near the shore which is opposite the Quartier of the Rue Saint Andrée, and at a point not very far distant from the secluded neighborhood of the Barrière du Roule.†[5]

The atrocity of this murder, (for it was at once evident that murder had been committed,) the youth and beauty of the victim, and, above all, her previous notoriety, conspired to produce intense excitement in the minds of the sensitive Parisians. I can call to mind no similar occurrence producing so general and so intense an effect. For several weeks, in the discussion[s] of this one

---

* The Hudson.   † Weehawken.

---

o but *(A)*   q *parfumerie. (A)*
p *Omitted (A)*   r three years/five months *(A, B, D)*
                               s discussing *(A)*

THE MYSTERY OF MARIE ROGET

absorbing theme, even the momentous political topics of the day were forgotten. The Prefect made unusual exertions; and the powers of the whole Parisian police were, of course, tasked to the utmost extent.

Upon the first discovery of the corpse, it was not supposed that the murderer would be able to elude, for more than a very brief period, the inquisition which was immediately set on foot. It was not until the expiration of a week that it was deemed necessary to offer a reward; and even then this reward was limited to a thousand francs. In the mean time the investigation proceeded with vigor, if not always with judgment, and numerous individuals were examined to no purpose; while, owing to the continual absence of all clue to the mystery, the popular excitement[t] greatly increased. At the end of the tenth day it was thought advisable to double the sum originally proposed; and, at length, the second week having elapsed without leading to any discoveries, and the prejudice which always exists in Paris against the Police having given vent to itself in several serious *émeutes*,[6] the Prefect took it upon himself to offer the sum of twenty thousand francs "for the conviction of the assassin," or, if more than one should prove to have been implicated, "for the conviction of any one of the assassins." In the proclamation setting forth this reward, a full pardon was promised to any accomplice who should come forward in evidence against his fellow; and to the whole was appended, wherever it appeared, the private placard of a committee of citizens, offering ten thousand francs, in addition to the amount proposed by the Prefecture.[7] The entire reward thus stood at no less than thirty thousand francs, which will be regarded as an extraordinary sum when we consider the humble condition of the girl, and the great frequency, in large cities, of such atrocities as the one described.

No one doubted now that the mystery of this murder would be immediately brought to light. But although, in one or two instances, arrests were made which promised elucidation, yet nothing was elicited which could implicate the parties suspected; and they were discharged forthwith.[8] Strange as it may appear, the

---

t   excitement became *(A)*

TALES: 1843–1844

third week from the discovery of the body had passed, and passed without any light being thrown upon the subject, before even a rumor of the events which had so agitated the public mind, reached the ears of Dupin and myself.[9] Engaged in researches which had absorbed our whole attention, it had been nearly a month since either of us had gone abroad, or received a visiter, or more than glanced at the leading political articles in one of the daily papers. The first intelligence of the murder was brought us by G——, in person.[10] He called upon us early in the afternoon of the thirteenth of July, 18—, and remained with us until late in the night. He had been piqued by the failure of all his endeavors to ferret out the assassins. His reputation — so he said with a peculiarly Parisian air — was at stake. Even his honor was concerned. The eyes of the public were upon him; and there was really no sacrifice which he would not be willing to make for the development of the mystery. He concluded a somewhat droll speech with a compliment upon what[u] he was pleased to term the *tact* of Dupin, and made him a direct, and certainly a liberal proposition, the precise nature of which I do not feel myself at liberty to disclose, but which has no bearing upon the proper subject of my narrative.

The compliment my friend rebutted as best he could, but the proposition he accepted at once, although its advantages were altogether provisional. This point being settled, the Prefect broke forth at once into explanations of his own views, interspersing them with long comments upon the evidence; of which latter we were not yet in possession. He discoursed much, and beyond doubt, learnedly; while I hazarded an occasional suggestion as the night wore drowsily away. Dupin, sitting steadily in his accustomed arm-chair, was the embodiment of respectful attention. He wore spectacles, during the whole interview; and an occasional glance beneath their green glasses,[11] sufficed to convince me that he slept not the less soundly, because silently, throughout the seven or eight leaden-footed hours which immediately preceded the departure of the Prefect.

In the morning, I procured, at the Prefecture, a full report of

---

u   which *(A)*

THE MYSTERY OF MARIE ROGET

all the evidence elicited, and, at the various newspaper offices, a copy of every paper in which, from first to last, had been published any decisive information in regard to this sad affair. Freed from all that was positively disproved, this mass of information stood thus:

Marie Rogêt left the residence of her mother, in the Rue Pavée St. Andrée, about nine o'clock in the morning of Sunday, June the twenty-second, 18—.[12] In going out, she gave notice to a Monsieur Jacques St.ᵛ Eustache,* and to him only, of her intention to spend the day with an aunt who resided in the Rue des Drômes.[13] The Rue des Drômes is a short and narrow but populous thoroughfare, not far from the banks of the river, and at a distance of some two miles, in the most direct course possible, from the *pension* of Madame Rogêt. St. Eustache was the accepted suitor of Marie, and lodged, as well as took his meals, at the *pension*. He was to have gone for his betrothed at dusk, and to have escorted her home. In the afternoon, however, it came on to rain heavily; and, supposing that she would remain all night at her aunt's, (as she had done under similar circumstances before,) he did not think it necessary to keep his promise.[14] As night drew on, Madame Rogêt (who was an infirm old lady, seventy years of age,) was heard to express a fear "that she should never see Marie again;" but this observation attracted little attention at the time.[15]

On Monday, it was ascertained that the girl had not been to the Rue des Drômes; and when the day elapsed without tidings of her, a tardy search was instituted at several points in the city, and its environs.[16] It was not, however, until the fourth day from the period of her disappearance that any thing satisfactory was ascertained respecting her. On this day, (Wednesday, the twenty-fifth of June,) a Monsieur Beauvais,† who, with a friend, had been making inquiries for Marie near the Barrière du Roule, on the shore of the Seine which is opposite the Rue Pavée St. Andrée,[17] was informed that a corpse had just been towed ashore by some fishermen, who had found it floating in the river. Upon seeing the

---

* Payne.
† Crommelin.

ᵛ *Omitted (A)*

TALES: 1843–1844

body, Beauvais, after some hesitation, identified it as that of the perfumery-girl. His friend recognized it more promptly.[18]

The face was suffused with dark blood, some of which issued from the mouth. No foam was seen, as in the case of the merely drowned. There was no discoloration in the cellular tissue. About the throat were bruises and impressions of fingers. The arms were bent over on the chest and were rigid. The right hand was clenched; the left partially open. On the left wrist were two circular excoriations, apparently the effect of ropes, or of a rope in more than one volution. A part of the right wrist, also, was much chafed, as well as the back throughout its extent, but more especially at the shoulder-blades. In bringing the body to the shore the fishermen had attached to it a rope; but none of the excoriations had been effected by this. The flesh of the neck was much swollen. There were no cuts apparent, or bruises which appeared the effect of blows. A piece of lace was found tied so tightly around the neck as to be hidden from sight; it was completely buried in the flesh, and was fastened by a knot which lay just under the left ear. This alone would have sufficed to produce death. The medical testimony spoke confidently of the virtuous character of the deceased. She had been ʷsubjected, it said, toʷ brutal violence. The corpse was in such condition when found, that there could have been no difficulty in its recognition by friends.[19]

The dress was much torn and otherwise disordered. In the outer garment, a slip, about a foot wide, had been torn upward from the bottom hem to the waist, but not torn off. It was wound three times around the waist, and secured by a sort of hitch in the back. The dress immediately beneath the frock was of fine muslin; and from this a slip eighteen inches wide had been torn entirely out — torn very evenly and with great care. It was found around her neck, fitting loosely, and secured with a hard knot. Over this muslin slip and the slip of lace, the strings of a bonnet were attached; the bonnet being appended. The knot by which the strings of the bonnet were fastened, was not a lady's, but a slip or sailor's knot.[20]

---

w . . . w   subjected to *(A)*

THE MYSTERY OF MARIE ROGET

After the recognition of the corpse, it was not, as usual, taken to the Morgue, (this formality being superfluous,) but hastily interred not far from the spot at which it was brought ashore.[21] Through the exertions of Beauvais, the matter was industriously hushed up, as far as possible; and several days had elapsed before any public emotion resulted. A weekly paper,* however, at length took up the theme;[22] the corpse was disinterred, and a re-examination instituted; but[x] nothing was elicited beyond what has been already noted. The clothes, however, were now submitted to the mother and friends of the deceased, and fully identified as those worn by the girl upon leaving home.[23]

Meantime, the excitement increased hourly. Several individuals were arrested and discharged. St. Eustache fell especially under suspicion; and he failed, at first, to give an intelligible account of his whereabouts during the Sunday on which Marie left home. Subsequently, however, he submitted to Monsieur G——, affidavits, accounting satisfactorily for every hour of the day in question.[24] As time passed and no discovery ensued, a thousand contradictory rumors were circulated, and journalists busied themselves in *suggestions*. Among these, the one which attracted the most notice, was the idea that Marie Rogêt still lived — that the corpse found in the Seine was that of some other unfortunate.[25] It will be proper that I submit to the reader some passages which embody the suggestion alluded to. These passages are *literal* translations from L'Etoile,† a paper[y] conducted, in general, with much ability.[26]

"Mademoiselle Rogêt left her mother's house on Sunday morning, June the twenty-second, 18—, with the ostensible purpose of going to see her aunt, or some other connexion, in the Rue des Drômes. From that hour, nobody is proved to have seen her. There is no trace or tidings of her at all. * * * * There has no person, whatever, come forward, so far, who saw her at all, on that day, after she left her mother's door. * * * * Now, though we have no evidence that Marie Rogêt was in the land of the living after nine o'clock on Sunday, June the twenty-second, we have proof that, up to that hour, she was alive. On Wednesday noon, at twelve, a female body was discovered afloat on the shore of the Barrière du Roule. This was, even if we presume that Marie Rogêt was thrown into the river within three hours after she left her mother's house, only three days from the time she left

* The "N. Y. Mercury."
† The "N. Y. Brother Jonathan," edited by H. Hastings Weld, Esq.

---

x   and *(A)*   y   small daily print *(A)*

TALES: 1843-1844

her home — three days to an hour. But it is folly to suppose that the murder, if murder was committed on her body, could have been consummated soon enough to have enabled her murderers to throw the body into the river before midnight. Those who are guilty of such horrid crimes, choose darkness rather than light. * * * * Thus we see that if the body found in the river *was* that of Marie Rogêt, it could only have been in the water two and a half days, or three at the outside. All experience has shown that drowned bodies, or bodies thrown into the water immediately after death by violence, require from six to ten days for sufficient decomposition to take place to bring them to the top of the water. Even where a cannon is fired over a corpse, and it rises before at least five or six days' immersion, it sinks again, if left alone. Now, we ask, what was there in this case to cause a departure from the ordinary course of nature? * * * * If the body had been kept in its mangled state on shore until Tuesday night, some trace would be found on shore of the murderers. It is a doubtful point, also, whether the body would be so soon afloat, even were it thrown in after having been dead two days. And, furthermore, it is exceedingly improbable that any villains who had committed such a murder as is here supposed, would have thrown the body in without weight to sink it, when such a precaution could have so easily been taken."[27]

The editor here proceeds to argue that the body must have been in the water "not three days merely, but, at least, five times three days," because it was so far decomposed that Beauvais had great difficulty in recognizing it. This latter point, however, was fully disproved.[28] I[z] continue the[a] translation:

"What, then, are the facts on which M. Beauvais says that he has no doubt the body was that of Marie Rogêt? He ripped up the gown sleeve, and says he found marks which satisfied him of the identity. The public generally supposed those marks to have consisted of some description of scars. He rubbed the arm and found *hair* upon it — something as indefinite, we think, as can readily be imagined — as little conclusive as finding an arm in the sleeve. M. Beauvais did not return that night, but sent word to Madame Rogêt, at seven o'clock, on Wednesday evening, that an investigation was still in progress respecting her daughter. If we allow that Madame Rogêt, from her age and grief, could not go over, (which is allowing a great deal,) there certainly must have been some one who would have thought it worth while to go over and attend the investigation, if they thought the body was that of Marie. Nobody went over. There was nothing said or heard about the matter in the Rue Pavée St. Andrée, that reached even the occupants of the same building. M. St. Eustache, the lover and intended husband of Marie, who boarded in her mother's house, deposes that he did not hear of the discovery of the body of his intended until the next morning, when M. Beauvais came into his chamber and told him of it. For an item of news like this, it strikes us it was very coolly received."[29]

In this way the journal endeavored to create the impression of

---

z   We *(A)*   a   our *(A)*

THE MYSTERY OF MARIE ROGET

an apathy on the part of the relatives of Marie, inconsistent with the supposition that these relatives believed the corpse to be hers. Its insinuations amount to this: — that Marie, with the connivance of her friends, had absented herself from the city for reasons involving a charge against her chastity; and that these friends, upon the discovery of a corpse in the Seine, somewhat resembling that of the girl, had availed themselves of the opportunity to impress the public with the belief of her death. But[b] L'Etoile was again over-hasty. It was distinctly proved that no apathy, such as was imagined, existed; that the old lady was exceedingly feeble, and so agitated as to be unable to attend to any duty; that St. Eustache, so far from receiving the news coolly, was distracted with grief, and bore himself so frantically, that M. Beauvais prevailed upon a friend and relative to take charge of him, and prevent his attending the examination at the disinterment. Moreover, although it was stated by L'Etoile, that the corpse was re-interred at the public expense — that an advantageous offer of private sepulture was absolutely declined by the family — and that no member of the family attended the ceremonial: — although, I say, all this was asserted by L'Etoile in furtherance of the impression it designed to convey — yet *all* this was satisfactorily disproved.[30] In a subsequent number of the paper, an attempt was made to throw suspicion upon Beauvais himself. The editor says:

"Now, then, a change comes over the matter. We are told that, on one occasion, while a Madame B —— was at Madame Rogêt's house, M. Beauvais, who was going out, told her that a *gendarme* was expected there, and that she, Madame B., must not say anything to the *gendarme* until he returned, but let the matter be for him. * * * * In the present posture of affairs, M. Beauvais appears to have the whole matter locked up in his head. A single step cannot be taken without M. Beauvais; for, go which way you will, you run against him. * * * * * For some reason, he determined that nobody shall have any thing to do with the proceedings but himself, and he has elbowed the male relatives out of the way, according to their representations, in a very singular manner. He seems to have been very much averse to permitting the relatives to see the body."[31]

[c]By the following fact, some[c] color was given to the suspicion thus thrown upon Beauvais.[d] A visiter at his office, a few days prior

---

b   But the *(A)*
c . . . c   Some *(A)*

d   Beauvais, by the following fact. *(A)*

TALES: 1843–1844

to the girl's disappearance, and during the absence of its occupant, had observed *a rose* in the key-hole of the door, and the name *"Marie"* inscribed upon a slate which hung near at hand.[32]

The general impression, so far as we were enabled to glean it from the newspapers, seemed to be, that Marie had been the victim of *a gang* of desperadoes — that by these she had been borne across the river, maltreated and murdered.[33] Le Commerciel,* however, a print of extensive influence, was earnest in combating this popular idea. I quote a passage or two from its columns:

"We are persuaded that pursuit has hitherto been on a false scent, so far as it has been directed to the Barrière du Roule. It is impossible that a person so well known to thousands as this young woman was, should have passed three blocks without some one having seen her; and any one who saw her would have remembered it, for she interested all who knew her. It was when the streets were full of people, when she went out. * * * It is impossible that she could have gone to the Barrière du Roule, or to the Rue des Drômes, without being recognized by a dozen persons; yet no one has come forward who saw her outside of her mother's door, and there is no evidence, except the testimony concerning her *expressed intentions,* that she did go out at all. Her gown was torn, bound round her, and tied; and by that the body was carried as a bundle. If the murder had been committed at the Barrière du Roule, there would have been no necessity for any such arrangement. The fact that the body was found floating near the Barrière, is no proof as to where it was thrown into the water. * * * * * A piece of one of the unfortunate girl's petticoats, two feet long and one foot wide, was torn out and tied under her chin around the back of her head, probably to prevent screams. This was done by fellows who had no pocket-handkerchief."[34]

A day or two before the Prefect called upon us, however, some important information reached the police, which seemed to overthrow, at least, the chief portion of Le Commerciel's argument. Two small boys, sons of a Madame Deluc, while roaming among the woods near the Barrière du Roule, chanced to penetrate a close thicket, within which were three or four large stones, forming a kind of seat, with a back and footstool. On the upper stone lay a white petticoat; on the second a silk scarf. A parasol, gloves, and a pocket-handkerchief were also here found. The handkerchief bore the name "Marie Rogêt." Fragments of dress were discovered on the brambles around. The earth was trampled, the bushes were broken, and there was every evidence of a struggle. Between the thicket and the river, the fences were found taken down, and the

* N. Y. "Journal of Commerce."

THE MYSTERY OF MARIE ROGET

ground bore evidence of some heavy burthen having been dragged along it.[35]

A weekly paper, Le Soleil,* had the following comments upon this discovery — comments which merely echoed the sentiment of the whole Parisian press:

"The things had all evidently been there at least three or four weeks; they were all mildewed down hard with the action of the rain, and stuck together from mildew. The grass had grown around and over some of them. The silk on the parasol was strong, but the threads of it were run together within. The upper part, where it had been doubled and folded, was all mildewed and rotten, and tore on its being opened. * * * * The pieces of her frock torn out by the bushes were about three inches wide and six inches long. One part was the hem of the frock, and it had been mended; the other piece was part of the skirt, not the hem. They looked like strips torn off, and were on the thorn bush, about a foot from the ground. * * * * * There can be no doubt, therefore, that the spot of this appalling outrage has been discovered."[36]

Consequent upon this discovery, new evidence appeared. Madame Deluc testified that she keeps a roadside inn not far from the bank of the river, opposite the Barrière du Roule. The neighborhood is secluded — particularly so. It is the usual Sunday resort of blackguards from the city, who cross the river in boats. About three o'clock, in the afternoon of the Sunday in question, a young girl arrived at the inn, accompanied by a young man of dark complexion. The two remained here for some time. On their departure, they took the road to some thick woods in the vicinity. Madame Deluc's attention was called to the dress worn by the girl, on account of its resemblance to one worn by a deceased relative. A scarf was particularly noticed. Soon after the departure of the couple, a gang of miscreants made their appearance, behaved boisterously, ate and drank without making payment, followed in the route of the young man and girl, returned to the inn about dusk, and re-crossed the river as if in great haste.

It was soon after dark, upon this same evening, that Madame Deluc, as well as her eldest son, heard the screams of a female in the vicinity of the inn. The screams were violent but brief. Madame D. recognized not only the scarf which was found in the thicket,

* Phil. "Sat. Evening Post," edited by C. J.[e] Peterson, Esq.

e *Peterson's middle name was Jacobs,*   *original texts (B, C, D)*
hence J is printed for the I of the

TALES: 1843–1844

but the dress which was discovered upon the corpse.[37] An omnibus-driver, Valence,* now also testified that he saw Marie Rogêt cross a ferry on the Seine, on the Sunday in question, in company with a young man of dark complexion. He, Valence, knew Marie, and could not be mistaken in her identity. The articles found in the thicket were fully identified by the relatives of Marie.[38]

The items of evidence and information thus collected by myself, from the newspapers, at the suggestion of Dupin, embraced only one more point — but this was a point of seemingly vast consequence. It appears that, immediately after the discovery of the clothes as above described, the lifeless, or nearly lifeless body of St. Eustache, Marie's betrothed, was found in the vicinity of what all now supposed the scene of the outrage. A phial labelled "laudanum," and emptied, was found near him. His breath gave evidence of the poison. He died without speaking. Upon his person was found a letter, briefly stating his love for Marie, with his design of self-destruction.[39]

"I need scarcely tell you," said Dupin, as he finished the perusal of my notes, "that this is a far more intricate case than that of the Rue Morgue; from which it differs in one important respect. This is an *ordinary,* although an atrocious instance of crime. There is nothing peculiarly *outré* about it. You will observe that, for this reason, the mystery has been considered easy, when, for this reason, it should have been considered difficult, of solution. Thus, at first, it was thought unnecessary to offer a reward. The myrmidons[40] of G—— were able at once to comprehend how and why such an atrocity *might have been* committed. They could[f] picture to their imaginations a mode — many modes — and a motive — many motives; and because it was not impossible that either of these numerous modes and motives *could* have been the actual one, they have taken it for granted that one of them *must.* But the ease with which these variable fancies were entertained, and the very plausibility which each assumed, should have been understood as indicative rather of the difficulties than of the facilities which must attend elucidation. I have before observed that it is by prominences above the plane of the ordinary, that reason feels her way, if at all, in her

* Adam.

THE MYSTERY OF MARIE ROGET

search for the true,[41] and that the proper question in cases such as this, is not so much 'what has occurred?' as 'what has occurred that has never occurred before?' In the investigations at the house of Madame L'Espanaye,[g]* the agents of G——were discouraged and confounded by that very *unusualness* which, to a properly regulated intellect, would have afforded the surest[h] omen of success; while this same intellect might have been plunged in despair at the[i] ordinary character of all that met the eye in the case of the perfumery-girl, and yet[j] told of nothing but easy triumph to the functionaries of the Prefecture.

"In the case of Madame L'Espanaye[k] and her daughter, there was, even at the beginning of our investigation, no doubt that murder had been committed. The idea of suicide was excluded at once. Here, too, we are freed, at the commencement, from all supposition of self-murder. The body found at the Barrière du Roule, was found under such circumstances as to leave us no room for embarrassment upon this important point. But it has been suggested that the corpse discovered, is not that of the Marie Rogêt for the conviction of whose assassin, or assassins, the reward is offered, and respecting whom, solely, our agreement has been arranged with the Prefect. We both know this gentleman well. It will not do to trust him too far. If, dating our inquiries from the body found, and thence tracing a murderer, we yet discover this body to be that of some other individual than Marie; or, if starting from the living Marie, we find her, yet find her unassassinated — in either case we lose our labor; since it is Monsieur G—— with whom we have to deal. For our own purpose, therefore, if not for the purpose of justice, it is indispensable that our first step should be the determination of the identity of the corpse with the Marie Rogêt who is missing.

[l]"With the public the arguments of L'Etoile[l] have had weight; and that the journal itself is convinced of their importance would

* See "Murders in the Rue Morgue."

---

f   would *(A)*
g   Espanage, *(A)*
h   sweet *(A)*
i   the *especially (A)*
j   *Omitted (A)*

k   Espanage *(A)*
l . . . l   "I know not what effect the arguments of 'L'Etoile' may have wrought upon your own understanding. With the public they *(A)*

TALES: 1843–1844

appear from the manner in which it commences one of its essays upon the subject — 'Several of the morning papers of the day,' it says, 'speak of the *conclusive* article in Monday's Etoile.'[42] To me, this article appears conclusive of little beyond the zeal of its inditer. We should bear in mind that, in general, it is the object of our newspapers rather to create a sensation — to make a point — than to further the cause of truth. The latter end is only pursued when it seems coincident with the former. The print which merely falls in with ordinary opinion (however well founded this opinion may be) earns for itself no credit with the mob. The mass of the people regard as profound only him who suggests *pungent contradictions* of the general idea. In ratiocination, not less than in[m] literature, it is the *epigram* which is the most immediately and the most universally appreciated. In both, it is of the lowest order of merit.

"What I mean to say is, that it is the mingled epigram and melodrame of the idea, that Marie Rogêt still lives, rather than any true plausibility in this idea, which have[n] suggested it to L'Etoile, and secured it a favorable reception with the public.[43] Let us examine the heads of this journal's[o] argument; endeavoring to avoid the incoherence with which it is originally set forth.

"The first aim of the writer is to show, from the brevity of the interval between Marie's disappearance and the finding of the floating corpse, that this corpse cannot be that of Marie. The reduction of this interval to its smallest possible dimension, becomes thus, at once, an object with the reasoner. In the rash pursuit of this object, he rushes into mere assumption at the outset. 'It is folly to suppose,' he says, 'that the murder, if murder was committed on her body, could[p] have been consummated soon enough to have enabled her murderers to throw the body into the river before midnight.'[44] We demand at once, and very naturally, *why?* Why is it folly to suppose that the murder was committed *within five minutes* after the girl's quitting her mother's house? Why is it folly to suppose that the murder was committed at any given period of the day? There have been assassinations at all hours. But, had the murder taken place at any moment between nine o'clock in

---

m   *Omitted (A)*   o   this journal's/the *(A)*
n   has *(A)*   p   would *(A)*

THE MYSTERY OF MARIE ROGET

the morning of Sunday,[45] and a quarter before midnight, there would still have been time enough 'to throw the body into the river before midnight.' This assumption, then, amounts precisely to this — that the murder was not committed on Sunday at all — and, if we allow L'Etoile[q] to assume this, we may permit it any liberties whatever. The paragraph beginning 'It is folly to suppose that the murder, etc.,' however it appears as printed in L'Etoile, may be imagined to have existed actually *thus* in the brain of its inditer — 'It is folly to suppose that the murder, if murder was committed on the body, could have been committed soon enough to have enabled her murderers to throw the body into the river before midnight; it is folly, we say, to suppose all this, and to suppose at the same time, (as we are resolved to suppose,) that the body was *not* thrown in until *after* midnight' — a sentence sufficiently inconsequential in itself, but not so utterly preposterous as the one printed.

"Were it my purpose," continued Dupin, "merely to *make out a case* against this passage of L'Etoile's argument, I might safely leave it where it is. It is not, however, with L'Etoile that we have to do, but with the truth. The sentence in question has but one meaning, as it stands; and this meaning I have fairly stated: but it is material that we go behind the mere words, for an idea which these words have obviously intended, and failed to convey. It was the design of the journalist to say that, at whatever period of the day or night of Sunday this murder was committed, it was improbable that the assassins would have ventured to bear the corpse to the river before midnight. And herein lies, really, the assumption of which I[r] complain. It is assumed that the murder was committed at such a position, and under such circumstances, that *the bearing it* to the river became necessary. Now, the assassination might have taken place upon the river's brink, or on the river itself; and, thus, the throwing the corpse in the water might have been resorted to, at any period of the day or night, as the most obvious and most immediate mode of disposal. You will understand that I suggest nothing here as probable, or as coincident with my own opinion.

---

q   it *(A)*   r   we *(A)*

TALES: 1843–1844

My design, so far, has no reference to the *facts* of the case. I wish merely to caution you against the whole tone of L'Etoile's *suggestion,* by calling your attention to its *ex parte* character at the outset.

"Having prescribed thus a limit to suit its own preconceived notions; having assumed that, if this were the body of Marie, it could have been in the water but a very brief time; the journal goes on to say:

> 'All experience has shown that drowned bodies, or bodies thrown into the water immediately after death by violence, require from six to ten days for sufficient^s decomposition to take place to bring them to the top of the water. Even when a cannon is fired over a corpse, and it rises before at least five or six days' immersion, it sinks again if let alone.'[46]

"These assertions have been tacitly received by every paper in Paris, with the exception of Le Moniteur.*[47] This latter print endeavors to combat that portion of the paragraph which has reference to 'drowned bodies' only, by citing some five or six instances in which the bodies of individuals known to be drowned were found floating after the lapse of less time than is insisted upon by L'Etoile. But there is something excessively unphilosophical in the attempt on the part of Le Moniteur, to rebut the general assertion of L'Etoile, by a citation of particular instances militating against that assertion. Had it been possible to adduce fifty instead of five examples of bodies found floating at the end of two or three days, these fifty examples could still have been properly regarded ᵗonly as exceptionsᵗ to L'Etoile's rule, until such time as the rule itself should be confuted. Admitting the rule, (and this Le Moniteur does not deny, insisting merely upon its exceptions,) the argument of L'Etoile is suffered to remain in full force; for this argument does not pretend to involve more than a question of the *probability* of the body having risen to the surface in less than three days; and this probability will be in favor of L'Etoile's position until the instances so childishly adduced shall be sufficient in number to establish an antagonistical rule.[48]

"You will see at once that all argument upon this head should

* The "N. Y. Commercial Advertiser," edited by Col. Stone.

---

s   *Omitted (A)*   t . . . t   as exceptions alone *(A)*

THE MYSTERY OF MARIE ROGET

be urged, if at all, against the rule itself; and for this end we must examine the *rationale* of the rule.[49] Now the human body, in general, is neither much lighter nor much heavier than the water of the Seine; that is to say, the specific gravity of the human body, in its natural condition, is about equal to the bulk of fresh water which it displaces. The bodies of fat and fleshy persons, with small bones, and of women generally, are lighter than those of the lean and large-boned, and of men; and the specific gravity of the water of a river is somewhat influenced by the presence of the tide from sea. But, leaving this tide out of question, it may be said that *very* few human bodies will sink at all, even in fresh water, *of their own accord.* Almost any one, falling into a river, will be enabled to float, if he suffer[u] the specific gravity of the water fairly to be adduced in comparison with his own—that is to say, if he suffer[v] his whole person to be immersed, with as little exception as possible. The proper position for one who cannot swim, is the upright position of the walker on land, with the head thrown fully back, and immersed; the mouth and nostrils alone remaining above the surface. Thus circumstanced, we shall find that we float without difficulty and without exertion. It is evident, however, that the gravities of the body, and of the bulk of water displaced, are very nicely balanced, and that a trifle will cause either to preponderate. An arm, for instance, uplifted from the water, and thus deprived of its support, is an additional weight sufficient to immerse the whole head, while the accidental aid of the smallest piece of timber will enable us to elevate the head so as to look about. Now, in the struggles of one unused to swimming, the arms are invariably thrown upwards, while an attempt is made to keep the head in its usual perpendicular position. The result is the immersion of the mouth and nostrils, and the inception, during efforts to breathe while beneath the surface, of water into the lungs. Much is also received into the stomach, and the whole body becomes heavier by the difference between the weight of the air originally distending these cavities, and that of the fluid which now fills them. This difference is sufficient to cause the body to sink, as a general rule; but is insufficient

---

u   suffers *(A)*   v   suffers *(A)*

TALES: 1843–1844

in the cases of individuals with small bones and an abnormal quantity of flaccid or fatty matter. Such individuals float even after drowning.

"The corpse, being supposed at the bottom of the river, will there remain until, by some means, its specific gravity again becomes less than that of the bulk of water which it displaces. This effect is brought about by decomposition, or otherwise. The result of decomposition is the generation of gas, distending the cellular tissues and all the cavities, and giving the *puffed* appearance which is so^w horrible. When this distension has so far progressed that the bulk of the corpse is materially increased without a corresponding increase of *mass* or weight, its specific gravity becomes less than that of the water displaced, and it forthwith makes its appearance at the surface. But decomposition is modified by innumerable circumstances — is hastened or retarded by innumerable agencies; for example, by the heat or cold of the season, by the mineral impregnation or purity of the water, by its depth or shallowness, by its currency or stagnation, by the temperament of the body, by its infection or freedom from disease before death. Thus it is evident that we can assign no period, with any thing like accuracy, at which the corpse shall rise through decomposition. Under certain conditions this result would be brought about within an hour; under others, it might not take place at all. There are chemical infusions by which the animal frame can be preserved *forever* from corruption; the Bi-chloride of Mercury is one. But, apart from decomposition, there may be, and very usually is, a generation of gas within the stomach, from the acetous fermentation of vegetable matter (or within other cavities from other causes) sufficient to induce a distension which will bring the body to the surface. The effect produced by the firing of a cannon is that of simple vibration. This may either loosen the corpse from the soft mud or ooze in which it is imbedded, thus permitting it to rise when other agencies have already prepared it for so doing; or it may overcome the tenacity of some putrescent portions of the cellular tissue; allowing the cavities to distend under the influence of the gas.

---

w   to (B, C) *misprint*

THE MYSTERY OF MARIE ROGET

"Having thus before us the whole philosophy of this subject, we can easily test by it the assertions of L'Etoile. 'All experience shows,' says this paper, 'that drowned bodies, or bodies thrown into the water immediately after death by violence, require from six to ten days for sufficient decomposition to take place to bring them to the top of the water. Even when a cannon is fired over a corpse, and it rises before at least five or six days' immersion, it sinks again if let alone.'[50]

"The whole of this paragraph must now appear a tissue of inconsequence and incoherence. All experience does *not* show that 'drowned bodies' *require* from six to ten days for sufficient decomposition to take place to bring them to the surface. Both science and experience show that the period of their rising is, and necessarily must be, indeterminate. If, moreover, a body has risen to the surface through firing of cannon, it will *not* 'sink again if let alone,' until decomposition has so far progressed as to permit the escape of the generated gas. But I wish to call your attention to the distinction which is made between 'drowned bodies,' and 'bodies thrown into the water immediately after death by violence.' Although the writer admits the distinction, he yet includes them all in the same category. I have shown how it is that the body of a drowning man becomes specifically heavier than its bulk of water, and that he would not sink at all, except for the struggles by which he elevates his arms above the surface, and his gasps for breath while beneath the surface — gasps which supply by water the place of the original air in the lungs. But these struggles and these gasps would not occur in the body 'thrown into the water immediately after death by violence.' Thus, in the latter instance, *the ˣbody, as a general rule,ˣ would not sink at all* — a fact of which L'Etoile is evidently ignorant. When decomposition had proceeded to a very great extent — when the flesh had in a great measure left the bones — then, indeed, but not *till* then, should we lose sight of the corpse.

"And now what are we to make of the argument,ʸ that the body found could not be that of Marie Rogêt, because, three days only

---

x . . . x   *body (A)*   y   argument of the journal, *(A)*

TALES: 1843–1844

having elapsed, this body was found floating? [z]If drowned, being a woman, she might never have sunk; or having sunk, might have re-appeared in twenty-four hours, or less. But no[z] one supposes her to have been drowned; and, dying before being thrown into the river, she might have been found floating at any period afterwards whatever.

" 'But,' says L'Etoile, 'if the body had been kept in its mangled state on shore until Tuesday night, some trace would be found on shore of the murderers.'[51] Here it is at first difficult to perceive the intention of the reasoner. He means to anticipate what he imagines would be an objection to his theory — viz: that the body was kept on shore two days, suffering rapid [a]decomposition — *more* rapid than if immersed in water.[a] He supposes that, had this been the case, it *might* have appeared at the surface on the Wednesday, and thinks that *only* under such circumstances it could so have appeared. He is accordingly in haste to show that it *was not* kept on shore; for, if so, 'some trace would be found on shore of the murderers.' I presume you smile at the *sequitur*. You cannot be made to see how the mere *duration* of the corpse on the shore could operate to *multiply traces* of the assassins. Nor can I.

" 'And furthermore it is exceedingly improbable,' continues our journal, 'that any villains who had committed such a murder as is here supposed, would have thrown the body in without weight to sink it, when such a precaution could have so easily been taken.'[52] Observe, here, the laughable confusion of thought! No one — not even L'Etoile — disputes the murder committed *on the body found*. The marks of violence are too obvious. It is our reasoner's object merely to show that this body is not Marie's. He wishes to prove that *Marie* is not assassinated — not that the corpse was not. Yet his observation proves only the latter point. Here is a corpse without weight attached. Murderers, casting it in, would not have failed to attach a weight. Therefore it was not thrown in by murderers. This is all which is proved, if any thing is.[b] The question of identity is not even approached, and L'Etoile has been at great pains merely to gainsay now what it has admitted only a moment before. 'We

---

z . . . z   No *(A)*   b   be. *(A)*
a . . . a   decomposition. *(A)*

THE MYSTERY OF MARIE ROGET

are perfectly convinced,' it says, 'that the body found was that of a murdered female.'[53]

"Nor is this the sole instance, even in this division of his subject, where our reasoner unwittingly reasons against himself. His evident ᶜobject, I have already said,ᶜ is to reduce, as much as possible, the interval between Marie's disappearance and the finding of the corpse. Yet we find him *urging* the point that no person saw the girl from the moment of her leaving her mother's house. 'We have no evidence,' he says, 'that Marie Rogêt was in the land of the living after nine o'clock on Sunday, June the twenty-second.'[54] As his argument is obviously an *ex parte* one, he should, at least, have left this matter out of sight; for had any one been known to see Marie, say on Monday, or on Tuesday, the interval in question would have been much reduced, and, by his own ratiocination, the probability much diminished of the corpse being that of the *grisette.*ᵈ It is, nevertheless, amusing to observe that L'Etoile insists upon its point in the full belief of its furthering its general argument.

"Reperuse now that portion of this argument which has reference to the identification of the corpse by Beauvais.[55] In regard to the *hair* upon the arm, L'Etoileᵉ has been obviously disingenuous. M. Beauvais, not being an idiot, could never have urged, in identification of the corpse, simply *hair upon its arm.* No arm is *without* hair. The ᶠ*generality* of theᶠ expression of L'Etoile is a mere perversion of the witness' phraseology. He must have spoken of some *peculiarity* in this hair. It must have beenᵍ a peculiarity of color, of quantity, of length, or of situation.

" 'Her foot,' says the journal, 'was small — so are thousands of feet. Her garter is no proof whatever — nor is her shoe — for shoes and garters are sold in packages. The same may be said of the flowers in her hat. One thing upon which M. Beauvais strongly insists is, that the clasp on the garter found, had been set back to take it in. This amounts to nothing; for most women find it proper to take a pair of garters home and fit them to the size of the limbs

---

c . . . c object *(A)*	f . . . f *general (A)*
d grisette. *(A)*	g must have been/was *(A)*
e our paper *(A)*	

TALES: 1843–1844

they are to encircle, rather than to try them in the store where they purchase.'[56] Here it is difficult to suppose the reasoner[h] in earnest. Had M. Beauvais, in his search for the body of Marie, discovered a corpse corresponding in general size and appearance to the missing girl, he would have been warranted (without reference to the question of habiliment at all) in forming an opinion that his search had been successful. If, in addition to the point of general size and contour, he had found upon the arm a peculiar hairy appearance which he had observed upon the living Marie, his opinion might have been justly strengthened; and the increase of positiveness might well have been in the ratio of the peculiarity, or unusualness, of the hairy mark. If, the feet of Marie being small, those of the corpse were also small, the increase of probability that the body was that of Marie would not be an increase in a ratio merely [i]arithmetical, but in one highly geometrical, or[i] accumulative. Add to all this shoes such as she had been known to wear upon the day of her disappearance, and, although these shoes may be 'sold in packages,' you so far augment the probability as to verge upon the certain. What, of itself, would be no evidence of identity, becomes through its corroborative position, proof most sure. Give us, then, flowers in the hat corresponding to those worn by the missing girl, and we seek for nothing farther. If only *one* flower, we seek for nothing farther — what then if two or three, or more? Each successive one is multiple evidence — proof not *added* to proof, but *multiplied* by hundreds or thousands.[57] Let us now discover, upon the deceased, garters such as the living used, and it is almost folly to proceed. But these garters are found to be tightened, by the setting back of a clasp, in just such a manner as her own had been tightened by Marie, shortly previous to her leaving home. It is now madness or hypocrisy to doubt. What L'Etoile says in respect to this abbreviation of the garter's being an usual occurrence, shows nothing beyond its own pertinacity in error. The elastic nature of the clasp-garter is self-demonstration of the *unusualness* of the abbreviation. What is made to adjust[j] itself, must of necessity require [k]foreign adjustment[k] but rarely. It must have

---

h   journal *(A)*
i . . . i   direct, but in one highly *(A)*

j   accomodate *(A)*
k . . . k   accomodation *(A)*

THE MYSTERY OF MARIE ROGET

been by an accident, in its strictest sense, that these garters of Marie needed the tightening described. They alone would have amply established her identity. But it is not that the corpse was found to have the garters of the missing girl, or found to have her shoes, or her bonnet, or the flowers of her bonnet, or her feet, or a peculiar mark upon the arm, or her general size and appearance — it is that the corpse had each, and *all collectively.* Could it be proved that the editor of L'Etoile *really* entertained a doubt, under the circumstances, there would be no need, in his case, of a commission *de lunatico inquirendo.*⁵⁸ He has¹ thought it sagacious to echo the small talk of the lawyers, who, for the most part, content themselves with echoing the rectangular precepts of the courts. I would here observe that very much of what is rejected as evidence by a court, is the best of evidence to the intellect. For the court, guiding itself by the general principles of evidence — the recognized and *booked* principles — is averse from swerving at particular instances. And this steadfast adherence to principle, with rigorous disregard of the conflicting exception, is a sure mode of attaining the *maximum* of attainable truth, in any long sequence of time. The practice, *in mass,* is therefore philosophical; but it is not the less certain that it engendersᵐ vast individual error.*⁵⁹

"In respect to the insinuations levelled at Beauvais, you will be willing to dismiss them in a breath. You have already fathomed the true character of this good gentleman. He is a *busy-body,* with much of romance and little of wit. Any one so constituted will readily so conduct himself, upon occasion of *real* excitement, as to render himself liable to suspicion on the part of the over-acute, or the ill-disposed. M. Beauvais (as it appears from your notes) had some personal interviews with the editor of L'Etoile, and offended him by venturing an opinion that the corpse, notwithstanding the

---

* "A theory based on the qualities of an object, will prevent its being unfolded according to its objects; and he who arranges topics in reference to their causes, will cease to value them according to their results. Thus the jurisprudence of every nation will show that, when law becomes a science and a system, it ceases to be justice. The errors into which a blind devotion to *principles* of classification has led the common law, will be seen by observing how often the legislature has been obliged to come forward to restore the equity its scheme had lost." — *Landor.*

---

l   had *(A)*   m   engenders frequently *(A)*

TALES: 1843–1844

theory of the editor, was, in sober fact that of Marie.[60] 'He persists,' says the paper,[n] 'in asserting the corpse to be that of Marie, but cannot give a circumstance, in addition to those which we have commented upon, to make others believe.' Now, without re-adverting to the fact that stronger evidence 'to make others believe,' could *never* have been adduced, it may be remarked that a man may very well be understood to believe, in a case of this kind, without the ability to advance a single reason for the belief of a second party. Nothing is more vague than impressions of individual identity. Each man recognizes his neighbor, yet there are few instances in which any one is prepared to *give a reason* for his recognition. The editor of L'Etoile had no right to be offended at M. Beauvais' unreasoning belief.[61]

"The suspicious circumstances which invest him, will be found to tally much better with my[o] hypothesis of *romantic busy-bodyism,* than with the reasoner's suggestion of guilt. Once adopting the more charitable interpretation, we shall find no difficulty in comprehending the rose in the key-hole; the 'Marie' upon the slate; the 'elbowing the male relatives out of the way;' the 'aversion to permitting them to see the body;' the caution given to Madame B——, that she must hold no conversation with the *gendarme* until his return (Beauvais'); and, lastly, his apparent determination 'that nobody should have anything to do with the proceedings except himself.' It seems to me unquestionable that Beauvais was a suitor of Marie's; that she coquetted with him; and that he was ambitious of being thought to enjoy her fullest intimacy and confidence. I shall say nothing more upon this point; and, as the evidence fully rebuts the assertion of L'Etoile, touching the matter of *apathy* on the part of the mother and other relatives — an apathy inconsistent with the supposition of their believing the corpse to be that of the perfumery-girl — we shall now proceed as if the question of *identity* were settled to our perfect satisfaction."[62]

"And what," I here demanded, "do you think of the opinions of Le Commerciel?"[63]

"That, in spirit, they are far more worthy of attention than any

---

n   the paper,/our journal, *(A)*   o   our *(A)*

THE MYSTERY OF MARIE ROGET

which have been promulgated upon the subject. The deductions from the premises are philosophical and acute; but the premises, in two instances, at least, are founded in imperfect observation. Le Commerciel wishes to intimate that Marie was seized by some gang of low ruffians not far from her mother's door. 'It is impossible,' it urges, 'that a person so well known to thousands as this young woman was, should have passed three blocks without some one having seen her.' This is the idea of a man long resident in Paris — a public man — and one whose walks to and fro in the city, have been mostly limited to the vicinity of the public offices. He is aware that he[p] seldom passes so far as a dozen blocks from his own *bureau*, without being recognized and accosted. And, knowing the extent of his personal acquaintance with others, and of others with him, he compares his notoriety with that of the perfumery-girl, finds no great difference between them, and reaches at once the conclusion that she, in her walks, would be equally liable to recognition [q]with himself in his.[q] This could only be the case were her walks of the same unvarying, methodical character, and within the same *species* of limited region as are his own. He passes to and fro, at regular intervals, within a confined periphery, abounding in individuals who are led to observation of his person through interest in the kindred nature of his occupation with their own. But the walks of Marie may, in general, be supposed discursive. In this particular instance, it will be understood as most probable, that she proceeded upon a route of more than average diversity from her accustomed ones. The parallel which we imagine to have existed in the mind of Le Commerciel would only be sustained in the event of the two individuals'[r] traversing the whole city. In this case, granting the personal acquaintances to be equal, the chances would be also equal that an equal number of personal rencounters would be made. For my own part, I should hold it not only as possible, but as very far more than probable, that Marie might have proceeded, at any given period, by any one of the many routes between her own residence and that of her aunt, without meeting a single individual whom she knew, or by whom she was

---

p   he *(A)*
q . . . q   with himself. *(A)*

r   individuals *(D) misprint*

TALES: 1843–1844

known. In viewing this question in its full and proper light, we must hold steadily in mind the great disproportion between the personal acquaintances of even the most noted individual in Paris, and the entire population of Paris itself.

"But whatever force there may still appear to be in the suggestion of Le Commerciel, will be much diminished when we take into consideration *the hour* at which the girl went abroad. 'It was when the streets were full of people,' says Le Commerciel, 'that she went out.' But not so. It was at nine o'clock in the morning.[64] Now at nine o'clock of every morning in the week, *with the exception of Sunday*, the streets of the city are, it is true, thronged with people. At nine on Sunday, the populace are chiefly within doors *preparing for church*. No ˢobserving personˢ can have failed to notice the peculiarly deserted air of the town, from about eight until ten on the morning of every Sabbath. Between ten and eleven the streets are thronged, but not at so early a period as that designated.

"There is another point at which there seems a deficiency of *observation* on the part of Le Commerciel. 'A piece,' it says, 'of one of the unfortunate girl's petticoats, two feet long, and one foot wide, was torn out and tied under her chin, and around the back of her head, probably to prevent screams. This was done by fellows who had no pocket-handkerchiefs.' Whether this idea is, or is not well founded, we will endeavor to see hereafter; but by 'fellows who have no pocket-handkerchiefs,' the editor intends the lowest class of ruffians. These, however, are the very description of people who will always be found to have handkerchiefs even when destitute of shirts. You must have had occasion to observe how absolutely indispensable, of late years, to the thorough blackguard, has become the pocket-handkerchief."[65]

"And what are we to think," I asked, "of the article in Le Soleil?"[66]

"That it is aᵗ pityᵘ its inditer was not ᵛborn a parrot — in which case he would have been the most illustrious parrot of his race.ᵛ He

---

s . . . s   one of observation, *(A)*
t   a vast *(A, B, D)*
u   pity that *(A)*

v . . . v   more minute. It is easy to surmise, and as easy to assert. *(A)*

THE MYSTERY OF MARIE ROGET

has merely repeated[w] the individual items of the already published opinion; collecting them, with a laudable industry, from this paper and from that.[67] 'The things had all *evidently* been there,' he says, 'at least, three or four weeks, and there can be *no doubt* that the spot of this appalling outrage has been discovered.'[x] The facts here re-stated by Le Soleil, are very far indeed from removing my own doubts upon this subject, and we will examine them more particularly hereafter in connexion with another division of the theme.

"At present we must occupy ourselves with other investigations. You cannot fail to have remarked the extreme laxity of the examination of the corpse. To be sure, the question of identity was readily determined, or should have been; but there were other points to be ascertained. Had the body been in any respect *despoiled?* Had the deceased any articles of jewelry about her person upon leaving home? if so, had she any when found? These are important questions utterly untouched by the evidence;[68] and there are others of equal moment, which have met with no attention. We must endeavor to satisfy ourselves by personal inquiry. The case of St.[y] Eustache must be re-examined. I have no suspicion of this person; but let us proceed methodically. We will ascertain beyond a doubt the validity of the *affidavits* in regard to his whereabouts on the Sunday. Affidavits of this character are readily made matter of mystification. Should there be nothing wrong here, however, we will dismiss St.[z] Eustache from our investigations. His suicide, however corroborative of suspicion, were there found to be deceit in the affidavits, is, without such deceit, in no respect an unaccountable circumstance, or one which need cause us to deflect from the line of ordinary analysis.

"In that[a] which I now propose, we will discard the interior[b] points of this tragedy, and concentrate our attention upon its outskirts.[c] Not the least usual error, in investigations such as this, is

---

w   repeated what others have done, (without establishing any incontrovertible proofs) *(A)*
x   *After this* Here, again, he speaks but from suspicion, and brings nothing to bear conclusively upon the matter. *(A)*

y   Saint *(A)*
z   Saint *(A)*
a   the analysis *(A)*
b   *interior (A)*
c   *outskirts. (A)*

TALES: 1843–1844

the limiting of inquiry to the immediate, with total disregard of the collateral or circumstantial[d] events. It is the mal-practice of the courts to confine evidence and discussion to the bounds of apparent relevancy.[e] Yet experience has shown, and a true philosophy will always show, that a vast, perhaps the larger portion of truth, arises from the seemingly irrelevant.[69] It is through the spirit of this principle, if not precisely through its letter,[70] that modern science has resolved to *calculate upon the unforeseen*. But perhaps you do not comprehend me. The history of human knowledge has so uninterruptedly shown that to collateral, or incidental, or accidental events we are indebted for the most numerous and most valuable discoveries, that it has at length become necessary, in any prospective view of improvement, to make not only large, but the largest allowances for inventions that shall arise by chance, and quite out of the range of ordinary expectation. It is no longer philosophical to base, upon what has been, a vision of what is to be. *Accident* is admitted as a portion of the substructure.[f] We make chance a matter of absolute calculation.[g] We subject the unlooked for and unimagined, to the mathematical *formulae* of the schools.

"I repeat that it is no more than fact, that the *larger* portion[h] of all truth has sprung from the collateral; and it is but in accordance with the spirit of the principle involved in this fact, that I would divert inquiry, in the present case, from the trodden and hitherto unfruitful ground of the event itself, to the cotemporary circumstances which surround it. While you ascertain the validity of the affidavits, I will examine the newspapers more generally than you have as yet done. So far, we have only reconnoitred the field of investigation; but it will be strange indeed if a comprehensive survey, such as I propose, of the public prints, will not afford us some minute points which shall establish a *direction* for inquiry."

In pursuance of Dupin's suggestion, I made scrupulous examination of the affair of the affidavits. The result was a firm conviction of their validity, and of the consequent innocence of St.[i]

---

d *circumstantial (A)*
e *relevancy. (A)*
f subtructure. *(A) misprint*
g certainty. *(A)*
h proportion *(A)*
i Saint *(A)*

THE MYSTERY OF MARIE ROGET

Eustache.[71] In the mean time my friend occupied himself, with what seemed to me a minuteness altogether objectless, in a scrutiny of the various newspaper files. At the end of a week he placed before me the following extracts:[72]

"jAbout three years and a half ago,j a disturbance very similar to the present, was caused by the disappearance of this same Marie Rogêt, from the *parfumerie* of Monsieur Le Blanc, in the Palais Royal. At the end of a week, however, she re-appeared at her customary *comptoir*, as well as ever, with the exception of a slight paleness not altogether usual. It was given out by Monsieur Le Blanc and her mother, that she had merely been on a visit to some friend in the country; and the affair was speedily hushed up. We presume that the present absence is a freak of the same nature, and that, at the expiration of a week, or perhaps of a month, we shall have her among us again." — *Evening Paper — Monday, June 23.**

"An evening journal of yesterday, refers to a former mysterious disappearance of Mademoiselle Rogêt. It is well known that, during the week of her absence from Le Blanc's *parfumerie,* she was in the company of a young naval officer, much noted for his debaucheries. A quarrel, it is supposed, providentially led to her return home. We have the name of the Lothario in question, who is, at present, stationed in Paris, but, for obvious reasons, forbear to make it public." — *Le Mercurie — Tuesday Morning, June 24.*†[73]

"An outrage of the most atrocious character was perpetrated near this city the day before yesterday. A gentleman, with his wife and daughter, engaged, about dusk, the services of six young men, who were idly rowing a boat to and fro near the banks of the Seine, to convey him across the river. Upon reaching the opposite shore, the three passengers stepped out, and had proceeded so far as to be beyond the view of the boat, when the daughter discovered that she had left in it her parasol. She returned for it, was seized by the gang, carried out into the stream, gagged, brutally treated, and finally taken to the shore at a point not far from that at which she had originally entered the boat with her parents. The villains have escaped for the time, but the police are upon their trail, and some of them will soon be taken." — *Morning Paper — June 25.*‡[74]

"We have received one or two communications, the object of which is to fasten the crime of the late atrocity upon Mennais;§ but as this gentleman has been fully exonerated by a legal inquiry, and as the arguments of our several correspondents appear to be more zealous than profound, we do not think it advisable to make them public." — *Morning Paper — June 28.***[75]

"We have received several forcibly written communications, apparently from various sources, and which go far to render it a matter of certainty that the

* "N. Y. Express." † "N. Y. Herald." ‡ "N. Y. Courier and Inquirer."
§ Mennais was one of the parties originally suspected and arrested, but discharged through total lack of evidence.
** "N. Y. Courier and Inquirer."

---

j . . . j   Two or three years since, *(A)*

TALES: 1843–1844

unfortunate Marie Rogêt has become a victim of one of the numerous bands of blackguards which infest the vicinity of the city upon Sunday. Our own opinion is decidedly in favor of this supposition. We shall endeavor to make room for some of these arguments hereafter." — *Evening Paper — Tuesday, June 31*.‡[76]

"On Monday, one of the bargemen connected with the revenue service, saw an empty boat floating down the Seine. Sails were lying in the bottom of the boat. The bargeman towed it under the barge office. The next morning it was taken from thence, without the knowledge of any of the officers. The rudder is now at the barge office." — *Le Diligence — Thursday, June 26.*§[77]

Upon reading these various extracts, they not only seemed to me irrelevant, but I could perceive no mode in which any one of them could be brought to bear upon the matter in hand. I waited for some explanation from Dupin.

"It is not my present[k] design," he said, "to *dwell* upon the first and second of these extracts. I have copied them chiefly to show you the extreme remissness of the police, who, as far as I can understand from the Prefect, have not troubled themselves, in any respect, with an examination of the naval officer alluded to. Yet it is mere folly to say that between the first and second disappearance of Marie, there is no *supposable* connection. Let us admit the first elopement to have resulted in a quarrel between the lovers, and the return home of the betrayed. We are now prepared to view a second *elopement* (if we *know* that an elopement has again taken place) as indicating a renewal of the betrayer's advances, rather than as the result of new proposals by a second individual — we are prepared to regard it as a 'making up' of the old *amour,* rather than as the commencement of a new one. The chances are ten[l] to one, that he who had once eloped with Marie, would again propose an elopement, rather than that she to whom proposals of elopement had been made by one individual, should have them made to her by another. And here let me call your attention to the fact, that the time elapsing between the first ascertained, and the second supposed elopement, is ᵐa few months more thanᵐ the general period of the cruises of our men-of-war. Had the lover been interrupted in his

‡ "N. Y. Evening Post." § "N. Y. Standard."

k *Omitted (A)* m . . . m precisely *(A)*
l ten thousand *(A)*

THE MYSTERY OF MARIE ROGET

first villainy[n] by the necessity of departure to sea, and had he seized the first moment of his return to renew the base designs not yet altogether [o]accomplished — or not yet altogether accomplished *by him?*[o] Of all these things we know nothing.

"You will say, however, that, in the second instance, there was *no* elopement as imagined. Certainly not — but are we prepared to say that there was not the frustrated design? Beyond St.[p] Eustache, and perhaps Beauvais, we find no recognized, no open, no honorable suitors of Marie. Of none other is there any thing said. Who, then, is the secret lover, of whom the relatives (*at least most of them*) know nothing, but whom Marie meets upon the morning of Sunday, and who is so deeply in her confidence, that she hesitates not to remain with him until the shades of the evening descend, amid the solitary groves of the Barrière du Roule? Who is that secret lover, I ask, of whom, at least, *most* of the relatives know nothing? And what means the singular prophecy of Madame Rogêt on the morning of Marie's departure? — 'I fear that I shall never see Marie again.'[78]

"But if we cannot imagine Madame Rogêt privy to the design of elopement, may we not at least suppose this design entertained by the girl? Upon quitting home, she gave it to be understood that she was about to visit her aunt in the Rue des Drômes, and St.[q] Eustache was requested to call for her at dark. Now, at first glance, this fact strongly militates against my suggestion; — but let us reflect. That she *did* meet[r] some companion, and proceed with him across the river, reaching the Barrière du Roule at so[s] late an hour as three o'clock in the afternoon, is known.[79] But in consenting so to accompany this individual, [t](*for whatever purpose — to her mother known or unknown,*)[t] she must have thought of her expressed intention when leaving home, and of the surprise and suspicion aroused in the bosom of her affianced suitor, St.[u] Eustache, when, calling for her, at the hour appointed, in the Rue des Drômes, he should find that she had not been there, and when,

n	villany *(A, B, C, D)*	r	meet with *(A)*
o . . . o	accomplished? *(A)*	s	at so/atso *(A)*
p	Saint *(A)*	t . . . t	*Omitted (A)*
q	Saint *(A)*	u	Saint *(A)*

TALES: 1843–1844

moreover, upon returning to the *pension* with this alarming intelligence, he should become aware of her continued absence from home. She must have thought of these things, I say. She must have foreseen the chagrin of St.ᵛ Eustache, the suspicion of all. She could not have thought of returning to brave this suspicion; but the suspicion becomes a point of trivial importance to her, if we suppose her *not* intending to return.

"We may imagine her thinking thus — 'I am to meet a certain person for the purpose of ʷelopement, or for certain other purposes known only to myself.ʷ It is necessary that there be no chance of interruption — there must be sufficient time given us to elude pursuit — I will give it to be understood that I shall visit and spend the day with my aunt at the Rue des Drômes — I willˣ tell St.ʸ Eustache not to call for me until dark — in this way, my absence from home for the longest possible period, without causing suspicion or anxiety, will be accounted for, and I shall gain more time than in any other manner. If I bid St.ᶻ Eustache call for me at dark, he will be sure not to call before; but, if I wholly neglect to bid him call, my time for escape will be diminished, since it will be expected that I return the earlier, and my absence will the sooner excite anxiety. Now, if it were my design to return *at all* — if I had in contemplation merely a stroll with the individual in question — it would not be my policy to bid St.ᵃ Eustache call; for, calling, he will be *sure* to ascertain that I have played him false — a fact of which I might keep him for ever in ignorance, by leaving home without notifying him of my intention, by returning before dark, and by then stating that I had been to visit my aunt in the Rue des Drômes. But, as it is my design *never* to ᵇreturn — or not for some weeks — or not until certain concealments are effected — theᵇ gaining of time is the only point about which I need give myself any concern.'ᶜ ⁸⁰

---

v   Saint *(A)*
w . . . w   elopement. *(A)*
x   well *(B, C, D) misprint*
y   Saint *(A)*
z   Saint *(A)*
a   Saint *(A)*
b . . . b   return, the *(A)*

c   *After this is another paragraph:*
"Such thoughts as these we may *imagine* to have passsed through the mind of Marie, but the point is one upon which I consider it necessary now to insist. I have reasoned thus, merely to call attention, as I said a minute ago, to the culpable remissness of the police. *(A)*

THE MYSTERY OF MARIE ROGET

"You have observed, in your notes, that the most general opinion in relation to this sad affair is, and was from the first, that the girl had been the victim of *a gang* of blackguards.[81] Now, the popular opinion, under certain conditions, is not to be disregarded. When arising of itself — when manifesting itself in a strictly spontaneous manner — we should look upon it as analogous with that *intuition* which is the idiosyncrasy of the individual man of genius. In ninety-nine cases from the hundred I would abide by its decision. But it is important that we find no palpable traces of *suggestion*. The opinion must be rigorously *the public's own;* and the distinction is often exceedingly difficult to perceive and to maintain. In the present instance, it appears to me that this 'public opinion,' in respect to *a gang,* has been superinduced by the collateral event which is detailed in the third of my extracts.[82] All Paris is excited by the discovered corpse of Marie, a girl young, beautiful and notorious. This[d] corpse is found, bearing marks of violence, and floating in the river. But it is now made known that, at the very period, or about the very period, in which it is supposed that the girl was assassinated, an outrage similar in nature to that endured by the deceased, although less in extent, was perpetrated, by a gang of young ruffians, upon the person of a second young female. Is it wonderful that the one known atrocity should influence the popular judgment in regard to the other unknown? This judgment awaited direction, and the known outrage seemed so opportunely to afford it! Marie, too, was found in the river; and upon this very river was this known outrage committed. The connexion of the two events had about it so much of the palpable, that the true wonder would have been a *failure* of the populace to appreciate and to seize it. But, in fact,[e] the one atrocity, known to be so committed, is, if any thing, evidence that the other, committed at a time nearly coincident, was *not* so committed. It would have been a miracle indeed, if, while a gang of ruffians were perpetrating, at a given locality, a most unheard-of wrong, there should have been another similar gang, in a similar locality, in the same city, under the same circumstances, with the same means and appliances, engaged in a wrong of precisely the same aspect, at precisely the same period of time![83] Yet

---

d   The *(A)*   e   in fact,/to the philosophical, *(A)*

TALES: 1843–1844

in what, if not in this marvellous train of coincidence, does the accidentally *suggested* opinion of the populace call upon us to believe?[84]

"Before proceeding farther, let us[f] consider the supposed scene of the assassination, in the thicket at the Barrière du Roule. This thicket, although dense, was in the close vicinity of a public road. Within were three or four large stones, forming a kind of seat with a back and footstool. On the upper stone was discovered a white petticoat; on the second, a silk scarf. A parasol, gloves, and a pocket-handkerchief, were also here found. The handkerchief bore the name, 'Marie Rogêt.' Fragments of dress were seen on the branches around. The earth was trampled, the bushes were broken, and there was every evidence of a violent struggle.[85]

"Notwithstanding the acclamation[g] with which the discovery of this thicket was received by the press, and the unanimity with which it was supposed to indicate the precise scene of the outrage, it must be admitted that there was some very good reason for doubt. That it *was* the scene, [h]I may or I may not[h] believe — but there was excellent reason for doubt.[86] Had the *true* scene been, as Le Commerciel suggested,[87] in the neighborhood of the Rue Pavée St. Andrée, the perpetrators of the crime, supposing them still resident in Paris, would naturally have been stricken with terror at the public attention thus acutely directed into the proper channel; and, in certain classes of minds, there would have arisen, at once, a sense of the necessity of some exertion to redivert this attention. And thus, the thicket[i] of the Barrière du Roule having been already suspected, the idea of placing the articles where they were found, might have been naturally entertained. There is no real evidence, although Le Soleil[j] so supposes, that the articles discovered had been more than a very few days in the thicket;[88] while there is much circumstantial proof that they could[k] not have remained there, without attracting attention, during the twenty days elapsing between the fatal Sunday and the afternoon upon which they were found by the boys.[89] 'They were all *mildewed* down hard,' says Le

---

f   us now *(A)*   i   thickets *(A)*
g   acclammation *(A) misprint*   j   Soliel *(A) misprint*
h...h   I *(A)*   k   would *(A)*

THE MYSTERY OF MARIE ROGET

Soleil, adopting the opinions of its predecessors, 'with the action of
the rain, and stuck together from *mildew*. The grass had grown
around and over some of them. The silk of the parasol was strong,
but the threads of it were run together within. The upper part,
where it had been doubled and folded, was all *mildewed* and rotten,
and tore on being opened.' In respect to the grass having 'grown
around and over some of them,' it is obvious that the fact could[l]
only have been ascertained from the words, and thus from the recollections, of two small boys; for these boys removed the articles
and took them home before they had been seen by a third party.[90]
But grass will grow, especially in warm and damp weather, (such
as was that of the period of the murder,) as much as[m] two or three
inches in a single day. A parasol lying upon a newly turfed ground,
might, in a[n] week, be entirely concealed from sight by the upspringing grass.[91] And touching that *mildew* upon which the editor of
Le Soleil[o] so pertinaciously insists, that he employs the word no
less than three times in the brief paragraph just quoted,[p] is he[q]
really unaware of the nature of this *mildew?* Is he to be told that
it is one of the many classes of *fungus,* of which the most ordinary[r]
feature is its upspringing and decadence within twenty-four hours?

"Thus we see, at a glance, that what has been most triumphantly
adduced in support of the idea that the articles had been 'for at least
three or four weeks' in the thicket, is most absurdly null as regards
any evidence of that fact. On[s] the other[t] hand, it is exceedingly difficult to believe that these articles could have remained in the thicket
specified, for a longer period than a single week — for a longer period than from one Sunday to the next. Those who know any thing
of the vicinity of Paris, know the extreme difficulty of finding *seclusion,* unless at a great distance from its suburbs. Such a thing as an
unexplored, or even an unfrequently visited recess, amid its woods
or groves, is not for a moment to be imagined. Let any one who,
being at heart a lover of nature, is yet chained by duty to the dust
and heat of this great metropolis — let any such one attempt, even

---

l   would *(A)*
m   *Omitted (A)*
n   a single *(A, B, D)*
o   Soliel *(A) misprint*
p   just quoted,/quoted just now — *(A)*

q   the editor *(A)*
r   remarkable *(A)*
s   But, on *(A)*
t   otner *(D) misprint*

TALES: 1843–1844

during the weekdays, to slake his thirst for solitude amid the scenes of natural loveliness which immediately surround us. At every second step, he will find the growing charm dispelled by the voice and personal intrusion of some ruffian or party of carousing blackguards. He will seek privacy amid the densest foliage, all in vain. Here are the very nooks where the unwashed most abound — here are the temples most desecrate.[u] With[v] sickness of the heart the wanderer will flee back to the polluted Paris as to a less odious because less incongruous sink of pollution. But if the vicinity[w] of the city is so beset during the working days of the week, how much more so on the Sabbath! It is now[x] especially that, released from the claims of labor, or deprived of the customary opportunities of crime, the[y] town blackguard seeks the precincts of the town, not through love of the rural, which in his heart he despises, but by way of escape from the restraints and conventionalities of society. He desires less the fresh air and the green trees, than the utter *license* of the country. Here, at the road-side inn, or beneath the foliage of the woods, he indulges, unchecked by any eye except those of his boon companions, in all the mad excess of a counterfeit hilarity — the joint offspring of liberty and of[z] rum. I say nothing more than what must be obvious to every dispassionate observer, when I repeat that the circumstance of the articles in question having remained undiscovered, for a longer period than from one Sunday to another, in *any* thicket in the immediate neighborhood of Paris, is to be looked upon as little less than miraculous.

"But there are not wanting other grounds for the suspicion that the articles were placed in the thicket with the view of diverting attention from the real scene of the outrage. And, first, let me direct your notice to the *date* of the discovery of the articles. Collate this with the date of the fifth extract made by myself from the newspapers.[92] You will find that the discovery followed, almost immediately, the urgent communications[a] sent to the evening paper. These communications, although various, and apparently from various

---

u   rife with desecration. *(A)*
v   With a deadly *(A)*
w   vicinage *(A)*
x   *Omitted (A)*

y   the lower order of the *(A)*
z   *Omitted (A)*
a   communication *(A)*

THE MYSTERY OF MARIE ROGET

sources, tended all to the same point — viz., the directing of attention to *a gang* as the perpetrators of the outrage, and to the neighborhood of the Barrière du Roule as its scene.[b] Now here, of course, the suspicion is not that, in consequence of these communications, or of the public attention by them directed, the articles were found by the boys; but the suspicion might and may well have been, that the articles were not *before* found by the boys, for the reason that the articles had not before been in the thicket; having been deposited there only at so late a period as at the date, or shortly prior to the date of the communications, by the guilty authors of these communications themselves.

"This thicket was a singular — an exceedingly singular one. It was unusually dense. Within its naturally walled enclosure were three extraordinary stones, *forming a seat with a back and footstool.* And this thicket, so full of a natural art, was in the immediate vicinity, *within a few rods,* of the dwelling of Madame Deluc, whose boys were in the habit of closely examining the shrubberies about them in search of the bark of the sassafras. Would it be a rash wager — a wager of one thousand to one — that *a day* never passed over the heads of these boys without finding at least one of them ensconced in the umbrageous hall, and enthroned upon its natural throne? Those who would hesitate at such a wager, have either never been boys themselves, or have forgotten the boyish nature. I repeat — it is exceedingly hard to comprehend how the articles could have remained in this thicket undiscovered, for a longer period than one or two days; and that thus there is good ground for suspicion, in spite of the dogmatic ignorance of Le Soleil,[c] that they were, at a comparatively late date, deposited where found.[93]

"But there are still other and stronger reasons for believing them so deposited, than any which I have as yet urged. And, now, let me beg your notice to the highly artificial arrangement of[d] the articles. On the *upper* stone lay a white petticoat; on the *second* a silk scarf; scattered around, were a parasol, gloves, and a pocket-handkerchief bearing the name, 'Marie Rogêt.' Here is just such an arrangement as would *naturally* be made by a not-over-acute person

---

b theatre. *(A)*
c Soliel *(A) misprint*

d or disposal of *(A)*

TALES: 1843–1844

wishing to dispose the articles *naturally*. But it is by no means a *really* natural arrangement. I should rather have looked to see the things *all* lying on the ground and trampled under foot. In the narrow limits of that bower, it would have been scarcely possible that the petticoat and scarf should have retained a position upon the stones, when subjected to the brushing to and fro of many struggling persons. 'There was evidence,' it is said, 'of a struggle; and the earth was trampled, the bushes were broken,' — but the petticoat and the scarf are found deposited as if upon shelves. 'The pieces of the frock torn out by the bushes were about three inches wide and six inches long. One part was the hem of the frock and it had been mended. They *looked like strips torn off.*' Here, inadvertently, Le Soleil[e] has employed an exceedingly suspicious phrase. The pieces, as described, do indeed 'look like strips torn off;' but purposely and by hand. It is one of the rarest of accidents that a piece is 'torn off,' from any garment such as is now in question, by the agency *of a thorn*. From the very nature of such fabrics, a thorn or nail becoming entangled in them, tears them rectangularly — divides them into two longitudinal rents, at right angles with each other, and meeting at an apex where the thorn enters — but it is scarcely possible to conceive the piece 'torn off.' I never so knew it, nor did you. To tear a piece *off* from such fabric, two distinct forces, in different directions, will be, in almost every case, required. If there be two edges to the fabric — if, for example, it be a pocket-handkerchief, and it is desired to tear from it a slip, then, and then only, will the one force serve the purpose. But in the present case the question is of a dress, presenting but one edge. To tear a piece from the interior, where no edge is presented, could only be effected by a miracle through the agency of thorns, and no *one* thorn could accomplish it. But, even where an edge is presented, two thorns will be necessary, operating, the one in two distinct directions, and the other in one. And this in the supposition that the edge is un-hemmed. If hemmed, the matter is nearly out of the question. We thus see the numerous and great obstacles in the way of pieces being 'torn off' through the simple agency of 'thorns;' yet we are required

---

e Soliel *(A) misprint*

THE MYSTERY OF MARIE ROGET

to believe not only that one piece but that many have been so torn. 'And one part,' too, *'was the hem of the frock!'* Another piece was *'part of the skirt, not the hem,'* — that is to say, was torn completely out, through the agency of thorns, from the unedged interior of the dress! These, I say, are things which one may well be pardoned for disbelieving; yet, taken collectedly, they form, perhaps, less of reasonable ground for suspicion, than the one startling circumstance of the articles' having been left in this thicket at all, by any *murderers* who had enough[f] precaution to think of removing the corpse. You will not have apprehended me rightly, however, if you suppose it my design to *deny* this thicket as the scene of the outrage. [g]There might have been a wrong *here,* or, more possibly, an accident at Madame Deluc's.[g] [94] But,[h] in fact, this is a point of minor importance. We are not engaged in an attempt to discover the scene, but to produce the perpetrators of the murder. What I have adduced, notwithstanding the minuteness with which I have adduced it, has been with the view, first, to show the folly of the positive and headlong assertions of Le Soleil,[i] but secondly and chiefly, to bring you, by the most natural route, to a further contemplation of the doubt whether this assassination has, or has not been, the work of *a gang.*

"We will resume this question by mere allusion to the revolting details of the surgeon examined at the inquest. It is only necessary to say that his published *inferences,* in regard to the number of the ruffians, have been properly ridiculed as unjust and totally baseless, by all the reputable anatomists of Paris. Not that the matter *might not* have been as inferred, but that there was no ground for the [j]inference: — was there not much for another?[j] [95]

"Let us reflect now upon 'the traces of a struggle;'[96] and let me ask what these traces have been supposed to demonstrate. A gang. But do they not rather demonstrate the absence of a gang? What *struggle* could have taken place — what struggle[k] so violent and so enduring as to have left its 'traces' in all directions — between a weak and defenceless girl and the *gang* of ruffians imagined? The silent grasp of a few rough arms and all would have been over. The

---

f   enough of *(A)*
g . . . g *Omitted (A)*
h For, *(A)*

i   Soliel, *(A)*
j . . . j inference. *(A)*
k *Omitted (A)*

TALES: 1843–1844

victim must have been absolutely passive at their will. You will here bear in mind[l] that the arguments urged against[m] the thicket as the scene, are applicable, in chief part, only against it as the scene of an outrage committed by *more than a single individual*. If we imagine but *one* violator, we can conceive, and thus only conceive, the struggle of so violent and so obstinate a nature as to have left the 'traces' apparent.

"And again. I have already mentioned the[n] suspicion to be excited by the fact that the articles in question were suffered to remain *at all* in the thicket where discovered.[97] It seems almost impossible that these evidences of guilt should have been accidentally left where found. There was sufficient presence of mind [o](it is supposed)[o] to remove the corpse; and yet a more positive evidence than the corpse itself (whose features might have been quickly obliterated by decay,) is allowed to lie conspicuously in the scene of the outrage — I allude to the handkerchief with the *name* of the deceased.[98] If this was accident, it was not the accident *of a gang*. We can imagine it only the accident of an individual. Let us see.[99] An individual has committed the murder. He is alone with the ghost of the departed. He is appalled by what lies motionless before him. The fury of his passion is over, and there is abundant room in his heart for the natural awe of the deed. His is none of that confidence which the presence of numbers inevitably inspires. He is *alone* with the dead. He trembles and is bewildered. Yet there is a necessity for disposing of the corpse. He bears it to the river, but leaves behind him the other evidences of guilt; for it is difficult, if not impossible to carry all the burthen at once, and it will be easy to return for what is left. But in his toilsome journey to the water his fears redouble within him. The sounds of life encompass his path. A dozen times he hears or fancies the step of an observer. Even the very lights from the city bewilder him. Yet, in time, and by long and frequent pauses of deep[p] agony, he reaches the river's brink, and disposes of his ghastly charge — perhaps through the medium

---

l   mind that I *admit* the thicket as the
scene of the outrage; and you will
immediately perceive *(A)*
m   *against (A)*

n   the strong and just *(A)*
o . . . o   *Omitted (A)*
p   long *(A)*

THE MYSTERY OF MARIE ROGET

of a boat. But *now* what treasure does the world hold — what threat of vengeance could it hold out — which would have power to urge the return of that lonely murderer over that toilsome and perilous path, to the thicket and its blood-chilling recollections? He returns *not,* let the consequences be what they may. He *could* not return if he would. His sole thought is immediate escape. He turns his back *forever* upon those dreadful shrubberies, and flees as from the wrath to come.[100]

"But how with a gang? Their number would have inspired them with confidence; if, indeed, confidence is ever wanting in the breast of the arrant blackguard; and[q] of arrant blackguards alone are the supposed *gangs* ever constituted. Their number, I say, would have prevented the bewildering and unreasoning terror which I have imagined to paralyze the single man. Could we suppose an oversight in one, or two, or three, this oversight would have been remedied by a fourth. They would have left nothing behind them; for their number would have enabled them to carry *all* at once. There would have been no need of *return.*

"Consider now the circumstance that, in the outer garment of the corpse when found, 'a slip, about a foot wide, had been torn upward from the bottom hem to the waist, wound three times round the waist, and secured by a sort of hitch in the back.'[101] This was done with the obvious design of affording *a handle* by which to carry the body. But would any *number* of men have dreamed of resorting to such an expedient? To three or four, the limbs of the corpse would have afforded not only a sufficient, but the best possible hold. The device is that of a single individual; and this brings us to the fact that 'between the thicket and the river, the rails of the fences were found taken down, and the ground bore evident traces of some heavy burden having been dragged along it!'[102] But would a *number* of men have put themselves to the superfluous trouble of taking down a fence, for the purpose of dragging through it a corpse which they might have *lifted over* any fence in an instant? Would a *number* of men have so *dragged* a corpse at all as to have left evident *traces* of the dragging?

---

q   for (*A*)

TALES: 1843–1844

"And here we must refer to an observation of Le Commerciel; an observation upon which I have already, in some measure, commented. 'A piece,' says this journal, 'of one of the unfortunate girl's petticoats was torn out and tied under her chin, and around the back of her head, probably to prevent screams. This was done by fellows who had no pocket-handkerchiefs.'[103]

"I have before[r] suggested that a genuine blackguard is never *without* a pocket-handkerchief.[104] But it is not to this fact that I now especially advert. That it was not through want of a handkerchief for the purpose imagined by Le Commerciel, that this bandage was employed, is rendered apparent by the handkerchief left in the thicket; and that the object was not 'to prevent screams' appears, also, from the bandage having been employed in preference to what would so much better have answered the purpose. But the language of the evidence speaks of the strip in question as 'found around the neck, fitting loosely, and secured with a hard knot.'[105] These words are sufficiently vague, but differ materially from those of Le Commerciel. The slip was eighteen inches wide, and therefore, although of muslin, would form a strong band when folded or rumpled longitudinally. And thus rumpled it was discovered. My inference is this. The solitary murderer, having borne the corpse, for some distance, ˢ(whether from the thicket or elsewhere)ˢ by means of the bandage *hitched* around its middle, found the weight, in this mode of procedure, too much for his strength. He resolved to drag the burthen — the evidence goes to show that it *was* dragged. With this object in view, it became necessary to attach something like a rope to one of the extremities. It could be best attached about the neck, where the head would prevent its slipping off. And, now, the murderer bethought him, unquestionably, of the bandage about the loins.[106] He would have used this, but for its volution about the corpse, the *hitch* which embarrassed it, and the reflection that it had not been 'torn off' from the garment. It was easier to tear a new slip from the petticoat. He tore it, made it fast about the neck, and so *dragged* his victim to the brink of the river. That this 'bandage,' only attainable with trouble and

---

r   already *(A)*   s . . . s   *Omitted (A)*

THE MYSTERY OF MARIE ROGET

delay, and but imperfectly answering its purpose — that this bandage was employed *at all,* demonstrates that the necessity for its employment sprang from circumstances arising at a period when the handkerchief was no longer attainable — that is to say, arising, as we have imagined, after quitting the thicket, ᵗ(if the thicket it was),ᵗ and on the road between the thicket and the river.

"But the evidence, you will say, of Madame Deluc, (!)ᵘ points especially to the presence of *a gang,* in the vicinity of the thicket, at or about the epoch of the ᵛmurder. This Iᵛ grant. I doubt if there were not a *dozen* gangs, such as described by Madame Deluc, in and about the vicinity of the Barrière du Roule at *or about* the period of this tragedy. But the gang which has drawn upon itself the pointed animadversion, although the somewhat tardy ʷand very suspiciousʷ evidence of Madame Deluc, is the *only* gang which is represented by that honest and scrupulous old lady as having eaten her cakes and swallowed her brandy, without putting themselves to the trouble of making her payment. *Et hinc illæ iræ?*[107]

"But what *is* the precise evidence of Madame Deluc? 'A gang of miscreants made their appearance, behaved boisterously, ate and drank without making payment, followed in the routeˣ of the young man and girl, returned to the inn *about dusk,* and recrossed the river as if in great haste.'[108]

"Now this 'great haste' very possibly seemed *greater* haste in the eyes of Madame Deluc, since she dwelt lingeringly and lamentingly upon her violated cakes and ale[109] — cakes and ale for which she might still have entertained a faint hope of compensation. Why, otherwise, since it was *about dusk,* should she make a point of the *haste?* It is no cause for wonder, surely, that even a gang of blackguards should make *haste* to get home, when a wide river is to be crossed in small boats, when storm impends, and when night *approaches.*

"I say *approaches;* for the night had *not yet arrived.* It was only *about dusk* that the indecent haste of these 'miscreants' offended the sober eyes of Madame Deluc. But we are told that it was upon

---

t . . . t *Omitted (A)*   w . . . w *Omitted (A)*
u (!) *omitted (A)*   x   rout *(A) misprint*
v . . . v murder, I *(A)*

TALES: 1843–1844

this very evening that Madame Deluc, as well as her eldest son, 'heard the screams of a female in the vicinity of the inn.' And in what words does Madame Deluc designate the period of the evening at which these screams were heard? 'It was *soon after dark,*' she says. But 'soon *after* dark,' is, at least, *dark;* and '*about dusk*' is as certainly daylight. Thus it is abundantly clear that the gang quitted the Barrière du Roule *prior* to the screams overheard (?)[y] by Madame Deluc.[110] And although, in all the many reports of the evidence, the relative expressions in question are distinctly and invariably employed just as I have employed them in this conversation with yourself, no notice whatever of the gross discrepancy has, as yet, been taken by any of the public journals, or by any of the Myrmidons of police.

"I shall add but one to the arguments against *a gang;* but this *one* has, to my own understanding at least, a weight altogether irresistible. Under the circumstances of large reward offered, and full pardon to any King's evidence,[111] it is not to be imagined, for a moment, that some member of *a gang* of low ruffians, or of any body of men, would not long ago have betrayed his accomplices. Each one of a gang so placed, is not so much greedy of reward, or anxious for escape, as *fearful of betrayal.* He betrays eagerly and early that *he may not himself be betrayed.* That the secret has not been divulged, is the very best of proof that it is, in fact, a secret. The horrors of this dark deed are known only to [z]*one,* or two,[z] living human beings,[a] and to God.

"[b]Let us sum up[b] now the meagre yet certain fruits of our long analysis. We have attained the idea [c]either of a fatal accident under the roof of Madame Deluc, or[c] of a murder perpetrated, in the thicket at the Barrière du Roule, by a lover, or at least by an intimate and secret associate of the deceased.[112] This associate is of swarthy complexion. This complexion, the 'hitch' in the bandage, and the 'sailor's knot,' with which the bonnet-ribbon is tied, point to a seaman. His companionship with the deceased, a gay, but not

---

y   (?) *omitted (A)*
z . . . z   *one (A)*
a   being, *(A)*
b . . . b   And *who* that one? It will not

be impossible — perhaps it will not be
difficult to discover. Let us sum up *(A)*
c . . . c   *Omitted (A)*

THE MYSTERY OF MARIE ROGET

an abject young girl, designates him as above the grade of the common sailor. Here the well written and urgent communications to the journals are much in the way of corroboration. The circumstance of the first elopement, as mentioned by Le Mercurie, tends to blend the idea of this seaman with that of the 'naval officer' who is first known to have led the unfortunate into crime.[d][113]

"And here, most fitly, comes the consideration of the continued absence of him of the dark complexion. Let me pause to observe that the complexion of this man is dark and swarthy; it was no common swarthiness which constituted the *sole* point of remembrance, both as regards Valence and Madame Deluc. But why[e] is this man absent? Was he murdered by the gang?[f] If so, why are there only *traces* of the assassinated *girl?* The scene of the two outrages will naturally be supposed identical. And where is his corpse? The assassins would most probably have disposed of both in the same way. But it may be said that this man lives, and is deterred from making himself known, through dread of being charged with the murder. This consideration might be supposed to operate upon him now — at this late period — since it has been given in evidence that he was seen with Marie — but it would have had no force at the period of the[g] deed. The first impulse of an innocent man would have been to announce the outrage, and to aid in identifying the ruffians. This, *policy* would have suggested. He had been seen with the girl. He had crossed the river with her in an open ferry-boat. The denouncing of the assassins would have appeared, even to an idiot, the surest and sole means of relieving himself from suspicion. We cannot suppose him, on the night of the fatal Sunday, both innocent himself and incognizant of an outrage committed. Yet only under such circumstances is it possible to imagine that he would have failed, if alive, in the denouncement of the assassins.

"And what means are ours, of attaining the truth? We shall find

---

d *After this* We are not forced to suppose a premeditated design of murder or of violation. But there was the friendly shelter of the thicket, and the approach of rain — there was opportunity and strong temptation — and then a sudden and violent wrong, to be concealed only by one of darker dye. *(A)*
e *why (A)*
f *the gang? (A)*
g the dark *(A)*

TALES: 1843–1844

these means multiplying and gathering distinctness as we proceed.[h] Let us sift to the bottom this affair of the first elopement. Let us know the full history of 'the officer,' with his present circumstances, and his whereabouts at the precise period of the murder. Let us carefully compare with each other the various communications sent to the evening paper, in which the object was to inculpate *a gang*. This done, let us compare these communications, both as regards style and MS., with those sent to the morning paper, at a previous period, and insisting so vehemently upon the guilt of Mennais. And, all this done, let us again compare these various communications with the known MSS. of the officer.[114] Let us endeavor to ascertain, by repeated questionings of Madame Deluc and her boys, as well as of the omnibus-driver, Valence, something more of the personal appearance and bearing of the 'man of dark complexion.' Queries, skilfully directed, will not fail to elicit, from some of these parties, information on this particular point [i](or upon others)[i] — information which the parties themselves may not even be aware of possessing.[115] And let us now trace *the boat* picked up by the bargeman on the morning of Monday the twenty-third of June, and which was removed from the barge-office, without the cognizance of the officer in attendance, and *without the rudder*, at some period prior to the discovery of the corpse.[116] With a proper caution and perseverance we shall infallibly trace this boat; for not only can the bargeman who picked it up identify it, but the *rudder is at hand*. The rudder *of a sail-boat* would not have been abandoned, without inquiry, by one altogether at ease in heart. And here let me pause to insinuate a question. There was no *advertisement* of the picking up of this boat. It was silently taken to the barge-office, and as silently removed. But its owner or employer — how *happened* he, at so early a period as Tuesday morning, to be informed, without the agency of advertisement, of the locality of the boat taken up on Monday, unless we imagine some connexion with the *navy* — some personal permanent connexion leading to cognizance of its minute interests — its petty local news?

---

h   proceed — provided that our preparatory analysis of the subject has not greatly diverged from the principles of truth. *(A)*

i . . . i   *Omitted (A)*

THE MYSTERY OF MARIE ROGET

"In speaking of the lonely assassin dragging his burden to the shore, I have already suggested the probability of his availing himself *of a boat*.[117] Now we are to understand that Marie Rogêt *was* precipitated from a boat. This would naturally have been the case. The corpse could not have been trusted to the shallow waters of the shore. The peculiar marks on the back and shoulders of the victim tell of the bottom ribs of a boat.[118] That the body was found without weight is also corroborative of the idea.[119] If thrown from the shore a weight would have been attached. We can only account for its absence by supposing the murderer to have neglected the precaution of supplying himself with it before pushing off. In the act of consigning the corpse to the water, he would unquestionably have noticed his oversight; but then no remedy would have been at hand. Any risk would have been preferred to a return to that accursed shore. Having rid himself of his ghastly charge, the murderer would have hastened to the city. There, at some obscure wharf, he would have leaped on land. But the boat — would he have secured it? He would have been in too great haste for such things as securing a boat. Moreover, in fastening it to the wharf, he would have felt as if securing evidence against himself. His natural thought would have been[j] to cast from him, as far as possible, all that had held connection with his crime. He would not only have fled from the wharf, but he would not have permitted *the boat* to remain. Assuredly he would have cast it adrift. Let us pursue our fancies. — In the morning, the wretch is stricken with unutterable horror at finding that the boat has been picked up and detained at a locality which he is in the daily habit of frequenting — at a locality, perhaps, which his duty compels him to frequent. The next night, [k]*without daring to ask for the rudder,*[k] he removes it. Now *where* is that rudderless boat? Let it be one of our first purposes to discover. With the first glimpse we obtain of it, the dawn of our success shall begin. This boat shall guide us, with a rapidity which will surprise even ourselves, to him who employed it in the midnight of the fatal Sabbath. Corroboration will rise upon [l]corroboration, and the murderer[l] will be traced."

---

j   have been/be *(A)*
k . . . k   *Not italicized (A)*

l . . . l   corroboration. *The murderer (A)*

TALES: 1843–1844

[For reasons which we shall not specify, but which to many readers will appear obvious, we have taken the liberty of here omitting, from the MSS. placed in our hands, such portion as details the *following up* of the apparently slight clew obtained by Dupin. We feel it advisable only to state, in brief, that the result desired was brought to pass; and[m] that the Prefect fulfilled punctually, although with reluctance, the terms of his compact with the Chevalier. Mr. Poe's article concludes with the following words. — *Eds.**n][120]

It will be understood that I speak of coincidences *and no more*. What I have said above upon this topic must suffice. In my own heart there dwells no faith in præter-nature. That Nature and its God are two, no man who thinks, will deny. That the latter, creating the former, can, at will, control or modify it, is also unquestionable. I say "at will;" for the question is of will,[o] and not, as the insanity of logic has assumed, of power.[p] It is not that the Deity *cannot* modify his laws, but that we insult him in imagining a possible necessity for modification. In their origin these laws were fashioned to embrace *all* contingencies which *could* lie in the Future. With God all is *Now*.[121]

I repeat, then, that I speak of these[q] things only as of coincidences. And farther: in what I relate it will be seen that between the fate of the unhappy Mary Cecilia Rogers, [r]so far as that fate is known,[r] and the fate of one Marie Rogêt [s]up to a certain epoch in her history,[s] there has existed a parallel in the contemplation of whose wonderful exactitude the reason becomes embarrassed. I say all this will be seen. But let it not for a moment be supposed that, in proceeding with the sad narrative of Marie from the epoch just mentioned, and in tracing to its *dénouement* the mystery which

---

* Of the Magazine in which the article was originally published.

---

m   that an individual assassin was convicted, upon his own confession, of the murder of Marie Rogêt, and *(A)*

n   *The starred footnote is omitted in A. The reader is reminded that Poe added this and all other footnotes, except that on the motto, and the one referring to "The Murders in the Rue Morgue," in*

his second printing of the story, Tales (1845). *See note 120.*

o   *will, (A)*

p   *power. (A)*

q   *certain (A)*

r . . . r   *so far as that fate is known, (A)*

s . . . s   *up to a certain epoch in her history, (A)*

THE MYSTERY OF MARIE ROGET

enshrouded her, it is my covert design to hint ᵗat an extension of the parallel,ᵗ or even to suggest that the measures adopted in Paris for the discovery of the assassin of a grisette, or measures founded in any similar ratiocination, would produce any similar result.

For, in respect to the latter branch of the supposition, it should be considered that the most trifling variation in the facts of the two cases might give rise to the most important miscalculations, by diverting thoroughly the two courses of events; very much as, in arithmetic, an error which, in its own individuality, may be in-appreciable, produces, at length, by dint of multiplication at all points of the process, a result enormously at variance with truth. And, in regard to the former branch, we must not fail to hold in view that the very Calculus of Probabilities to which I have re-ferred, forbids all idea of the extension of the parallel: — forbids it with a positiveness strong and decided just in proportion as this parallel has already been long-drawn and exact. This is one of those anomalous propositions which, seemingly appealing to thought altogether apart from the mathematical, is yet one which only the mathematician can fully entertain. Nothing, for example, is more difficult than to convince the merely general reader that the fact of sixes having been thrown twice in succession by a player at dice, is sufficient cause for betting the largest odds that sixes will not be thrown in the third attempt.¹²² A suggestion to this effect is usually rejected by the intellect at once. It does not appear that the two throws which have been completed, and which lie now absolutely in the Past, can have influence upon the throw which exists only in the Future. The chance for throwing sixes seems to be precisely as it was at any ordinary time — that is to say, subject only to the influence of the various other throws which may be made by the dice. And this is a reflection which appears so ex-ceedinglyᵘ obvious that attempts to controvert it are received more frequently with a derisive smile than with anything like respectful attention. The error here involved — a gross error redolent of mis-chief — I cannot pretend to expose within the limits assigned me at present; and with the philosophical it needs no exposure. It may be sufficient here to say that it forms one of an infinite series of

t . . . t   *an extension of the parallel, (A)*   u   *exceedingly (A)*

TALES: 1843–1844

mistakes which arise in the path of Reason through her propensity for seeking truth *in detail.*

NOTES

Title: Throughout the texts of the tale and in the manuscript table of contents for PHANTASY-PIECES Poe used the circumflex in "Rogêt," but none of the printed texts collated carried the accent in the title, which in each case is printed in large capitals. Practice among scholars in referring to the tale differs; some follow the title literally as printed; others adopt the circumflex, which seems to be the form intended by Poe.

Motto: The English translation Poe found in a book he reviewed in *Graham's* for December 1841, Sarah Austin's *Fragments from German Prose Writers* (London, reprinted in New York, 1841), p. 97. He improved the translator's style slightly. In "Poe's Knowledge of German," *Modern Philology*, June 1904, Gustav Gruener traced the original to "Moralische Ansichten," in *Novalis Schriften* edited by Ludwig Tieck and Friedrich Schlegel (first edition, Berlin, 1802, II, 532). Other fragments from Novalis — correctly, Friedrich von Hardenberg, 1772–1801 — in Mrs. Austin's book are used in "A Tale of the Ragged Mountains" and "Marginalia," no. 164 (*Democratic Review*, April 7, 1846, p. 270).

1. "The facts of the case as given by Poe are in the main correct," says Wimsatt; "that is, he reproduces rather faithfully what he read in the widely published documents I have listed" (*PMLA*, March 1941, p. 233). Poe did indeed follow "in minute detail" many of the "essential" facts, but more than once he deliberately altered them and proceeded to develop his arguments on the fictitious basis; see, for example, n. 12 below. His repeated references to a second confession are not substantiated by the evidence found.

2. Poe refers again to the Calculus of Probabilities at the end of his story, and dallies with mathematical probability several times between. Wimsatt (n. 32) says that "French writers of Poe's time hailed him with delight as a *pupil* of Laplace," but I think it unlikely that he went directly to the works of that mathematical philosopher.

3. Avowedly writing fiction, Poe gave his characters French (or French-sounding) names and helped himself, with fiction-writer's license, to actual Parisian streets and landmarks, inventing others. The liberties he took disturbed some French readers; see n. 17 below. The "essential" facts of Mary Rogers' background here used — widowed mother, boarding house, offer of employment — along with other interesting details quoted from the *Sunday News* are mentioned in the New York *Brother Jonathan*, August 14, 1841. *Brother Jonathan* was published weekly, on Saturday, but it had a daily edition, the *Tattler*, from which — as well as from many unrelated papers — it printed excerpts, often explicitly credited.

4. *Brother Jonathan*, August 14, 1841, refers to this first disappearance of

TALES: 1843–1844

J. Lorimer Graham copy of *Tales,* with manuscript changes of 1849; *(D) Works* (1850), I, 262–280.

The J. Lorimer Graham copy of the *Tales (C)* is followed. Griswold's version *(D)* is merely a reprint of an unrevised copy of the *Tales (B)* and has no independent authority; it introduces three typographical errors.

Reprints

Chambers' Edinburgh Journal, November 30, 1844, abridged from *The Gift.* The abridgment was copied by: *Littell's Living Age* (Boston), January 18, 1845; the *Spirit of the Times* (Philadelphia), January 20 and 22, 1845; and the *New York Weekly News,* January 25, 1845, labeled *"Chambers' Journal via Littell's Living Age"* (for the last, see G. Thomas Tanselle, *Publications of the Bibliographical Society of America,* Second Quarter 1962).

Translation

Magasin pittoresque, August 1845, as "Une Lettre volée," and reprinted in *L'Echo de la Presse,* August 25, 1845.

THE PURLOINED LETTER. [C]

Nil sapientiae odiosius acumine nimio.

Seneca.

At Paris, just after dark one gusty evening in the autumn of 18—, I was enjoying the twofold luxury of meditation and a meerschaum,[1] in company with my friend C. Auguste Dupin, in his little back library, or book-closet, *au troisième,*[a] No. 33, *Rue Dunôt, Faubourg St. Germain.*[2] For one hour at least we had maintained a profound silence; while each, to any casual observer, might have seemed intently and exclusively occupied with the curling eddies of smoke that oppressed the atmosphere of the chamber. For myself, however, I was mentally discussing certain topics which had formed matter for conversation between us at an earlier period of the evening; I mean the affair of the Rue Morgue, and the mystery attending the murder of Marie Rogêt.[b] I looked upon it, therefore, as something of a coincidence, when the door of our apartment was thrown open and admitted our old acquaintance, Monsieur G——, the Prefect of the Parisian police.[3] We gave him a hearty welcome; for there was nearly half as

---

Motto omitted in A
a   *troisième,* (*A, B, C, D*)

b   Roget. (*A*)

·974·

THE PURLOINED LETTER

much of the entertaining as of the contemptible about the man, and we had not seen him for several years. We had been sitting in the dark, and Dupin now arose for the purpose of lighting a lamp, but sat down again, without doing so, upon G.'s saying that he had called to consult us, or rather to ask the opinion of my friend, about some official business which had occasioned a great deal of trouble.

"If it is any point requiring reflection," observed Dupin, as he forebore to enkindle the wick, "we shall examine it to better purpose in the dark."

"That is another of your odd notions," said the Prefect, who had a fashion of calling every thing "odd" that was beyond his comprehension, and thus lived amid an absolute legion of "oddities."

"Very true," said Dupin, as he supplied his visiter with a pipe, and rolled towards him a^c comfortable chair.

"And what is the difficulty now?" I asked. "Nothing more in the assassination way, I hope?"

"Oh no; nothing of that nature. The fact is, the business is *very* simple indeed, and I make no doubt that we can manage it sufficiently well ourselves; but then I thought Dupin would like to hear the details of it, because it is so excessively *odd*."

"Simple and odd," said Dupin.

"Why, yes; and not exactly that, either. The fact is, we have all been a good deal puzzled because the affair *is* so simple, and yet baffles us altogether."

"Perhaps it is the very simplicity of the thing which puts you at fault," said my friend.

"What nonsense you *do* talk!" replied the Prefect, laughing heartily.

"Perhaps the mystery is a^d little *too* plain," said Dupin.

"Oh, good heavens! who ever heard of such an idea?"

"A little *too* self-evident."

"Ha! ha! ha! — ha! ha! ha! — ho! ho! ho!" roared^e our visiter, profoundly amused, "oh, Dupin, you will be the death of me yet!"[4]

---

c   a very *(A)*   e   roared out *(A)*
d   *Omitted (D)*

TALES: 1843–1844

"And what, after all, *is* the matter on hand?" I asked.

"Why, I will tell you," replied the Prefect, as he gave a long, steady, and contemplative puff, and settled himself in his chair. "I will tell you in a few words; but, before I begin, let me caution you that this is[f] an affair demanding the greatest secrecy, and that I should most probably lose the position I now hold, were it known that I confided it to any one."

"Proceed," said I.

"Or not," said Dupin.

"Well, then; I have received personal information, from a very high quarter, that a certain document of the last importance, has been purloined from the royal apartments. The individual who purloined it is known; this beyond a doubt; he was seen to take it. It is known, also, that it still remains in his possession."

"How is this known?" asked Dupin.

"It is clearly inferred," replied the Prefect, "from the nature of the document, and from the non-appearance of certain results which would at once arise from its passing *out* of the robber's possession; — that is to say, from his employing it as he must design in the end to employ it."

"Be a little more explicit," I said.

"Well, I may venture so far as to say that the paper gives its holder a certain power in a certain quarter where such power is immensely valuable." The Prefect was fond of the cant of diplomacy.

"Still I do not quite understand," said Dupin.

"No? Well; the disclosure of the document to a third person, who shall be nameless, would bring in question the honor of a personage of most exalted station; and this fact gives the holder of the document an ascendancy over the illustrious personage whose honor and peace are so jeopardized."

"But this ascendancy," I interposed, "would depend upon the robber's knowledge of the loser's knowledge of the robber. Who would dare—"

"The thief," said G., "is the Minister D——, who dares all things, those unbecoming as well as those becoming a man. The

---

f   *Omitted (D)*

THE PURLOINED LETTER

method of the theft was not less ingenious than bold. The document in question — a letter, to be frank — had been received by the personage robbed while alone in the royal *boudoir*. During its perusal she was suddenly interrupted by the entrance of the other exalted personage from whom especially it was her wish to conceal it. After a hurried and vain endeavor to thrust it in a drawer, she was forced to place it, open as it was, upon a table. The address, however, was uppermost, and, the contents thus unexposed, the letter escaped notice. At this juncture enters the Minister D——. His lynx eye immediately perceives the paper, recognises the handwriting of the address, observes the confusion of the personage addressed, and fathoms her secret. After some business transactions, hurried through in his ordinary manner, he produces a letter somewhat similar to the one in question, opens it, pretends to read it, and then places it in close juxtaposition to the other. Again he converses, for some fifteen minutes, upon the public affairs. At length, in taking leave, he takes also from the table the letter to which he had no claim. Its rightful owner saw, but, of course, dared not call attention to the act, in the presence of the third personage who stood at her elbow. The minister decamped; leaving his own letter — one of no importance — upon the table."

"Here, then," said Dupin to me, "you have precisely what you demand to make the ascendancy complete — the robber's knowledge of the loser's knowledge of the robber."

"Yes," replied the Prefect; "and the power thus attained has, for some months past, been wielded, for political purposes, to a very dangerous extent. The personage robbed is more thoroughly convinced, every day, of the necessity of reclaiming her letter. But this, of course, cannot be done openly. In fine, driven to despair, she has committed the matter to me."

"Than whom," said Dupin, amid a perfect whirlwind of smoke, " no more sagacious agent could, I suppose, be desired, or even imagined."

"You flatter me," replied the Prefect; "but it is possible that some such opinion may have been entertained."

"It is clear," said I, "as you observe, that the letter is still in possession of the minister; since it is this possession, and not any

TALES: 1843–1844

employment of the letter, which bestows the power. With the employment the power departs."

"True," said G.; "and upon this conviction I proceeded. My first care was to make thorough search of the minister's hotel;[5] and here my chief embarrassment lay in the necessity of searching without his knowledge. Beyond all things, I have been warned of the danger which would result from giving him reason to suspect our design."

"But," said I, "you are quite *au fait* in these investigations. The Parisian police have done this thing often before."

"O yes; and for this reason I did not despair. The habits of the minister gave me, too, a great advantage. He is frequently absent from home all night. His servants are by no means numerous. They sleep at a distance from their master's apartment,[g] and, being chiefly Neapolitans, are readily made drunk.[6] I have keys, as you know, with which I can open any chamber or cabinet in Paris. For three months a night has not passed, during the greater part of which I have not been engaged, personally, in ransacking the D—— Hotel. My honor is interested, and, to mention a great secret, the reward is enormous. So I did not abandon the search until I had become fully satisfied that the thief is a more astute man than myself. I fancy that I have investigated every nook and corner of the premises in which it is possible that the paper can be concealed."

"But is it not possible," I suggested, "that although the letter may be in possession of the minister, as it unquestionably is, he may have concealed it elsewhere than upon his own premises?"

"This is barely possible," said Dupin. "The present peculiar condition of affairs at court, and especially of those intrigues in which D—— is known to be involved, would render the instant availability of the document — its susceptibility of being produced at a moment's notice — a point of nearly equal importance with its possession."

"Its susceptibility of being produced?" said I.

"That is to say, of being *destroyed*," said Dupin.

"True," I observed; "the paper is clearly then upon the

---

g   apartments, *(A)*

THE PURLOINED LETTER

premises. As for its being upon the person of the minister, we may consider that as out of the question."

"Entirely," said the Prefect. "He has been twice waylaid, as if by footpads, and his person rigorously searched under my own inspection."

"You might have spared yourself this trouble," said Dupin. "D——, I presume, is not altogether a fool, and, if not, must have anticipated these waylayings, as a matter of course."

"Not *altogether* a fool," said G., "but then he's a poet, which I take to be only one remove from a fool."[7]

"True," said Dupin, after a long and thoughtful whiff from his meerschaum, "although I have been guilty of certain doggrel myself."

"Suppose you detail," said I, "the particulars of your search."[8]

"Why the fact is, we took our time, and we searched *every where*. I have had long experience in these affairs. I took the entire building, room by room; devoting the nights of a whole week to each. We examined, first, the furniture of each apartment. We opened every possible drawer; and I presume you know that, to a properly trained police agent, such a thing as a *secret* drawer is impossible. Any man is a dolt who permits a 'secret' drawer to escape him in a search of this kind. The thing is *so* plain. There is a certain amount of bulk — of space — to be accounted for in every cabinet. Then we have accurate rules. The fiftieth part of a line could not escape us. After the cabinets we took the chairs. The cushions we probed with the fine long needles you have seen me employ. From the tables we removed the tops."

"Why so?"

"Sometimes the top of a table, or other similarly arranged piece of furniture, is removed by the person wishing to conceal an article; then the leg is excavated, the article deposited within the cavity, and the top replaced. The bottoms and tops of bedposts are employed in the same way."

"But could not the cavity be detected by sounding?" I asked.

"By no means, if, when the article is deposited, a sufficient wadding of cotton be placed around it. Besides, in our case, we were obliged to proceed without noise."

"But you could not have removed — you could not have taken

TALES: 1843-1844

to pieces *all* articles of furniture in which it would have been possible to make a deposit in the manner you mention. A letter may be compressed into a thin spiral roll, not differing much in shape or bulk from a large knitting-needle, and in this form it might be inserted into the rung of a chair, for example. You did not take to pieces all the chairs?"

"Certainly not; but we did better — we examined the rungs of every chair in the hotel, and, indeed, the jointings of every description of furniture, by the aid of a most powerful microscope. Had there been any traces of recent disturbance we should not have failed to detect it instantly.[h] A single grain of gimlet-dust,[i] for example, would have been as obvious as an apple. Any disorder in the glueing — any unusual gaping in the joints — would have sufficed to insure detection."

"I presume[j] you looked to the mirrors, between the boards and the plates, and you probed the beds and the bed-clothes, as well as the curtains and carpets."

"That of course; and when we had absolutely completed every particle of the furniture in this way, then we examined the house itself. We divided its entire surface into compartments, which we numbered, so that none might be missed; then we scrutinized each individual square inch throughout the premises, including the two houses immediately adjoining, with the microscope, as before."

"The two houses adjoining!" I exclaimed; "you must have had a great deal of trouble."

"We had; but the reward offered is prodigious."

"You include the *grounds* about the houses?"

"All the grounds are paved with brick. They gave us comparatively little trouble. We examined the moss between the bricks, and found it undisturbed."[k]

"You looked among D——'s papers, of course, and into the books of the library?"

---

h *instanter. (A)*
i gimlet-dust, or saw-dust, *(A)*
j "I presume/"Of course *(A)*
k *After this are two additional paragraphs:*

"And the roofs?"
"We surveyed every inch of the external surface, and probed carefully beneath every tile." *(A)*

THE PURLOINED LETTER

"Certainly; we opened every package and parcel; we not only opened every book, but we turned over every leaf in each volume, not contenting ourselves with a mere shake, according to the fashion of some of our police officers.[9] We also measured the thickness of every book-*cover,* with the most accurate admeasurement, and applied to each[1] the most jealous scrutiny of the microscope. Had any of the bindings been recently meddled with, it would have been utterly impossible that the fact should have escaped observation. Some five or six volumes, just from the hands of the binder, we carefully probed, longitudinally, with the needles."

"You explored the floors beneath the carpets?"

"Beyond doubt. We removed every carpet, and examined the boards with the microscope."

"And the paper on the walls?"

"Yes."

"You looked into the cellars?"

"We did."[m]

"Then," I said, "you have been making a miscalculation, and the letter is *not* upon the premises, as you suppose."

"I fear you are right there," said the Prefect. "And now, Dupin, what would you advise me to do?"

"To make a thorough re-search of the premises."

"That is absolutely needless," replied G———. "I am not more sure that I breathe than I am that the letter is not at the Hotel."

"I have no better advice to give you," said Dupin. "You have, of course, an accurate description of the letter?"

"Oh yes!" — And here the Prefect, producing a memorandum-book, proceeded to read aloud a minute account of the internal, and especially of the external appearance of the missing document. Soon after finishing the perusal of this description, he took his departure, more entirely depressed in spirits than I had ever known the good gentleman before.

In about a month afterwards he paid us another visit, and found us occupied very nearly as before. He took a pipe and a chair and entered into some ordinary conversation. At length I said, —

---

1   them *(A)*

m   "We did."/"We did; and, as time and labour were no objects, we dug up

every one of them to the depth of four feet." *(A)*

TALES: 1843–1844

"Well, but G——, what of the purloined letter? I presume you have at last made up your mind that there is no such thing as overreaching the Minister?"

"Confound him, say I — yes; I made the re-examination, however, as Dupin suggested — but it was all labor lost, as I knew it would be."

"How much was the reward offered, did you say?" asked Dupin.

"Why, a very great deal — a *very* liberal reward — I don't like to say how much, precisely; but one thing I *will* say, that I wouldn't mind giving my individual check for fifty thousand francs to any one who could obtain me that letter. The fact is, it is becoming of more and more importance every day; and the reward has been lately doubled. If it were trebled, however, I could do no more than I have done."

"Why, yes," said Dupin, drawlingly, between the whiffs[n] of his meerschaum, "I really — think, G——, you have not exerted yourself — to the utmost in this matter. You might — do a little more, I think, eh?"

"How? — in what way?"

"Why — puff, puff — you might — puff, puff — employ counsel in the matter, eh? — puff, puff, puff. Do you remember the story they tell of Abernethy?"

"No; hang Abernethy!"

"To be sure! hang him and welcome. But, once upon a time, a certain rich miser conceived the design of spunging upon this Abernethy for a medical opinion.[10] Getting up, for this purpose, an ordinary conversation in a private company, he insinuated his case to the physician, as that of an imaginary individual.

" 'We will suppose,' said the miser, 'that his symptoms are such and such; now, doctor, what would *you* have directed him to take?'

" 'Take!' said Abernethy, 'why, take *advice,* to be sure.' "

"But," said the Prefect, a little discomposed, "*I* am *perfectly* willing to take advice, and to pay for it. I would *really* give fifty thousand francs[o] to any one who would aid me in the matter."

---

n   which *(D) misprint*   o   francs, every *centime* of it, *(A)*

THE PURLOINED LETTER

"In that case," replied Dupin, opening a drawer, and producing a check-book, "you may as well fill me up a check for the amount mentioned. When you have signed it, I will hand you the letter."

I was astounded. The Prefect appeared absolutely thunderstricken. For some minutes he remained speechless and motionless, looking incredulously at my friend with open mouth, and eyes that seemed starting from their sockets; then, apparently recovering himself in some measure, he seized a pen, and after several pauses and vacant stares, finally filled up and signed a check for fifty thousand francs, and handed it across the table to Dupin. The latter examined it carefully and deposited it in his pocketbook; then, unlocking an *escritoire,* took thence a letter and gave it to the Prefect. This functionary grasped it in a perfect agony of joy, opened it with a trembling hand, cast a rapid glance at its contents, and then, scrambling and struggling to the door, rushed at length unceremoniously from the room and from the house, without having uttered aᵖ syllable since Dupin had requested him to fill up the check.

When he had gone, my friend entered into some explanations.

"The Parisian police," he said, "are exceedingly able in their way. They are persevering, ingenious, cunning, and thoroughly versed in the knowledge which their duties seem chiefly to demand. Thus, when G—— detailed to us his mode of searching the premises at the Hotel D——, I felt entire confidence in his having made a satisfactory investigation — so far as his labors extended."

"So far as his labors extended?" said I.

"Yes," said Dupin. "The measures adopted were not only the best of their kind, but carried out to absolute perfection. Had the letter been deposited within the range of their search, these fellows would, beyond a question, have found it."

I merely laughed — but he seemed quite serious in all that he said.

"The measures, then," he continued, "were good in their kind, and well executed; their defect lay in their being inapplicable to

---

p   a solitary *(A)*

TALES: 1843-1844

the case, and to the man. A certain set of highly ingenious resources are, with the Prefect, a sort of Procrustean bed,[11] to which he forcibly adapts his designs. But he perpetually errs by being too deep or too shallow, for the matter in hand; and many a schoolboy is a better reasoner than he. I knew one about eight years of age, whose success at guessing in the game of 'even and odd' attracted universal admiration. This game is simple, and is played with marbles. One player holds in his hand a number of these toys, and demands of another whether that number is even or odd. If the guess is right, the guesser wins one; if wrong, he loses one. The boy to whom I allude won all the marbles of the school. Of course he had some principle of guessing; and this lay in mere observation and admeasurement of the astuteness of his opponents. For example, an arrant simpleton is his opponent, and, holding up his closed hand, asks, 'are they even or odd?' Our schoolboy replies, 'odd,' and loses; but upon the second trial he wins, for he then says to himself, "the simpleton had them even upon the first trial, and his amount of cunning is just sufficient to make him have them odd upon the second; I will therefore guess odd; — he guesses odd, and wins. Now, with a simpleton a degree above the first, he would have reasoned thus: 'This fellow finds that in the first instance I guessed odd, and, in the second, he will propose to himself, upon the first impulse, a simple variation from even to odd, as did the first simpleton; but then a second thought will suggest that this is too simple a variation, and finally he will decide upon putting it even as before. I will therefore guess even;' — he guesses even, and wins. Now this mode of reasoning in the schoolboy, whom his fellows termed 'lucky,' — what, in its last analysis, is it?"

"It is merely," I said, "an identification of the reasoner's intellect with that of his opponent."

"It is," said Dupin; "and, upon inquiring of the boy by what means he effected the *thorough* identification in which his success consisted, I received answer as follows: 'When I wish to find out how wise, or how stupid, or how good, or how wicked is any one, or what are his thoughts at the moment, I fashion the expression of my face, as accurately as possible, in accordance with the expression of his, and then wait to see what thoughts or sentiments arise in my mind or heart, as if to match or correspond with the ex-

THE PURLOINED LETTER

pression.'[12] This response of the schoolboy lies at the bottom of all the spurious profundity which has been attributed to Rochefoucault,[q] to La Bruyère,[r] to Machiavelli, and to Campanella."[13]

"And the identification," I said, "of the reasoner's intellect with that of his opponent, depends, if I understand you aright, upon the accuracy with which the opponent's intellect is admeasured."

"For its practical value it depends upon this," replied Dupin; "and the Prefect and his cohort fail so frequently, first, by default of this identification, and, secondly, by ill-admeasurement, or rather through non-admeasurement, of the intellect with which they are engaged. They consider only their *own* ideas of ingenuity; and, in searching for anything hidden, advert only to the modes in which *they* would have hidden it. They are right in this much — that their own ingenuity is a faithful representative of that of *the mass;* but when the cunning of the individual felon is diverse in character from their own, the felon foils them, of course. This always happens when it is above their own, and very usually when it is below. They have no variation of principle in their investigations; at best, when urged by some unusual emergency — by some extraordinary reward — they extend or exaggerate their old modes of *practice,* without touching their principles. What, for example, in this case of D——, has been done to vary the principle of action? What is all this boring, and probing, and sounding, and scrutinizing with the microscope, and dividing the surface of the building into registered square inches — what is it all but an exaggeration *of the application* of the one principle or set of principles of search, which are based upon the one set of notions regarding human ingenuity, to which the Prefect, in the long routine of his duty, has been accustomed? Do you not see he has taken it for granted that *all* men proceed to conceal a letter, — not exactly in a gimlet-hole bored in a chair-leg — but, at least, in *some* out-of-the-way hole or corner suggested by the same tenor of thought which would urge a man to secrete a letter in a gimlet-hole bored in a chair-leg? And do you not see also, that such *recherchés*[s]

TALES: 1843–1844

nooks for concealment are adapted only for ordinary occasions, and would be adopted only by ordinary intellects; for, in all cases of concealment, a disposal of the article concealed — a disposal of it in this *recherché* manner, — is, in the very first instance, ᵗpresumable and presumed;ᵗ and thus its discovery depends, not at all upon the acumen, but altogether upon the mere care, patience, and determination of the seekers; and where the case is of importance — or, what amounts to the same thing in the policial eyes, when the reward is of magnitude, — the qualities in question have *never* been known to fail. You will now understand what I meant in suggesting that, had the purloined letter been hidden any where within the limits of the Prefect's examination — in other words, had the principle of its concealment been comprehended within the principles of the Prefect — its discovery would have been a matter altogether beyond question. This functionary, however, has been thoroughly mystified; and the remote source of his defeat lies in the supposition that the Minister is a fool, because he has acquired renown as a poet. All fools are poets; this the Prefect *feels;*[14] and he is merely guilty of a *non distributio medii*[15] in thence inferring that all poets are fools."

"But is this really the poet?" I asked. "There are two brothers, I know; and both have attained reputation in letters. The Minister I believe has written learnedly on the Differential Calculus. He is a mathematician, and no poet."

"You are mistaken; I know him well; he is both. As poet *and* mathematician, he would reason well;ᵘ as mere mathematician, he could not have reasoned at all, and thus would have been at the mercy of the Prefect."

"You surprise me," I said, "by these opinions, which have been contradicted by the voice of the world. You do not mean to set at naught the well-digested idea of centuries. The mathematical reason has long beenᵛ regarded as *the* reason *par excellence.*"

" *'Il y a à parier,'*ʷ " replied Dupin, quoting from Chamfort, " *'que toute idée publique, toute convention reçue, est une sottise,*

---

t...t presumed and presemable; *(A)*
u well; as poet, profoundly; *(A)*
v long been/been long *(A)*

w *parièr,' (A, B, C, D)* accent *deleted editorially*

THE PURLOINED LETTER

car elle a convenu[x] *au plus grand nombre.*[y][16] The mathematicians, I grant you, have done their best to promulgate the popular error to which you allude, and which is none the less an error for its promulgation as truth. With an art worthy a better cause, for example, they have insinuated the term 'analysis' into application to algebra. The French are the originators of this particular deception; but if a term is of any importance — if words derive any value from applicability — then 'analysis' conveys 'algebra' about as much as, in Latin, *'ambitus'* implies 'ambition,' *'religio'* 'religion,' or *'homines honesti,'* a set of *honorable* men."[17]

"You have a quarrel on hand, I see," said I, "with some of the algebraists of Paris; but proceed."[18]

"I dispute the availability, and thus the value, of that reason which is cultivated in any especial form other than the abstractly logical. I dispute, in particular, the reason educed by mathematical study. The mathematics are the science of form and quantity; mathematical reasoning is merely logic applied to observation upon form and quantity. The great error lies in supposing that even the truths of what is called *pure* algebra, are abstract or general truths. And this error is so egregious that I am confounded at the universality with which it has been received. Mathematical axioms are *not* axioms of general truth. What is true of *relation* — of form and quantity — is often grossly false in regard to morals, for example. In this latter science it is very usually *un*true that the aggregated parts are equal to the whole. In chemistry also the axiom fails. In the consideration of motive it fails; for two motives, each of a given value, have not, necessarily, a value when united, equal to the sum of their values apart. There are numerous other mathematical truths which are only truths within the limits of *relation*. But the mathematician argues, from his *finite truths*, through habit, as if they were of an absolutely general applicability — as the world indeed imagines them to be. Bryant, in his very learned 'Mythology,' mentions an analogous source of error, when he says that 'although the Pagan fables are not believed, yet we forget ourselves continually, and make inferences from them

---

x *convenue (A, B, C, D) corrected*   y *This sentence not italicized (A)*
editorially

TALES: 1843–1844

as existing realities.'[19] With the algebraists,[z] however, who are Pagans themselves, the 'Pagan fables' *are* believed, and the inferences are made, not so much through lapse of memory, as through an unaccountable addling of the brains. In short, I never yet encountered the mere mathematician who could be trusted out of equal roots, or one who did not clandestinely hold it as a point of his faith that $x^2 + px$ was absolutely and unconditionally equal to q. Say to one of these gentlemen, by way of experiment, if you please, that you believe occasions may occur where $x^2 + px$ is *not* altogether equal to q, and, having made him understand what you mean, get out of his reach as speedily as convenient, for, beyond doubt, he will endeavor to knock you down.

"I mean to say," continued Dupin, while I merely laughed at his last observations, "that if the Minister had been no more than a mathematician, the Prefect would have been under no necessity of giving me this check.[a] I knew him, however, as both mathematician and poet, and my measures were adapted to his capacity, with reference to the circumstances by which he was surrounded. I knew him as a courtier, too, and as a bold *intriguant*. Such a man, I considered, could not fail to be aware of the ordinary policial modes of action. He could not have failed to anticipate — and events have proved that he did not fail to anticipate — the waylayings to which he was subjected. He must have foreseen, I reflected, the secret investigations of his premises. His frequent absences from home at night, which were hailed by the Prefect as certain aids to his success, I regarded only as *ruses,* to afford opportunity for thorough search to the police, and thus the sooner to impress them with the conviction to which G——, in fact, did finally arrive — the conviction that the letter was not upon the premises. I felt, also, that the whole train of thought, which I was at some pains in detailing to you just now, concerning the invariable principle of policial action in searches for articles concealed — I felt that this whole train of thought would necessarily pass through the mind of the Minister. It would imperatively lead him to despise all the ordinary *nooks* of concealment. *He* could not, I

---

z   algebraist, *(A)*
a   *After this* Had he been no more   than a poet, I think it probable that he
would have foiled us all. *(A)*

THE PURLOINED LETTER

reflected, be so weak as not to see that the most intricate and remote recess of his hotel would be as open as his commonest closets
to the eyes, to the probes, to the gimlets, and to the microscopes of
the Prefect. I saw, in fine, that he would be driven, as a matter of
course, to *simplicity,* if not deliberately induced to it as a matter
of choice. You will remember, perhaps, how desperately the Prefect laughed when I suggested, upon our first interview, that it was
just possible this mystery troubled him so much on account of its
being so *very* self-evident."

"Yes," said I, "I remember his merriment well. I really
thought he would have fallen into convulsions."

"The material world," continued Dupin, "abounds with very
strict analogies to the immaterial; and thus some color of truth
has been given to the rhetorical dogma, that metaphor, or simile,
may be made to strengthen an argument, as well as to embellish
a description. The principle of the *vis inertiæ,*[20] for example,[b]
seems to be identical in physics and metaphysics. It is not more true
in the former, that a large body is with more difficulty set in mo-
tion than a smaller one, and that its subsequent *momentum*[c] is
commensurate with this difficulty, than it is, in the latter, that
intellects of the vaster capacity, while more forcible, more constant, and more eventful in their movements than those of inferior
grade, are yet the less readily moved, and more embarrassed and
full of hesitation in the first few steps of their progress. Again:
have you ever noticed which of the street signs, over the shop-
doors, are the most attractive of attention?"

"I have never given the matter a thought," I said.

"There is a game of puzzles," he resumed, "which is played
upon a map. One party playing requires another to find a given
word — the name of town, river, state or empire — any word, in
short, upon the motley and perplexed surface of the chart. A
novice in the game generally seeks to embarrass his opponents by
giving them the most minutely lettered names; but the adept
selects such words as stretch, in large characters, from one end of
the chart to the other. These, like the over-largely lettered signs

---

b example, with the amount of   consequent upon it, *(A)*
momentum proportionate with it and   c   *impetus (A)*

TALES: 1843–1844

and placards of the street, escape observation by dint of being excessively obvious; and here the physical oversight is precisely analogous with the moral inapprehension by which the intellect suffers to pass unnoticed those considerations which are too obtrusively and too palpably self-evident. But this is a point, it appears, somewhat above or beneath the understanding of the Prefect. He never once thought it probable, or possible, that the Minister had deposited the letter immediately beneath the nose of the whole world, by way of best preventing any portion of that world from perceiving it.[21]

"But the more I reflected upon the daring, dashing, and discriminating ingenuity of D——; upon the fact that the document must always have been *at hand,* if he intended to use it to good purpose; and upon the decisive evidence, obtained by the Prefect, that it was not hidden within the limits of that dignitary's ordinary search — the more satisfied I became that, to conceal this letter, the Minister had resorted to the comprehensive and sagacious expedient of not attempting to conceal it at all.

"Full of these ideas, I prepared myself with a pair of green spectacles,[22] and called one fine morning, quite by accident, at the Ministerial hotel. I found D—— at home, yawning, lounging, and dawdling, as usual, and pretending to be in the last extremity of *ennui.* He is, perhaps, the most really energetic human being now alive — but that is only when nobody sees him.

"To be even with him, I complained of my weak eyes, and lamented the necessity of the spectacles, under cover of which I cautiously and thoroughly surveyed the[d] apartment, while seemingly intent only upon the conversation of my host.

"I paid especial attention to a large writing-table near which he sat, and upon which lay confusedly, some miscellaneous letters and other papers, with one or two musical instruments and a few books. Here, however, after a long and very deliberate scrutiny, I saw nothing to excite particular suspicion.

"At length my eyes, in going the circuit of the room, fell upon a trumpery fillagree card-rack of pasteboard, that hung dangling by a dirty blue ribbon[e] from a little brass knob just beneath the

---

d the whole *(A, B, D)*   e riband, *(A)*

THE PURLOINED LETTER

middle of the mantel-piece. In this rack, which had three or four compartments, were five or six visiting cards and a solitary letter. This last was much soiled and crumpled. It was torn nearly in two, across the middle — as if a design, in the first instance, to tear it entirely up as worthless, had been altered, or stayed, in the second. It had a large black seal, bearing the D—— cipher *very* conspicuously, and was addressed, in a diminutive female hand, to D——, the minister, himself. It was thrust carelessly, and even, as it seemed, contemptuously, into one of the upper[f] divisions of the rack.

"No sooner had I glanced at this letter, than I concluded it to be that of which I was in search. To be sure, it was, to all appearance, radically different from the one of which the Prefect had read us so minute a description. Here the seal was large and black, with the D—— cipher; there it was small and red, with the ducal arms of the S—— family. Here, the address, to the Minister, was diminutive and feminine; there the superscription, to a certain royal personage, was markedly bold and decided; the size alone formed a point of correspondence. But, then, the *radicalness* of these differences, which was excessive; the dirt; the soiled and torn condition of the paper, so inconsistent with the *true* methodical habits of D——, and so suggestive of a design to delude the beholder into an idea of the worthlessness of the document; these things, together with the hyperobtrusive situation of this document, full in the view of every visiter, and thus exactly in accordance with the conclusions to which I had previously arrived; these things, I say, were strongly corroborative of suspicion, in one who came with the intention to suspect.

"I protracted my visit as long as possible, and, while I maintained a most animated discussion with the Minister, on[g] a topic which I knew well had never failed to interest and excite him, I kept my attention really riveted upon the letter. In this examination, I committed to memory its external appearance and arrangement in the rack; and also fell, at length, upon a discovery which set at rest whatever trivial doubt I might have entertained. In scrutinizing the edges of the paper, I observed them to be more

---

f   uppermost *(A, B, D)*   g   upon *(A, B, D)*

TALES: 1843–1844

chafed than seemed necessary. They presented the *broken* appearance which is manifested when a stiff paper, having been once folded and pressed with a folder, is refolded in a reversed direction, in the same creases or edges which had formed the original fold. This discovery was sufficient. It was clear to me that the letter had been turned, as a glove, inside out, re-directed, and re-sealed.²³ I bade the Minister good morning, and took my departure at once, leaving a gold snuff-box upon the table.

"The next morning I called for the snuff-box, when we resumed, quite eagerly, the conversation of the preceding day. While thus engaged, however, a loud report, as if of a pistol, was heard immediately beneath the windows of the hotel, and was succeeded by a series of fearful screams, and the shoutings of aʰ mob. D—— rushed to a casement, threw it open, and looked out. In the meantime, I stepped to the card-rack, took the letter, put it in my pocket, and replaced it by a *fac-simile,* ⁱ(so far as regards externals,)ⁱ which I had carefully prepared at my lodgings;ʲ imitating the D—— cipher, very readily, by means of a seal formed of bread.

"The disturbance in the street had been occasioned by the frantic behavior of a man with a musket. He had fired it among a crowd of women and children. It proved, however, to have been without ball, and the fellow was suffered to go his way as a lunatic or a drunkard. When he had gone, D—— came from the window, whither I had followed him immediately upon securing the object in view. Soon afterwards I bade him farewell. The pretended lunatic was a man in my own pay."

"But what purpose had you," I asked, "in replacing the letter by a *fac-simile?* Would it not have been better, at the first visit, to have seized it openly, and departed?"

"D——," replied Dupin, "is a desperate man, and a man of nerve. His hotel, too, is not without attendants devoted to his interests. Had I made the wild attempt you suggest, I mightᵏ never have left the Ministerial presence alive. The good people of Paris mightˡ have heard of me no more. But I had an object apart from

---

h   a terrified *(A, B, D)*
i . . . i   *Omitted (A)*
j   lodgings ;/lodgings — *(A, B, D)*

k   should *(A)*
l   would *(A)*

THE PURLOINED LETTER

these considerations. You know my political prepossessions. In this matter, I act as a partisan of the lady concerned. For eighteen months the Minister has had her in his power. She has now him in hers;[m] since, being unaware that the letter is not in his possession, he will proceed with his exactions as if it was. Thus will he inevitably commit himself, at once, to his political destruction. His downfall, too, will not be more precipitate than awkward. It is all very well to talk about the *facilis descensus Averni*;[24] but in all kinds of climbing, as Catalani[n] said of singing, it is far more easy to get up than to come down.[25] In the present instance I have no sympathy — at least no pity — for him who descends. He is that *monstrum horrendum*,[26] an unprincipled man of genius. I confess, however, that I should like very well to know the precise character of his thoughts, when, being defied by her whom the Prefect terms 'a certain personage,' he is reduced to opening the letter which I left for him in the card-rack."

"How? did you put any thing particular in it?"

"Why — it did not seem altogether right to leave the interior blank — that would have been insulting. D——,[o] at Vienna once, did me an evil turn, which I told him, quite good-humoredly, that I should remember. So, as I knew he would feel some curiosity in regard to the identity of the person who had outwitted him, I thought it a pity not to give him a clue. He is well acquainted with my MS., and I just copied into the middle of the blank sheet the words —

—— Un[p] dessein si funeste,
S'il n'est digne d'Atrée, est digne de Thyeste.

They are to be found in Crébillon's 'Atrée.' "[27]

NOTES

Motto: The Latin quotation ascribed to Seneca has not been located. Poe used it first in the 1843 version of "The Murders in the Rue Morgue," near the end of the tale (see variants on p. 568), but omitted it in later texts. It means "Nothing is more hateful to wisdom than too much cunning." Compare Dupin's

m hers;/hers — *(A, B, D)*	p —— Un/" '—— ——Un
n Catalini *(A) misprint*	*(B, D)*
o To be sure, D——, *(A)*	

INDEX